HOPE'S VENGEANCE

Ricki Thomas

A Wild Wolf Publication

Published by Wild Wolf Publishing in 2012
Copyright © 2011 Ricki Thomas
This second edition published by Wild Wolf Publishing in
2016

Second Print

ISBN: 978-1-907954-19-1
Also available in E-Book Edition

www.wildwolfpublishing.com

Also from this author:

Unlikely Killer

Rings of Death

Deadly Angels

Bonfire Night

Black Park

Bloody Mary

Holiday of the Dead (contributor)

Wild Wolf's Twisted Tails (contributor)

Guilty Parties (contributor)

The Road More Travelled (contributor)

Session One

"So why are you here to see me?" Dawn relaxed into the chair and crossed her slender legs, the worn, charcoal jeans tight over her knees.

Hope sat opposite, stiff and unsmiling. "You know why; it's been headlines for months."

"I don't read headlines. You came to me, remember, so tell me in your words why you are here to see me?"

Hope remained rigid, a sardonic sneer beneath irritated eyes. She huffed, exaggerated and rude. "I've recently been freed from Talavera Bruce prison in Rio after being set up by my best friend. Having paid for her lavish wedding earlier this year, and having known her for over twenty years, I thought that was a bit of a liberty."

Dawn said nothing, scanning Hope's face, her body language; it was clear her latest and most famous client was going to be a tough one. With fists clenched from unreleased anger and her jaw tense, Hope retained more than she allowed out. Dawn studied the woman, sweet, attractive, but hollow cheeked and eyes that belied a deep inner pain. Dawn was excellent at her job and liked a challenge, so was looking forward to working through the anguish.

Hope noticed the scrutiny and crossed her arms, comfortable in the protection of the physical barrier. "Well?"

Dawn sensed the petite and casually dressed woman's ambivalence. "You're paying me, I'm your counsellor. It's not me who needs to talk, but you." The sequins on her tie-dye tunic glistened in the September rays that streamed through the window.

"Completely confidential?" Soft and childlike. Nervous.

Dawn let her breath out with hopeful relief; they had crossed a line. "Yep."

Timidly grateful, Hope relaxed and the wall between them tumbled gently. "I've known Lucy since my last year at junior school. That's what hurts the most, we've been friends for so long. She's had a rough time and I tried to make things better because I can afford to now."

"Now?"

The half-smile belied the irony. "I haven't always been this successful, you know. I've had plenty of lean years to draw from. But now I have money, I want to make the people around me happy."

"And you thought paying for Lucy's wedding would make her happy?"

"I knew it would. It did."

Hope retreated once more, eyes glazing, and Dawn was eager to keep her talking. She would have to watch that tendency. "Tell me from the start how it happened."

The prompt worked and Hope was back in the room. She took a few deep breaths to steel herself and began. "It all started on New Year's Day, just after the bells had rung the year in. A friend of mine, Helen, had arranged a surprise party to cheer me up."

"A worthwhile friend."

Dawn's aside was met with a satirical snort. "I say friend - and she has turned out to be a good one - but she's actually my third husband's 'other' wife. Anyway, that's for another session, I want to deal with Lucy's betrayal first."

"That's fine, you tell me what you want to tell me."

"It had just gone midnight when Lee proposed to Lucy. It was so romantic, down on bended knee, flowers, the works. Neither of them had been married before and I guess I wanted to do something to make it extra special for them, so because I've got a big house with massive gardens, I offered to host the reception there."

Hope searched Dawn's face, insecurely seeking approval of her success, her wealth, but the unimpressed, friendly smile didn't waver. "That's very generous. She must mean a lot to you."

Irritated, Hope sneered again. "Meant." She shuffled in her seat, playing with the explanation carefully before letting it go. "Lucy has been there for me through some very difficult times and I needed her to know how grateful I was. I guess I even want to forgive her now, even after all of this, but I think I need your help for that."

"Tell me about the wedding."

Hope gave her first smile, genuine and delicate, but also animated and alive. "It was going to be a summer wedding, but Lucy found out she was pregnant in the New Year so they brought the date forward."

8

"Lovely, was it her first baby?"

"No, third. She had Callum young, then Christopher in her mid-twenties. Neither are Lee's. Anyway, she didn't want to be heavily pregnant in the photos so we decided on the eighth of April. I live in a small village and the church is just around the corner, it's really pretty, so they said they wanted to get married there. I was happy about that and we used my address for the banns. I was Matron of Honour." Hope quietened, retreating again.

"She obviously treasured your friendship. At the time, anyway."

The agony in Hope's eyes was fierce and Dawn was taken aback by the challenging stare. She realised she would need to plough through many layers before she reached the core of her client's pain. Rippling with sarcasm, Hope said, "If she did, she had a funny way of showing it."

Eager to dispel the grey atmosphere, stagnant, still, Dawn hastily backtracked, ensuring her tone remained light and positive. "So you helped to plan the wedding?"

Sighing, she wearily continued. "I arranged the caterers, a local firm, and the DJ we'd used at the New Year's Eve party. Lucy wanted to use the barn rather than the house, she said it was far enough from the neighbours to avoid any complaints about the music, but close enough to the kitchen for the caterers. It suited me perfectly because it wouldn't affect our family life."

"Our? Who lives with you?"

"Come on, Dawn, you must read *Hello*, doesn't everyone?"

Dawn chuckled, the mass of tumbling curls swaying over the ethnic, velvet waistcoat, blonde contrasting with burgundy. "No way, it's not my thing."

Hope grinned widely, crinkling laughter lines softening the harshness and revealing the unexpectedly beautiful woman beneath, and Dawn guessed she had passed one of Hope's tests. "No, I guess you don't. I have three kids. I had Penny when I was eighteen, then there's Olive and my gorgeous little Bern."

"Lovely. How old are they?"

"Bern's seven, he's a loveable little rogue. Penny's thirteen now and Olive's nine. Have you got any?"

Dawn shook her head. "So you were holding the reception in the barn."

9

"I was shocked when I saw the guest list, she'd invited hundreds, but I stuck to my word and just arranged a marquee as well. I had the best local florist in to adorn everything with fresh flowers, mainly red roses because that was the theme Lucy wanted, and I had the bakery do a five-tiered cake, showered with tiny handmade sugar-paste roses."

"That must have cost a fortune." Dawn knew her client was wealthy, but the shock was genuine.

Hope nodded and, rueful, her eyes dropped to the floor. "She was worth it. At least, I thought she was. She bought the dress herself, had it made by somebody in Reading where she lives. It was stunning, really unusual, elaborate. Although she was four months pregnant, her bump didn't show, which was a surprise because the dress was fitted. It was an excellent design. It followed the theme of the wedding, with tiny red rosebuds tumbling down her back and along the train. She kept it a secret so when I saw her on the wedding day, she looked so stunning it brought tears to my eyes." Hope took a deep breath, her jaw severe, willing tears away. "I was so proud of her."

Seconds ticked by as Hope drew calming, deep breaths, gathering her anguish and locking it away. "Penny and Olive were bridesmaids, along with Lucy's nieces, Tequila and Sangria." Her eyes flashed, looking for a smile, but Dawn was composed. "My daughters wore scarlet dresses and the two little girls were in pink. I had the florist sprinkle pink and red petals from the gate to the barn, just a little surprise to take Lucy's breath away."

"I can hear the bitterness in your voice, you obviously tried very hard to make this a special day for her."

"I did." Frustration replaced the scorned expression. "You know, I was busy too, winter and spring, finishing the book. The publisher kept returning the manuscript, demanding alterations. They agreed it was ready to go to print only a week before the wedding. I was busy at work and trying to arrange the perfect bloody wedding at the same time. And I did it, the book, the wedding, I did it for her. And that's how she bloody repaid me."

"What's the book about?" Dawn had read the bestseller and been impressed with both the style and content.

"It's called '*Are Things What They Seem?*'. It's about bullying and the devastating effects it has on society. Not just bullying at school, but in the workplace, home, even the streets. It sold well."

Dawn smiled at the understatement. "Was it your first book?" She knew the answer but needed to keep Hope talking.

"No, second. My first was... hold on a minute, you're not going to tell me you haven't heard of the first one? No one could miss the scandal that surrounded that one, reader of *Hello* or not."

Dawn sighed impatiently. *"Women and Violence, Is There a Solution?* Hope, you need to understand that I want to hear things from you, not third-rate journalists. Yes, I know your books, yes, I've read them both. They're fantastic, you raise so many important issues, but I want to hear how you feel, do you understand that?"

Hope was unsure whether to feel chastised or delirious. Over the past few years when she had tried to express her feelings, deaf ears had dismissed her ignorantly, so the role of unassuming mother, cleaner, worker - the silent one in the background, blending into the wall, seen but not heard - was the person who arose naturally now, a contrast to her early, determined days. Now she had been given permission to speak, to express herself. To feel. They may have met only half an hour before, but Dawn was different and she liked her quirkiness, her funkiness. For the first time in forever, Hope was ready to let someone in.

Bursting with years of pent-up anguish, the sigh of relief was almost visible and the whiteness left Hope's knuckles. She leaned back on the chair. Dawn repressed her own relief, aware she needed to stay in the role of protector if Hope were to continue to relax. Five silent minutes passed, Dawn biding her time, guessing Hope was preparing a landslide.

Eventually it came. "Lucy came to stay on the Friday, we had a drink, had a laugh in the evening. It was fun. We got up early on the Saturday, had a long, lazy breakfast: fruit, meats, cheeses. Bucks fizz." She chuckled gently, childishly embarrassed. "We had a good laugh, you know. We went upstairs to my suite after breakfast for a full-on pampering session. We had hairdressers, a make-up lady, and I'd bought loads of new products - expensive stuff - so we could all feel beautiful. It was great. Special." She sighed remorsefully.

"I'd hired a couple of Daimlers so we could arrive at the church in style. People stopped and stared as we went past, it must have looked impressive, the ribbons, the flowers." Dawn shifted in her seat, eagerly listening to the tale she had already studied in the tabloids.

11

"Lucy's eldest, Callum, gave her away, he looked so smart in his suit. We followed them down the aisle and I was so proud of her, her elegance, her beauty. My best friend." Anger flashed and her voice cracked. "It makes me sick now to think of it." Hope's knuckles whitened once more and she swallowed heavily, choking back tears she refused to cry.

"Lee seemed so genuine at the reception, he kept thanking me, over and over, in fact it became quite embarrassing in the end. I'd arranged for some silver service waiting staff and they presented the guests with Champagne, then saw to our every need while we ate. The food was commendable; the chefs certainly knew how to feed the five thousand with style."

Dawn leant forward, fingers entwined, quizzical. "Let me get this right, you paid for all of this?"

"It was my wedding present to them, Lucy meant a lot to me." Hope shrugged nonchalantly, oblivious that she had tugged up her sleeve to scratch her arm, revealing thick scars of self-harm. Dawn filed them mentally; there was more to Hope's troubles than a spell in prison or a twisted friend. "The day was perfect, special. Everyone who came said they had a fantastic time, there was lots of laughter, hugs, pleasantries. I was really proud, of Lee and Lucy, of Callum, of my kids."

"What about you? You arranged it all."

Another deep sigh. "I guess I was proud of me. No, fuck that, I'll be honest: I was jealous. No, that's too strong. Envious then. Is that selfish?"

"Because she got to be princess for the day?" Dawn relished the admission. This was truth, this was feeling, emotion. She was cracking through the shell.

"No, I'm not the type to be a princess, I prefer the spotlight to stay off me. I was envious - and I still am, more so after what's happened - I was envious that nobody has ever lavished that sort of attention on me, made me feel special and worthwhile. It makes me feel selfish saying that."

"You arranged and paid for a dream wedding for your friend, I doubt anyone could describe you as selfish."

Rolling her sleeve back into place, Hope grasped a plastic cup of water from the table and took a sip before gulping it down. She wiped her mouth with the back of her hand and, dismissing the compliment, continued, "After the wedding I felt like I was in a

12

void. Lee and Lucy had honeymooned in Rio and gone back to Reading afterwards, my book had been accepted. I had nothing to do, nothing important, except bum around the house, being a mum, being a housewife. That's never been enough for me. I'd been toying with the idea of writing a book on conspiracy theories for years so I played about, researching bits on the net, but my heart wasn't in it. So when I got a call from Lee in May telling me they were going back to Rio as they'd enjoyed the honeymoon so much, I jumped at the chance of joining them. That was a big mistake."

"Fill me in here, I need some background. Did you pay for the initial trip?"

"No, Lee did. And he paid for this one, me as well. Board, flights. I objected at first, but Lucy pleaded, said they wanted to thank me for the wedding, that they could afford it because Lee had been given a massive bonus at work. It all seemed believable, never occurred to me there'd be a hidden agenda."

"No, why would it?" Dawn recalled the opposing slant the papers had taken and her stomach churned, hearing the details from the victim through clenched teeth, raw with anger. "So you went?"

"Yes, end of June. Faith looked after the kids." Dawn's eyes asked the question. "My sister."

"Are there just the two of you?"

The ironic tinkle again. "No. Charity's the eldest, then Faith, me, and Happiness is sixteen. Our other sister, Honesty - you've probably read about her - died on New Year's Eve, five years ago in December. She was shot in the head, close range."

Momentarily unprofessional, Dawn couldn't stop the gasp from escaping. "You mean Little Honesty? The singer who was killed by a stalker."

"The very same." White knuckles, grating voice, but this time with an involuntary shudder, which Dawn couldn't help but share.

"Have you ever talked that through with a counsellor? That must have been a tremendous loss, she was only young."

"Twenty."

"And such a violent death." Dawn recalled the disbelief that had swept the country as if it were yesterday; everybody had loved Little Honesty. There had been nothing not to love.

"The bastard. She was the nicest, sweetest person that ever walked this earth. He should have taken me, not her. Anyone but her. Not my Honesty."

"I can see you were close."

"I idolised her, she was my angel. I adored that girl." Hope shifted on the seat, crossing her arms in self-defence. "Look, can we change the subject, I'm finding this hard?"

Dawn checked her watch and laid her notepad and pen on the coffee table. "Of course." Astonished by how fast the hour had passed, Hope noted the finality and pulled a chequebook from her bag, opening it, pen hovering. "Is the same time next week alright for you?"

Hope nodded, scribbling the amount in her wayward handwriting. "I'm paying you upfront for ten sessions, okay?" Grabbing her coat, her bag from the floor, Hope dropped the cheque and scurried from the room.

Dawn shuddered as the air cleared, the heavy cloud that had choked her for the past hour, and realised she was relieved Hope had gone. There were so many unanswered questions, so much depth to the woman, and she was intrigued to hear the full story, but still the overwhelming sensation was relief. Dawn drew a deep breath; she had just enough time for a quick coffee before the next client.

Session Two

After a short greeting, a few preliminaries, they settled into their seats and Dawn struggled to conceal her shock over Hope's condition: she was a mess. The naked face that had been neatly painted the week before was reddened, eyes swollen and sunken. Her unkempt dark waves were scraped back and her clothes crumpled and scruffy. Her demeanour was timid, belittled to a corner, hiding from the world, from herself. "Hope?"

The anger that had dominated the previous week's session was gone, her knuckles weren't white, the snarl absent and her eyes unchallenging. Dawn's immediate task was to deduce whether a new tragedy had happened, or if this was a result of dredging up the past the week before. But if Hope didn't talk, neither could progress. "What's happened?"

Sounds of life drifted through the sealed window - a drill boring through tarmac on the road outside, children merrily shouting in the school playground nearby, impatient cars shooting past - but Hope was in a void, silenced by a steely resolve not to cry. Twenty minutes passed with every tear restrained, every sob bravely swallowed. She breathed no explanation, not even a sigh, and Dawn was concerned of Hope's mental state. Maybe she needed more than a counsellor. Should she refer her to a psychiatrist? Dawn doodled nonchalantly on her pad, while Hope's inner torment struggled to find the right words.

Twenty-five minutes. A sip of water, followed by a gulp. That was it, a breakthrough. The simple act had revealed so much about the woman and Dawn now understood that Hope always tested the water before continuing, physically and mentally. The ensuing sigh proved her theory. "I've made an appointment to visit Lucy at Eastwood Park Prison."

The revelation was unexpected and Dawn swallowed to control her response. She had suspected difficulties in dealing with Honesty's untimely death, or unexplored memories of the hell in Rio - anything but the generous statement. "Why?"

15

"I need closure. I need to forgive her before I can move on. I'm paying you to help me move on, but I can't do that without forgiving her."

"That's very astute." Dawn felt a surge of respect and her intrigue deepened.

"You know, the holiday in Rio was heavenly. It's a beautiful city, the sights are tremendous, awesome, and the people are generous and kind. The hotel was dreamlike, the food, the company, the staff. The holiday was wonderful. Lee and Lucy - there was no indication, no signs that I missed. I've mulled through it all, I had the time to, stuck in that prison day in day out, two months of my life wasted, missing my kids. I was innocent, but they treated me like a criminal. They were all smiles at Galeao Airport, right to the end, Lucy and Lee. They had it planned to perfection. We were about to board when Lee spotted - that's the word he used - a friend, a Brazilian guy, so he asked me to take his and Lucy's hand luggage onto the plane, said they'd meet me on board in a few minutes.

I mean, we'd been through customs, passport control, everything, I had no reason to think anything untoward at all, I was happy to help out while they said their goodbyes. But I guess they must have already heard alarm bells, because as soon as I picked up the bags security was there, big guys, scary, talking, ranting, babbling and I couldn't understand them. They wrenched the bags away, dragging me from the departure lounge. I was terrified. I looked at Lucy, at Lee, but they just watched, they said nothing. Lucy smiled, and that's when I knew."

"You knew?"

"I'd been set up. It was cocaine, inner linings in both bags. You know, they almost got away with it, getting through customs, but they must have known there were suspicions. So they let me take the rap. The legal system in Brazil has zero tolerance to drug trafficking, you're caught with drugs, you're locked up, simple as that."

Hope drew a deep breath and stood slowly, wandering to the window, gazing sightlessly. Stark sunlight that shone through the branches of a tree danced on her pale skin, highlighting the grey that littered her scruffily trapped hair. She was a tiny woman, small-boned and skinny. Her features were delicate, yet distinctive, her jaw jutting with tension. Protected by crossed arms, she was alone in the room, talking to nobody, not even herself, and her words haunted the atmosphere. "It took the British Embassy two months to prove my innocence."

Dawn was undecided: prompt or not? The decision was taken from her. "Prison conditions were everything you read about in the magazines. Filthy, pungent, dirty. Cockroaches everywhere, unpalatable food, the stench of shit pervading constantly, urine, body odour, filth." A gentle chuckle at the irony. "Best diet I've ever done." Hope grabbed at the skin underneath her ribs - there was no fat, her body sinew and bones - and then scratched at her chest, arms, legs subconsciously. "Lying on the mattress, a stupid piece of piss stained foam on the floor, I'll never forget the feeling of cockroaches crawling on my skin at night, too many to swat away. I was innocent, Dawn, innocent." Her voice cracked and she became tiny again, folding into the chair, crossed arms shielding her from the world.

Dawn struggled now; what words could pacify an experience like that? She remained quiet, waiting for Hope to find strength once more. "It sounds contrived, but I missed the kids more than anything. Missed their arms around me, hearing their voices, being part of their lives. They all grew up while I was away. I missed a chunk of their lives that I can never get back."

"Who looked after them during all this?"

The sip of water, followed by the gulp, and the plastic cup was drained. "Faith and Adam."

"Adam?"

"Her husband, my sister's husband. They stayed on after I was due back, Faith was instrumental in getting me freed. I owe her everything."

Dawn shook her head. "You don't owe anyone, Hope, this happened to you, you're the victim."

The hour was nearly up, the silence at the beginning having wasted precious time, but Dawn was loath to let it stop, her client being in such a turmoil. She decided to extend the session for a short while and let natural progression decide when it ended; she would deal with the fallout from her boss later.

"You know, when my lawyer told me I was free, I couldn't even raise a smile. It was like all my emotion had gone. No tears, no laughing, no punching the air. They gave me some clothes, I changed out of the jumpsuit, put them on. But I didn't give a shit about washing, make-up, brushing my hair. I just slobbed out of that hell with a complete disregard of things that had mattered before."

"You've got self-respect back, though, you were beautifully turned out last week." Dawn had inadvertently insulted Hope and she swore inwardly.

"I had an interview with a journalist after the session last week." Hope tugged at the scruffy leggings. "This garbage is the real me now." Her dainty fingers raked through the greasy hair, releasing more tendrils to frame the distraught face. "This garbage, this is me. I'm fucking disgusting."

"So what stops you from cleaning yourself up, do you think you're punishing yourself?"

The sudden analysis was unexpected and Hope hastily withdrew, mulling the words for a minute with a furrowed brow. "Maybe. You'd have to understand the low I got to. The first week in prison, maybe two, maybe three, I tried to keep clean, I was sure the injustice would be sorted out quickly. I had hope then. But as the days passed it dawned on me that the nightmare wasn't going to just go away, there was a real potential that I could be locked away for the next twenty years, surrounded by squalor and filth." She clasped her hand to her chest, bearing honesty. "You see, I'm a good person, I have a good heart and I care, I always have, but life's treated me badly, horribly. The shit that's happened to me the past few years has just piled in, hard and fast, you wouldn't believe some of the things that have happened."

She was being challenged, but Dawn had no idea what question Hope wanted her to ask. She deflected diplomatically to keep the conversation flowing. "Try me."

"Rape. Twice."

"That must have been awful for you."

"Of course it was bloody awful." For the first time this session the white knuckles were back, anger flashing from Hope's eyes, fierce, deadly blue flames, and Dawn had to physically stop herself from wincing. "Especially the second one, that was more than awful. It was horrific."

A misplaced maternal instinct surfaced and Dawn quelled the urge to hug the pain from the woman; it took her by surprise. She swallowed hard, leaning back, hands neatly in her lap. "Do you want to tell me?"

18

Hope inadvertently rolled her sleeve up, reminding Dawn of the previous week, of the long scars that littered her arms, some healed and silvery, some angry and purple. Scars from the sharpest blades to release the deepest, hidden pain. Again, she suspected Hope's history was cavernous. Hope dug her long, un-manicured nails into her flesh, which whitened. "It was just after Christmas, coming up two years ago. I was in my office - I use one of the bedrooms as an office - and it was late. The kids were in bed and I was doing the second draft of Women and Violence. Al - he was my third husband; we're divorced now - was downstairs." Hope shuddered. "I tell you, he was a bastard, he stole more than half my inheritance money from Honesty, but I guess that's another story for another day."

She lifted the empty plastic cup and replaced it on the table. "Do you want some more water?" Dawn indicated the water cooler beside the door.

Hope shook her head. Her fingers returned to her arm and pinched the skin roughly. She crossed her legs, wrapping her foot around her calf, shielding herself from the violation. "I heard a noise at the window, a tapping, scratching." Dawn flinched as a nail pierced the skin, releasing a bead of blood. "I was curious, thought it might be a bird, so I went over and pulled the curtain aside. It was so quick; I didn't know what was happening. There was a bang and glass went everywhere. A man scrabbled through, black clothes, balaclava. He'd cut himself on the glass but didn't seem to care. It suddenly occurred to me to scream, shout for Al, but when I tried no noise came out. Then he had me, hand over my mouth. I was struggling to breathe. I tried to bite, I was fighting, but he was big. His grip on me tightened and I was trapped."

Hope bit into her fist, the imprints remaining when the nails returned to the bleeding arm. "He was strong, had me on the floor easily, and his hand was in my trousers, tearing them off, my knickers. He forced his dick inside, it ripped, every movement he made felt like it was tearing me in two, and it went on forever. Every time he pushed it in the pain was awful, but something weird happened, because I felt like I knew him, he seemed familiar. Then it dawned on me that I knew his smell, but I was too terrified to place where from. Then he came. He'd clearly enjoyed it - the noise he made was animal - and then he pulled out." Her tone flattened,

19

the pain too explored to hurt any more. "He was gone in seconds, through the door, down the stairs. I heard the front door slam."

The session was ten minutes over and the next client was due soon; Dawn had to find a way to close. "I lay there crying, just lay there. For ages. I couldn't understand it. Why Al hadn't stopped him when he ran downstairs. It didn't make sense. I felt him trickle out of my body. I felt his fucking sperm trickle out.

"Then Al came in. His hair was all over the place and I remember thinking that was odd. He came over and hugged me, held me tightly, and I was choked, I couldn't say a word. I was angry at him because he didn't protect me, but then I noticed his erection. Seeing me, half-undressed, crying and vulnerable, it'd turned him on. And that's when I placed the smell. The smell of the rapist. The smell of my husband."

The claws now tore at Hope's cheek, digging deep, imprinting bitterness, and Dawn's jaw sagged as she realised what Hope meant. "I screamed. Running. Running. Away from the house, away from him, just away." The anger flashed again, steel eyes glaring at Dawn, a twisted sneer, challenging. Slowly, deliberately, she whispered, "You see, I've been through things you can never understand."

The air hung, a grey cloud dripping with vitriol.

Hope moved swiftly, a split second to collect her things, and she was gone.

The receptionist mouthed from the doorway that the next client had arrived. Dawn acknowledged with a nod, but still hadn't released the breath she had taken with Hope's final words.

In nine years as a counsellor, she had never experienced such a burning rage, such depth, so many layers. She needed to compose herself before continuing her day.

Session Three

Nervous, Dawn hated that she didn't want to see her client. Over the past week she had deliberated Hope's anger, the scars on her arms, the bitterness, and had concluded that although the rape was vicious and significant, there was still more to the problem. Although professionally capable of raising Hope from the depths, she was concerned about dealing emotionally with the acerbic anger that pulsed from the woman. She had considered asking Hope to find another counsellor several times, but worried the rejection might send her over the edge.

She bustled around the room, fussing needlessly, longing for the next hour to be history. The receptionist announced Hope's arrival and Dawn felt a heavy presence, a dark veil of depression. Hope entered, timid yet overwhelming. Dawn indicated the seat and they sat in silence, grasping for an opening.

Dawn started. "What you told me last week was a terrible experience for you. Do you want to explore it in here?" Tinged with guilt; she had shown an adverse reaction, which a good counsellor should never do.

"I was unfair to you, Dawn, I wanted to shock you. I was angry. I've dealt with it. It was easy, because he destroyed any love I had for him that day, and I knew I hadn't deserved that mistreatment. Obviously, I reported it, there was plenty of evidence and he was arrested. I mean, at first I couldn't understand why. I went through our relationship, thinking it over, looking for signs, and yes, I had to admit that he'd had sadistic tendencies that I guess I'd excused him for. If I'd said no before, he'd always respected that.

"I was relieved when he was arrested, at least in custody he couldn't get me again, and my solicitor also got an injunction so he couldn't come anywhere near me. I just concentrated on the kids, on the book, on marketing myself, getting an agent. I kept busy. It was what happened next that really knocked me for six, because I didn't see it coming at all. In fact, I must be so bloody naïve, the amount of shit I miss."

"Go on." Dawn braced herself. The bitterness was returning and she realised anger always preceded a shock statement. At least she now had a warning sign to keep her reactions in check.

But the anger subsided quickly, expelled in a huge sigh. A sip of water and a gulp. "My accountant asked me for a meeting a week or so after the rape. Well, when he arrived, he showed me my business statements for the previous month."

"Business?"

"I was an independent financial advisor before I began writing, I ran a successful business. Only gave it up when I heard Woman and Violence was going to be published."

"Right." Dawn crossed her legs, leaning back, and Hope mirrored her; they were in tune and the trepidation she had felt before the session melted away.

"There was just over eight hundred thousand missing from my account."

Dawn tried unsuccessfully to withhold a gasp, berating herself for her unprofessionalism. "That's a lot of money."

"My sister Honesty was a rich lady when she died, she'd made a fortune from her music and investments. She'd divided her estate between Mum, Charity, Faith, Happiness and me, and I inherited just over a million pounds. I have always seen it as blood money so I never touched a penny, but Al clearly didn't share my values."

"Your husband? The one who raped you?"

"Nice character, huh." Hope swallowed hard, a little cough, and took a sip, surprising Dawn by not following with a gulp. "He hadn't even bothered to cover his tracks; the transfers were all made to his personal account."

"You must have been furious."

"I was a fool. I'd let myself love him. That's what happens when you love people: they hurt you."

"Only bad people, Hope, there are good people too."

Dawn wished her words back when she saw the fire return to Hope's eyes. "I did love him though, everything about him, and sometimes I struggle to tally what he did to me with the man I thought he was, the one I loved. When we got together it seemed the sun shined more, the sky was bluer, and it was such a beautiful, whirlwind affair." The flames died and a smile tweaked the edges of her lips as she recalled the love story. "I'd been single for years and I didn't want to be, nor did Frank, my first husband. Penny's father.

22

We sort of came to an agreement: we'd get married again, but as companions, not lovers. We'd been planning the wedding for the best part of a year." Dawn considered this to be pivotal to Hope's character, that she would deliberately deny herself an important part of matrimony. A form of self-punishment and a clear symptom of sexual dysfunction. Dawn was eager to discover the cause.

"I don't know what happened, but over the months things sort of went stale. Frank's a very stubborn man, he can be childish, and he started having what I can only describe as tantrums. It grated on me, silliness irritates me, and I guess the more I pulled away, the worse he got."

"So he was vying for your attention?" Dawn tapped the pen on the pad and scribbled a quick note.

"I suppose. It must have been late February, early March, because my plaster cast had just come off."

"Oh?"

"A silly accident. I'd fallen down the stairs after a few too many one night and broken my leg." She patted her lower thigh. "It was embarrassing, really. Anyway, me and Frank, we went to see a band we liked in London, the Hamsters. They're not one of the biggies, but a touring pub band, they do rock covers: Hendrix, Gary Moore, ZZ Top, that type of thing. They're good fun."

"They sound it, I like rock." Dawn smiled.

"I guessed that, you wear some wicked clothes." Hope coveted the taupe velvet waistcoat, the ripped drainpipe jeans that enhanced Dawn's athletic, masculine figure tucked neatly into knee high boots.

"Thanks. I didn't think clothes were your thing, I'm surprised you noticed."

Hope smiled shyly, eyes dropping to the floor. "I used to dress similarly, until, well..." She clawed unwittingly at the baggy leggings that fell from her skinny frame.

She was retreating and Dawn needed to snap her back. "So, you'd gone to London."

"Yes, we were watching the band, but there was a guy there, he was drunk, really bad. He kept shoving me from behind, then when I moved, he stood in front of me, waving his arms around, dancing about. Totally wrecked. He was pissing me off, so when the band stopped for a break, Frank and I got talking to Al because the guy was pissing him off too.

"Well, I thought nothing more of it, we went home, rare night out over. Over the next month Frank was getting to me with his tantrums and I got to the stage where I realised I couldn't go through with marrying him again, I wanted to call it off, but I didn't know how.

"We had plans to go back to London to see the band again, but when we got there, Frank threw the mother of all paddies and stormed off. I was in a dilemma: did I stay and watch, or take the train back home. I was a bit scared to tell the truth, I'm not good in crowds on my own."

Dawn scribbled the possibly relevant snippet on her pad discreetly while Hope sipped and gulped. "Then I saw Al, not that I knew his name then, and decided to go and say hi. Well, I was stunned, he went all goofy, sort of flustered, like guys do when they fancy a girl. I was wearing tight jeans and a sexy top, heels, I guess I looked the business. So I took his number when he offered it. That was that, I thought, a quick ego boost to be chatted up.

"I did a lot of thinking on the way home. It's a long journey, as I'm sure you know, three hours or so by train, and it gave me ample time to weigh things up. By the time I arrived home I'd decided to call the wedding off, it would have been a mistake to go through with it."

"That's a big decision to make."

"I know. I forced myself to accept I didn't love Frank the right way, and marrying him would be lying to myself, lying to him."

Dawn breathed a silent sigh of relief; her client did have some common sense after all. "How did he take it?"

"He was good, we talked it through. He still had his house in Newbury so he packed up, got a new job and moved back down south. Our relationship was strained for a while, but we get on now. After all, we still have Penny together, it's better for her if her parents aren't at each other's throats."

Dawn nodded. "Yep, that's good, keeping it real for the children. That takes maturity."

Hope shook her head, scanning the carpet sightlessly. "I was lonely after Frank left. I mean, I knew it was the right thing to do, but the walls still seemed to close in on me."

Dawn sat straight. "That's an interesting thing to say. What do you mean?"

Her enthusiasm wasn't returned. Hope shrugged, dismissive. "Nothing really, it's just the way I describe being alone."

It described more, but Dawn would have to wait for further exploration until Hope was ready. "I guess Al's number was burning my pocket. He was tall, big built, like he could protect me." A significant statement again; Dawn was suddenly learning a huge amount about her client. "I phoned him and we talked for hours. He was clever, really intelligent, and had a great sense of humour. I hadn't laughed like that in years. Soon we were talking every night, and two weeks later he came up to stay with me.

"It was like being hit by a landslide, that first evening we spent together. We just gazed into each other's eyes, holding hands, talking, but oblivious to anything, everything else. I literally had to drag myself away to put the kids to bed. We slept together that night and it felt so perfect, so right." Hope's dreamy eyes watered and she focused on the middle distance as her story faltered.

Keep the conversation going, keep Hope in the room. "How long ago was this?"

Hope counted on her fingers. "Three and a half years ago."

"Right, still quite recent, then."

Hope nodded stoically. "Every Christmas had come at once for me, I gave my all to him. After a couple of weeks, we decided to get married."

"That's not long to make a decision like that."

"No, and as my mum said at the time, 'marry in haste, repent at leisure'. But I was in love, I was blinkered. And if I'm honest, I guess I wanted to shock people." Their eyes met, Hope searching for reassurance and understanding. She didn't get it; Dawn hid her confusion, intending to discuss some of the revelations with her boss. Hope sighed and continued. "We married three weeks later. He packed in his job and moved in with me."

Dawn rubbed her forehead, brow furrowed, searching for words. "Hope, bear with me, but why would you want to get married to someone you barely know to shock people?"

A detached shrug, and Dawn could have sworn she saw a flicker of a smile. She suspected she was being played; she would have to learn not to react, it was feeding Hope's fire. "No, forget that, I can see where you're coming from." She couldn't. "So you were married. Your mother had already voiced her objections, what did she make of it?"

25

A wave of the hand and a snarl. "What fucking right did she have to comment, she married the fucking lesbian lover none of us knew about four months later."

Dawn was taken aback by the prejudice and added it to her list of matters to be explored. "What annoyed you most: the fact she's a lesbian, or that she didn't tell you about her lover?"

Hope softened, lowering her eyes. "I don't know. To be honest it was a lovely wedding, obviously not legally binding - same sex marriages weren't then - and Belinda does make her very happy."

"Do you want to tell me about it?" Dawn and Hope checked the clock simultaneously: twenty minutes left.

Hope shook her head. "No, save that for another day, I'll get Al out of my system this week. Bastard." She crossed her legs tightly, squeezing the calves together, the rape predominant.

"Okay, tell me more about Al."

"He'd moved in, he was living in my house and I couldn't get enough of him. Not just sexually, although we certainly got our fair share of that. I mean him, just looking at him, holding him, I always wanted to be touching him, his hand, his arm, his face. I felt like half a person when he wasn't beside me."

"You sound as if you were dependent on him."

"I suppose I was, I wanted him to hold the world away, keep me from harm, from the nastiness."

"And it turns out he was the one who harmed you the most, was the nastiest. That must have been difficult to take." Dawn nodded, sympathetic.

The familiar rueful smile flickered. "You haven't heard the last bit, Dawn, the nail in the coffin. I'm such a bloody mug, so fucking naïve." She was retreating again.

"Tell me." The prompt was futile; Dawn hadn't coaxed her back. She tried again, louder. "He's viciously raped you and stolen the best part of a million pounds, what can possibly top that?"

"Bigamy."

Don't react! Don't react! Don't react! Dawn's head screamed and she desperately tried to keep her expression blank.

"It was four months after he'd been arrested, he was on bail awaiting a trial by jury. He'd managed to get the case deferred by saying I was lying, that I'd given my permission to transfer the

26

money. He said I'd signed the paperwork and now regretted giving him the money."

"Surely a handwriting analysis…"

"He'd done an excellent job with my signature. Three independent graphologists, and each one refused to commit either way. It was his bastard lying word against mine." Growling, ferocious.

"It was late one night, winter was approaching, it was cold. I got a phone call from a woman with a southern accent, said she was looking for Alistair Brown. I was intrigued, some woman after my bastard ex, so I asked who was calling. You know, I thought it was hilarious when she said his wife, thought it was a crank call, but she asked why I was laughing, so I said, 'because I'm his wife'. I tell you, Dawn, the language she used was ripe, torrents of abuse, swearing, shouting. Truth was, I was smoking a joint at the time, it makes me dead laid back, so I just sort of calmed her down."

Dawn raised her eyebrow and a fierce glare shot her surprise down. "Don't get judgemental on me, the law's wrong on cannabis, it's harmless."

"Hey, you're paying me for my counselling skills, not a lecture. It's confidential in here, say what you like."

"I feel suicidal."

The intense blue of Hope's eyes bored into her own and she refrained from returning the glare, irritated by her client's flippancy and terrified by her intelligence. "No you don't, you just know that if you did I would be duty bound to inform someone. Don't mess with me, Hope, it's counterproductive."

Hope chuckled. The charged atmosphere settled and Dawn composed herself. "So you calmed the woman down."

"We arranged to meet at a cafe in London the next day."

"A long journey for what could easily have been a crank call."

Hope's eyes sparkling joyously. "You don't get it. If there was any potential she was telling the truth, that was it, he'd be nailed. I couldn't recover all my money - he was an excellent liar - so this could be pure revenge."

Dawn was uncomfortable, the vehemence almost vulgar.

"She was a little worn around the edges, Helen, but pretty - well, attractive. Older than me."

"Have you mentioned her before? I seem to remember the name." Dawn realised the unusual confidence Hope suddenly had was the source of her discomfort, she was uncommonly in charge.

"I think I mentioned the party she arranged last New Year's Eve, the one where Lee proposed to Lucy."

"Yep, that's right. So you met up with her."

"We eyed each other up, but not aggressively. We sat, had a coffee. Seems they'd been married five years and had two kids. He'd told her two years before that he was moving to Norfolk for a job, and although she thought it strange to move north for work when salaries were so high in London, she was too busy with the kids to object much. She'd been easily pacified when he said he'd find a nice house and she could follow him later."

Dawn was stunned, Hope was way too bright to be drawn into a scam like that. It didn't make sense. "Surely he must have still seen her, otherwise alarm bells would have been ringing."

A gentle snigger which didn't register in her eyes. "Yes, and I'm a mug too. He said he needed to go to London once a month to get his supply of weed. He was the one who started me on it; I was always anti-drugs before I met him. I'd give him a few hundred pounds, I mean, I didn't know how much the bloody stuff cost, did I? I trusted him. I'm a bloody fool."

"Do you still take it? Now you're not with Al."

"No."

Dawn sensed the lie and stifled a sigh. "So he was successfully stringing you both a line."

"Up to this point, yes. It was unnecessary, but she showed me a photo just to be certain we were talking about the same man. Then we talked, me and Helen, we talked for hours. Half of me wanted to hate her."

"Why? She'd done nothing wrong, she was a victim too." Dawn leaned on her arm, fingers drumming her lips.

Hope shrugged and sighed, deep, reluctant. "Truth? I think even though he'd raped me, part of me still loved him. God, that's the first time I've ever admitted that."

"What about now?"

She shook her head. Then nodded. "I don't know. Maybe. Maybe not. Maybe I love the man I thought he was still. Maybe I'm flatlining, no vital signs, nothing. Some days I hurt like hell, some days I feel nothing."

"How do you deal with the days that hurt?"

"I drink." The abruptness left an uncomfortable atmosphere, a barrier between the two women. Hope had overstepped her personal limit and revealed a secret she had wanted to keep close. Did Dawn ignore or pursue?

Ignore. Dawn reasoned it would come out later once Hope trusted her. "So did you contact the police?"

Relief emanated from Hope, her body relaxing; she had got away with the blunder. "Of course, but there was more to it than that. You see, after having coffee I went back to her place. She lived in Putney, where we'd seen the band, you know, the Hamsters. Her house was disgraceful, a right mess, completely run down, and it shocked me that she lived in such squalor.

"Her kids - hers and Al's, two little boys - came running out to see her. She hugged them and I felt an odd tenderness towards her. I mean, I already liked her, but now I felt compassion too for her circumstances. Dawn, I genuinely liked her.

"The wallpaper was peeling away inside the house, there was damp everywhere, and it stank, musty with mould. There was a stack of inhalers on the table and Helen told me that Dean, the youngest, was asthmatic. Something snapped in me, I really wanted to help her, so I made a suggestion, and the next thing, they were all coming back with me to Norfolk. I paid for the train tickets and brought them all back to my house."

"To live?"

"No, they stayed a week, like a mini holiday, but they've been up regularly since then. Helen loves it up here, says the air's cleaner, and Dean's asthma improves when he stays, so recently she went on the housing list, she's trying to get somewhere as near to my place as possible. She's one of my best friends now. Strange, that, isn't it?"

Dawn nodded, it was definitely an odd scenario. "Could she do a house swap, is that a way forward?"

Hope shook her head. "No, no, the house in Putney, it's hers. Well, was. This is another thing the police are still investigating, you know, fraud. She bought it with Al before they got married, but he persuaded her it would be 'financially beneficial', apparently, to sign it to his sole name. She's an idiot like me, she trusted him. He was so good at getting you to trust him. Cases like this are long and tough, difficult to prove, it's ongoing." Hope checked her watch: the minute hand had reached the hour and she shifted in her seat.

Dawn set the pad and pen on the table. "Right, that feels like a good place to end the session, is that okay with you?"

"Yes."

They stood, Hope stooping to retrieve her bag from beside the chair, while Dawn held the door open. As Hope passed her, smiling, Dawn laid a hand on her shoulder. "I think we covered a great deal of ground today."

Session Four

Dawn filled two plastic cups from the water cooler and set them on the coffee table, before opening the window a crack. It was cold outside, the frost covering the roads and trees only just beginning to recede with the stark warmth of the winter sun, but the pumped heating overcompensated leaving a cloying atmosphere in the room. The gentle breeze relaxed the oppressiveness, but suddenly a new warmth was inescapable; Hope had arrived.

Dawn's smile was genuine, yet questioning. She had not seen her client so positive in the month they had been meeting and a tinge of optimism, unsure what for, registered. Hope beamed as she sat confidently, and they basked in the contented air for a minute. Dawn leaned forward, her smile wide. "It's lovely to see you happy. What's happened?"

"God, Dawn, I've been dying to tell you: my youngest sister, Happiness, has got a record contract." Eager and excited. "FMI, who Honesty recorded with before she was killed, offered her a three-album deal."

Dawn's eyes widened, jaw set tight, teeth rigidly clenched. Jealous. Her own band had been recording for over five years, demos sent to anybody who would listen, sessions at any pub that would pay them, and she knew a three-album deal for a newcomer in this day and age was unheard of. Unable to speak in case her envy showed, she fixed an affable grin, willing it to reach her eyes.

Disappointed by the lack of enthusiasm to her news, Hope remained smiling, but the light in her eyes dulled. She elaborated, desperate to impress. "It's virtually unheard of nowadays, a three-album deal for a first timer."

"I know." Dripping with resentment. Dawn's behaviour was unprofessional and it scared her that she could be so rude to a client. She chastised herself, empathy slapping the resentment, and the tension in her shoulders and jaw relaxed. "I know, Hope, and it's wonderful news. I'm really pleased for her, and for you. How old is she again?" The friendliness had returned.

"Sixteen." Hope's eyes twinkled, dancing once more. "Her band's called Vivity. Well, it's not really a band, just her and this boy

31

called Tony. He plays keyboards, and he records somehow through the computer…"

"Soundcards." The bitterness surfaced again; Dawn scorned bands that weren't 'real' musicians. But she was aware that bringing her personal life into the session was wrong. She needed to discuss this with Pat; her boss was a great leveller when problems arose.

"That's it, yes. Soundcards. The band's been going a couple of years, and in the summer they sent a demo to FMI, then a talent scout saw them play at a school gig and that was it."

When Hope had first mentioned Honesty's death, they had changed the subject because it upset her, yet now she was animated about Happiness's lucky break, and despite it being hurtful to Dawn, she should talk about it for as long as she needed. The urge to get up and leave swamped the counsellor.

Oblivious to Dawn's torment, Hope continued animatedly. "They signed in London last Wednesday and they're rushing out the new single in time for Christmas. The bigwigs are giving them full publicity, aiming for a Christmas number one."

La la la la la laaaaaaaaa! Dawn's inner child wanted to stick fingers in her ears and shout loudly.

"I'm so pleased for her, she's worked so hard for this. She always wanted to be a singer and she's got a beautiful voice."

Laaaa laaaaa, de daaaa daaaaa! Restrain yourself Dawn, what are you doing? Be professional. Too late. "Does it not scare you at all, after what happened to Little Honesty?"

Silence.

Dawn mentally slapped herself hard around the face, knowing the bitchy remark deserved it in reality too. The twinkle left her client's eyes, the bright smile replaced by grief. Her shoulders sagged, shrinking into the seat. Brimming with remorse, Dawn wanted to explain, to admit her vicious jealousy, justify herself. "Oh, hell… Hope, I'm so sorry, I didn't mean to upset you."

Dawn scanned the broken figure, desperate to catch some blue from underneath the sad, heavy lids, make contact somehow, but the silence whipped her, beating guilt into her. Hope had been so animated, so confident - healthy, glowing - and Dawn's malicious envy had deflated her. Now she was tiny. Frail and grey.

Hope hung her head, defensive arms clutching her knees tightly, and her lips curled down, a caricature of a child's miserable drawing scribbled messily on paper.

32

Stilled, a statue of pain.

Silent, but for the breeze whispering through, dodging Hope's form to preserve her lifelessness.

Words raced through Dawn's mind, desperate to backtrack, to breathe life into Hope again, but every idea was drowned by her own scream of 'guilty'. She dropped her head in shame, surveying specks on the carpet rather than establish eye contact.

After a lifetime, Dawn became aware of a prickling, burning sensation smouldering the top of her head, singeing her skin, heating her brain. She glanced up and the pure, venomous anger that flamed from Hope's eyes seared her own. The intensity was too fierce to sustain and she looked away.

"Yes." Growling, guttural. "Of course it scares me. Every single day of my life."

The vehemence directed into Dawn's soul was terrifying and tears sprung to her eyes. She had been beating herself, thrashing out the guilt, but now Hope ferociously grasped the crop with the intimidating glare. A gasp escaped, her heart stalling.

"Imagine it, Dawn, put yourself in my shoes." Every word calculated, imprinting like a rubber stamp on Dawn's brain. "Happiness sounds just like Honesty. If you close your eyes you'd think Honesty had never died. Whenever she opens her mouth and that beautiful noise tumbles out, it jerks my heart because it reminds me how much I miss my angel. And then I feel ashamed, because I should be proud of her, not wishing she'd shut the fuck up."

"Hope, you're wrong…"

Fire. The savage flame stung Dawn into silence. "I love my sister very much. But not enough. Because I have this veil, you see." Hope rose to her feet, the usual fragility replaced by a mountainous power, grand, masterful. She ruled the room. "This veil. It's dark, it's a blanket. It lies over me, between me and the world, between me and my sisters, between me and everybody. It folds into every part of me leaving no gaps and it protects me from pain." Clutching her chest, the anguish was physical. "It stops people…" the blueness caught Dawn's eyes and it was impossible to break the connection, "from hurting me."

A swish of material, a slam, and the dense atmosphere evaporated immediately. Now the statue, breath frozen in her chest, Dawn was unable to comprehend what had just happened.

33

The Boss

Although clean and tidy, the room was cluttered. Bleached mint walls hosted several notice boards, each littered with yellowing scraps, the tatty corners turned and smudged with greasy fingerprints. Comfortable, worn armchairs sat unsymmetrically on the industrial carpet, with a few small tables dotted around. Beside the window, an out-of-place range of mottled grey kitchen cupboards housed a kettle, some crockery and a small sink.

Pat took the steaming coffees from the side and glided towards her protégé, setting them carefully on a scuffed teak coffee table. Despite her vast size she had an elegance about her, a way of moving from A to B without disturbing the air. Her hefty form slipped gracefully onto a chair. "My dear, you slipped up. We may be counsellors but we're human too, and I know how hard you and the boys have worked to get a record contract."

Dawn shook her head, unsure how to convey her feelings accurately. "No." Slow, deliberate. Hesitant. Pat's chubby fingers patted her hand, which felt as if it were being brushed with silk. "No."

"Come on, dear, we all have bad days. Accept this as one of yours and move on."

Dawn shook her head, a thousand words in her head that she couldn't arrange sensibly. "No."

Pat sighed, steeling herself to state the inevitable. "Have you considered passing this client to a colleague?"

"No." Dawn was shocked by the speedy response, especially as she had in fact frequently considered waving Hope away like a bad smell. But something had happened in that room today. Dawn was clueless as to what, but was also compelled. She needed to know Hope's story. She needed to see Hope.

Clueless to the unspoken words, Pat took the response literally. "Well, dear, perhaps that might be something you should…"

"You don't get it. When I said that today, when I callously threw the dead sister in, I did it to hurt her. It wasn't for me, the jealousy, it wasn't about me. It was about hurting her."

35

Pat's plump arm flowed to the coffee cup and drifted it back to her lips, taking a sip through the fleshy redness.

Dawn sighed guiltily, confused by the revelation. "She's the strongest person I have ever known, Pat. She's tiny, like a little mouse. Dainty, sweet, vulnerable, timid. But she's strong."

A light sweep of the arm and the empty cup was on the table.

"When she's not defensive her anger, her sadness, bitterness, it's massive. She terrifies me, but somehow I like her. Respect her. But she scares me. And there's something about Hope that makes you want to crush her."

"To hurt her?"

"To hurt her."

Again, Pat let out a long sigh. "I think you should pass her over, dear. As a counsellor, it's imperative you don't let the client in, because as soon as you do, you stop being impartial. You're one of the best counsellors I've ever trained and I don't want you to ruin your reputation, especially with such a high-profile client."

Dawn's sigh met with Pat's, hanging together in the stagnant air. "I hear what you're saying. Let me have another session with her, if I feel she's getting to me again, I'll bite the bullet and pass her on. Is that fair?"

"I guess so, but don't mess things for yourself, just be careful." Pat's oversized body wisped from the chair and was gone.

In the quiet clutter of the homely room, Dawn debated and contemplated, and by the time she had finished her coffee, she had decided she couldn't let Hope go, and it didn't matter how badly she behaved, how unprofessional she was, or how much Hope wheedled and churned inside her, she had to be the one who heard the story.

Session Five

Sitting on the chair, Dawn nervously checked her watch, uneasy that Hope was late. Clients who personally paid for counselling rarely missed the beginning of a session and it crossed Dawn's mind more than once that Hope had decided to quit after the disastrous previous week. She twiddled her fingers, crossed and uncrossed her legs, played with her hair, before taking her pad and doodling. Pen pressing firmly, a maze unfolded on the page, bigger, thicker, wider, more paths surrounding the tiny centre, hemming it in, hiding it... she was in the centre, she was surrounded by deep lines, blocking, trapping... Stop! Dawn tore the page from the book, scrunching it angrily before slamming it in the bin.

Laying the pad down, the indented scores of the maze visible in the pale sunlight, Dawn wandered to the door, nodding to the receptionist. Gayle shook her head, returning to her filing. "Damn." She pushed the door to and marched slowly - backwards, forwards, backwards, forwards - before stopping at the window to scan the road, left to right. There she was. Dawn's heart leapt, a shiver along her spine.

She rushed back to her seat, desperate to regain some composure before her nemesis began the onslaught. Dawn scraped candyfloss-pink tipped fingers through her golden curls, neatening the waywardness, shaping the mayhem. She forced her shoulders firm, back straight, and crossed her booted ankles, the new leather creaking as it settled. But the strained control was belied by fidgeting fingers, picking at gems, at sequins, threads on the waistcoat.

A waft of fresh, wintry air burst into the room, quickly engulfed by the dry warmth, and Hope, her nose reddened from cold, peeled off her top layer - gloves, hat, scarf, coat. "I'm really sorry I'm late, I've just come from the James Paget and the traffic was bloody awful."

Dawn leaned forward, concern furrowing her brow. "Why have you been to the hospital, everything okay, I hope?"

The scarlet of her nose dissipated, gradually reducing to pink as the heat sunk into her skin, and her manner was brusque, a contrast to the victim or bully stances Dawn had witnessed before. Hope rubbed her hands together, blowing on them. "Good and bad, really. My sister and her daughter are both there for different things."

"Oh, how awful. What's wrong?" Genuine empathy.

Hope's power was impressive today, her aura glistening and presence godlike. She leaned towards her counsellor and spoke purposefully, eyes narrowed. "Dawn, you and I both know that you fucked up last week, but forget it with the fake sentiment. I don't like shallow."

Dawn recoiled inwardly. Two sentences, two slapped cheeks. Her heart pounding. It was imperative she gained control of the conversation again. With the greatest effort, she controlled her breathing and fixed a confident expression, smiling, ensuring it reached the eyes. "Last week I asked an acceptable question at what was perhaps an inappropriate time, but I don't believe it warrants that accusation." Hope chuckled, testing Dawn, challenging. The counsellor collected her inner strength and continued bravely. "If you do feel I was in the wrong, I can give you the name and number of my supervisor and you can speak with her."

Grinning, Hope slid her mobile from her pocket and tossed it into the air, catching it easily. "No need, already done it. Pat agreed that you fucked up and apologised profusely on your behalf. So you don't need to." She winked and replaced the phone. "My eldest sister, Charity, she's just had a miscarriage. She's pretty upset because she'd made it past the twelve-week mark, so had relaxed a bit."

Dawn had miraculously retained her composure. "I'm guessing it's not her first, then. How old is she?"

"Thirty-six, and no, she's had five."

"Ouch."

"Ouch. First was straight after Honesty died. It was the shock, I reckon, not that they were close; Charity isn't close to any of us."

"You mentioned her daughter was in hospital too."

"Leukaemia, bless her, she's only three."

Dawn nodded. Now the conversation had softened, a whole new facet was opening before her: Family Hope. Organised Hope. Not the little, scruffy, unloved child. Not the aggressive, anger fuelled dragon. Not the smart, pre-interview superstar. But a busy, orderly, organised do-it-all, be-there-for, say-the-right-things family member.

"They've recently run tests on all of us to see whether anyone can donate some bone marrow, and we found out today that Keith's perfect match."

"Is he a brother?"

"Her dad, Charity's husband. Too late for her baby though, she lost it late last night; started bleeding early evening, went to hospital ten-ish and lost the baby soon afterwards. I should think it's probably down to stress again."

The standard cliché was on the tip of Dawn's tongue - *how does that make you feel?* - but Hope wouldn't fall for that one. The only way she had found to get her client to open up and drop the barriers was to get her talking as if she were debating her problems within herself. Yet this efficient facet of Hope didn't appear to have real emotion, only the socially acceptable motions. If Hope were presented with a baby in this mode she would coo; with a lost child, she would fuss. A chance meeting with an old colleague? She would pass the time of day and discuss the weather. Dawn had low hopes for the outcome of this session.

"You mentioned Charity isn't close to any of you, but she's just miscarried and you were there for her straight away; I'd say that's pretty close, wouldn't you?" Dawn prayed she wouldn't get a curt rebuttal. Hope was becoming brave, and when she directed her anger it seemed physically threatening.

Yet... Dawn boggled as her client transformed before her eyes, her rigid pose softened, melting, and the stiff upper lip relaxed. Hope's sigh was long, drawn out. "We had a hard time, you know, us kids. Mum, my father, they weren't the best parents in the world, they were selfish, they didn't put us kids first. My kids always come first, no matter what."

Hope crossed her arms, bringing her knees in tight, childish and vulnerable. Again, she had changed her hat and Victim Hope had arrived, an echo of a bad childhood. It was important for Dawn to know the whole story, but Hope had stalled, silent and lost. What avenue would be best: Charity, or their parents? "Where does Charity come into that dynamic?"

"It's not her fault, really, she never did anything to prompt it. We've discussed it in the past few years." Dawn felt a gnawing trepidation, suspecting that Daddy's Little Secret was about to be revealed. "She was their first. She wasn't planned, so they married quickly and told everyone she'd come early. Faith followed two years later, then me two years after that. Mum says she used to dote on her three girls, but I don't ever remember feeling doted on and nor does Faith. Everything was always about Charity. She was the pretty one, the clever one, the sportiest, the funniest, the 'anything you can think of that makes her better than us' one. My father's a hard man, he's emotionless, but you can see the love for Charity in his eyes. It's never been there for me, and Faith isn't in touch with him either."

"Let me clarify this, are we talking father and child love, or incestuous love here?"

Hope chuckled, a tinkling, infectious giggle, hand cupped over her mouth like a child, and Dawn couldn't help but join in, her suspicions evidently wrong. "I could call Dad a lot of things, but a child molester isn't one of them. No, Charity's legs - mine and Faith's too for that matter - were kept firmly together. We were all innocent until we wanted to be guilty."

Although a reassuring response, something about the statement niggled Dawn. Sexuality was a problem for Hope and it wasn't a result of the two rapes she had suffered. Her memory jolted, Dawn collected her pad from the table and made a note to question the first rape. It had never been discussed after the severity of the second one. "So you felt your dad didn't love you?"

Another smirk, ironic this time. "My father. A dad behaves like a dad." Intrigued. Dawn had definitely heard Hope call him dad when denying any abusive behaviour and she scribbled a note. "My father was distant. He went to work, went to the pub, played golf, had an amateur radio hut. He was out before we got up and we were in bed before he got in. All I knew when I was a kid was this grumpy man who we were threatened with if we were naughty."

"Did he hit you when you were naughty?"

That flashing anger, the ocean blue boring into Dawn's mind, and her instinct was to flinch, but she sat firm, determinedly retaining the power in the partnership. "What is it with you, Dawn? Would that little cliché fit in perfectly with your training? Then you can sum me up as a child sex abuse victim, pat me on the head and send me on my readjusted way? Fuck off! Dad, my father, he wasn't a good father, in fact he was a selfish, two-timing bastard who left us all for shit after he fucked off with Sandra. Penniless, we were, in a fucking council house in a fucking shithole down south, with no fucking money and rags for clothes.

"But let's get some clarity into your pigeonhole mind here. My father never laid a finger on any one of us. He never got drunk and beat us. He never got drunk and beat my Mum. He got drunk, but he was - probably still is for that matter - a decent man. Just one who discarded us when he got a better offer than my mother."

Another uncomfortable breakthrough, and Dawn took the torrent on the chin. She easily tolerated bad language and recognised that such outbursts opened doors inside Hope's mind, helped her by releasing emotion for them both to analyse. "Okay, I've heard you."

The fists were down and Hope was passive again, steeling herself for the next instalment. "I was a quiet kid, but naughty. I remember, even though I was only seven, when he left for good. I used to play up and Mum would lose her rag, and then she would say she'd tell my father when he got home, standard stuff. So if I was naughty, I got to see my dad, that's the way I saw it."

"Bad attention is as good as good attention." Dawn leant back, relaxed and interested.

"I started school early because I was quite bright; they used to do that in those days if the parents pushed hard enough. I missed being home and there was a boy who used to call me names. It always made me cry, and then I'd wet myself. When Mum dropped me off at school, I'd walk along the inside of the railings when she went home, crying because I didn't want her to leave me. She always told me to stop being silly, to go and play.

"About the same time I noticed that however badly I behaved, Mum stopped threatening me with Dad, and I thought I'd been so naughty he'd gone away, and I didn't want that, I just wanted him to love me. I still do."

"So he'd left your mum?"

"Not yet. He'd gone to work away from home, we were staying back until the house sold. We were away from him for six months." Hope smiled wistfully, taking a sip then finishing the water, wiping her mouth before putting the cup down. "I didn't understand it when we moved to Exeter, where Dad's job was. We started going to the pub with Mum and Dad all the time, there was a playroom, and sometimes I looked through the door and Dad would have his arm around this woman we later knew as Sandra."

Dawn's eyes widened. "Your mum was there?" The story was obviously painful and Dawn was intrigued that Hope wasn't tense or angry, but resigned to the memory, as if she had mulled it over so many times she couldn't be bothered any more.

She exhaled slowly, shoulders low. "Dad had met Sandra as soon as he'd moved to Exeter. She was married, two kids, and she got pregnant during their affair. Her husband, Sam, said the baby was Dad's, Dad said it was Sam's. I don't know how it happened. I'm an adult now and I wouldn't tolerate such a situation, but Sam and Mum just accepted the affair and life went on. We all spent lots of time together, the four adults, the five kids. I got on really well with Sam and Sandra's daughter, Vel, we became best friends for that period of my life."

Dawn smiled gently.

"Well, when baby Felicity was born it all carried on, then I don't know what happened, but Sam walked out on Sandra, just disappeared. I never saw him again."

"Did you like him?"

"No, he was a revolting alcoholic, he'd get pissed and throw up really noisily in the bathroom. It used to make my stomach churn just hearing it."

The bitterness brought Dawn to attention and she sat straight. Hope had spoken through gritted teeth, pale hands in fists with whitened knuckles. It was brief, but significant. She relaxed in an instant, the episode over, but Dawn wondered if this was the root of the suspected sexual dysfunction. For a moment, she debated asking but chose not to after the previous outburst.

"It happened really quickly. Sam was gone, then Dad moved into Sandra's house with Vel, Fred and Felicity. We moved to a tiny house in Reading, a dump that stank of damp, mould. It was dark, dingy. Horrid."

"So that was your mum, you and your two older sisters, right?"

"The way I saw it, Dad didn't want us any more, he wanted Sandra's kids. That's the way Charity and Faith saw it too, but Charity was especially angry because we'd gone from being wealthy to poor. We had to go to the new school in our old uniforms because Mum couldn't afford to buy us new ones, so right from the start the other kids teased us. I used to stand by the wall and cry, I just couldn't understand what we'd done wrong."

42

"You understand now though, don't you, that it wasn't your fault?"

Apologetic and small, Hope walked to the water cooler, her footsteps silent, and refilled her cup, sipping. "Yes, but I'm still angry at him."

With no outward signs, Dawn noted. She glanced at her watch; the session was five minutes over. "It's a good time to stop, isn't it?"

Hope nodded, her fragility painful as she stooped to collect her bag, a contrast to the bustle of efficiency that had arrived half an hour before. She left like a ghost, a slight wisp of nothingness. Dawn set her pad on the table and clutched her head, breathing deeply -in, out - trying to dispel the overwhelming sensation of abandonment. She could physically feel Hope's anguish. And it hurt.

Fifteen minutes passed, and eventually she resolved to phone Hope during the week to suggest they change the time of their sessions to the last before lunch; counselling a client immediately after Hope was too difficult.

Dawn was emotionally drained.

Session Six

Dawn had pulled on a long jumper over her thick jeans that morning, but regretted it now in the stiflingly warm room. She rolled up her sleeves and opened the window slightly, just as Hope came through the door. They smiled at each other and sat. Neither spoke for a minute, then Hope rested her head on her hand. "I saw Lucy."

Dawn felt it inappropriate to speak; Hope would continue when she was ready. It took a while.

"She said she was sorry. She cried." Hope stood, hands clasped behind her back, and paced slowly between the window and door. "She begged me to forgive her."

"Did you? Could you?"

Hope laughed - genuine, gentle and without a hint of sarcasm - and stopped, facing Dawn. "I've known Lucy since I was eleven, we met at junior school the summer before we moved up to high school. I went to the grammar and she went to the comp, but we stayed in touch.

"Dawn, we grew up together, we had babies together, we helped each other. I loved her." She sat, head in hand again. "The tears, god, that girl can act, but they weren't for me. She wasn't sorry for what she'd put me through, put my kids, my family through. She was sorry because she's stuck in prison for the next five years. If she had been sorry for her actions, for her part in my nightmare, I would have forgiven her, but she wasn't. To forgive her would be to absolve her.

"I don't love her any more. Visiting her in prison was closure. I did it, it's over, Brazil's over. It happened and I can't change it, so I don't want it to affect my life any more."

Dawn grinned widely. "I'm so proud of you. Letting it go is a massive step towards a happier future."

A fleeting smile, and determination shone from Hope's eyes. "I know. I booked the counselling with you because I wanted to get away from Brazil, and we've achieved that."

A flicker of worry rippled across Dawn's brow. "That sounds final."

Hope beamed, reassuring. "No, it felt so good last week to go through what happened when I was young, so cathartic, it really helped. Dawn, I want to keep seeing you, I want to explore..." Hope tugged the sleeve of her baggy jumper up, displaying the scarring Dawn had already seen, "I want to explore why I do this. I want to know why it makes me feel better."

"Do you still do it?"

"If I say yes you'll consider having me sectioned. I've been to prison once; I don't want to again."

Dawn laughed. "Nice answer."

Hope's smile faltered and she dipped her head, peeping from under long, dark lashes. Childish, timid. "Will you keep seeing me?"

Dawn almost patted her hand but held back, remembering the rules. "Of course I'll keep seeing you. Hope, I will keep seeing you for as long as you want, and if it takes years, then it takes years." Hope's shy smile returned. "Now, where do you want to start?"

"I'd like to pick up from last week, I want to go through it all, step by step, work it all out."

"Then that's what we'll do." A knock on the door. Dawn winked, trotting to open it. The receptionist passed her a tray set with two steaming mugs of coffee, sachets of sugar and a side-plate of biscuits. Dawn thanked her and laid the tray on the table. "I thought it unfair for you to keep drinking icy water when the weather's as bad as this."

Hope gasped, her jaw hanging. "You did this for me?"

Dawn nodded, but her smile faded when tears tumbled down her client's cheeks. Wiping them with her sleeve, Hope fished in her bag, giving up when Dawn placed a box of tissues on the table. Hope took a handful and dabbed at the wetness, wiping her reddened nose. But the tears continued and, a private person, she was embarrassed.

Avoiding eye contact for her client's dignity, Dawn waited for her to control the sobbing, and eventually she prompted, "Why did my arranging coffee make you cry?"

A grimace and a fresh crop of tears rolled, soaked immediately into a waiting tissue. "I don't know. I guess I'm not used to someone being nice to me any more."

"Okay, take your time." Dawn suppressed the surprising urge to hug her client, waiting patiently for Hope to compose herself, listening to the rhythmic clock and awkward sobbing.

Five minutes passed, and Hope's shoulders stopped heaving as she calmed herself firmly. "I am so sorry about that. I feel so silly." She dabbed at her damp cheeks, wiping her nose, throwing the tattered tissue in the bin and dragging out a fresh one. Dawn smiled, dismissing the unnecessary apology. They each took a mug from the tray and Dawn hungrily surveyed the biscuits.

"Last week I saw my parents' shameful behaviour from a child's point of view instead of with the adult reasoning I've attached to it as I've grown up. It gave me an opportunity to say goodbye to it."

Dawn set her drink down and leaned forward, her expression intense. "Do you realise how amazing that is, that you could do that, that you could let it go?"

Hope tittered shyly. "Not amazing, but I'm a little bit proud of myself."

"And so you should be." She stirred another sugar into her drink and sipped, taking a second biscuit.

"I don't know how you can eat all those biscuits and stay so slim; I'm getting fat just looking at them."

Dawn eyed the skinny frame, bones jutting from underneath the oversized jumper. Hope's prominent cheekbones made her eyes appear huge, her neck scrawny, and the leggings she favoured were baggy, knees sharp where they bent. "Do you think you're fat?"

"I have to watch what I eat; I could do with losing a few pounds." Hope patted her concave tummy as Dawn penned a quick note on her pad.

"Last week you told me you moved to Reading. Why there?"

"It's where Mum grew up."

"Ah, of course, her parents." Dawn leant back, relaxed.

Hope swallowed a mouthful of coffee, shaking her head and waving her hand. "No, they'd moved to the south coast, Brighton, years before. I think Mum thought she had some friends there or something. Actually, to tell you the truth, I never asked." She finished the coffee and set the mug down. "I hated Reading. When we were with Dad, we always had a big house, with huge gardens to play in and our own rooms, and we lived in villages with playgrounds and greens. We had new clothes, good food, we went

46

to restaurants, days out. Now he was doing all that with Vel, Fred and Felicity, and we were in a tiny, damp shithole in a smelly town with noisy cars right outside the door and neighbours shouting at their kids and each other. I hated it.

"We went to Exeter once a year to stay with them, Dad and Sandra, and Vel and me got on like a house on fire, so I always looked forward to the holidays. Sandra was like Mum used to be, happy, smiley, cooked us dinner, kissed us goodnight. She used to give me six kisses before bed, one on my forehead," Hope emphasised by pointing, "one on each cheek, one on the chin, one on the nose, then one on my lips."

A light switched off, sullen sadness sweeping over her, but no rage, just the resigned stance from the week before. It occurred to Dawn that this period of Hope's life had been so low, she was too tired to have any emotion over it now. "Did you love Sandra? Do you?"

The intense fire returned, burning from the blueness. Her knuckles were white, fists clenched, lips curled to a sneer. "Fuck off, did I, I fucking hated her. She stole my dad. Velda, Frederick, fucking Felicity. They had my dad, I had nothing. I had a fucking waster of a mother who drank and smoked away our food money, our clothes money. The fucking house reeked of smoke, choking, it was horrid. She drank vodka from the bottle all day, every day. You know, I don't know who fathered Honesty, I'm not sure Mum even knows. She says Sam's the father, but there was always some new bloke sniffing around, taking her to bed, shagging her noisily so we all had to hold our hands over our ears."

Dawn needed to calm the situation somehow, finding it difficult to think rationally when the anger was in the room. It was harsh, it hurt, scared her. No, terrified her. She spoke evenly, catching the tremor before it left her lips. "Hope, you told me it helped to be the child again; tell me the story from when you moved to Reading. How old were you?"

Instantly serene, as if the sun were shining in the room, and Dawn gasped, amazed by the transition. How did that happen? "I was seven. Just seven. We moved straight after my birthday. Me, Faith, Charity, none of us knew what was happening, it was all so quick. It was like a rug had been pulled from under us. We came home from school and the house was empty, Dad and Mum were in a car waiting for us. Mum had prepared some sandwiches and we

47

ate them in the back while Dad drove; we thought they'd got back together. We giggled, joked, laughed in the back, while Dad drove and Mum gazed at the fields through the window. We thought it was an adventure."

Haunting, the words tailed off and Dawn prompted, "So where were you going?"

"Reading. The fields stopped and there were lots of houses, the air got thicker, smelly, like I'd never known before. Big buildings, people, cars everywhere, it was horrid, I'd never seen anything like it. Then the car stopped outside a blackened terraced house. The garden was overgrown, and a 'To Let' sign waved in the breeze. Stick an 'I' in that and that's exactly the type of shit the house was." Hope sniggered, sneering.

"Dad stayed in the car while Mum opened the door, then she told us it was our new home. She was smiling like we should be pleased, but fuck off were we. The three of us walked around, taking in the tiny rooms, the tatty furniture. There were three bedrooms, the smallest only had room for a bed and chest of drawers. Charity chose that one. There was only one bed in the next one, Mum said she'd get another but me and Faith would have to share until she could get the money. I still to this day don't know how our things got over there, but our teddies and clothes were all there, waiting for us."

Hope breathed deeply, preparing herself, and Dawn discreetly checked her watch: twenty minutes left. "That was the start of the nightmare, walking through the door and hearing the word 'home'. The next part started straight after. Dad drove away, Mum came in, got a bottle of vodka from a cupboard and poured a glass out. I was scared, because that was what Sam had always drunk before he was sick, so I started crying. Mum patted me on the head, then she hugged me and said it would be alright. After she'd had about half the bottle she started crying, then she got angry and sent us to bed. We didn't even have any covers on the bed and the mattress stank. Faith and I cried ourselves to sleep, but at least we had each other to cuddle."

Hope sauntered to the water cooler. "Things didn't improve. Soon she was drinking from early morning, getting through a bottle a day. We had no food in the house, so ate as much as we could at school because we had free meals; I always went up for seconds." A soft chuckle. "Probably why I'm so fat now." Dawn remained stern.

48

Refreshed, Hope sat again, relaxing back on the chair. "We discovered jumble sales, me and my sisters, we'd steal a bit of money from Mum's purse when she was passed out and go to jumble sales. Then we had something to wear to school and the teasing stopped, so we began to fit in. We got used to Mum always being drunk, crying, but then her tummy got huge. Charity said she was pregnant, but we didn't believe her.

"Then one night, Mum woke us up at two in the morning, said she had to go to hospital because it was time. An ambulance came, then two policemen; Mum got in the ambulance and they went off. The police said they had to stay until a social worker got there. We were taken to another place, to this woman, big, fat she was. I thought we'd done something wrong again, had lost our mum now, I was so scared. I loved her, you know, just because she stopped being a nice mum, I still loved her."

"You say that in the past tense?"

The sardonically raised eyebrow silenced Dawn. "She was back just in time for Christmas with my new baby sister. I adored Honesty from the word go, her little scrunched up face, jet black hair, tiny fingers and toes. She was beautiful."

Dawn stretched out her hands, questioning. "Can I clarify something here? You say your mum was drunk all the time, but then came home with a baby?"

"That's the one. Terrible, huh. We didn't know the significance at the time, but she was lucky Honesty came out okay." Incredulous, Dawn settled back against the chair. "We started to take it in turns to miss school, me and Faith. Mum always told us to go in the morning, but when we did, sometimes we'd come back home and Honesty would be screaming while Mum was asleep, drunk. So we made sure one of us was always on hand for our sister. Charity refused to help, said her schoolwork was important and she wasn't going to miss it. We used to fight, me and Charity, because I said Honesty was important too, but she didn't care."

"Did anyone know you were missing school to look after the baby? I mean, social workers, anyone?" Unchecked, Dawn was visibly shocked.

"Eventually, yes, we got a social worker each and Mum got some help. She still drank then, but only in the evenings."

"How awful, Hope, what a horrible comedown. You must have been so scared." Dawn glanced at her watch. "It's almost time to finish, but can I ask a couple of questions, just to get things straight in my head?" She had to see the reactions again, see if Hope's body language gave anything away.

"Fire away." A wide, confident smile.

"Sandra, did you ever forgive her?"

Hope shrugged, indifferent. "She means nothing to me. I don't believe in adultery, she did it, she wrecked a family, she wrecked our lives. I won't even let her register on my emotional scale."

Dawn was perplexed: Hope was blaming the affair firmly on Sandra, yet when she described her father leaving, the bottle spun in his direction; that would have to be explored. "Right. The other thing I noticed was your adverse reaction when I mentioned Sam."

Hope rolled her eyes. "Did he ever touch me, I know. Dawn, you seem intent on making me a victim of sexual abuse. Stop it. I'm not. No one went there, okay? Sam never laid a finger on me, nor did my father, nor did anyone. My first boyfriend took my virginity when I was ready, end of story."

Dawn grinned. "You got me."

Hope stood, thanked her, and left.

The Staff Room

The coffee on the table was cold, forgotten. With no morning clients, Dawn had curled on a chair, feet on the table, and become gripped by a book she had found on the shelf, searching for something - anything - to confirm her suspicions that Hope had been sexually abused, despite her denial. The signs were abundant in the way she talked, her behaviour, but it was still a gut feeling.

As if levitating, Pat glided into the room and Dawn swiftly moved her feet from the table. "Don't do that on my account, dear." Blushing, Dawn placed the book face down on the table and stretched, arms wide, long legs outstretched. She yawned and took the coffee, huffing. "Damn."

"Cold, eh?" In an admirable flowing sequence, the air appearing unmoved, Pat filled the kettle and switched it on, collected two mugs, spooned in some coffee and added milk.

Dawn rose, stretching again - this time arms and back - and strolled to the kitchen area, her streetwise strut contrasting her boss's elegance. She tipped the cold drink away and placed the mug in the sink. "I forgot all about it."

Pat brushed Dawn's shoulder with a cotton wool hand and glanced at the table. "What are you reading that has you so engrossed?" She poured boiling water into the mugs, stirring, and they took the drinks to the table.

"Child Sexual Abuse by David Finkelhor, I found it in the bookcase." Pat raised an eyebrow, waiting for elaboration, and Dawn felt silly. She sighed. "A client of mine. She denies it. I don't know why I keep going on about it, she's getting pissed off with me." Pat was intolerant to swearing and Dawn glanced up, biting her tongue, hoping her boss would let it go. She did. "I don't know."

Pat took her coffee in her plump hands, the warmth reddening them further, and cocked her head. Her prim curls were tight against her head - neat, old - and her lips worked gently as she thought. "Repression, maybe?"

Dawn shook her head vigorously. "Don't believe in it, sorry."

"For a reason?"

"It's unproven. Even Freud dismissed his own theory eventually."

Pat drained her cup and floated back to the kitchenette. "Two thoughts, dear, two thoughts. Firstly, don't dismiss anything; just because it hasn't been proven, doesn't mean it doesn't exist. People swore the world was flat once, remember." Dawn nodded, the reasoning sinking in. "And secondly, Hope will tell you her problems; you'll get to the bottom of it, just give it time."

Dawn gaped, stuttering. "How do you know I'm talking about Hope?"

Pat sailed to the door, the air about her untouched, and paused before opening it wide. "Dawn, she's all you ever think about nowadays. She's gotten hold of you and you've let her." The door closed and Dawn suddenly felt more alone than ever. She shuddered.

Session Seven

Confident and expressive, Dawn paced - back and forth, back and forth - repeating, "Hope, I can't see you any more. Hope, I can't see you any more." She growled, waving her fist in frustration. "Hope, I fucking can't fucking see you any fucking more because I'm a fucking failure."

She reddened when she realised Gayle was leaning through the open door, sniggering. "Finished?"

"Pah, damn it." Dawn threw herself onto a chair. "She's here, isn't she?"

"Yes she is, and I hope she didn't overhear your little outburst."

Elbows on knees, head in hands. "I wish she had, it would make this easier. Show her in, Gayle, let's get this over with."

Suddenly, wintry sun flooded through the window and bathed Hope in a halo of warmth as she entered, an uncommon, cheerful smile beaming. "Hi, Dawn." She sat, concerned. "Are you okay?"

Dawn sighed heavily. "Hope, I... I..." She stood, smoothing hands on her jeans, stopping at the knee. "I... I... Shit, I can't do this. Look, Hope, I..." Dawn lowered her head, beaten. The best thing for Hope would be to hand her to another counsellor, but Dawn couldn't let her go. She needed to see her, to feed off her, to bask in her strength. "Damn."

Weighing the unusual situation up, she thought of the fantastic rapport they shared, the trust. Maybe Hope needed her too, maybe she was the only person who could help her, the only person who could understand her many layers, the chasmic depths. Pat's words echoed in her head: *'She's gotten hold of you and you've let her.'* The relationship was too intense. But the thought of not seeing Hope again, not suckling from her unique power... Life without Hope would be a life without a soul now; it was too late to retreat.

Frantic, she searched for a feasible question and the unplanned words tripped from her lips. "I wanted to ask you about the first rape." Her eyes implored her client to ignore the telling silence before the question, and the contemplation on Hope's face -

53

furrowed brow beneath the chestnut fringe - indicated she had got away it.

Grateful. Relieved. Dawn watched Hope mentally play with her answer, lost in her memories, comforted by the familiar sip from the plastic cup, knowing the gulp that followed would launch a painful outpouring. And Hope began. "I was twenty. Funny enough, I met the guy through Lucy." A short, ironic tinkle. "Not very good for me, is she."

Confused, Dawn debated the hold Hope had on her, as if she had cast a spell. She was just a client, that was all. Famous, yes, but Dawn wasn't the type to be star struck. Why couldn't she let her go? Maybe somebody needed to force the point. Maybe she should tell Pat what was going on, then she would intervene and place Hope with another counsellor, maybe even another firm.

"Dawn?" Hope shook her counsellor's arm. "Someone just knocked at the door." Her attention jolted back and she shrugged Hope's hand away, swooping to the door, taking the coffee-laden tray. "Dawn, you're really jumpy today, what's up?"

"Hope, what do you think of the occult?" Coming from nowhere, the question stunned Dawn and a shiver ran along her spine.

Perplexed, Hope held her palms up, shrugging. "I don't know. I guess I'm on the fence."

"What about witchcraft? Do you believe in witchcraft?" Dawn's heart raced, thudding above the ticking clock, the white noise of the world outside. Where was this heading? What was she doing?

Hope shrugged again, eyebrow raised and grimacing. "I don't know. No, I guess not, no. Three hundred candles, a sprig of rosemary and a disembowelled frog to make someone love you? It's piffle, I guess."

Suddenly unable to breathe, Dawn lumbered towards the door, sweat on her brow. "Can you just give me a minute? I need to do something."

"Of course." Dawn staggered out, lungs aching from the lack of oxygen. She slumped to the floor, deep breaths straining her ribcage, pallid hands scraping her beading forehead.

Panted words whispery, she repeated her new mantra - once, twice, over and over - reprogramming the glitch in her brain.

"Nothing sinister going on. Nothing sinister going on. Nothing sinister going on."

There was no spell, no power, no sorcery. Hope was just a normal woman, a regular client. She was just a counsellor, a fine one, and she was going to go back into the room like a professional and continue to help this troubled woman to be at peace with herself.

With a final deep breath, the palpitations subsiding, Dawn re-entered the room, finding Hope calmly relaxed in the folds of the chair, smiling peacefully.

"Are you okay?" The serenity replaced with concern.

Dawn inhaled deeply, her golden curls bobbing as she returned to her chair. "I'm fine. I'm sorry about that, had an urgent phone call to make. I'll give you an extra five minutes at the end to make up for it. Now, where were we?"

"You asked me about the first rape."

Nodding enthusiastically, Dawn leaned forward, chin on hand, fingers drumming her sparkly pink lips.

"Lucy and I went to different high schools, so we lost touch for a couple of years, no falling out or anything, just the way kids do. I bumped into her again when we were nineteen. You see, when I was seventeen I bought a flat in Maidenhead with my first husband, Frank. Anyway, we split up, leaving me a single mum to Penny, working in Reading, so when we sold the house I put my share of the profit into a flat in Reading so I could be nearer my family. Not that they were much help, but that's a different story."

Dawn waved. "Just to clarify, you're nineteen, failed marriage, baby, moved to Reading. Right?"

Hope nodded. "A few weeks after moving back I bumped into Lucy. We were both pushing buggies and we had a chuckle that we'd both become parents so young. Anyway, she'd got a council house about two miles from me on the Dee Park Estate and I started going to her place. She always had friends popping by, so we'd put Penny and Callum upstairs to bed and go and get pissed, groups of us, it was a laugh. Just a laugh.

"One of the guys, Peter, we used to talk. He was nice - I thought so anyway - and everyone guessed he was gay. He wasn't effeminate, in fact he was a big bloke, but he never hit on any of the girls and he certainly never hit on me. We just talked.

55

"I was going through a rough patch at work before it happened and a group of us had arranged to go out pubbing and get pissed."

Hope shook her head, fingers squeezing her temples. "I need to go back a bit to explain first. You see, Frank and I split up shortly after I conceived Penny and he refused to have anything to do with the pregnancy or the baby. It had upset me at first."

Dawn straightened, waving her hands. "How far are you going back? You're only nineteen at this point, or is it twenty. Let me get this straight. You and Frank were married, right, were you seventeen when you married?"

Hope shook her head. "No, eighteen, as soon as I turned eighteen."

"And you split up?"

Hope laughed, embarrassed. "Eighteen." She sipped her coffee. "We found out just before we got married that I was pregnant. I was ecstatic. I know I was young, but I'd always wanted to be a mum. Anyway, when I told Frank he was furious."

"So I'm guessing it wasn't planned." Dawn was hooked on the story, completely recovered from her earlier blip.

"No, I was on the pill. He told me to have an abortion but I wanted to keep the baby, and he said he'd leave me if I did, the wedding would be off."

Dawn grimaced inadvertently; she had been in a similar situation and had foolishly met his wishes, a decision she regretted every day, especially since discovering she was infertile the year before.

"I promised him I'd arrange one after the honeymoon, and I did, but when it came to it I couldn't go through with it. I thought he'd come round to the idea of having a baby, but he didn't, he just left, went back to his mum and dad's. I didn't see him again for a long time."

"When did he first meet Penny? You're in touch now, aren't you?" Dawn finished her coffee and retrieved her pad and pen from the table, along with a chocolate biscuit.

Hope nodded. "It was New Year's Eve. She was six months old. He came over unexpectedly with a bottle of wine saying he wanted to make amends, make it up to me for not being there. Penny was asleep in her cot so he looked in on her, said she was beautiful." Her eyes clouded, a soft smile edging her lips. "She was a beautiful baby. She's gorgeous now; a bit chubby, but it's only puppy fat."

Hope swallowed hard while feeling her protruding ribs and Dawn watched with interest. "Anyway, I didn't want Frank back, I was coping with motherhood and working full-time as well, why upset the applecart? But then his mum, Rita, turned up the next day. She was gutted because Frank had only told her the night before after visiting me that she had a granddaughter."

The words fell out before Dawn could stop them. "He sounds like a bit of a shit, if you ask me."

Hope giggled. "I know, he was a right idiot when he was young. He's okay now, turned out quite decent in the end, but I don't know what I saw in him. Anyway, now Rita knew about Penny she wanted to be a part of her life and that suited me. She started having her every other weekend, every Tuesday night, and three days a week while I was at work."

"Wow, good mother-in-law to have."

"She was. Like I said, I'd been managing fine, but I hadn't gone out for over a year, I had no social life, and the childminding costs really hit my pocket. So Rita helped me financially and socially, really. On one of the weekends Rita had Penny, Lucy's mum had taken Callum so we could go out. There was a huge group, all the regulars who hung around at Lucy's. We went to the pub, had way too many, it was a fun evening. But I was having big problems at work because a contract accountant kept hitting on me, was threatening that if I didn't sleep with him he'd get me fired. So as I got drunker, I started to feel down and I went outside away from the noise, the laughter. I think I needed some tears, but I've always found it difficult to cry, well, since I was about seven or eight, anyway."

Dawn remembered the tears from before and glanced at Hope, questioning.

Hope laughed. "I know what you're thinking, but that was a one off, I was really down that day. Normally I have to get really pissed and be alone before I can cry, it's like I have to decide that I need to, then put a date in my diary." She chuckled merrily, unaware of the significance to Dawn.

"Anyway, Peter followed me out, said he'd seen me looking upset. He didn't drink alcohol and suggested we go for a drive, he would stop at an off licence to get me some brandy and I could

57

offload my burdens in private. I jumped at the chance, I trusted him. I thought he was gay."

Hope's voice trailed and the tears she had said were difficult threatened. Dawn was perplexed by the mass of contradictions that came from her client. "I know what you're thinking: I just said I found it difficult to cry and now I'm fighting hard not to."

"You're right, I was. Why don't you just let them out?" She pushed a box of tissues across the table. "You'll feel a lot better."

Hope bit on her fist, unaware of the pain in her desperation not to lose face, but it was too late. They spilled down her cheeks, over her chin, dripping uncaught to her leggings, copious and unchecked. She took a handful of tissues and spoke through her shame. "We got the booze, I was drinking from the bottle. I was a bit of a pisshead when I was young." She glanced at Dawn from under her fringe, seeking reassurance. "He drove, I drank, and pretty soon my mood had lifted and I was laughing. We turned the music right up; it was Def Leppard and I love them. Gods of War in the jet-black early hours of the morning, so loud it felt like my ears were going to burst. I felt free. Happy.

"We ended up on Hayling Island somehow, it was deserted, silent. Obviously we turned the music down. I'd drunk half the bottle and was slurring, I'd been pissed before we'd even got the brandy. I needed the loo, so he found a car park with some public toilets and pulled up. Well, when I came out he'd turned the car off, the lights, and was sitting in the back. He told me to get in, said it was more comfortable for him without the pedals by his feet. I genuinely believed he was no threat, so I did."

Hope swallowed, jaw tense and eyes deadened to a slate grey. With a gravelly voice, she said, "He started caressing me, you know, my chest, legs. I was intrigued, I thought he was gay, and here he was making a move on me. I'd never even considered if he was good-looking or not, the question had never registered. I put my hand out and he stopped. We said nothing, I just looked at him, debating whether I fancied him or not. To be honest, I realised I did. He was tall and dark with a kind face. Chubby, but kind, with a cute smile. I took my hand away so he could continue."

Another dry swallow, a grimace. "Something changed. Quickly. It went from gentle to harsh. He was pawing at me, grabbing me hard. It hurt. I tried to push him away, kept saying stop - get off me, you're hurting me - but he kept on. Scratching, biting,

58

biting my tits, my bum. It was really painful and I was scared. I tried for the door handle but he'd locked the car. I was scrabbling about, trying to unlock it, but he forced his body onto me and I'm only small, I was trapped. He bit me so hard in places it broke the skin. He didn't bother to take my pants off, just lifted my skirt and moved them aside. Did the business. I kept fighting but it just seemed to pleasure him more."

The tears had stopped; whatever inner barrier Hope used to stop her memories hurting had sprung into place. Dawn studied the quiet mouse before her; no timidity this time, no crossed arms or hugged knees. Just a resigned nothingness. She guessed Hope was reliving the rape in her mind and there was nothing she could reach out to her with. Nobody in the world could make the recollection less painful, only sit and listen, reassure her that it wasn't her fault.

"It took ages. Ages. When he finished he said 'Thanks for that' and got out of the car, zipped himself away, lifted his arms and flexed his biceps. He said, 'Do you like my muscles?', then got back into the driver's seat. I righted my skirt and got in the front."

"You got back in the car with him?" Dawn's eyes were wide.

She shrugged. "I was in the middle of a deserted island, miles from home. Penny was coming home in six hours. What else could I do?"

Dawn shook her head slowly. "Did you report it?"

That ironic laugh and a brief flash of anger. "Don't be stupid, I was wearing a leather mini skirt and high heels, and I was pissed as a fart."

Dawn leaned forward earnestly. "The police always take these accusations seriously, they…"

The fire silenced her, Hope's anger flaming furiously. Growling, menacing. "Fine. I go to a police station. My words are slurred, I can't walk in a straight fucking line. I'm dressed like a fucking prostitute and I tell them I've been raped. You getting the picture here? So they take the slut seriously, they dump her on a trolley, shove more things inside just to make the pain a bit more unbearable. They get the evidence they need, because there was plenty of that, with the bites, the bruises, the shedload of semen."

"So there you are, you've got evidence, you've got a case." They both recoiled, stunned that Dawn had shouted.

Her teeth clenched, an ominous, bitter snarl, "And then it comes to court. Single parent. Not so much prejudice now, but there was in those days. Bad track record; I did my time sleeping around, I was a right tart, I shagged loads of guys. Wouldn't take the defence long to tarnish me, would it?"

"So you let him get away with it then, maybe to do it again to some other girl. Maybe he's still doing it." Rarely did Dawn lose her temper, but today her anger was blood red and shooting from both barrels.

Hope jumped up, grabbing her bag. "I don't have to fucking take this. I didn't let him get away with it, Dawn, why can't you understand that? Society let him get away with it. If people took rape as seriously as it should be taken, then it wouldn't matter if I was drunk, or wearing a mini skirt, or a single mum, or promiscuous. The fact I'd been viciously violated should have been the only consideration. But the law isn't fair and we have to accept that the law is real life."

Dawn raised her hands, apologetic, shaking her head. "Hope, you're right. I know you're right and I'm sorry. Sit down, let's get through this." She glanced at her watch: time was up but there were still the promised extra five minutes. "Look, I get as rattled as you about rape and it hurts me to hear how dreadfully you've been treated. I didn't become a counsellor by accident, I don't have a hard heart and I'm human. I want to help you through this."

Hope sat slowly, clutching her bag to her chest, the physical barrier back in place. "I never wore a mini skirt again. It made me grow up. It made me realise that if I was sexy and flirty, giggly, it made me realise that they could easily take more than I wanted to give. I hate being vulnerable. It doesn't matter how famous I am, how much my words make a difference, how dowdily I dress, how quiet I am. I'm a victim of my size. If they want it, they can have it, because they can always overpower me."

Dawn sighed. "That's a heavy burden to live with, it's a paranoid way of looking at things."

"I've been Pollyanna in my time, naïve, hopeful, optimistic, upbeat. The same shit happens to you whether you anticipate it or not. But if you anticipate it, it doesn't hurt as much, because you've already prepared yourself mentally for it."

"So you're saying nothing can hurt you now because you expect the worst?"

"Exactly."

The Last Chance

Dawn unwrapped the foil from the sandwich she had prepared that morning, examining the triangle in her hand, wondering where her hunger had gone. It was no good, she had no appetite at all. She dropped the sandwich onto its wrapper and pushed it aside. "There's a cheese salad sandwich here if anyone's hungry."

A few murmured replies rippled through the room and the sandwich remained unclaimed. Dawn wriggled down in the chair, slumping comfortably, her mind full of Hope, as it always seemed to be nowadays. She closed her eyes, imagining herself in Hope's place, how terrified she must have been. Or maybe she already had barriers up at that age, didn't let it affect her. Who knows?

She was jolted from her dreaming by a wisp of silken skin on her arm, and bending uncomfortably by her side was her boss. "Can I see you for a moment in my office please, dear."

Pat would normally chat in the staff room, so Dawn, following the large woman, knew something was wrong. Pat closed the door and sat behind her desk, the copious folds of her dress floating into place with the same elegance as their model. She motioned for Dawn to sit and rested her elbows on the desk, plump fingertips pressing together. "I heard you shouting."

She had expected this and was prepared. "I didn't lose control." Lying didn't come easily and Dawn hoped the heat she felt on her face didn't show.

"It didn't sound that way. I want you to pass Hope to a colleague." The soft words danced across the desk, unaware of the consternation they caused Dawn.

Forceful, a flick-knife springing at danger, Dawn stood, shouting and wild, completely out of character. Dawn's calmness was her greatest quality, yet now she yelled her defence, insisting her behaviour had been the only way to stir Hope into talking, that they had made breakthroughs by the dozen, that if Pat moved Hope to another counsellor now she would see it as rejection, would make matters worse. And there it was: the truth.

The ever-ready smile on Pat's chubby face remained constant throughout the torrent. When Dawn had finally finished her tirade,

62

she debated, fingertips tapping a rhythm together. "Okay, you obviously feel strongly about this. We'll try another solution. I want you to write a report on this client, I want to know everything: what's been covered, any progress, her mental state, how you see your form of counselling progressing and helping her. You have two days. Once I've read the report, I'll base my decision of whether to move her or not on the content."

Dawn sagged with relief; she still had a chance to stay with Hope. "Thanks, Pat, I'll start it this evening." She would have to call the boys and cancel the gig they had lined up at The Pig and Whistle, but somehow this was more important.

From the moment she and her brother, Rick, had formed Reveal, she had not missed band practice even once, let alone a paying gig. Dawn shrugged the uncomfortable realisation away.

Session Eight

Dawn's track record as a counsellor was impeccable and she had risked professional suicide by belittling the intensity she and Hope shared in the report, but if she had written the truth, she wouldn't be waiting for Hope now. Pat sat in the corner, blending into the walls like a mountainous piece of furniture, insistent on attending the session. Dawn had had no choice in the decision and it made her nervous, aware she had to be in complete control. But she didn't like being in control with Hope; it worked better if she let herself go, if Hope let herself go. Her client walked in, bringing warmth to the dullness that simpered through the window that shielded them from the unusually high winds.

At first Hope didn't notice Pat, her obese form clad head to toe in beige, a monumental shadow on the matching emulsioned walls, but Dawn was quick to indicate their company, as if warning Hope to behave herself. "This is my next in line, Pat Hinds, she wants to sit in on the session if that's okay with you."

Hope shrugged indifferently, but Dawn sensed the ambivalence that she also felt. Hope clarified her sentiment by sitting with her back towards Pat on a different chair than normal and clicking her umbrella open, settling it over her shoulder as a barrier. Dawn suppressed an impertinent smile, while Pat jotted the slight on her notebook.

"So, how are you?" Hope was unusually smart, a quality navy suit bulking her tiny body, hair neatly tamed bar a few stragglers that had escaped in the wind, and her face was painted prettily.

Hope crossed her legs, dainty ankles tapering into high patent courts. "Good thanks, much better after discussing things with you last week." Hope winked, and Dawn realised Hope was about to play a game with her for Pat's benefit. She grinned widely, eagerly awaiting this week's rollercoaster.

"Have you thought about what you want to talk about today?"

Hope slowly turned half circle, eyes boring into Pat, who winced under the intensity. "I have now." Deliberate, calculated. "I want to talk about being *fat*." Pat's jaw dropped, hanging lamely

64

from her chubby cheeks, creating a further chin, and Hope returned her gaze to her counsellor.

Dawn struggled to find words to fill the uncomfortable silence, while her client smirked contentedly. Eventually, Hope helped. "I was first diagnosed as anorexic when I was thirteen."

Dawn exhaled gratefully. "That's very young."

"I was very troubled. I was a skinny kid anyway, so not eating became a problem quite quickly."

"How did it start? Do you know, or did it just happen?" Dawn stretched out her legs - long, lean - suspecting every word Hope uttered was staged.

"Mum and my father had a friend I remembered from Exeter, but he'd met a woman called Eileen and moved to Frensham in Surrey. I don't know why they picked me, but just after my thirteenth birthday, Gordon came and picked me up - just me, not my sisters - and took me to Frensham. Mum said I was having a holiday. I'd never met Eileen before, but I was stunned when she opened the door as we pulled into the driveway." Once more, Hope glared at Pat. "She was - well, almost now - the fattest woman I'd ever seen."

Pat reddened, discreetly slipping a tissue from her pocket and removing a sweet from her mouth, swallowing hard, eyes on the floor. Dawn had never witnessed anything like it and felt sudden pity for her shamed boss.

Hope remained composed, returning to Dawn. "She was nice, Eileen, so friendly. She bought me a dress - maroon, it was - and some new shoes. I didn't see much of Gordon, just Eileen. She taught me how to make roux sauce. It was evening when we arrived and dinner was ready. She got these massive plates from the cupboard and served up three foot-long sausages for me, plus a mound of mash and three different types of vegetable, drenched in gravy. I took my plate through and sat at the dining table. Dinner looked and smelled gorgeous.

"I waited until Gordon and Eileen had sat down and started eating. The mash was gorgeous and creamy, so rich, and it almost melted into the gravy. Then something weird happened: I looked up and there was this huge blob in front of me, she wasn't even chewing, just shovelling piles of food into her face. Her arms wobbled as she moved the fork back and forth, and she wasn't tasting the food, just piling it in as if there were no tomorrow. I felt sick. It made me sick just watching her, her blubber, her greed.

"After half a plate she noticed I wasn't eating and got concerned, asking if I wasn't hungry. I said no, told her I'd eaten before I came. Over the next couple of days, I noticed that she never stopped eating. And it was a stupid game too, the sort of 'ooh, I shouldn't do, but I'll just have one little cake, one won't hurt.' But she'd finish that one and start on something else. Crisps. Chocolate. Cake. Cheese. Crackers. Sandwiches. Biscuits. You name it, it went into that big, flabby gob."

"So your reaction to this woman's problem was to deny yourself food?" Dawn rested her elbows on her knees, leaning forward, eager to quell the vicious attack on her boss.

"I didn't eat. I pretended to. Put food in my mouth when they were watching, then took it out and threw it when they weren't. Once I got home it was easy. Mum was in full alcoholic mode by this time, she never cooked us a meal, so I told the school I was eating at home and they just accepted it. It was fine. I was in control and I vowed I'd never get fat."

Hope stood and stretched, running her hands down her tiny body as if smoothing the suit, but the action enhanced her slimness, and Dawn recognised she was still gibing Pat. She strolled to the window, calm and confident, and gazed through. "It's easy, not eating. You just tell yourself how disgusting it is." Again, she focused on Pat. "You just need self-control. I have good self-control. You tell yourself how disgusting food is, how it goes through your body and ends up as shit. My mum was fat then, too. Not as gross as Eileen, or others I've seen, but fat. After I'd stayed with Eileen I noticed that when Mum had one biscuit, she always finished the packet. Same with chocolate bars; she just ate and ate and ate. Fat people make me sick."

Aware that Hope was trying to humiliate her, Pat was annoyed. "It's interesting you find larger people indistinguishable, dear, as if they lose their identity." Dawn fired Pat a disgusted glare; sitting in on a counselling session should not mean joining in, and she didn't like her toes being trodden on.

Hope smiled, firmly in control of the situation. "Oh, no, not indistinguishable at all. Eileen was a lovely, jolly lady. My mother was a suicidal alcoholic. But neither of them had any self-control, that's the indistinguishable part."

66

"Self-control and slimness seem to be very important to you, maybe to the point of obsession, don't you think?" Pat had engaged now and was verbally taking Hope into the ring to send her down, blow by blow. Insignificant in the audience, Dawn was furious, but would have to save their inevitable argument for later, in private.

The gentle laugh, crystal bells tinkling with superiority. "You think somebody can't be slim without having OCD? So that's what you tell yourself when you're stuffing your face in McDonalds and KFC. It's not me with the control problem, love."

The punch had landed squarely on the chin and Pat squirmed into a defensive stance. "I have personally never eaten from either of those establishments."

"But you admit you're fat?"

Dawn paled as the altercation unfolded, bitter vitriol spilling from both parties, aghast that her boss - one of the best counsellors she had ever known - had allowed herself to be drawn into a personal dispute. She waved to catch Pat's attention, stop the battle, but was invisible in the crossfire.

"My weight has nothing to do with you."

"Neither mine you, but you felt it appropriate to mention it when you accused me of being obsessive."

"That's not what I said."

"Admit it, you don't go home to a bowl of green salad, do you?"

"What I eat is my business."

Hope squared her shoulders, appearing tall, strong, powerful, an antithesis of the skinny and frail victim who usually attended the sessions. "And what I say to my counsellor is my business. You are the one who's poking into my business, not the other way around." Her eyes were intense, cold, yet burned Pat, searing her with their fierceness.

A defeated gulp rippled through the fleshy chins as Pat struggled to answer. Embarrassed, she glanced at Dawn, whose supportive nod barely registered, before stuttering, "You were asked at the beginning of the session if you minded me being here. You could have said yes."

Hope strolled - slow, calm, confident - until she reached the seated woman. Although tiny, she seemed to tower over Pat, looming threateningly close, hands clasped behind her back. "If I had said yes, you would have placed me with another counsellor because you don't think Dawn's up to the job. And I don't want another counsellor. Dawn is helping me immensely. She's good, she gets me to open up. But you, you just want to ruin it, for me and for Dawn."

Pat's eyes flickered between the two women. Without speaking, she took her bag and glided elegantly from the room, head high, without a backwards glance. Her job done, Hope marched to her usual chair as if the interaction had been an everyday occurrence. Confused, Dawn had never witnessed such a powerful - weird - exchange and had no idea what came next. Whispering, "Why did you do that?"

"I'll bet she didn't mention that she phoned me the other day, asked how we were getting on. She mentioned the report she'd made you do." Hope had an air of superiority when she wore a suit, her posture upright and assured. "In the first session I asked you if this was confidential and you said yes. Well, it can't be if you go and write it all down for Miss Piggy out there to read."

"It's only for Pat, no one else would…"

A blaze of blue fire silenced her. "I tell *you* things, not her, or her boss, or the papers, or the gossip magazines." Quiet, but firm and direct. "Every single word you have written about me is potentially a front cover story for the tabloids. Don't think for a second that your little receptionist will think twice about my file's confidentiality when the journalists are offering her twenty thousand just to slip them a snippet or two. I want that report burned, Dawn. I want that report back, and burned."

"Hope, I…"

"Now."

The Report

Dawn stepped gingerly into Pat's office, unsure whether she would be under fire for her client's behaviour, and was shocked to note Pat's red-rimmed eyes, her face blotchy. Unopened crisp bags and chocolate bars were in the bin beside the desk, and Pat followed her stare, edging the bin under the table with a podgy foot. "What do you want, Dawn?" Her usual friendliness was absent, her voice cutting and gravelly.

Dawn clasped her hands together, fingers entwined, sheepish. "She wants the report. She wants to burn it."

Pat waved, petulant. "Well she can't have it."

Dawn edged closer. "Please, Pat, she has good reason, if it were to get into the wrong hands..."

A sudden movement, graceful still, and Pat stood beside Dawn, hands on wide hips, confrontational and uncomfortably close. "She can *not* have it." She stepped back, replacing the anger with impassivity. "Anyway, after what I've seen today, I'm considering having her sectioned."

Dawn gasped, her cherry-pink stained lip hanging lamely. "What? She's in no way mentally unstable. You've made this personal, Pat, you want revenge because she indirectly insulted you."

Wagging her finger, losing control once more. "Not at all, I'm more professional than that." Specks of spittle sprayed with each word. "That woman is dangerous, she needs to be locked away. She's evil."

Dawn was aghast, this was ridiculous. "Bollocks, is she. She called you fat and you can't handle that." Dawn kicked the bin, uneaten confectionary, biscuits and snacks spilling over the carpet. "Look at that, and that's just what you brought to pig out on today. She's right, you're morbidly obese, you have no self-control, and you do eat when you think you're not being watched. But that's no reason to lock one of my clients up where she doesn't belong."

Pat slammed the report on her desk with her fist and Dawn moved to pick it up, but Pat snatched it back. "I've read it, Dawn.

She's clearly depressed, probably anorexic by the size of her, and are those kids really safe with a drug smuggler?"

"You twisted bitch, you know she was exonerated of that. Does that woman who just spoke to you appear to be depressed? She seemed very confident to me."

"Then let's see what a psychiatrist makes of her, shall we? I'll pass the report to Surinda Jahal, see what she makes of it."

Neither woman had noticed Hope enter the room. Dawn towered over her, lanky and slim in high black boots, and Pat, short but cumbersome, dwarfed her. Hope's voice was level, firm. "You will pass that report to nobody. I am paying Dawn to be my counsellor, and what I say in that room is for her ears only. Give me that report."

Pat shoved the file under a chunky arm. "No."

"Then you die."

The words echoed through the stunned silence. No moving, no breathing.

Then, the corners of her lips crinkling to an ambiguous smile, Hope turned and left the room.

Session Nine

Scared now, Dawn didn't want to see her, but knew she had to. She paced the room, back, forth, the report lying ominously on the table. The building was quiet, the usual buzzing white noise silenced by Pat's untimely death. Gayle popped her head through the door, her normal sunny smile replaced with sombre grief, the usual chirpiness now a singular, sad tone. "Your client's arrived."

The diminutive figure slipped through the doorway, timid, shy, her pallor grey, floating like a ghost to her usual seat. Dawn remained standing. "How did you do it?"

"God, I knew it. I didn't, Dawn, I swear. It was a freak accident." Hope had read the local headlines with shock, how high winds had blown a tile loose and it had fallen onto Patricia Hinds, breaking her skull and killing her instantly.

Dawn restarted the pacing, blonde curls swaying with her unfeminine gait. Gone was the usual funky, ethnic outfit, replaced with a sober Aran jumper, boyfriend jeans and flat ankle boots. She had not mentioned Hope's statement the week before to anybody; how could she, they would think she was nuts. But the coincidence was incredible. Too incredible.

"I cried too, you know. Not for her, I didn't like her, but because I knew you'd think it was my fault somehow." Plaintive, a mewing kitten. "It wasn't."

Dawn was angry. She had respected her boss, her work and calm manner, her mentorship. "She didn't deserve it, Hope, she was a good woman, an excellent counsellor. Why did you kill her?"

Hope hugged her knees to her chest, her dulled eyes hidden beneath the overgrown fringe. "I didn't kill her. I couldn't. I can't make the wind take tiles off and throw them at specific people. Come on, where's your common sense?"

Dawn looked to the ceiling, breathing heavily. "That's why I want to know how you did it."

"I didn't." She was weary with the inevitable questioning, wishing back her threat the week before, and tears threatened, prickling.

71

"Witchcraft? Was it witchcraft? Or voodoo? How did you do it?" Dawn raised her hands, animated with disgusted fury. Hope glanced subconsciously at the report and Dawn snatched the folder, hugging it tight, protecting Pat's final encounter. Snarling, she ripped the report in two, in four, eight, sixteen, throwing the shreds around her feet, scattering Hope's history with disbandment. "Satisfied? You didn't have to kill her; she'd given it back. We'd discussed it over a coffee and she'd seen your reasoning. You didn't have to kill her." The shouting ended, but the resulting silence was deafening, an uncomfortable wedge driven between the two women.

Hope cried silent tears, abundantly coursing over her pallid skin, soaking into the leggings at the bent knees. Tugging a tissue from the box, she dabbed at her wet cheeks. "I didn't kill her."

"So what was the threat for last week, then? That's too much of a bloody coincidence, and you know it."

Hope exhaled slowly, resigned. "When I said that, I meant professionally. I was going to get my solicitor involved and take some kind of legal action out on her, the publicity would have killed her counselling career."

Dawn growled, punching the back of her chair, and slumped onto it, sagging, head down. "Shit." Tugging her hands through her curls, creating a frizz Hope hadn't seen before. "I never thought of it that way."

"No."

A single tear escaped, her face contorted in agony as she tried to retain her professionalism, then her body convulsed uncontrollably, and soon she was howling, unable to contain the grief any longer, guilty and distraught. Hope snatched another tissue from the box and passed it to Dawn with a reassuring squeeze of her hand. Seven pent-up days of tears tumbled unchecked, tormented sobs of bereavement spilling.

Head in hands, Dawn was oblivious to Hope silently reclaiming the scraps of paper from the floor to ensure her secrets stayed in the room. The clock on the wall ticked softly in the background, a metronome beating away the minutes.

Scanning the carpet for rogue shreds of her memories, Hope pocketed her torn words and sat beside Dawn, clutching her hand.

Mother and child.

The counselling could be resumed at a later date when Dawn was ready.

Bereft, overflowing with emptiness, Dawn snuggled against Hope's maternal shoulder and gradually the shuddering relaxed as the tears subsided.

Minutes passed without words or movement.

Today, Dawn needed Hope.

Session Ten

The open grief had gone and Dawn's sense of style was back, the tight black jeans tucked into knee high stiletto boots, a golden, sequinned waistcoat covering a black polo-necked sweater. A steaming mug of vegetable cup-a-soup warmed her hands as she awaited her client's arrival. She didn't have to wait long; Hope breezed into the room, cheerful, immaculate and smiling.

Dawn downed the dregs of the thick soup, set the mug down and stood, gesturing a seat. Hope tried to speak but Dawn shook her head. "No, me first please. Look, I want to apologise for my behaviour last week." Hope waved her hand, dismissive, vying to get a word in edgeways, but Dawn's spillage continued. "I can promise it won't happen again, and it goes without saying that I won't charge you for that session."

"Dawn, stop it. I don't mind, okay. As you've said before, you're human too. It's forgotten, it's in the past. Let's move forward." Her soothing voice relaxed Dawn and she sat. A few moments passed, and Hope smiled, upbeat. "There's been an exciting development I've been dying to tell you about." Dawn was grateful for the reprieve and eager to start. "Do you remember I mentioned that Al was being done for fraud?"

"Al is husband number…"

"Three. Bigamist husband, overall wanker, rapist and thief." Dawn tried not to, but a giggle escaped; swearing seemed erroneous from the smart-suited woman, hair tied in a neat chignon, her delicate features enhanced by the severe style. "He'd got Helen, the other wife, to transfer the house into his name."

Dawn nodded vigorously and the low sun caught the sequins on her waistcoat, showering shiny droplets onto the walls. "Yes, yes."

"He was found guilty this week. His prison sentence has increased five years and the house is to be transferred solely into her name. I'm really pleased for her, it means she can sell it and move up here as soon as possible."

"That's great news, it'll be good for you to have a friend close by." Silence fell, Dawn waiting for Hope, Hope waiting for Dawn.

74

Eventually, Dawn changed the subject. "You're very smart today, have you got an interview?"

"Cosmopolitan. We're having lunch at the Italia Nostra, you know, the Italian on St Giles."

"Very nice, I like it there, the oven-baked crespelle is my favourite, it's delicious."

Hope chuckled. "I don't like Italian food, none of it, pasta, pizza. Gives me an excuse just to have a side salad so I won't put on weight." Hope patted her stomach and Dawn's smile faded. Noticing, Hope explained, "I have to eat out a lot, meeting agents, publishers, journos, all sorts. If I ate what I really wanted to eat I'd be the size of a house."

Various sentences ran through Dawn's mind, choosing which was most appropriate. "Two weeks ago, the run in with Pat," the name caught in her throat and she coughed lightly, "how much was true, about hating food, anorexia, all of that."

Hope was uncomfortable, and Dawn wondered if she was embarrassed by the way she had treated Pat, or shamed by a poor relationship with food. "In answer to your question: no, I don't feel remorse about the business with Miss Hinds. She was in the wrong and my privacy was violated." Dawn recoiled; had she voiced the question inadvertently? She was sure it had been simply a thought, but how else would Hope know? She was perturbed, yet her intrigue in her client grew. "I do have a poor relationship with food. I make myself sick after eating; the physical bloat makes me feel disgusting. I try to avoid food if possible, situations where I have to eat. I tell the kids I'll eat later, or I've already eaten. The act of masticating, swallowing, shitting, I try to avoid it all."

Should she challenge Hope's awareness of her inner thoughts? No, of course not, she was being silly. "Do you want to discuss it, try and work out why you feel that way?" She must have said it out loud without realising.

Hope's gentle tinkle lit the room. "I know why, and I told you and Miss Hinds: Eileen; my mother. All the other fatties of this world. You know, Mum had a fine figure when she was with my father. I don't remember, but I've seen the photos. She's taller than me by a couple of inches; I'm the runt of the family." Hope chuckled, but Dawn's heart ached for her lack of self-confidence. "Before Honesty was born she just drank all day, ate nothing but junk, always sweet things. Her weight went up and up, she just sat on the sofa, day in, day out, scoffing, getting pissed, dragging us kids up purely by presence rather than interaction. I hated it, the wobbling flesh, the smell of sweat and sores, leaked urine. Her body was covered in boils, pus filled acne everywhere, her face, neck, back. I mean, she pulled herself together eventually and gradually slimmed down, but her worst was during my impressionable years. I was well and truly anorexic by the time she began dieting."

"Were you hospitalised?" The metallic-blue nail varnish glistened as her fingers drummed her mauve lips.

Hope caught Dawn's eye, holding the stare. "I'm way too clever for that. When they diagnosed me as anorexic, the school watching to make sure I ate lunch, my sisters watching to make sure I ate dinner, weekly weigh-ins - fuss, fuss, fuss - I hated that. I had to get them off my back somehow. I went to jumble sales and got baggy clothes, wore layers and put stones in my pockets when they weighed me, got clever at making myself sick. I can even do it without using my fingers by swallowing hard, or eat marmite with a spoon out of the jar; that never fails."

"Have you any idea how much food you actually digest, calories, or whatever?" Hope swallowed, strolling to the water cooler, pouring a cup. "Oh, sorry, I forgot to ask Gayle to bring some coffee in, do you want…"

"No, thanks, water's fine." Dawn realised she had never seen Hope eat any of the biscuits brought in to compliment the coffee. "I don't eat much. If I get the tummy pains, I'll eat a mouthful of something. Maybe of tuna mayo, or a crisp, a bite of an apple. As soon as it reaches my stomach the pains stop. I maybe have ten bites a day."

"What about this afternoon, with you eating out, what will you do? Surely you can't get away with a mouthful or two, someone would pick up on that, mention it in their article?" Dawn shrugged, concerned.

Hope laughed, formal with the confidence the suit gave her, the Efficient Hope who had first appeared a few weeks previously. But the trust between the two women had grown since then, an easiness that brought honesty, exposing the rotting skeletons. "Dawn, I've been anorexic and bulimic for the best part of twenty years. I'm an expert at avoiding food without being noticed and at covering my tracks if I chuck."

"What makes you keep doing it? I mean, being sick strains your heart, rots your teeth, starving makes you ill."

Hope stood abruptly, holding her arms wide. "Do you think I look unhealthy?" Baring her teeth. "Do these look rotten?" Lifting her blouse to reveal a beautifully toned stomach, devoid of stretch marks, skin tight over the bones, but not revolting as Dawn had expected. "I'm a naturally tiny person. I'm five foot nothing and a size four, my frame is small. But I'm strong as an ox, very fit, and I have a wonderful dentist." Dawn frowned, quizzical, and Hope tugged at her teeth. "Crowns. Impervious to stomach acid. I have money, remember."

Dawn raised her arms in submission. "Okay, you're happy the way you are, I'll let it drop unless you want to talk about it again. Can we talk about your mother? You've mentioned she's now come out as a lesbian. Do you want to explore your relationship with her?"

Leaning her elbows on the armrests, Hope's jacket sleeves fell slightly to reveal several plasters on her forearms and Dawn averted her eyes; another subject for another day. Deep in thought, Hope contemplated whether to honour her mother with paid time. "Yes, why not."

"Were you close when you were a child?" Dawn crossed her legs.

"Yes. Until my father left, set us up in that shithole in Reading, Mum was great, good, she used to cuddle me, us, give us time."

"You can see as an adult, though, that your mother must have been severely depressed after the break-up with your father, judging by the behaviour you've spoken about."

Nodding vigorously. "Of course. I know that, I can give credence to that, it's obvious. But that doesn't make it okay. Fine, she was suffering, but so were we. Me, Faith, Charity, and then little Honesty too. She, or society, our relatives, everybody. We were children, they should have been looking out for us. Someone should have helped us."

"You feel like everybody let you down."

The first flash in a long while; Dawn had hit a wound and the bitterness was clear. "I don't *feel* like everybody let us down, they did let us down. Fact."

77

"Okay, fair enough. How old were you again when you moved to Reading?"

"Seven. Seven innocent years. Then I had no choice but to grow up. I was an adult by the time I was eight."

"But sometimes you're still a vulnerable child now." Dawn hadn't intended to say it aloud. Hope roughly scraped a tear away, annoyed at her loss of control. "Take me through how you grew up so quickly, tell me what it was like."

An ironic snort, and Hope closed her eyes. "Where do I start?" She slumped into the chair, lifting her legs until she was curled into a tiny parcel, tightly wrapped and dainty. "I sort of ignored it at first. When we first moved, I was having problems at school, we all were, you know, Mum making us wear our old uniforms, things like that. We all got bullied. So home was more of an escape then, whether Mum was drunk or not. Well, when we discovered jumble sales, got new clothes, I dropped my posh accent and picked up the Reading slang, which made me fit in more." Dawn raised her eyebrows, her client's crystal vowels were perfect BBC English. "Soon I had a few friends, especially Tracy, she was great. She lived just around the corner from me and I spent most of my time after school playing at hers. I rarely brought her home, because I was embarrassed by the smell, by Mum. The whole house reeked of cigarettes and alcohol and she was passed out more often than not."

Dawn checked her watch discreetly; they had plenty of time. "Am I right in remembering that your mum was pregnant at this point?"

Hope opened her eyes and a sadness drifted through, a vacant sorrow that touched Dawn's heart. "Her tummy was getting bigger, but so was all of her, and I was only seven, the youngest, I had no idea there was a baby in there." A deep sigh. "Everything changed when Honesty was born, the whole dynamic of the household. Mum let herself go even further. We, well, me and Faith, took it in turns to skip school, make sure Honesty was fed and clean."

"How old were you now?"

"I was seven and a half when Honesty was born." Her voice grated, pain rattling from hidden depths. "I loved her so much. Why did that bastard take her away?" She breathed deeply, moments to minutes, reburying the hurt before it gripped too tight. Dawn quietly collected two cups of ice-cold water, shivering from their

78

chill as she carried them to the table. Hope's eyes were closed, the edges of her lips down, tense and unhappy.

A silent minute passed before she was ready to continue. "Tracy went to lots of youth groups; she was always at something or other. When Mum was passed out I would go with her. They were run by the school, I think." Teeth gritted, she growled, "One by the church."

"That's one thing I've been meaning to ask, actually." Dawn leaned forward, chin on hands. "Religion. You all have classic Catholic names, is it important to you?" The room temperature dropped rapidly and Dawn shuddered.

Hope dropped her legs and sat upright, daggers from her eyes stabbing Dawn. Her nails dug into the armrests, scratching, wounding, and she spoke clearly, slowly. "I detest religion."

Reeling, the anger ferocious, Dawn had clearly opened a festering wound. The physical effect of Hope's incredible fury was something Dawn had never witnessed before. Fisted hands shaking uncontrollably, speedy, shallow breaths, a glimmer of sweat on her brow. And her eyes were dangerous pools of black, wide and wild. "I don't want to talk about religion."

"Okay, okay, no problem." A wave of fear passed and she hugged herself against the chill in the room. "Let's go back. You went to some groups."

The rage was gone, but Dawn would not forget. Religion was undoubtedly the core of Hope's wrath, but why? An elaborate fairy tale, a few moralistic nods. Maybe some parts were hypocritical, but not worth such an extreme level of angst. If she couldn't mention religion, she would have to dance around the subject some other way.

As if nothing had happened, Hope said, "The Friendly Club was one. One of the leaders, Griffin, he liked me, took me under his wing. He let me talk to him, tell him about what it was like at home."

"Did he do anything about the situation at home, call in Social Services or anything?"

"He didn't have to. Mum took an overdose when Honesty was two months old. We went to a children's home while she was in hospital. It was horrid. You know, she was always passed out, drunk, but at least we were at home, at least we felt secure in our surroundings. Going to that place was dreadful. It was the only one they could find that could accommodate all four of us and it was for kids younger than us, well, me, Faith and Charity. Charity was the oldest there."

"How long were you there?"

A dismissive wave. Hope was relaxed again, but her feet remained on the floor. "Only two nights. Mum had her stomach pumped, a rap on the knuckles and a promise of a counsellor in maybe two years; you know how the NHS is."

Dawn knew better than to nod, but she understood. If a person were seriously suicidal they had no hope with the waiting lists and lack of resources.

"Because Honesty was a baby they insisted on keeping her in a different wing to us. We sat there, in this room, bloody unwanted pieces of shit, surrounded by toys too young for us, kids too loud for us, wishing we were at school, at home, with our mum, with our dad. But the nights were the killer. We had a room to ourselves, it was small and had bunk beds and a mattress on the floor. Charity had the top bunk, Faith the bottom and I had the mattress. Once all the noise and bustle had died down and the toddlers had gone to sleep, all we could hear was Honesty's plaintive cry. Faith and I, we both tried to go to her but they told us off, sent us back to bed, but we knew she needed us, she missed us."

Hope's face contorted, holding back tears, and Dawn suspected that if she hadn't been immaculately made-up for the interview, she would no longer be inhibited about releasing them. "Faith and I cuddled up on her bunk, we cried, just wanting to console our baby, shower her with love and let her know she wasn't alone. She wanted her mummy. She wanted us." She swallowed hard, her sore throat apparent from the grating in her voice. She reached for the water, now warmed enough to drink, and sipped, gulped, draining the cup.

"Mum was back from hospital when we were brought home. She was sober. Clean, dressed, her hair was brushed. She had some new glasses. Our new social worker, her name was Jeanne, she wrote down her number and told us to call if we needed her, fat fucking load of good that was because Mum kept a lock on the phone." The familiar ironic snort. "But she was good, Jeanne, because she came round regularly, talked to Mum, to all of us, and cooed over Honesty. It felt like she really cared."

"Did your mum respond to the help?"

80

Hope leant heavily on the armrest, chin settling into her hand, and let out a deep, fatigued sigh. "Sometimes. She tried. She still drank, but she had the occasional good day and they were great. I loved her on those days. She started going to something called Gingerbread, which was for single parents. I started going to a thing called the Girl's Group. And I still went to the Friendly Club. Griffin started coming over after I told him about Mum's overdose. He was my special friend."

Dawn's brow furrowed. "Oh? How old was he?"

Hope smiled lightly, a picture of innocence as she shrugged. "I don't know, never asked. I guess he would have been in his twenties. Wore those man sandal things, I call them Jesus Creepers, bloody ugly things."

"You say he started to come to your house, under what guise? I mean, what was the Friendly Club? Who ran it?"

Hope laughed, holding a hand up, a 'stop' sign. "Woah, one question at a time." She chuckled a little more, oblivious to Dawn's apprehension. "Um, Friendly Club?" Patting her lips in thought. "Ah, yes, church. St Paul's Church. It was a spin off from Sunday School." A glance at Dawn. "It's okay, they never did anything religious there, it was just a bunch of kids playing about. I just went to keep Tracy company."

"So in what capacity did Griffin start visiting you at home?" Dawn's misgivings were loud, but Hope couldn't hear them.

"He was a trainee vicar, I think. But he didn't just visit me, he talked to Mum, too."

"Faith? Charity?"

Recollecting, then a proud, childlike smile. "No, just me and Mum."

In unison, they glanced at the clock; the session was up. At a loss for words, Dawn had some terrible suspicions, but would have to tread carefully. She so wished Pat were alive to bounce questions, ideas; her heart wrenched and she willed the hurt away. Returning her attention to her client, the chequebook was out and Hope was scribbling on it. "No, Hope, I'm not charging you for last week, so you've paid to session eleven."

Hope tore the cheque off and held it out for Dawn. "I'm paying for last week. It may not have been about me, but I got a lot out of it. You were so frank and open with your emotions, it made me realise that I can be with you too. I would have cried today, but," she pointed exaggeratedly to her face, "the make-up would have been ruined and it took an hour to do." She laughed. "This cheque is for the next ten sessions. You're really helping me, Dawn."

Dawn took the cheque. "I'm pleased you're seeing this through, you're making real headway."

Smiling, Hope stood and shook Dawn's hand when she rose to join her. She went to leave, efficient and organised once more, but swung back at the door. "Oh, I meant to tell you, I can't come next week, we're going down to Mum's for a pre-Christmas get together."

"Oh, lovely. Okay, two weeks. Where's Mum's, by the way?"

"Cornwall."

"Nice." The two women held eye contact for a while; the conversation didn't seem complete. "Look, do me a favour," Hope cocked her head, "can you spend some time on your own with your mum to discuss Griffin? Just to see what she has to say about him."

Cornwall

Hope had gathered her children together, towing present-stuffed suitcases to the car, and set off on the long journey to Cornwall. Although the main event was on Saturday, they left on Friday to break the drive with a night in Marlow on the way. Reading would have been a more sensible place to stay as it was en-route, but the town reminded Hope of her disastrous childhood. And Lucy.

Danesfield House was a beautiful place, wasted on the children, but Hope had dreamed of staying there in her twenties, never imagining that such opulent dreams would come true. She awoke on Saturday refreshed from an unbroken sleep in the sumptuous bed and, once breakfasted, they continued the journey. The views over Salisbury Plain and the Dartmoor National Park were stunning, the air crisp and chill, the sharp glow from the low winter sun blinding behind them.

After a tiring few hours, they finally reached Pendoggett, driving through automatic gates to reach the mansion Wanda Ferris had bought with the inheritance money after Honesty's untimely death. It was a beautiful home with ornate stonework and newly whitewashed render, approximately two hundred years old. Hope surveyed the landscaped gardens along the lengthy driveway, admiring the clever mix of colours and textures, stunning under the cold sun.

Grand white pillars framed a huge stepped approach to the main entrance, shielding heavy oak doors, but Hope and the children walked to a small, unostentatious side door, under strict instructions that the central hall was only to be used by the traumatised families who lived in the women's refuge her mother had created in the bulk of the house. Wanda's living area was modest compared to the rest of the property: a living room, five en-suite bedrooms, and a large farmhouse kitchen, complete with a massive oak table.

Hope was the last of the siblings to arrive and the first ten minutes were consumed by kisses, hugs and small talk. Wanda's wife, Belinda, a marvel with youngsters, whisked the grandchildren away, bribing them with fizzy drinks and goodies, leaving the husbands to chatter over a whisky, while Wanda showed her daughters how the refuge was developing. Stepping through an internal door, the girls found themselves in a substantial hallway. In its prime, the walls would have been bedecked with mouldings and precious family paintings, but were now littered with noticeboards and information leaflets. Beside the main door was a reception desk, and behind were the charity's administration offices.

Strolling through the corridors, Hope was astounded by her mother's weight gain. Since marrying Belinda, content and secure, the years of dieting were a distant memory. The charity was her guiding light and Wanda's pride in the venture was palpable. She had a true passion for the first time: helping women and children who had suffered the beating fists and manipulative scorn of domestic violence. "We've got twenty-seven rooms now we've converted the reception rooms and the old servant's quarters. Most have four beds, enough for a woman and three children. If she should have more than three, we have z-beds, which we can find a place for in the larger rooms. I'll show you this one, it's empty; we have a family arriving later."

Wanda unlocked the door using a weighty ring of keys and they entered the fresh, homely room. Walls decorated in cream, the beds were made neatly, a small sofa fronted a television, and a kitchenette in the corner provided a kettle, sink and microwave oven. A further door led to a shower-room, functional and white, with a smattering of colour-coordinated cosmetics.

"It's very luxurious, Mum, don't you think it's a bit much? I mean, half these women are druggies and thieves."

Wanda's glare silenced Charity. "These women are victims of domestic violence. They have been beaten and hospitalised repeatedly until finally taking the brave step to flee their bullying partners. They come from all walks of life, but the one thing they share is strength. My duty is to treat them with dignity, showing them love, support, kindness and respect. I haven't had a problem with any of the families so far, not one has taken advantage of my hospitality, and we have nearly a hundred percent success rate at rehabilitating the families in a safe and suitable environment."

Charity skulked away, rebuked and hostile, but Wanda bathed in the proud warmth of her other three daughters, blue eyes twinkling behind glasses, smiling chubby cheeks. After showing them the canteen and busy kitchen, the tour culminated with the ballroom, which was bedecked with sparkling decorations and a towering Austrian pine, branches weighted with tinsel and baubles. "We'll be having dinner this afternoon, then partying in here with the ladies and their children after. It should be a great evening."

Gobsmacked, Charity held a hand up, eyes wide. "Er, now, hold on a minute, let me get this straight: you want me to bring my Ava, only just in remission from leukaemia, into a room full of druggies and yobs for a party. You have got to be joking, Mother." Happiness giggled, alongside Hope and Faith's gasps, and Wanda frowned, mouth firm, but Charity wasn't about to back down. "No way, you can party without us. I'm not mixing with the likes of this riff-raff."

Breaking the tense atmosphere, a gentle voice tinkled from the doorway. "Mrs Ferris, the latest family, the," Gilly, the receptionist, checked her notepad, "Reeves, have arrived."

A cacophony of whining, crying children could be heard nearby. A final glower at her eldest child, Wanda settled a beaming smile on her face and strode from the room, raising her arms welcomingly. "Mrs Reeves, oh, hello, you must by Kyle, aren't you a big boy, and you must be Jake. Come on, let's go and see your new room." The sobbing was replaced by chuckling as they headed up the stairs.

A Family Meal

Belinda proudly carried an oversized turkey to the table, setting it centrally amongst the crackers, party poppers, vegetable dishes and candles. A gentle and soft-spoken woman, she mothered Wanda, shrouding her in security and love, helping her to stay away from the demon bottle that had almost stolen her life on many occasions. Cooking was Belinda's talent and she had anticipated this day excitedly since Wanda had first chosen the date. Since Honesty's death, the annual Christmas get-togethers had become a welcome tradition for the family and were generally fun occasions. But this was the first year Wanda would be including her 'ladies' in the evening celebrations, which led to bellicose conversation from Charity and her husband, Keith, who disagreed with the development.

The large family squeezed tightly around the extensive table and, briefly surveying her flock before commencing - her eldest, with Keith and Ava; Faith and Adam with their children, Kitty and Reuben; Hope, with Penny, Olive and Bern; Happiness, who was lucky to have found a break in her hectic schedule to attend the party; and lastly her beloved Belinda - Wanda stood to say grace, as she always did since Honesty's death.

Hope glanced around as her mother prayed. She hated religion and was proud to be an atheist, but it surprised her that every other family member, including her own offspring, had their eyes closed and hands together. As happened so often, Hope felt like the black sheep and a pang of loneliness made her shudder.

After the commotion of serving - spooning, ladling, pouring - everyone had plates full to bursting with traditional Christmas fayre and they tucked in with gusto, the complementary wine flowing abundantly. Laughter, joking, catching up, the delicious food simply added to the wonderful occasion.

They sat for two hours, stuffed, before Ava began to whimper from tiredness, and Charity and Keith excused themselves to go and settle their daughter in her temporary bed. Gradually the group dispersed and Belinda began the arduous task of preparing the plates and platters for the dishwasher. Wanda placed her arms about her waist from behind, kissing her wife's auburn tresses. "Thank you for today, Bel."

The Party

The music was loud and thudding, the recovering women dancing drunkenly to the beat, carefree and happy, devoid of the threat of violence. With most of the youngsters in bed, the mothers were relishing their freedom, drinking copiously - punch, cider, wine, beer - safe in the knowledge they could let their hair down without fisticuffs before bed.

Wanda and Belinda had proudly hosted the evening, meeting and greeting, dancing, serving the buffet, providing drinks. Hope had enjoyed herself, but Dawn's final words rang in the back of her mind continuously, haunting and taunting. Not able to approach the subject sober, she took advantage of the flowing alcohol, unable to understand the trepidation she felt. Griffin had just been a friend, so why did the prospect of discussing him cause such angst?

She grabbed a bottle of Australian Shiraz and two glasses from the table before finding her laughing mother. "Mum, can we have a chat? In private."

Wanda excused herself from a small group of women and led the way through the main hall to the door that separated her private area from the refuge. Hope placed the glasses on the table that had seen so much hilarity earlier, the polished wood a contrast to the colourful tablecloths that had adorned it so prettily. She filled each glass to the brim, needing the alcohol to say what she had to say, to hear what she had to hear.

"Mum, you know the Brazil business this year?" Wanda took a gulp of wine, nodding appreciatively as the full, round flavour hit her. "I've been having counselling for a couple of months to try and get it out of my system. I wanted to talk it through with someone, rationalise Lucy's betrayal, get over it and move on." Wanda supped some more, seemingly disinterested, which niggled Hope; a mother who openly cared for everybody, nurtured the weak, the sad, the hurt, yet had no interest in her own daughter's problems. She wanted to rebel, like she had done as a child, to get a reaction. Attention. Hope sipped - a taster - then downed her drink, refilling both glasses. The bottle was almost empty.

"She told me to speak to you about Griffin." Wanda winced and looked away, jaw set firm. Hope faltered, fearful. "Why the reaction?"

Wanda removed her glasses and rubbed her eyes, teeth gritted, before replacing them and facing Hope directly. "You were always the selfish one, Hope Ferris."

Astonished by the statement, Hope's correction was instinctive. "Brown."

"It was always about you. You were so naughty, so demanding, always wanted to be centre of attention. You still do it now. Three marriages, just so everyone can look at you on your wedding day. I wouldn't be surprised if you planned the Brazil thing just to get yourself in the papers. Your stupid book, Women and Violence, making money out of those poor women's suffering. You're so selfish."

Hope's jaw had dropped, eyes wide, stunned, as if the past twenty-five years had been swiped away and she was a child again, thigh smarting from a slap. "Why are you doing this?"

"He didn't do anything to you, it was all your devious imagination, just to get yourself some attention." Wanda gulped her drink, grabbing the bottle and refilling her glass. Hope poured the dregs into her own glass. "He was innocent. He was a good man. And you tried to accuse him of such disgusting things. Honestly, you've always been a nasty piece of work. Selfish." Wanda downed her drink and stumbled to the larder, grasping a bottle of cheap vodka, before returning to the table.

Hope laid a hand on her mother's, a little too harshly. "Mum, I need to know, what did I say to you? How old was I? What happened?"

A blazing blue tongue of fire - a glare Hope had directed at Dawn so many times - shot from her mother, but Hope was too confused to return the fury. Her brow furrowed as Wanda stood, swaying above her, threatening, intimidating. She took a deep breath and shouted, "I've asked myself time and time again why God took Honesty and not you, because she was special and you're a pathetic drama queen. It should have been you, not her."

Hope shrank, shoulders hunched, becoming small and nervous, apologetic. Her eyes were dark pools of sadness. "I agree with you, Mum, and I've wished it so often." Gentle, like a breeze.

Through gritted teeth, she bellowed, "If Charity had said Griffin had hurt her, I would have believed her, because she wasn't always away with the fairies like you were. But you, it was just attention grabbing. Always seeking to be the centre of the universe, that's you."

The door opened and Belinda peeped through, concerned. "Is everything okay? I could hear you shouting from down the hallway."

Wanda burst into tears, crocodiles coursing down her cheeks, and Belinda rushed to her side, throwing her arms around her. "There, there, love, it's okay, it's okay."

Head hung low, stooping and broken, Hope silently backed away, snatching and hiding a knife from the side as she neared the door. Oblivious to the whooping celebration in the ballroom, she climbed the creaking servants' stairs and crept to her designated bedroom.

Momentarily, she was comforted by the soft sounds of her sleeping children - little Bern, the covers down to his waist, and Olive, tightly wrapped with just the top of her head peeping on the pillow. Penny was still at the party, determined to play until the early hours.

Hope quietly retrieved a bottle of single malt from her suitcase and took it to the en-suite bathroom after collecting a used glass from the side. Locking herself in, she poured a hefty measure and took a sip, shuddering at the bitterness, knocking it back. She refilled the glass.

Sitting on the tiled floor, she lifted her skirt and rolled her tights down, silvery scars littering both legs. She sliced the knife deeply into her thigh. Deeper, deeper. The agony was incredible, but the internal pain hurt more, the knowledge she was unlovable. Another slash. Three, another, another. The other thigh - one, two, three, four. Thick blood oozed from the wounds and dribbled to the slate floor, taking with it the anger, rejection and hurt, away from her heart, ready to be cleared away and forgotten.

The bleeding was cathartic. The whisky numbed the torment.

Hope was good: she managed not to cry.

Session Eleven

Dawn was surprised that she was looking forward to Hope's session, amazed that two weeks without her strength seemed too long, but the tiny, hunched woman who entered was feeble, distraught. "Hope, what on earth has happened?"

Hope slumped onto the chair, pulling her legs up tightly until she was a small ball of defensiveness. "I asked my mum."

Dawn glanced at her notes from the previous session, reminding her of the question: Griffin. Her heart sank, but she recognised another step had been taken, something more they could work on. "What did she say? How did it go?"

"She said I'm selfish." Hope ran her hands up and down her thighs, and although the cuts were six days old, they still hurt. Silence echoed, Dawn unsure whether to prompt, or let Hope arrange her next sentence in private. The ticking clock was rhythmic, a gentle heartbeat. "My mother was really nasty to me when I mentioned his name, but I've thought through the conversation over and over this past week and I believe that Griffin did something to me that he shouldn't have done. That I told Mum and she covered it up."

"Right. What makes you think that? Can you remember the conversation?" Dawn leant forward eagerly, wishing she had been a fly on the wall.

"Not word for word, no, I was too shocked by Mum's reaction. But she said I'd accused him of disgusting things, and that he was a good man who didn't deserve to be slated like that. She said I was a naughty child and had made things up in my devious imagination. She said if Charity had said something like that, she would have believed her, but not me."

"Fucking hell." Dawn hadn't stopped the reaction in time and was on her feet, looking to the ceiling. "Mothers like that don't deserve their kids." Realising she had let the revelation personally affect her, she snatched a glimpse at Hope, but she was indifferent, as if the words hadn't even registered. Relieved, Dawn promptly sat and crossed her arms.

"Dawn, you mentioned before that you suspected I had been sexually abused. Why?"

"Just things. I'm trained to spot things."

"No, don't cop out on me. I want to know what things, I want to know exactly why, because I need to research this for myself independently of you. If Griffin did something horrible to me when I was a kid, I want to know what it was. I want to know why."

Dawn flicked through her notes, sighing. It had been a gut feeling with no solid basis and eventually she admitted so. "I guess you being happy to marry Frank again just for security - a loveless marriage - it smacks of sexual dysfunction. Promiscuity. The cutting, that's common with abuse victims. Reliance on alcohol..."

"Who said I rely on alcohol? I never said that." Hope's eyes were ablaze and Dawn was astounded by her defensiveness.

She mentally prepared herself for the verbal battering she was sure would follow. "I can smell it on your breath. With the exception of the first session and the one where you had an interview with Cosmo afterwards, you have clearly had a lot to drink the night before. Maybe even in the morning, I don't know."

Hope was distraught, had been desperate to keep her secret. "But vodka isn't supposed to smell. How can you smell it?"

A light tap on the door and Dawn gratefully took the tray from Gayle, thanking her before sealing their privacy again. She set it on the table, spooning sugar into her mug on autopilot. "Hope, you just can, but that's irrelevant. What's your problem with alcohol? It's not illegal, so why don't you want people to know you drink?"

Hope swallowed hard, fearful, brow furrowed and breathing fast and light. "My second husband, Olive and Bern's father - Nigel, his name is - when I left him he got nasty. He knew I liked a drink and said he was going to go for custody using my drinking as the reason. I daren't let anyone know I drink in case he finds out and takes my babies away. Please don't make this public, Dawn, I couldn't live without my kids, I really couldn't. They hold me together." Each breath was so shallow it barely touched the lungs, her face pale and hands trembling.

Crossing the counsellor-patient boundary, Dawn grabbed her hands and stroked, caressing to deflect the anguish. "Calm down, Hope, it's confidential in here, I'm not going to say anything to anyone. Come on, deep breaths, slowly, hold it in, that's good, come on, deep breath, hold it in."

Following Dawn's instruction, Hope regained control. She clutched her upper left arm, fingernails digging deeply. "Is your arm sore?"

Hope shook her head, letting out a breath through blue, pursed lips. "Just a touch of heartburn, it's just stress. It'll pass in a minute."

Dawn stroked Hope's cold, waxy hands, concerned. "Do you get that pain often?" She wasn't sure if Hope had heard, but then she shrugged, dismissive. "You need to see a doctor about that. I mean it. Promise me you will." Hope nodded, chest full of air. "I mean it. Make an appointment this afternoon."

"Okay, don't nag me."

Dawn settled back against the cushioned chair, the softness moulding to fit her body. "Are you okay now?" Hope nodded. "You were going to tell me why you believe Griffin assaulted you in some way."

Hope followed Dawn's lead and relaxed into her own chair, arms palm up on the rests. "It's clear from what Mum said that I told her Griffin was doing something horrible to me. Dawn, I'm not a liar, I never have been, even though I've been accused of it many a time. If I told Mum he was hurting me, then he was hurting me. I would never have said anything like that for attention like she said I did."

"Okay, so from now on we'll play it that you were assaulted by Griffin, and we'll use that as a starting block. Does that sound okay?"

Hope nodded, intrigue and determination replacing the sadness she had originally brought into the room.

"Tell me, what do you remember about Griffin?"

Her eyes scrunched in recollection. "Not much, to be honest. I remember he wore Jesus Creepers, he had hairy toes. I don't remember his face, just his presence, you know, like when he was there doing the dishes with me, when he said I did the dishes just like he did."

"Do you know how old you were?"

Contemplation. "About seven, eight-ish. I was going to the Friendly Club and he stuck around us for a year or so. He was definitely there at Christmas, because I went carol singing with the

93

church, Mum did too. Little Honesty was in her pram; she was just a tiny baby at the time. I remember we went back to a different house every evening afterwards, had mince pies, drinks, that sort of thing." Dawn nodded, blowing her coffee, sipping. "We went to a service at the church on Christmas Eve, it was the Midnight Mass, we had oranges with candles in them - Christingles, they were called - and the church was dark. I felt comfortable there, I really enjoyed it, the drama, the uniqueness."

"But no face. What about your house, what do you remember about the house?"

"It was filthy and it stank because Mum drank and smoked so much. I remember the kitchen clearly, doing the dishes with Griffin. He said I did them just like he did..." She breathed gently, a ghost, lost.

"That sounds like a significant day, you've brought the dishes up a couple of times now. Can you remember what happened after you did the dishes? Where you went? What you did? Was your mum there? Sisters?"

Hope shook her head. "No, just doing the dishes, it ends there." Frustration took over. "I want to know how to get the memory back."

Dawn glanced at her watch: half an hour had passed. She had some ideas and wished Pat was still around to bounce off before involving Hope. Damn Pat for dying. She had suggested Hope may have repressed memories and Dawn had dismissed the idea offhand. "We need to tread carefully, because if your mind has erased or hidden your memories, it's trying to protect you." She hoped she sounded convincing, because this was uncharted territory in her counselling career. "You need to ask yourself if you really want to get those memories out, or whether you'd be better off leaving them be."

Hope picked at her leggings, each tug lifting the worn material to a little cone before gradually shrinking flat. She glanced at Dawn, at the sparkly waistcoat and black sweater, tight black jeans with knee high, stiletto boots. Her hair bobbed lightly with each breath, golden curls that framed a heavy set and attractive face, painted in bright, cheerful colours. "Dawn, you have a good life. You're confident enough to care about what you wear, about making yourself pretty, looking after yourself. You have pride and self-respect; it emanates from you. I want to be like that, but I feel

94

so dirty. Always do. I suspect I've been violated, but I don't know how. I don't know if he used his fingers, or his dick, or if he just looked. And the worst part is I don't know if I let him. Maybe even enjoyed it. I need to know. I need to know that I tried to stop him. I need to know what he did."

An instant decision; Dawn dragged a wooden chair to the circle. "Sit on this. I'm going to relax you." Hope obeyed. "Deeply relax you, then I want your mind to go back to your childhood. I'm not going to ask anything about Griffin, so don't worry, that's for a later date. Today, I want to know who you were aged seven and eight." Dawn had only ever read about the technique and had dismissed it alongside Freud's repressed memory theory, but today it seemed like the right thing to do. She had realised in the early days that impulsiveness and spontaneity worked best with Hope, and now her theory would be tested. "Close your eyes."

Her voice gentle, a transient breeze trickling through the room, and using soft words, Dawn talked her client into a trance. Hope's shoulders slumped, her back hunched, and her feet hovered just above the carpet. She was under.

Crossing her fingers that she wasn't being unethical, Dawn began. "You're going back to your childhood. You're seven years old and you live in Reading with your mum and sisters, Charity, Faith and Honesty. Are you there?"

Dawn's eyes widened as Hope moved her legs gently, back and forth, childlike. Her hands slipped to the edges of the chair, forcing her back straight, eyes tightly shut. "You're kicking your legs; are you happy?" The giggle of a young girl, bright and cheeky, a touch of shyness. "What are you wearing?"

"I got these from the jumble sale at the Church Hall. Do you like them?" Jerky and young, expressed questioningly as only a child can do.

Amazed, Dawn was certain Hope was truly a child again in her mind. "I like them, describe them to me."

"You're silly, you can see them. My brown skirt. It was 5p. And my jumper was 5p too." Her legs swung wildly, sweeping to the front, to the back. "I like school now I've got new clothes."

"Tell me about school."

A grin spread across Hope's face, almost toothy by default, and her legs kicked merrily; the child inside was happy. "Mrs Batty is my teacher and she says I'm a prodigy. I don't know what that means though, but I know it's good."

"Why does she say that?"

"Because I read grown-up books. Mum taught me to read when I was little, so now I read things for teenagers."

Dawn scribbled on her pad. "What about home? What's home like?"

"It's good. I stay off school a couple of days a week so I can look after Honesty. She's my little sister. She's a baby. I love her." It was interesting that young Hope enjoyed staying off school to mind her sister, yet adult Hope resented it.

"What does your mum do when you're looking after Honesty?"

"Mummy has to have special drinks so she can feed Honesty with her boobies." Hope giggled shyly, head cocked, testing the reaction to the rude word. Dawn remained silent. "Mummy needs to sleep a lot because having a baby is hard, so when she sleeps I cuddle Honesty and give her toys."

"Hope, what do you look like? What colour is your hair?"

Her hand shot up, winding the brunette hair around her fingers, tugging it this way and that, curling and freeing. "It's brown. Sometimes it's curly. Mummy wants to cut it but I run away because I don't want her to."

"Are you smiling? Tell me about your face."

The legs stopped swinging and hung lifelessly, toes pointing inwards, and her body melted into the chair, hands hugging her chest. "I don't have a face. I have hair but not a face. There's a black hole instead of a face."

There it was, the fish they had been baiting. "You must have eyes; what colour are your eyes?"

"I haven't got eyes. I can't have eyes because I haven't got a face."

"Can you see anything or are you blind?"

"I can see everything. I just don't have any eyes."

"Hope, tell me about your bedroom."

The legs began to sway again, rhythmic, careless. "I can't see my bedroom. I can see frost flowers on the window, but no bedroom."

Dawn had heard enough and started the careful process of bringing Hope back: gentle words in a soft tone, soothing. She was

96

also now certain that something had happened to her client, probably in her bedroom, and this abuse - whatever it was - had caused Hope to despise her face enough to block it out.

Hope had insisted she wanted to know the truth, but Dawn was unsure if that was wise, or how to progress, having not experienced, witnessed, or read about a similar circumstance. She needed to consult somebody before they trod further along this path. But Pat was gone and she had been the only wise sage in the company, her colleagues all thirty-somethings like herself. Who did she turn to? "Are you back with me?" Hope smiled, deeply relaxed. "Do you remember any of what just happened?"

Another smile, thoughtful, yet chillingly calm. "Yes, everything. It was a strange sensation, because I felt just like a child again, and I spoke like a child, but I'm an adult."

Dawn swallowed, coughing lightly, clearing her unblocked throat. Buying time. "What about the face? What did you make of that?"

Uncomfortably serene, Hope was *too* composed. "It was weird, like I was looking at myself and somebody had crayoned black over where my face should have been. A hole. Maybe that explains why I feel so ugly all the time; when people tell me I'm pretty, I know they're lying. I look in the mirror and hate what I see. I always feel dirty, like I don't wash enough. I always feel like I smell."

Dawn discreetly looked at her watch. "Hope, I want you to think seriously about this over the next week, about whether you really want to dredge up the past. I can help you move on without you ever knowing, you'd be healed without whatever pain the truth holds."

The determined streak was back and Hope viewed her counsellor with confidence and defiance. "You'd want to know, wouldn't you? You can't tell me honestly that you wouldn't, you'd be lying. He assaulted me. He might be still doing it to some poor kid out there. He was a trainee fucking vicar for Christ's sake, vicars have every opportunity with children because the very job they do instigates trust from all quarters. If I found out what he did, I could find him and prosecute. Then he'd never be able to do it to any other child."

Dawn shifted uncomfortably. The words thrown like sharpened darts made sense, but every bone in her body told her

97

Hope wasn't ready. For such a strong person, she just wasn't strong enough. "Hope, I can see your point, really I can, but I worry it might be too soon. Thing is, you've only just found out that you may have been abused after what, twenty-five years or so, that's a massive revelation to cope with already. I implore you to wait a while, use the counselling to accept the abuse before taking such a dramatic step."

Hope nodded, but a devious glint in her eye worried Dawn. Her mind raced, wondering how to stop her doing anything impulsive or damaging. "Hope, why don't you come and see me more than once a week for the foreseeable future, we can work this through together."

Hope grinned and it appeared genuine, but Dawn was still concerned. "I'm fine, really, I feel better than I have in a long time." She glanced at the clock. "I believe that's it for today, so I'll see you next Friday."

Hope collected her coat, gloves and scarf in a single movement and was at the door, leaving Dawn scant time to respond. "Hope, slow down, please." Hope turned back, shrugging the woollen jacket across her shoulders. "Promise me you'll not do anything stupid. Please."

Hope manipulated the scarf around her neck, deftly donning the gloves. Her expression was tranquil, the edges of a smile touching her lips. Something extraordinary had happened during the session and now Hope's eyes held a new and unprecedented danger. Black pools of peril, the intense fire within ready to reach out and kill. She smiled fleetingly, dimples briefly appearing on her slender cheeks, and winked elaborately. The door closed.

Mesmerised by the transformation she had witnessed, Dawn cradled her head in her hands, fingers grasping at the brown roots she had not had time to have bleached. "Jesus Christ, what have I done? Pat, I wish you were here."

The Phone Book

Helen heard Hope's car pull into the driveway and skipped to the front door, cracking it open. She had arrived in Saxlingham Nethergate two days before with her young sons, Darren and Dean, intending to spend the week property-hunting now her present house had finally been returned to its rightful owner. She was grateful to Hope, who had paid for decorators to come in and make the house saleable - if only on the surface - and promised she would repay her when the proceeds hit her bank account.

Hope darted inside, shivering from the cold. "How did it go?" Helen's eyes had a sparkle that had died years before, excited about moving north, close to her unlikely best friend.

Hope was shedding her outer layers onto chairs, falling to the floor. She was in a hurry. "I'll tell you later. I need to make a phone call in private. You go and get the kettle on, I'll be back in a minute."

Hope darted up the stairs, her low boots echoing her haste on the polished wooden steps, and a door slammed. In her office, Hope rifled through the Yellow Pages, searching for the help she was sure would cure her. "Hypnotherapy. Hypnotherapy. Hypno... Ah, here we are: hypnotherapy and regression services." Hope circled an advert, grasped the phone and dialled.

The University Book

Dawn was grateful to not have any clients for the afternoon. She had previously booked a half-day holiday to do her Christmas shopping, but that was irrelevant now. She needed to talk to somebody about Hope, about the technique she had used, about how to retrieve memories, or even if she should retrieve them. Her mind had darted from one person to the next, and the only man she could think of who was well enough qualified and may be willing to help was her old psychology tutor, Taylor Wilkinson. She couldn't remember why he had given her his home number all those years ago, but knew she had it somewhere.

She climbed the ladder, clasping a torch, and squeezed her large frame through the hatch, shining the light around, illuminating the boxes of memories and rubbish. Tearing open a box - two, three - she finally found the one containing her old study files and threw them from the box recklessly, searching. The navy one, battered at the edges and creased in the middle, squashed and tatty, was the goal and she tugged it open, flicking through the pages, picturing the number she could remember writing years before. There it was. She threw the file through the hatch, a dull thud as it landed on the bedroom carpet, and followed it down.

Grasping the folder, Dawn scurried downstairs to call him, hoping he hadn't moved house in the past nine years. She pressed the number and impatiently listened to the ringing, monotonous, repetitive. Answered. "Wilkinson."

Relief flooded her, tingling her fingers and toes. "Thank God. Mr Wilkinson, you might not remember me, but I was one of your pupils, Dawn Faraday. Please can we meet up. It's urgent, I can't stress that enough."

"Goodness, young lady, remember to breathe whilst you're talking. Yes, I remember you, and yes, of course we can meet." His good nature was apparent as he chuckled.

Tears prickled Dawn's eyes and she was aghast at how much emotion she felt. "Thank you, sir, thank you so much."

Mr Wilkinson

"Goodness, look at you, you're all grown up." Taylor Wilkinson stood beside his desk, arm outstretched for a friendly handshake. Dawn took his warm hand with gratitude and sat in the seat he indicated. "I can't believe how tall you are, I'm sure you've grown since university."

Dawn giggled; she had heard that so many times before. "I didn't stop growing until my mid-twenties, overtook both my parents, apparently. My brother says I'm the tallest in the family."

Concern furrowed his brow. "You're still not in touch with them?" She shook her head, waving dismissively, and he tactfully changed the subject. "What do you get up to nowadays, still messing about in a band? I seem to remember you had a beautiful singing voice." Mr Wilkinson was relaxed, foot on knee, slumped on his leather chair, and his openness comforted Dawn.

"Still in a band, yes, we're called Reveal, we play rock mainly." Worry fleeted across her face. The band. She had been skipping rehearsals, much to the annoyance of her brother and the rest of the band. Her heart was still behind it - she loved singing, raw music, performing, the whole scene - but her attention had been solely on Hope recently. She kept her tone bright. "We do local gigs, but still going for the big time if we ever get a lucky break."

Wilkinson raised an eyebrow but diplomatically stayed quiet; Dawn was unlikely to get a lucky break at her age. "Now, young lady, you sounded quite desperate on the phone, how can I help you?"

Dawn swallowed hard, where did she start? She had imagined the conversation so many times since the previous day, but still hadn't found a starting point. And there was confidentiality to think about too. "Mr Wilkinson…"

A friendly chuckle. "Young lady, you're an adult now, please call me Taylor."

Dawn smiled gratefully, pleased he was so amiable. "Taylor, I have a degree in clinical psychology and a diploma in counselling, and I'm a member of the British Association for Counselling and Psychotherapy."

"A true professional then, I'm proud you took your education so far." His eyes crinkled into a warm smile.

Dawn tried to find a way to phrase her dilemma. She hadn't been seeking approval or compliments, but that was how she had come across. She needed to take a different route, but how could one explain Hope? She scanned the functional room, debating inwardly. The walls were yellowed with age and well-worn bookcases dripped with traditionally bound classics and modern paperbacks, largely nonfiction. The Axminster carpet was tatty with age, a threadbare track between the door and antique oak desk. The biggest surprise was the absence of a computer; Taylor evidently shunned modern technology in favour of tried and trusted books in his thirst for knowledge.

"Taylor, I wasn't looking for praise just then, that must have sounded so big headed. I was just trying to show you that if I, with my high level of education, can't solve this problem, that's how deep a problem it is for me. God, even that sounds arrogant." Dawn shook her head, reprimanding herself. She was making a fool of herself and still hadn't reached the Hope dilemma.

Taylor picked up the phone and pressed number two firmly. "Angela, sweetheart, I don't suppose you'd bring in a tray of drinks, would you?" He caught Dawn's eye, mouthing 'tea or coffee', and she smiled. "Two coffees, yes, yes. Thank you, love, I really appreciate it." He replaced the handset and clasped his hands on the desk, regarding his former pupil. He had always respected Dawn. She was old for her years, despite her youthful wardrobe, and was intelligent, funny and unique. However, his compassion floated to her now; he had never seen her so disturbed, even before her final exams. He remained silent, knowing she would spill her troubles when she was ready.

Eventually, "I have a client and it appears she has repressed memories of abuse from a young age. I did something the other day and I'm not sure it was ethical."

"Oh?"

Dawn's eyes met the floor, ashamed and embarrassed, and she mumbled, "I regressed her." A glance for his reaction then back to the floor. "Not to the abuse - I wouldn't do that, I'm not qualified - just back to when she was seven, her home life, surroundings, how she felt about her family."

102

His fingers were outstretched, tips squeezed together in a pyramid. "So you've justified your actions to me, but not to yourself. What exactly is the problem? Be specific."

Guilty unease, her eyes begging him for help. "I think she's going to do something stupid. I think the whole revelation - it's only been a week since she found out - I think it's sending her over the edge. I don't know what to do."

A light tap on the door and a mature and impeccably neat lady stepped onto the threadbare trail, a silver tray in her outstretched hands. She smiled at Dawn, at her husband, warmly glowing with kindness, and retreated gracefully, leaving a wisp of musk in the room after closing the door.

Taylor debated Dawn's outburst, fingers drumming the leather blotter. "You say something stupid, what do you mean by that?"

"Not suicide. She self-harms, but she's not suicidal. I don't know. She wants to know what the guy did to her. She's desperate to know, but I think it's too soon. She's only just discovered the possible abuse after twenty-five years; I think she needs to come to terms with it before finding out any more details."

Taylor removed his glasses, setting them on the desk, and rubbed his eyes. "Yes, yes, I agree. You think she may try some other therapy to regain the memory, is that what scares you?"

She nodded vigorously. "Taylor, she has an anger I've never seen in anyone before. It's so deep, so vitriolic, she scares me sometimes. I'm not sure how much she's capable of once the fire inside is lit…" Dawn had voiced a worry she had never consciously considered before and it shocked her.

Taylor was intrigued, wishing he could meet the challenging client. He mulled the situation for a minute and gasped, incredulous. "You think she may try and get revenge on the abuser, don't you? It's not concern for your client's welfare, it's concern for his, isn't it?"

Dawn fidgeted. He had hit the nail on the head, but she wished he had phrased it in a way that didn't crucify her for siding with the enemy. Anger teetered; he had made her sound so cruel. "It's not like that. She's not like that. I mean, yes, I'm worried she'll track him down. In fact, yes, that's exactly what I'm here about. Oh, for God's sake, I just don't know."

His calmness was refreshing. "Does she know who the abuser was?"

"Yes, he was a trainee vicar, but she's only ever referred to him by his first name. I'm not sure she knows his surname."

His fingers continued to drum against the wood, a soothing patter. "Hmm, but that wouldn't take much finding out, though." He swung his chair gently left to right, contemplating, before offering the get out clause: "So let her. She's only your problem in the counselling sessions, what she chooses to do in her own time is her business."

Dawn was stunned. "Mr Wilkinson, are you telling me to ignore the danger signs? Is that even ethical?"

He regarded her, her enthusiasm and compassion, and understood her dilemma, but it was obvious she was emotionally tied to her client, and that danger sign was more imperative than any other. "Yes. And if this client keeps niggling you aside of work, you know you must transfer her to another counsellor. You have let things become personal."

The Surname

Hope's knuckles were white as she gripped the phone, teeth gritted with frustration. "Just tell me his surname, that's all I'm asking."

Wanda Ferris was equally annoyed, her voice curt. "Hope, let this go, will you. It's in the past, it all happened twenty-five years ago now, that's a lifetime away. It's time you let it go."

"Mother, you don't seem to understand, it's not in the past for me. It's my past, my present, my future. I need closure and to get that I need to know that I've done all I can to get retribution for what he did. Why can't you understand that? Why are you putting so much loyalty into a man who screwed your seven-year-old daughter, rather than protecting and helping me? You didn't act on what I told you a quarter of a century ago, you didn't try to stop him or alert the authorities, get me the help I needed. You're my mother and I need you to help me now. Help me to help myself. If you won't tell me what I told you back then, then at least tell me his surname. Just give me some answers, for god's sake, and make amends for your failings as a mother when I desperately needed you."

"Right," the anger shot down the line like a fireball and Hope tugged the phone from her ear, "I'll tell you his surname, but in return I never want to hear this business mentioned again. You do what messing you need to do, but leave me out of it. His name was Hall." The line went dead and involuntary tears - relief for the answer, grief for her mother's abandonment - streamed copiously, emptying her electrically charged emotions.

Hope breathed slowly, deeply, calming herself until she was ready for the next step. Less than a minute passed before eagerness overwhelmed the sadness and she turned to her computer, typing 'Griffin Hall vicar' into the search engine. Soon she knew the village he lived in, the church he preached at and his extra-curricular activities - all of which were under the guise of the church, and all involving children.

The Regression

Hope had a surreal calmness as she rested back on the encompassing, overstuffed chair. The room was pastel green with potted plants providing the only contrast, apart from the seat and the navy clad woman in front of her.

Mary was a nervous woman, demure and unassuming, but her voice had a wonderful tone, soothing like silk, reassuring, comforting, and Hope was confident she had chosen the right hypnotherapist from the three she had shortlisted. "Just a final recap to make sure I have your instructions correct." Molten chocolate vowels dripped deliciously and Hope's tension subsided. "You were sexually abused at the age of seven by a man named Griffin Hall. You want to be regressed to that age to revisit the abuse. You want it on tape because you intend to prosecute."

Hope nodded, smiling.

Mary continued, brow furrowed. "You do realise this could be traumatic; do you have help after this session."

She was becoming impatient. "Yes, yes, of course."

"If you like, I can place a block on your subconscious before I bring you round to stop you having flashbacks."

"That won't be necessary."

"Are you sure?"

Hope grinned enigmatically. "Look, I'm ready, I'm in control. I know what I'm doing."

The older woman sighed, pigeon eyes peeping from beneath a heavy fringe, pinched pouting lips enhancing wrinkles caused by years of tobacco abuse, and she switched the tape recorder on. Her dreamy, creamy voice lulled Hope, and step-by-step she soothed her to a distant plain, a place where an innocent child played. Hope could see herself dancing in the breeze, her summer dress, smock-stitched to the waist, billowing. Her red T-bar sandals reminded her of Dorothy in The Wizard of Oz, crinkled socks topping them scruffily beneath scabbed knees. Her dark hair was long, flowing and she scampered about, doing cartwheels, handstands. Carefree.

"Are you happy, Hope? Are you in a nice place?" Oozing into her semi-consciousness like an angel's harp.

106

"I'm playing. I'm running and skipping. I feel so free."

"You can play again later, but you need to go home now, can you do that for me?"

"Oh," a sulky child, "okay!" Hope's knees and arms jerked slightly. "I'm home."

"There's a man called Griffin who visits you, is he there?"

Hope's expression dulled, hands shielding her face. "He's doing something to Mummy. She's kneeling on the floor and he's pulling her head into his legs. They're making funny noises. I don't like it. Mummy's seen me. He's gone away from her. He's got a big thing sticking out. I'm scared. I'm running through the room now, I've passed them, I want to go to my room, I'm running up the stairs. Mummy's coming after me. I'm in my room and I've slammed the door. I can hear them talking outside. I'm scared. I don't want a smack."

Hope's legs were drawn to her chest, arms wrapping them, hands clasped tightly together, gripping. Her body shook uncontrollably, frightened tremors coursing. Her innocence glowed vividly as her words created a filthy atmosphere. "The door's opening. It's Griffin. I can hear Mummy going down the stairs. He's locked the door, I think he's going to smack me, I don't want a smack."

She broke into a wide smile, arms relaxing, legs falling to the floor. "It's okay, he's being nice, he's kneeling beside me. He's got my hand and is playing with my fingers. It tickles." Her body tensed once more. "His hand's gone up my skirt, I don't like it, his fingers are in my knickers. I'm pushing him away." Hope's arms jabbed the air, legs kicking to one side, the unseen attacker persisting. "He won't let me go, he's holding me down, I'm by the wall and I can't move, he's taken my knickers off. I want my mum. I want my mum. I want to get away. He's holding me down, he's doing things to my bottom and it hurts, I don't like it. No! No!"

The childish voice became a terrified scream, gurgling, terror-filled. Gruesome. "The big thing. The big purple thing. He's pushing it in my bottom. It hurts. Mummy, it hurts, it hurts."

Hope was spread over the chair, legs apart, silent sobs racking her chest as she relived her childhood rape. Mary hoped it would be over soon; her client was deeply distressed and she was eager to bring her round. But suddenly Hope jerked upright and her speech became slurred, her mouth no longer forming words properly.

Mary could barely understand what Hope was saying, the consonants unpronounced, but soon gathered from the body movement that she was being forced to perform oral sex. Her eyes were wide, petrified and she struggled to breathe. Trying to speak. Trying to fend off her abuser. Mary's heart jumped, sickness gnawing the pit of her stomach. She swallowed hard as she continued to witness the vile attack, checking the tape was recording twice so her client would never have to experience this horror in regression again.

The room became calm. Hope lay on her side, curled into a ball of despair and no more words were required. Mary's velvet voice crooned, gently bringing Hope from the nightmare, ready to deal with the forthcoming trial of police stations and statements.

Hope opened her eyes, sapphire crystals shining, warming the room, and an enigmatic smile returned to her lips. Mary rewound the tape, avoiding Hope's stare, unsure how to deal with the aftermath having never experienced such a show before. "Do you remember what just happened?"

The blueness darkened to ebony, eyes dead with no soul, but the smile remained. "I remember everything." Her calmness was unnerving and Mary fidgeted. The woman before her had suffered greatly and she had no idea what to say, but there was a danger to her aura too. Hope was a victim, without a doubt, but her meek manner shielded a fierce hatred and Mary wanted her away from her treatment room as soon as possible.

Luckily for her, Hope was in no mind to prolong the session either. She checked the tape had recorded adequately before leaving her number, stating the police would probably be in touch.

Mary shut the front door behind Hope as soon as she could without being rude and rushed back to the room, opening the window wide, despite the freezing winds, to clear the oppressive atmosphere. Leaning out, she took a deep breath - another, another - resolving to take a sleeping tablet later to block out any repercussions from the hideous meeting.

Session Twelve

Although the room was stiflingly warm, the atmosphere was chilly between Hope and Dawn. Each with a steaming coffee, they had greeted politely, but hadn't spoken since. Restless, they played with their hair, fidgeted with their fingers, picked at clothes, anything to avoid speech.

It was Dawn's job to get the session going, but she didn't know where to start. Something about Hope was different, a menacing cloud of vengeful peril. Dawn needed to root out what had happened in the past seven days, but Hope wasn't forthcoming. "I see you've dyed your hair." It was a pathetic icebreaker and Dawn chastised herself.

"Yes." Bored.

She tried again, smiling, friendly. "Are you ready for Christmas?"

Hope nodded, disinterested. "Yes."

Dawn bristled but remained bright. "Just two days to go. Are the kids looking forward to it?"

Hope glared at Dawn. "Of course."

Dawn didn't have the patience to spend an hour prompting this woman and considered cancelling the session and going to the pub with her colleagues for a Christmas drink instead. She tried to stop her disenchantment showing, smiling as she said, "Look, something's obviously happened in the past week, why don't you tell me about it instead of wasting the hour."

Hope sighed, irritated. "I've done a lot of homework this week and it's been very revealing, but I'm not sure I want to talk to you about it."

Dawn leaned forward, quizzical. "Okay, why's that?"

She shrugged, sulky.

Hope was testing her patience today and it was irksome, like dealing with a child. Her professionalism wavered, rolling her eyes, folding arms, vexed. "Right, we play games, do we? We spend the next hour with me trying to guess what changes you've had this week. Fine, if that's what you want, you're the client, but don't expect me to get overexcited about it."

109

Hope smirked and Dawn realised she had played into her hands. This was a new facet to Hope; the confidence and self-assurance had appeared before, but now there was a sinister quality, a danger. Dawn shuddered, apprehensive.

Hope sipped her coffee, back straight and ankles crossed neatly. She wore smart, well-fitting casuals that exacerbated her tiny figure: Levis teamed with a tight velveteen top and coordinating waistcoat, and knee high stiletto boots. Dawn hadn't seen her in jeans before.

Then it hit her: her own uniform had been copied. Dawn gaped, shivering, the ominous blackness in the room weighting the air, and a chilling, victorious smile settled on Hope's lips. Instinct screamed at Dawn to get out of the room, to get as far away as possible. She didn't want to counsel Hope any more.

"Yes you do." Dawn's brow crinkled, confused. "Counsel me. You do want to counsel me."

Her eyes widened, sure she hadn't said anything aloud; if she had, she had no recollection. Was this another game? Coincidence? Where had the statement come from? "What do you mean?" Her voice was weak, a touch of panic.

"You can't leave me now, we're too good together. We're a team and we work well."

Dawn studied the new woman before her. Mahogany waves that danced in the light and dramatic make-up that enhanced her natural beauty without brassiness. And an uncanny ability to read minds. She chose her words carefully, willing away the irrational trepidation. "Who said anything about leaving?"

"I can see it in your face. You don't feel comfortable with me today, I'm worrying you."

Her irritation returned and she shook her head. "Rubbish." Her client grated on her and Dawn's temper was brewing. "Look, I'm fed up with this, I don't want games. I just don't. I'm here to counsel you and if you don't want or need counselling, why don't we just move on and get on with our Christmas shopping?"

"Wow, and it's not even your time of the month."

Enough was enough. Dawn's patience snapped and she jumped to the door, opening it wide. "Come on. Session over."

The triumphant smile remained and Dawn was desperate to dodge the mesmerising blue that transfixed her, that compelled her to close the door and seal their privacy again. Assertive, hypnotising,

Hope's voice was quiet. "I want you to come on a journey with me, I want you to meet someone."

Dawn sat, resigned. "That's not how we…"

"It may not be, but we've never followed the sheep in our sessions before, so why start now?"

She was scared, terrified of the temptation to break the rules, but her willpower was gone. "When?"

Her expression unreadable, Hope shook her head slightly and her thick, russet locks flowed like liquid over her shoulders. "Tomorrow evening."

Dawn chuckled, incredulous. "Don't be ridiculous, it's Christmas Eve, I've got a gig with…"

"A gig?" Hope leaned forward with intrigue.

Dawn sighed. More unprofessionalism; she had allowed her personal life into the room and was determined not to elaborate. "Yes, so I can't go anywhere with you, sorry."

"Yes, you can. We're going to a place called Polton in Bedfordshire to attend Midnight Mass at St Peter's Church." The calculated agenda had been revealed matter-of-factly and the cold and clinical delivery forced another shudder through Dawn.

She crossed her arms, trying to remain in control, but her voice was wary, cracking. "You've found him, haven't you?"

"Yes. Griffin Hall, rector at St Peter's Church, Polton."

"Hope, what are you planning? You know you can't break the law; it won't do you any favours."

Hope tinkled prettily, but the humour failed to reach her eyes. "Who said anything about breaking the law? I just want to go and see what he's like, how he plays it, if he's got any more skeletons in his cupboard. I want you to see him."

Dawn downed her cold coffee, grimacing. "Nope, no can do. I've cancelled too many gigs recently; the lads would shoot me."

Hope's eyes bored into Dawn and she couldn't pull away, unwillingly spellbound. The breath was painfully tight in her chest, her body gasping for oxygen, but escape was impossible. "You will come with me. Tell me where you're playing and I'll meet you there. We'll drive down after the show."

Caught in headlights, Dawn wanted to object… The gig, her band, her private life… Hope should be separate from her personal affairs… She tried to break the spell, but the bind was too strong and she remained transfixed by the intense, sparkling eyes. "Hope, no. Please."

"You know, if you're any good I could have a word with Happiness about fixing you up with a scout from FMI."

A bribe. And she didn't want to drive to a stupid church ceremony on Christmas Eve, she wanted to get hammered with the lads. She had to resist. "We're playing at The Farmer's Arms in town, our set begins at eight." A shred of strength surfaced. "I'm not sure this a good idea."

The smile seemed genuine, but the atmosphere remained heady. "It's a great idea. I was regressed this week, on Monday." Dawn gasped, now understanding. "I relived the first assault, assuming there was more than one." Dawn was silent, dumbfounded. "It explains so much. All the things we've talked about in here. My parents and their messy divorce, my ex-husbands and their mistreatment, the rapes, they're just party to this. I've subconsciously put myself in the position of being used by people - abused by people - because I didn't feel worthwhile, and it's all down to what Griffin did when I was a child and my mother subsequently covering it up."

"That's a fair summary, there's probably a lot of truth in it." Dawn grasped a smidgeon of control from the filthy depths she had sunk to.

"The hypnotherapist taped the regression. I haven't listened to it, but I remember everything and it's vile. Griffin Hall is a sadistic, revolting individual."

"Are you going to go to the police?" The room darkened and a roll of thunder clapped outside, raindrops hammering against the window. Storms usually fascinated Dawn - the drama, the vulnerability - but today the atmosphere was sinister and goose-bumps rose on her arms.

Unperturbed, maybe unaware, Hope shrugged. "It was twenty-five years ago. I'll give the tape to the police, give them my story, they'll listen and say 'dear, dear', then they'll interview him, he'll deny it, and that will be it over. What's the point?"

Dawn thumped the arm of the chair. "God, Hope, you really piss me off with that attitude. You took the same stance with your first rape. Look, if you don't report it, you have no hope of stopping him, but if you do there's a chance, even if it's a small one, that you can. He's probably still doing it to other little girls, you know that."

"And that's my responsibility, is it? He assaulted me, so I have to bear the brunt of his actions for the rest of my fucking life, do I? Put yourself in my position, Dawn, how would you feel if you were in my shoes, knowing some idiot fucked you when you were seven, knowing you were violated, yet disbelieved when you tried to get help."

"I know exactly how you feel because it happened to me, in my case it was my uncle, my father's brother, and as a result the only member of my family who keeps in contact with me is my brother." The words had tumbled out urgently and she knew she had gone too far. Silence hung in the oppressed room, the air heavy, both women stunned by the admission.

The thunderstorm raged outside, fiery daggers of lightning swiftly followed by a bass drumroll, accompanied by rainy percussion. Their eyes occasionally met, sharing mutual understanding. As the minutes ticked by, Dawn realised the intimacy had been progressive in Hope's case, albeit unprofessional, because she held a new respect for her counsellor. Dawn was no longer an enemy who sympathised, but had no appreciation of the depth of wretchedness.

"Did you have counselling?" A wisp of a voice.

Dawn nodded without vigour, equally haunted. "Pat Hinds. Deceased."

Hope gasped, hand clasping her mouth as she looked away. "Shit. Now I know why you were so upset: she saved you, she was your hero."

"He did it until I was thirteen, when I fell pregnant with his baby. I tried to tell my parents it was his, but they thought I was covering up for a boy at school or something. They forced me to have an abortion, which I didn't want. It was botched and left me infertile. I can't have kids now." Jaw set firm, Dawn was in agony, regardless of the extensive time she had spent in therapy. "I went to university to study English Language, but changed to Psychotherapy after Pat counselled me. She made a difference to me, changed my life, and I wanted to help other people like that. I really want to help you. Now you can see that I do understand you, what you've been through." She patted her heart. "I feel for you in here."

"I've been cruel to you then, challenging you like I do. You're one of the sisters and I've mistreated you." Anguished, ridden with guilt.

"No, I was the same with Pat in the early days, angry at her, as if it were her fault."

"Why didn't you want an abortion if you were only thirteen?"

Dawn rose, her athletic body parting the charged atmosphere, and strolled to the window, her gait awkward, streetwise. Placing her hands on the pane, dribbles of rain separated by the glass, she said, "I was lucky to get this job, I'm sure Pat pulled some strings. She was my mentor."

"Did you report your uncle?"

"They put me in care. When my mother and father didn't believe me, I went to a teacher and she helped me to tell the police. My parents threw me out, so I was taken into care. But me, the teacher, we persevered and the police were great. He was imprisoned on three counts of indecent assault and one of rape of a minor. He got twelve years."

"Hell, you've had it rough." Hope stood, stretching, and joined Dawn at the window. For minutes, they lost themselves in the breath-taking storm. Rain battering the glass, sodden people scurrying frantically, angry flashes of white electric followed by booming explosions that rocked the foundations. "I always find storms cathartic; the uncontrollable drama gives me peace."

"Why do you want to see Griffin?"

"I told you, I want…"

Dawn grabbed her arm and forced eye contact. "No, not the acceptable, rehearsed version. Why are you really going?"

Looking to the floor, Hope swallowed hard, and suddenly the intense flames of blue bored into Dawn, burrowing into her brain, stopping her heart. Then the smile was back, enigmatic and mischievous, but fake and empty. "Griffin won't get twelve years, he won't get five, or three. In fact, not even three months. He's a respected rector now, who's going to believe me against a man of the cloth?"

"So you're getting revenge in another way?" Dawn's tension, along with her guiding role in the sessions, had dissipated; a leveller had passed between them and there was no going back. Hope no longer scared her, there was nothing to be scared of. They were together, allies in a cruel war, and Dawn was secure that Hope

114

would protect her from any onslaught. In return, she would support her client to the bitter end.

An icy smile, glowering, vindictive. "No revenge. Call it research. It'll be a surprise, but I can guarantee you'll enjoy it."

"Go to the police, Hope, please don't take this into your own hands." Dawn focused on the tumultuous weather again.

"It's more fun this way." Hope collected her winter outerwear from the chair. "The hour's almost up, I'll get off a bit early if that's okay. I've got some shopping to do, last minute presents, fruit and veg, that kind of thing. I'll need to prepare the meal before tomorrow evening, otherwise I'll be in the kitchen all Christmas Day. I'm looking forward to watching you play tomorrow." She tugged the door open, but turned back to Dawn, still soaking up the raging storm by the window. "By the way, do you sing rock?"

Dawn faltered. She loved talking about the band, in fact she adored everything about it - the singing, her talented bandmates, the gigs, recording - except the endless rejection letters. "Yes. The lads are fantastic musicians, they're tight, they bounce off each other."

Hope grinned and this time it met her eyes. She cocked her head, friendly and collusive, and left. Already missing the new warmth between the two, Dawn searched through the contacts on her mobile. She punched the green button and waited.

Taylor and Dawn

"You did what?" He was incredulous, moving the phone to the other ear in case he had misheard.

"I told her I'd also been abused sexually." Dawn was challenging, a surly teenager.

"You have got to stop seeing that client, you're too close, you should never reveal yourself in the sessions." Taylor paced his office, determined to wear the carpet further.

"It was a good move, it's made her trust me, we've got a new bond."

Taylor tugged at his balding white wisps in frustration. "For God's sake, listen to yourself. You have got to get off this case, my love, and pronto, you're too involved."

Dawn turned from the window, and although the door was wide open, eavesdroppers a threat, she made no move to close it. "No, I need to see her through this journey, Taylor, we're really getting somewhere. I'm going with her to see the man who abused her tomorrow, we're meeting at the gig I'm doing."

Dawn returned to the window, the storm raging violently still, and scoured the street for Hope's figure, wanting a final glimpse. Completely unaware that Hope had re-entered the room, soaking in the one-sided conversation.

"No, Taylor, you can't do that. Please don't, you'll ruin everything - No, you don't get it, she needs me - Taylor, don't, just don't tell - I haven't got a boss at the moment, no one's been appointed since Pat died - yes, Pat Hinds - It isn't a dangerous situation, and what's the problem if we get on well? Oh, fuck it." Furious, Dawn ended the call and spun around. Gobsmacked to see Hope at the door.

"What's going on?" A gentle but meaningful growl.

Nervous, a tale-telling child, Dawn smiled innocently. "You shouldn't have heard that. Why have you come back?"

Hope indicated the glove she had thrown onto her seat moments before in anticipation of Dawn's question and walked over to retrieve it. "Is this Taylor person trying to stop you seeing me?"

116

Dawn sighed, frustrated, ready to lay the truth on the table. "He's my old psychology tutor from university. He thinks our counselling sessions are unhealthy, that I should arrange for you to see another counsellor."

Hope's eyes held Dawn's, steadfast. "Are you going to?"

The danger in the partnership had gone and Dawn felt intricately bound to her client. "No, but…"

Fury now, flashing fire. "But?"

"It's not me, Hope. Taylor wants to tell my boss, get the firm to separate us."

Hope said nothing, but her lips contorted to an angry sneer, fists pumping, white knuckles, shoulders tense. The pools of blue-framed-ebony glistened in the dark room, the atmosphere heavy like the storm.

Slowly, her stare not leaving Dawn, she shrugged on her leather jacket, tassels bobbing from side to side. She pulled the baker-boy cap over her reddened waves and dragged the gloves on. Suddenly she was ten years younger, a funky rocker, quirky and hot. A sex bomb. "Taylor Wilkinson, you say?"

Hope left the room for the second time, and Dawn could have sworn she hadn't mentioned her tutor's surname.

Christmas Eve at Work

The morning sessions passed uneventfully, but Dawn's mind was on other things: the prospect of her acting manager reading her the riot act; and the forthcoming gig and subsequent journey to Bedfordshire. She said the right words, interjected in the right places, but was grateful when the third and last client left, enabling her to get on with the things that mattered, and the first stop was a nearby pub with her colleagues for a Christmas drink.

Sitting by a dark oak table, heady notes of stale lager weighing the room, Dawn was at ease in the once smoky inn, supping her pint as confidently as any man. Most of her colleagues abhorred the commonness of the working man environment, complaining bitterly when The Red Horse had been chosen as the company's local, but Dawn preferred a modest setting and was happy to converse with a drunken stranger, have an unexpected laugh.

Chris Blinkhorn, a fifty-something, weedy obsessive who was temporarily filling Pat Hind's shoes, sat opposite Dawn, randomly picking at bits of nothing on the table, smoothing his trousers on a regular basis to the count of ten, his left eye flickering in the process. Dawn had waited all day for him to reprimand her, lecture her on how she shouldn't get involved with clients, transfer Hope to colleague, but he hadn't even made eye contact. Taylor had been adamant on the phone that he intended to talk to her supervisor, so why was Chris avoiding her?

As she tugged on her tasselled leather jacket - a cheap and shoddy version of Hope's expensive one - she surmised she wouldn't know the fate of her and Hope's sessions until Christmas and New Year had passed.

The Gig

Dawn never felt more alive than when she was singing on stage. She was an excellent show-woman, her powerful voice strong and clear, and her sexily-clad body could make grown men cry. She strutted, grooved, ran and jumped, whooping the audience to a frenzy.

Reveal had been together for just over five years and had quite a following. Chaz, Dawn's good mate and ex-boyfriend, played bass guitar, a talented musician whose skills were only freed when he wasn't drunk or high, which was becoming less frequent. LeMan, with his wild, frizzy hair and puppy dog eyes was the craziest member of the band, battering the drums - and life itself - with enthusiasm and force. Both lead guitarists were brilliant: Ed, the quiet one; and Rick, Dawn's brother.

Rick and Dawn had co-founded several bands since their teenage years, Reveal being the tightest mix of personalities and musicians yet, and they were unusually close for siblings, but Rick's increasing sexual encounters with the groupies grated on her. They argued about it often, she felt he was taking advantage of their naivety and innocence, especially the youngsters, but he was adamant they knew what they were doing.

The heavy beat pounded the room, power chords resounding from brown-stained walls and impressive vocals and harmonies enrapturing the screaming audience. The girls and women in the crowd all had a favourite of the four handsome lads, many daydreaming they could meet, marry and make babies, and numerous men fantasised about taking the sexy singer to bed. Or an alleyway.

The set was a mixture of their original material and covered rock classics, and tonight they were on form, the musicians tightly-knit and Dawn's voice incredible. The result was beautifully professional and they ticked every box required to have a number one single. Except youth. Thirty was a milestone no wannabe should pass before making the big time.

On the undersized stage, the heat from the lights searing, Dawn was tired, unladylike sweat dripping from her brow, her throat grating and eyes stinging. She finished the song with a flourish and took a low bow, the crowd cheering and whooping for more. The lads followed her from the stage, giving the fans an appreciative and exhausted wave, and they accepted a welcome pint each from their manager, downing them quickly, greedy with thirst.

When they finally stepped back on the stage the audience went wild, the chanting for an encore rewarded. Chaz began his plucky, catchy riff to cheers, and soon Rick joined on his guitar. LeMan's frenzied drumming dropped into place, before Ed's power chord completed the introduction of AC/DC's *Livewire*, the feverish screaming now overpowered.

Dawn, who had been strutting across the stage, exaggeratedly nodding to the beat, stood in the centre and leant to the microphone, taking a deep breath. Suddenly, she froze, dropping the microphone, face paling. Her cue missed, the band, quick to improvise, repeated the introduction, glancing at their singer, concerned by her rare mistake.

The clammy sweat covering her torso, her face, increased, feeling demons burning her, searing her soul, and her breath lightened, shallow gasps, fear gripping, squeezing. Confused, staring into the audience, the hot lights blazing in her eyes, and the black, bouncing silhouettes disappeared - meaningless figures that didn't matter - as Dawn made eye contact with Hope.

They held each other's gaze for far too long. The anxious musicians, worried for their singer, carried the song, but the audience began to tire of the repetition.

Finally, Hope smiled, waving - an order to carry on with her job - and Dawn returned the smile, preparing herself at the microphone.

A subtle beat by LeMan, and Dawn took a deep breath. "Well if you're looking for trouble, I'm the gal you'll need, looking for satisfaction, I'm satisfaction guaranteed..."

Her vocals were impeccable, pitch perfect and powerful; Dawn was giving the greatest performance of her life - energy, rawness, sexiness - a fitting tribute to Bon Scott.

The five raunchy, thundering, awe-inspiring minutes were over too quickly and the crowd screamed for more, but Dawn, bowing low, exhausted and sticky, left the stage. The lads were gearing up for the usual finale, an excellently energetic cover of Led Zeppelin's Rock and Roll, and they kept playing, supposing Dawn wanted a drink. But after a minute of playing they petered out, with no choice but to shrug at their fans before also leaving the stage.

In the small, cramped bathroom that the landlord insisted was suitable as a dressing room, Dawn reached for a towel, dabbing at her face, arms, chest, before shrugging on a fluffy housecoat. The knock was anticipated and she tugged the door wide, welcoming Hope to the room.

Dawn took a flannel, soaping it, rubbing her face, her neck. "What did you think?"

"You're ace, really brilliant. I'll definitely mention you to Happiness and Tony." Dawn grinned, desperately hoping her musical luck had changed. "You're a good-looking bunch too, especially the lead guitarist on the right, he's hot."

Dawn chuckled, now towelling the sweat from her damp, unkempt ringlets. "That's my brother, Rick. Watch him, he's great looking, but he knows it, and he's a real ladies' man. I wouldn't go there with him if I were you."

Hope dismissed the warning, her face becoming stern, the contradicting smile not reaching her eyes. "Yes. But you're not me, are you. Men always fall in love with me. If I wanted to have him, he would be hooked, ladies' man or not. I'd have him eating out of my hand."

Worry skimmed Dawn's forehead, a protective surge for her brother, and she prayed that Hope wouldn't want to have him. Throwing the towel on the wooden bench, she resolved to get her out of the pub before Rick finished his customary pint and made his way back to the room. She checked her face in the mirror, fingers smoothing away the smudged mascara from under her eyes, and ran her hands through her hair, tugging through the dampened knots. She shrugged on her jacket, spraying deodorant about her body as an afterthought, and grabbed her bag. "Come on, let's go or we'll never get there in time."

Hope's eyes questioned the haste, studying her counsellor as she tugged the door handle, gesturing the exit, impatient. They stepped into the corridor, the carpet a soft welcome from the cold, cracked tiles of the bathroom, and Dawn's heart sank as she saw Rick and LeMan approaching. They waved, wide grins fuelled from the adrenaline high of playing live, and Dawn worriedly glanced beside her, but it was too late. Hope was making a beeline for her brother and she looked fantastic tonight in high heels, slim legs in drainpipe jeans enhancing her neat backside and her newly red hair glossy and bouncy. Dawn was helpless; Rick was about to get caught in the same headlights that had her entrapped. She cursed.

Dawn neared the mutually attracted pair, tugging at Hope's arm, insisting they leave instantly, and balked with dismay when Hope took an address card from her pocket and handed it to Rick. Their eyes locked, Hope inviting and flirty, Rick mesmerised and beguiled. "Call me."

Dawn succeeded in shuffling her charge towards the exit, with Hope glancing seductively over her shoulder, and despaired when he replied, "I will. I definitely will."

A Late Night Journey

The only sliver of light once they reached the countryside and lost the bright orange hue of the lampposts was from the new moon. They shared no words at first, Dawn depressed by her brother's latest flame, Hope deep in concentration. Eventually they reached the outskirts of Cambridge, and Polton was only a short journey away.

"Reveal's a great band." A competent driver, Hope concentrated on the road.

Dawn glanced at her chauffeur, her ambition instantly taking precedence over Rick's sexual conquests. "You really think so? Do you think we've got potential?"

Hope nodded. "Yes, I'd buy your stuff. You've got a great voice and those boys are dreamboats. Musically, they're so tight. I was really impressed with what I saw tonight. Who writes the original material?"

Dawn grinned, the compliment stroking her ego. "Me and Rick, mainly. Of course, Chaz and Ed have a say in it, adding bits and suggesting things, but it's me and Rick who come up with the ideas." Dawn hesitated every time she mentioned her brother, concerned about forcing him into Hope's consciousness.

The silence returned, the plush saloon sweeping through the English countryside, and Dawn relaxed into the soft leather seat, the heating and movement lulling her, eyes drooping, breathing rhythmic. Soon the urge to sleep won and her breaths deepened, a light snuffle. Comforted by Hope's presence in her dreams, alone and isolated, trapped inside the luxury car, only Hope and Dawn existed.

Unaware that her passenger had fallen asleep, Hope voiced her thoughts. "I'll have a word with Happiness about you, I'm sure she and Tony will come and see you play sometime. She's not into rock, but she appreciates good musicians. Him too."

No response came and Hope glanced at Dawn, smiling tenderly on seeing her asleep. She focused on the road, fiddling with the stereo for some music to pass the time. Finding a mellow and bluesy Primal Scream song, she sang along quietly.

The car raced along the black roads, headlights painting a limited picture ahead, while the radio, absent of adverts and Christmas tunes, kept Hope awake. Eventually St Peter's Church appeared, eerily lit by floodlights that enhanced its elaborate aged stone features. Hope parked on the side of the road and switched the lights off.

After a few calming breaths, she was ready to see the man who had taken her childhood, and through the low mist could see a figure greeting the villagers as they arrived. She tapped Dawn's shoulder, stirring her. "Wake up, sleepyhead." She pointed to the skinny figure, draped in robes, a welcoming smile on his face as he shook hands with his parishioners.

From nowhere a pain shot through Hope's chest, acute and crushing, and she clasped her arm, her face contorted, breathing laboured. Concerned, Dawn remembered her advice that Hope see a doctor. "Are you okay?"

Hope was transfixed by the clergyman, ignoring the griping pains, willing them away, oblivious to Dawn's worry. Viscous words thick with hatred: "That's Griffin."

Angela Wilkinson

The lights were dimmed but bright enough for the nurses to tend their patients. The monotonous and rhythmic beeping of the life support machine reassured Taylor, signalling his beloved wife was still alive.

The accident the previous day had been sudden and unexplained. Angela Wilkinson's car had skidded across a country lane and clipped a tree, rolling several times before settling upside down in a ditch. The weather was cold but not frosty, so the only feasible explanation was that an animal had run in front of the car and Angela, a keen nature lover, had been more concerned for its welfare than her own.

Sitting high in his tractor, a farmer had noticed the car minutes after the incident and summoned help. Untrained in first aid, all he could do in the long minutes while awaiting the ambulance was sit by the car and hold Angela's hand. She had lost consciousness on impact, unable to state what had happened or where she hurt, and he knew enough to not undo the seatbelt that supported her upturned body. He had caressed her skin, whispering soothingly in case she could hear, hoping she hung on to life.

The ambulance had arrived promptly, sirens blaring and lights flashing regardless of the empty lanes, and the paramedics had freed Angela's battered body, gently laying her onto a stretcher with her back and neck supported in case of spinal injury. Soon the only visible evidence of the accident had been the undercarriage and wheels of the Ford Fiesta, the violet paintwork hidden in the undergrowth, and a narrow track in the roadside weeds that had been trodden down by the rescuers.

Angela Wilkinson had needed an emergency blood transfusion on arriving at the Norfolk and Norwich Hospital due to severe internal injuries, and once stabilised, underwent surgery to repair her shattered spleen and tears in the diaphragm and duodenum. Numerous splinters from three smashed ribs were removed from the soft tissue.

Taylor had arrived as soon as possible, driving like a maniac to be with the woman he loved in her desperate hour. Tears had flowed copiously as he paced the corridor outside the operating theatre, lengthy minutes becoming hours, his senses sharp with endless cups of coffee. When finally allowed to see her, her eyes were still made-up and hair neat. She hadn't looked ill - not close to death as the nurses had warned - just peaceful, serene. Asleep.

She had been taken to intensive care and settled, numerous wires monitoring her condition and a tube in her throat to enable the ventilator to breathe for her, saving her precious energy. Over the hours her adult children had spent time with her, sobbing as they said what they had to in case she didn't make it. Determined not to leave Angela's side, their father patted them on the back comfortingly, assuring them he would do all he could to keep their mother alive.

It was nearly midnight on Christmas Eve and he had been at the hospital for thirty-four hours with no food; his appetite had vanished. The broken man sat clasping his wife's hand, rolling her wedding ring casually. Silent.

Nothing in the world mattered any more. Nothing but Angela.

Midnight Mass

Hope was desperately uncomfortable, not only from sitting on a hard, wooden pew at the back of the congregation, but from being inside a church. She couldn't deny that the service was as beautiful as she remembered from her childhood. Lights low, each worshipper brandished an orange representing the world tied with a red ribbon to symbolise the blood of Jesus, pierced with four sweets on cocktail sticks in honour of the four seasons and the fruits of the earth. A lit candle grew from the centre, a token to honour Christ and the light He sheds on the earth. The flickering shed a gentle glow on the ornate stained windows, the complex architecture, the religious statues that littered the church and the tired and hopeful congregation.

Leading the service, Griffin Hall had read a sermon, introduced hymns and quoted the psalms, and now he was wishing his flock well over the Christmas period. Hope and Dawn had curiously scrutinized the man as he had delivered his speeches. Tall and slim, a typical man-of-the-cloth uniform of greys and olives beneath his robes, he had silver streaks in his dark hair, particularly around the temples, and thickly-framed glasses balanced on a long, hooked nose. Hope cynically imagined he wore Jesus Creepers below the corduroy slacks that peeped from the hem of his robes.

The lights brightened, controlled by the overworked verger, and the organist played a gentle breeze of chords to guide the flock from the building. The throng of worshippers - old, young, tall, short, well-insulated against the cold, wintry wind - slowly shuffled along the aisle towards the imposing wooden doors at the entrance of the church, following the footsteps of their rector, who waited in the foyer to wish them farewell. Dawn stood, but sat again when she realised Hope had no intention of moving.

Gradually the congregation thinned until only a few stragglers remained and Griffin gazed at the two unfamiliar women. He smiled, but it wasn't returned and he made his way towards Dawn and Hope, curious of their identity and reticence to leave.

Stepping brusquely along the aisle, a slight limp causing him to sway unnaturally. "Ladies, thank you for attending our Midnight Mass, support of St Peter's is always gratefully appreciated."

His whiny voice threw long-forgotten memories at Hope, reminding her of his filthy presence in her childhood. She felt bile rising and her stomach muscles clenched; she had not eaten all day so there was nothing to bring up.

Except the bile.

Bitter acid stinging her throat, flooding her mouth, stripping her teeth.

Retching, and it was out. Greenish yellow, vile smelling, dripping from his robes, his collar, his chin. He recoiled, disgusted, blaspheming under his breath, furious.

Swiping an arm across his face, his chest, wiping away the vitriolic juice, the pungent odour lodged in his nostrils.

Dawn watched the scene with amazement.

Eventually he stopped fussing, resigned that the stench would linger until he got back to the rectory, and raised a questioning eyebrow at the woman who had revoltingly abused him.

Eyes a shocking blue - clear, wide, innocent - she was smiling. She stared, disconcerting, frightening, burrowing under his skin and into his psyche, and without losing eye-contact she took her handbag from the pew and marched purposefully from the church.

The Rectory

Dorothy Hall arranged the hot mince pies and sausage rolls neatly on doily covered plates and took them to the lounge for the small gathering of parishioners to snack on. Hosting post-Christingles drinks for the church helpers had been a tradition since her husband had become the rector five years before, one which everybody enjoyed; there was always a good turnout.

Griffin hadn't returned yet, but Dorothy was unperturbed as he always took time to ensure the church was securely locked after a recent spate of vandalism. Dorothy generously offered sherry to the guests, smiling affably, oblivious to the two new faces in the doorway.

Nervous and out of place, Dawn tugged Hope's arm, concerned about her client's hidden agenda. "What are you doing? Really, we should leave."

Hope glared at her, the intensity incredible - burning through pupil to retina, to brain - and roughly shrugged her arm away. "We're staying. Stick with me, act as if we belong here. You're going to enjoy this; just imagine it's your uncle we're doing it to, imagine the satisfaction you'd feel."

Dawn grimaced apprehensively, wondering why she had expected Hope to scurry away with her tail between her legs; she wasn't the type to shy away from a problem. Remembering she didn't have to drive, Dawn snatched a glass of sherry from the table and downed it, following it with another, and almost immediately her face warmed, flushing.

Hope was mingling but she stood out, her clothes vibrant and funky compared to the twin-sets and tweed that overwhelmed the room, and once more Dawn realised her own style had been emulated by her client. She was unsure whether to see it as a compliment or an irritation, but had to admit that Hope looked fantastic, the rock chick vibe suited her.

Hope felt a hand on her arm and looked at the diminutive, friendly woman beaming up at her. "Hello, dear, I'm Dorothy, Griff's wife. I don't believe we've met."

She smiled widely, eyes twinkling. "Oh, Dorothy, I've heard so much about you. It's lovely to finally meet you."

Her husband tended not to mention her, their marriage not the happiest union in the parish, and she regarded Hope quizzically. "So what have you been doing for the church that has led to an invite from Griff tonight."

The smile remained. "Oh, I helped decorate Griffin's robes this evening, a smattering of colour. Made him more Christmassy, you know."

Dorothy's smile waned, uncomfortable now yet unsure why, and said under her breath, "Nobody calls him Griffin, he hates it."

Grinning cheerfully, eyes crinkling, Hope raised her voice. "Au contraire, he loves it from me, reminds him of when I used to scream his name when he was having sex with me. 'Griffin', I used to shout, 'Stop, you're hurting me.' I mean, he's a big boy, isn't he?" The meaningless conversation in the room died, all eyes and ears on Hope's interaction with the rector's wife. Gobsmacked, Dawn was enjoying the exchange.

Dorothy stuttered, words abandoning her, until, "You... you... you must be mistaken, Griff's a rector, he wouldn't..."

Hope patted her arm, soulful eyes full of compassion. "Hey, it was a long time ago. I don't think he'd even met you then and I was only seven, after all." A collective gasp rang through the room, mouths dropping, eyes boggling, and Dorothy wrung her hands, squeezing. Hope's smile deadened, eyes harsh and jaw set firm, and she squared her shoulders; suddenly she was huge. Commanding, powerful. She slowly scanned the room, the silent crowd avoiding the steel blue as she took in each person, one by one. Everyone was mesmerised by the unfolding drama.

Finally, she spoke. "You can tell Griffin I'm back, tell him Hope didn't go away. And watch your children and grandchildren because he likes them young. I'm sure he runs lots of youth groups - am I right?"

"Dear Lord, he does as well." The exclaimer remained faceless but a concerned and congruent murmur fluttered through the room.

Hope ignored the rumbling undercurrent. "Tell Griffin that his life is over."

The Journey Back

Having taken advantage of the free alcohol, Dawn was lightheaded and dozed on the passenger seat, while Hope concentrated on the dark roads. The luxury car purred like a contented kitten, warmth pumped through vents to take the frosty edge from the air. Dawn moaned, head in hands, and Hope glanced at her. "Are you okay?"

Groaning, her hands returned to her lap. "Yes, I'm fine, just a headache. I had a few too many sherries back there." Quiet once more - one beat, two, three - Dawn turned to her client, brow furrowed. "You were unbelievable, Hope, but I don't understand why you brought me. I didn't do anything to help."

Another pause. "You're wrong. I couldn't have done it without you, you're my strength. Just knowing you were there gave me the courage to do what I did. I was shitting bricks when I was talking to his wife, what with everyone looking at me and everything."

Dawn snorted. "Get away! You were confident as hell, that was nothing to do with me."

"Yes, it was. I feed off you, you give me power, you give me nerves of steel. We're good for each other, we work together. You're going to help me get to the top of the world." Her gentle chuckle filled the car.

Dawn smiled with gratitude, pleased to have helped, yet more so to be on her way home to bed.

Session Thirteen

Fluorescent lights brightened the building, but with no one strutting around, paper in hand, ready to pass the time of day or catch up on the soap storylines, it was soulless. Having interrupted her holiday for this one session, Dawn paced the reception area, eager to see Hope.

She took one of the steaming mugs of vegetable soup from Gayle's desk, cupping her hands around the body, warming her reddened fingers. It was bitter outside, the northerly gusts blowing at forty miles per hour, roads smattered with snow and muddy slush. The sun was low, streetlights on regardless that it was late morning, and the heavy, lead clouds hung, stagnant, a vicious ice trap.

Hope bustled in, only her clear blue eyes and delicate pink nose visible beneath a Paddington duffle coat and woollen accessories. She sniffled as the heat hit her and dug into her pocket for a tatty tissue, which she held by her nose for a minute. Dawn took the second mug and offered it to Hope. "I made you a soup. It's so cold, I thought you'd need it." Hope thanked her gratefully, taking the drink in her gloved hands, and they headed for the usual room.

Once settled in their chairs, Hope still wrapped excessively, Dawn began the hour. "How was your Christmas?"

Hope nodded, tugging the woollen hat off and smoothing her dyed mahogany waves into place. "It was okay. My sister and her husband came over for the day with their daughter. They ended up staying the night because Keith had too much to drink."

"Right." Dawn took a gulp, chewing on the croutons and reconstituted carrot bits. "Which sister was it?"

"Charity. Charity, Keith, and their daughter Ava, the one who's in remission from leukaemia."

"Yes, I remember now. She had a miscarriage recently, didn't she?"

Hope peeled the lengthy scarf from her neck, winding it into a ball before dropping it next to her untouched soup. "Yes, she's on antidepressants now. To be honest, she's hard work. I know that

132

miscarriage is hard - I've been there - but the thing is, once it happens there's nothing you can do about it, it's gone, over, so why dwell on it. She needs to move on."

Dawn swallowed, buying time, arranging her comeback carefully. "Hope, it's not that easy for some women, repeated miscarriages can be soul destroying. She probably hasn't had enough time to grieve yet, it must still be raw."

Hope waved dismissively. "Charity has always had it easy up until now, the best of Mum, the best of our father. She had a whirlwind affair with Keith, they married in Barbados. He's rich and handsome, they have a gorgeous house in Beccles, the cars, the lifestyle, everything. So she's had a few miscarriages, her daughter is recovering from leukaemia, but that's it, everything else has been good."

Dawn stroked her chin, breathing deeply as she digested the intolerant torrent. "You're very jealous of her, aren't you? What is it? The money, that it came to her through marriage rather than hard work like yours did. Or is it the preferable attention she received from your parents? What is it?"

Hope's eyes were wide, shocked. "I'm not jealous." The murmur was nearly lost in the clanging of the heating system as it warmed up. Hope removed her gloves and stood to drag off her coat. Underneath the dowdy outerwear she looked fantastic, the nicest Dawn had seen her. A tight lacy top clung to her miniscule curves, a pair of well-fitting jeans hugging her legs, and several retro metal and black necklaces accentuated the recently found - or was it revamped - rock chick look. Her hair was big with bouncy waves and her skin glowed healthily. High, black stiletto boots sealed the image. A mini-me, thought Dawn, with more money.

Hope folded her coat and sat, taking the soup from the table. She warmed her hands on the mug, but had no inclination to drink the calorific liquid. "You need to understand Charity, and I've only done so in the past few years since she moved up this way. We weren't close as kids, Faith and I had a lot of resentment towards her, and she deliberately shut herself off from us."

Dawn leant forward, chin on hands. "Ah, but which came first, though. If she knows you resent her, she's going to be defensive. And if she's closed and defensive, you're going to think her aloof. It's a chicken and egg situation."

"No, it was always different, I can't remember it not being. It was like Mum and Dad were hers only, that she hated them giving us attention, especially Dad. When Mum praised us, she would leap in, stroking her own ego, stealing the attention, and if Mum didn't go with her she'd kick up an argument. It happened more and more when she became a teenager, she and Mum used to have physical fights, throwing things, hitting each other, it was horrid."

"Adolescents can be horrible, Hope, you should know that, your daughter's thirteen."

"I know, but Penny's nothing like that. Hard work, yes, I've caught her sneaking out at night, smoking and drinking on more than one occasion, but she has a healthy respect for me. She'd never hit me. No, Penny's chilled."

Hope quietened, lost in thought, and eventually addressed herself rather than Dawn. "She's been putting on weight recently, gotten quite chubby. I've got to take a look at her diet. It's only a bit of puppy fat, but it won't hurt to make sure she's eating properly."

Back with Dawn, Hope relaxed into the comfortable chair. "Charity is a snob, always has been. She's intolerant, rude and abrasive. It's her way. It was the money she missed, the lifestyle, and she was desperate for that back. Keith had to happen, and when she met him he ticked all the right boxes. Ridiculously rich, blond with blue eyes, tall, well built, arrogant, snobbish and fertile. She hooked him from the first date, there was no way she was letting him get away. They flew forty people over to Barbados when they married. Forty people, how fucking pretentious is that?"

"Would you have felt it so pretentious if you'd had an invite?"

Hope glared at Dawn. She had hit a raw nerve, but she wasn't about to rise to the bait. "Keith sold shares in his business in London to free up enough cash for them to buy their luxury house in Beccles without a mortgage. He still reaps in the profits, but works remotely. Maybe goes to London once a week, he stays at the apartment they have there. With Beccles only being twenty or so miles from my place we started to spend more time together and now we have an understanding of each other. An adult understanding. We're chalk and cheese, but we can be civil and even have the occasional laugh."

Running her fingers through her hair, Hope glanced up when the lights flickered, then at Dawn, who was also watching them.

Dawn went to the window and scanned outside; the streetlights were flickering. "It's notorious for power cuts around here." The shimmering died and the room darkened to charcoal grey, the two women silhouetted in the oppressiveness. "Shit, I'd better try and find a couple of candles."

Dawn returned empty handed several minutes later and sat heavily, crossing her legs. "If you had any idea how many candles I got for Christmas, but they're all at home and I can't find a single one here. Do you mind continuing in this half-light, or would you rather end the session?"

"I think it's quite nice, makes you think more when your senses are dulled. Anyway, candles are the enemy after Christmas day." Hope tutted.

"Oh, why's that?"

Dawn imagined the candles at the Midnight Mass had prompted bad memories to surface, so was pleasantly stunted when Hope laughed. "Keith knocked one over at Christmas dinner and it set the whole table alight. We controlled it without needing to call the fire service, but it was scary. Amazing how quickly things caught. I was stunned."

"Wow, was the meal ruined?"

"No, luckily we'd finished. He'd had a bit much to drink - well, that's an understatement, he was pissed - and he was messing about. Charity had a right go at him after, but she's a fine one to talk, she's got a reputation as a bit of an arsonist herself."

The familiar chuckle tinkled and Dawn nodded, prompting without words, absorbed. "She must have been about fourteen, I guess, she was in her bedroom, and Mum had gone out, probably to get more booze, she was in her alcoholic stage at the time. Anyway, Charity was setting up some candles for some kind of ritual or something. It was the same thing, she knocked one over and the room caught alight."

An underlying anger bubbled, Hope slowly shaking her head. "She didn't want anyone to know, she felt stupid, so instead of screaming so we knew to get out, she messed about trying to put it out herself with her bedside rug. So bloody irresponsible, she was then and is now." A deep sigh. "By the time she got out of the room the fire was out of control and her throat was too sore to shout. Luckily Mum came home and smelt the smoke, she screamed

135

for us to get out. I grabbed Honesty from her cot, she was woozy from smoke inhalation. It was scary."

"I bet, fire's so dangerous, people don't realise." The room fell silent and both women relaxed, comfortable in each other's presence. Dawn the counsellor, Hope the client. Hope the strong leader, Dawn the submissive slave? Friends? The boundaries had somehow become blurred.

"We had to move out for a month while the landlord did the repairs, the council put us in emergency accommodation. The whole of the first floor was burnt black, the furniture ruined. Our personal things, the boxed stuff - you know, memories, first drawings, school reports, special gifts and notes - Mum kept them in the loft and they were ruined. Even after all the plastering and decorating that had gone on, it always smelled acrid up there after that, kind of lodged in the back of your nostrils every time you passed the fifth step on the staircase."

Dawn rested her chin on her hand, contemplative. "Dynamics, Hope? Charity was in your own words the 'favourite', Mum and Dad thought she could do no wrong. And here she is messing with fire, destroying your house and personal belongings, even risking the lives of her siblings in her recklessness. Did the episode change the dynamics within the family, the way your parents viewed her, or you?"

Hope snorted, adopting the resigned manner that came to the fore whenever she spoke of her childhood at home. "Rewards, that's what she got. She went to live with Dad and Sandra. Mum didn't kick her out, he just decided she needed more attention than she was getting. He put her in private school, had an extension built on his house so she could have not just her own bedroom, but an en-suite and lounge area too."

Dawn's jaw dropped, an incredulous smile painted on her face. "You are joking this time, right?"

Hope shook her head dramatically, hammering the truth in her words home. "Sadly not. That's what Charity gets if she does wrong: rewards. Keith's the same with her. If she behaves out of line he treats her to things, excuses her social gaffs with depression, or miscarriage, or leukaemia, or the time of day, or the fact there's only one cloud in the sky rather than two."

"F… shit, sorry, I forgot where I was for a second, what with the darkness." Dawn's eyes dipped, embarrassed, remembering her role.

Now her chuckle was genuine. "Hey, don't worry, I've got a filthy mouth, why shouldn't you join in."

They sniggered in acknowledgement of the mediocre stab at humour. Straightening, professional again, Dawn crossed her legs and took a deep breath. "I'm getting a huge sense of resentment from you and it appears to be completely deserved, but at the end of the day it's dragging you down. You need to accept and let go if you want to progress."

Hope cupped her hands around the cooling mug, the soup still untouched. "Psychobabble. Progress where? Where exactly am I progressing?"

Dawn sighed. Being honest with herself? Yes, she was spouting rubbish. Moments ticked by as she contemplated which direction to take. "Okay, I'll try and rephrase it to make sense. At the moment, you are putting a lot of emotional energy into both being jealous, and…"

"I'm not jealous. Why would I be? I've got a successful career, I'm wealthy in my own right, I've got three gorgeous children, friends. Hell, I've even shifted time-honoured barriers when it comes to domestic violence and bullying."

Another sigh; Hope was hard work. "I know what you've got, but what you don't have is your parents' approval, their pride and support, and getting that means a lot to you."

Hope gritted her teeth, eyes watering, fists clenched, unable to speak should it open the dam for the tears to tumble. She strolled to the window, shoulders back, retaining her dignity. Dawn suspected another milestone had been reached, that her client could start accepting the way her parents behaved, her sister, the family set up. She was sympathetic for Hope, dealing with so much at the same time. As far as Dawn knew, she had not reported Griffin to the police yet, so that was still an inner torment, and it appeared her parents were a major cause of the troubles that not just Hope, but her siblings too, had to come to terms with.

"Truth is I hate her. I hate her snobbery, her conservatism, her lack of empathy and compassion. She's the most selfish person I've ever known, always has been. When she was pregnant with Ava I thought 'this is it, this is where she starts thinking about someone else rather than just herself', and there it was, Ava was born, but even though Charity's home all day they got a live-in nanny.

"Keith and Charity don't bathe her, or feed her, they wouldn't change her nappies, they don't put her to bed, read to her, they hardly see her. When she got leukaemia they saw it as an irritation. Ava has everything materially, gets anything she wants. If she wants a doll they buy it, a horse, they buy it, hell, if she wanted an apartment they'd go on out and buy one to her specification. But love, time, cuddles. No way. And now they want another baby."

Hope composed herself, emotionally drained, and her jaw tensed. "You know, my kids, they're always coming for hugs and snuggles, kisses and love. But when they visit Ava just looks at us as if we're aliens when that happens. She has no concept of physical love."

Dawn joined Hope at the window and they gazed through the glass, absorbing the leaden, charcoal sky, the puffy snowflakes dancing from the clouds and drifting this way and that before settling on the freezing ground. "From what you've told me about your childhood, I imagine the real problem you have with Ava and her situation is that you empathise with her from your own personal experience."

Hope regarded Dawn, her thickset jaw and strong nose, hazel eyes that flitted between green and brown depending on the light, and was impressed with her insight. "Go on."

Dawn faced Hope, sincere and animated. "Just look at it, you were all but ignored when you were a kid, if it wasn't rejection by your father, then it was the alcohol stealing your mother. You brought yourself up and had a major hand in bringing your sister up. When people have children, they try to ensure the child has whatever they lacked in their own childhood, whatever made them unhappy. It's commonplace and understandable."

"You're right there. I give my kids lots of attention, cuddles and love because it's what I didn't have when I was young."

"You've got it. But obviously you love your niece and want the best for her too, and you can see her not getting the things you crave yourself, the things you insist your children have. It burns you up."

They returned to the chairs in the shrouding darkness, the world forgotten. "So how do I get rid of the resentment and accept things so they don't bug me any more."

138

Crossing her legs, the well-worn denim stretching easily over the knees, Dawn smiled. "That's just it, Hope, that's what you need to do: accept it. I can't tell you how to do that, only you can work that out. Perhaps break things down into manageable chunks and work on it bit by bit. It'll take some hard work on your part - a lot of hard work - and you'll have to want it or it won't happen."

Lost in thought, isolated from the world and each other, the silence was pure without the white noise of buzzing electricity. Minutes passed with no interaction. Finally, "I can do that. I want it enough. I can do it, but it'll take time."

"Good, we can keep talking about it over the weeks if you think that will help."

Shaking her head, decisive. "No. You've told me what needs to be done and I'll find a way to do it. Charity, resentment, jealousy. You won't hear them from me again."

Dawn was intrigued by the orderly and resolute dismissal of a lifelong problem and wanted to question the disciplined surety, but suspected it wouldn't help. Hope focused on the coffee table, the mug of cold soup, reconstituted vegetables and sodden croutons bobbing on the surface. "The one thing I can't drop is Ava. In fact, I'm going to work harder with her. She's a dear little thing, tiny. Charity's a big girl, not fat, but tall and big boned. We look nothing like each other, I'm the runt of the family."

Dawn grimaced; it wasn't the first time Hope had belittled herself that way and it didn't tally with the strong woman who sat before her. "Keith's about six two, built like the proverbial brick shithouse, yet Ava was a weed when she was born. Charity went full term with her, she was just a tiny baby."

"How much did she weigh; can you remember?" The answer wouldn't mean anything to her, her inability to have children meant she had never become au-fait with the terminology, but it kept Hope talking.

"Five pound something, eight or nine, thereabouts. She had the dinkiest feet and hands. Tiny fingernails, teeny toes. She's a pretty little thing too, got her father's looks. Charity's attractive, but she's not pretty, whereas Keith's drop-dead gorgeous. Well, until he opens his mouth and the pompous shit comes out. No, I'm going to concentrate on Ava, include her in our family trips, show her physical love. Show her interactive fun, not lonely playing."

139

Dawn nodded, proud and heart-warmed. "Hope, you're a genuinely kind person, aren't you? If you let the hatred and anger go you could change the world, the position you're in."

Although the room was dim, Dawn saw the ocean blue turn steel-grey, and determined Hope was reborn. "I know. And that's what I intend to do."

No words seemed appropriate after the resolute statement, and Hope collected her things together, slipping the coat onto her shoulders, hat, gloves, scarf, wrapping herself like a present.

Murmuring a ghostly 'thanks', Hope left the room and a satisfied smile edged Dawn's lips. Real progress had been made today and she was pleased with herself, pleased with her client.

She couldn't wait until the next session.

Dorothy Takes Matters into Her Own Hands

The kettle was on, bread in the toaster, bacon frying in the pan, and the table was neatly laden with cereals and marmalades. Dorothy was keeping life normal but Griffin had fallen apart. He trudged through the door, dressing gown hanging loosely either side, unbothered with the belt, and slumped onto his usual chair.

Dorothy poured the boiling water into the teapot, mashing the bag with a spoon, squeezing out the strong Yorkshire flavour. She hastened it to the table and filled Griffin's cup, careful not to dribble any onto the saucer, topping the golden liquid with milk from an earthenware jug.

"Are you planning on working today?" A simple question that caused wretched turmoil for Griffin, his face contorting and wrinkles deepening into a grotesque sneer.

"How can I? You've heard the gossips, they've hung, drawn and quartered me. My innocence doesn't matter to them, they're vultures." His fist slammed against the waxed table to emphasise his bitterness.

Dorothy placed the toast in the silver rack, a tarnished present from their wedding day twenty-three years before, and opened the butter dish. "Griff, you can't carry on like this, avoiding everyone. You have a job to do, you're the rector, your parish needs you to take control."

He stood, fury rising. "Those people have been too quick to judge me, Dot, they haven't given me a chance."

Breaking an egg into the hot fat, she remained as calm and serene as ever. "You're innocent. The truth will always prevail."

Deflated, temper spent, he sank onto the seat and dragged a piece of toast onto his plate. Quiet. "Of course I'm innocent. You're right." He carefully buttered the toast, ensuring the fat reached each edge of the square, soaking in. "But I can't go back, not until this is sorted out."

Efficient and organised, she scooped the bacon and eggs onto a pre-warmed plate and handed it to her husband. "Then today I will sort it out, because you can't go on like this."

Dorothy swept from the room, leaving Griffin slouched on the seat, awash with self-pity. After a quick wash, she dressed in clothes that added years and tousled her unflattering permed curls until they sat neatly against her head. She tugged a silk headscarf over her hair, carefully knotting it below the chin, and donned her woollen Fearnought, the heavy material weighing down her sloping shoulders.

By the front door, she slipped on the waiting Hush Puppies that instantly warmed her feet and took her basket, handbag and umbrella. A tartan scarf with matching gloves, a resolute goodbye over her shoulder, and Dorothy Hall promptly left the rectory; she had a crisis to sort out.

The overnight snow had turned to slush on the main road through Polton, but the pavements were still fluffy white, except for a well-worn and slippery central passageway. Dorothy's ungainly figure came through the gate and marched to the bus stop, carefully avoiding the impacted ice. Chugging slowly, the bus arrived just as she did and she exchanged tittle-tattle with the driver while paying for her ticket, sitting near the front.

Pumping hot air for the freezing passengers, the bus rambled through country roads, winding left, then right and left again, the purring engine lulling Dorothy until her lazy eyelids drooped. Although only eleven miles, the journey took the best part of an hour and she dozed peacefully.

Bedford was warmer than Polton and Dorothy removed her scarf, stuffing it in the wicker basket looped over her forearm. She had dismounted in the suburb of Kempston and headed for the nearby police station. Once inside, the overzealous heating stifling, she marched purposefully to the desk sergeant and concisely voiced her complaint. He listened with interest, brow furrowing as the story deepened. "Mrs...?"

"Hall. Dorothy Hall."

He tapped the end of his pen against the reception desk, eyes not meeting hers. "To be honest I don't see what we can do. You don't know who the woman is so we can't have a word with her, and she's not really issued any real threats, has she?"

Dorothy's hackles were up - she had expected more concern for her husband in his desperate hour - and she checked the name badge. "Mr Adams..."

"Sergeant." He was finding the old woman tiresome and his coffee was getting cold.

"I don't know how familiar you are with Polton, young man, but it's a small town and the parish is very close, and in a small town with a close parish, gossip can get out of hand. My husband has been unable to work since this hussy brandished her ridiculous allegations because he is being hounded by his flock."

Adams stifled a snigger and drowned his coffee regardless of her presence. "In that case, the best thing you can do is see his superiors and explain the situation, ask for them to maybe issue a notice of innocence, or something to that effect."

Dorothy's jaw dropped and her grey eyes, magnified by the thick lenses of her glasses, widened. "You mean to tell me, young man, that you have no intention of taking any action at all?"

He sighed, replacing the mug on the desk. "If you give us the name of the woman who made the allegations we can have a word with her, but without that we're powerless."

She shot him a glare and a tut, turned on her low heels and stormed out. Relieved, Adams took his mug to the kitchen, refilling the kettle and switching it on. He prepared another coffee, occasionally checking if anyone was waiting in reception, but it was still empty when he returned to his seat.

Adams busied himself, checking the latest crime reports, scanning through the usual thefts and car crime, a couple of muggings, one stabbing, but the next report stood out. "Hope Brown, of Saxlingham Nethergate, reporting alleged childhood abuse by Rector Griffin Hall of St Peter's Church, Polton."

Moving the other reports aside, he leant back on his chair and carefully perused the statement, ensuring he didn't miss a detail. What he read was horrific.

Griffin Gets a Visit

DI Horseferry had been happy for Adams to attend when she questioned the rector, he was a good officer, and his colleague had been grateful to take desk duty instead of freezing on the streets.

They knocked on the oak door, admiring the impressive, rambling cottage, and were presently greeted by a tall man who introduced himself as the Rector Griffin Hall. He led them to his study, indicating seats beside an overstocked bookcase, and sat behind the desk, subconsciously asserting his authority.

Horseferry began, competent and commanding. "We have received a complaint regarding the alleged sexual assault of a minor twenty-five years ago."

Griffin rolled his eyes, forearms slumping to the desk, resigned. "It's a lie. I don't know who she is and I don't know why she's doing this. I don't know what her problem is with me but in God's name it's a lie."

"I need to ask you some questions, as I'm sure you'll understand we're duty bound to investigate every complaint, regardless of how unlikely it is." Adams was impressed with his senior's diplomacy, how she had instantly put the man at ease. "Have you ever worked at St Paul's Church in Reading."

"Yes, that's where I did my training, twenty-five, twenty-six or so years ago."

"Did you know of a family named Ferris?"

He shook his head slowly. "No, I can't say I recall the name, sorry."

Horseferry despised being lied to, it brought out the terrier in her. "Did you officiate at a children's club called the Friendly Club on Tuesday nights?"

Griffin smiled sweetly, eyes twinkling. "Yes, yes, I felt it important for children to have somewhere safe to go in the evenings and was instrumental in setting it up."

"Then you really should try harder to remember Hope Ferris. She attended the Friendly Club religiously, excuse the pun, for roughly a year." Her manner was harsh and Griffin's innocuous smile waned.

144

Head in hands, muttering under his breath, he deliberated for a minute. "Yes, now I think of it I do remember her. Timid little thing, shy, kept in the corners and didn't say or do much. Didn't have much time for her, she was quite whiny, quite an irritation. I wasn't displeased when she stopped coming." The saintly smile returned.

"Did you ever spend time at the Ferris's house."

"No," shaking his head, "no, not at all."

Horseferry sighed silently. The rector was a slimeball and cases like this where it was one person's word against the other irritated her. It was unlikely anything would ever come of the investigation. "Ms Ferris has detailed a vivid account of rape, followed by a serious sexual attack, when she was aged seven and she alleges you were her attacker."

He waved his hands, eyes sorrowful, mouth twisted. "No, it's rubbish, I tell you. I don't know what this woman has against me but it's all lies, it never happened. It's in her imagination. For some bizarre reason, she's trying to ruin my life and I don't know why. In fact, I should be suing her for defamation of character. Or libel. Or slander. Whatever. Officer, I want to put in a counter complaint, I want this woman arrested for what she's doing to me, for harassment." Agitated, Griffin lit a cigar, inhaling deeply, the nicotine relaxing his tense shoulders.

Horseferry rose. "Thank you, we'll be in touch. We'll see ourselves out." Adams followed his superior from the room, wondering why she had stopped the interview so hastily, and when they left the house, she offered an unprompted explanation. "I know what you're thinking, but I can assure you we were going to get nothing out of him in that kind of mood. Look, when we get back to the station I want you to contact Norwich, see if they can get the woman to do a video interview, that way we can see her body language. Tell them we need some proof, like a birthmark or a witness to him visiting, as much as possible. Tell them my gut feeling is guilty and I want to hammer the guy."

Griffin Gets a Letter

He didn't recognise the postmark on the envelope, but Griffin received a great deal of unexpected post and opened it without regard. The quality, crisp, white paper was headed with the address, contact details and logo of the Rumbourne Hotel in Thetford and Griffin was curious, reading avidly.

'Dear Rector Hall, I read about your recent troubles in the newspaper and the wicked accusations have shocked me to the core. I am American, currently resident in England while I study British culture, and in my travels I stayed at Polton and gratefully attended your Sunday sermon. I found you to be a wonderful man and leader, and I hereby offer you my total support as long as this despicable situation continues to raise its ugly head. Yours sincerely, Eva Brunel.'

Griffin grinned, pleased to have a supporter, and such a well-spoken and polite one too. He was fed up with the whole business and eager to put it behind him. His superiors had arranged for a flyer to be placed on the church notice board advocating his innocence in what was suspected to be a revenge attack by an unhinged individual, pleading that the parishioners ignore the accusations and accept their rector back to the church with no recriminations. He was due to preach the following Sunday for the first time since Midnight Mass.

He set the letter on the desk, straightening it firmly, unsure whether to file it or reply. He resolved to take some time away from the study to ponder the decision.

Griffin Replies

He had pottered around for a couple of hours, and amidst the mindless jobs, had taken dinner, had a short nap and fed the birds with bacon fat and toast crumbs leftover from breakfast. The unexpected letter voicing support consumed him and after some deliberation his decision was made: it would be polite to reply and thank the mysterious Eva for her support. After all, his parishioners hadn't shown such faith.

In the dimness of the desk light, the room dark now night had settled, he sat behind the desk with a blank piece of writing paper on the blotter before him, fountain pen poised. Unscrambling the jigsaw of words in his head, he eventually phrased them in a way he felt suitable:

'Dear Miss Brunel, I hope this letter will find you as I have no indication of your address but for that of the Rumbourne Hotel. I want to thank you wholeheartedly for your support in this matter. I have to admit that the past couple of weeks have been harrowing, with many I thought of as friends shunning me regardless of the truth. However, I have received a visit from the police and they are satisfied of my innocence. It was indeed lovely to hear from you. Yours sincerely, Rector Griffin Hall.'

It wasn't until he was tugging on his pyjama bottoms later that he realised he had not seen an article in the local newspaper about the events on Christmas Eve, and it was too mediocre a matter to be of interest to the national newspapers. He resolved to speak to a few of his more trustworthy parishioners the next day to see if anybody recalled the coverage, suspecting Dorothy had hidden it from him to spare his feelings. He glanced at her hefty form in the single bed under the window and a rare moment of tenderness tugged at his heart. He watched her, lightly snoring, for a few seconds, before changing his top and settling into his own single bed.

Hope's Version

The procedure had been explained and all she had to do was give her account of the abuse she had suffered at such a tender age. DI Jackie Lancer and Hope were alone, a camcorder on standby.

In the next room, a constable waited patiently for the story to unfold, viewing her actions and expressions on a monitor. Over the next hour she related the ugly scene she had relived in hypnotherapy, an account that tallied almost word for word with the written statement. Jackie marvelled at how well-rehearsed Hope's script seemed to be and her gut feeling was that the unemotional woman was either lying, or had a fanciful imagination. By the time Hope had finished, Jackie considered her to have no credibility.

Although she didn't share Claudia Horseferry's conviction that the attack was genuine, Jackie still needed to investigate and she scanned the list of questions the Bedford Police had requested she ask.

"Hope, just a couple of things. Firstly, can you think of any people who may have witnessed Griffin Hall visiting the house you lived in as a child? Maybe a neighbour or a playmate, your social worker maybe?"

Hope's eyes twinkled and she smiled smugly. "Yes, my mum and sisters, Charity and Faith. They'll all tell you how much time he spent at ours."

Dutifully, Jackie noted their names and contact details and continued, and each answer was delivered without hesitation. Jackie checked her watch; her stomach was growling and she was eager to get some lunch. "Okay, I have one final question. Can you remember anything about Griffin Hall's body - a birthmark, tattoo, scar - that might back up your, um, accusation?"

Here was the steamroller dismissal Hope had warned her counsellor of; Jackie Lancer clearly believed the abuse was a fantasy. Previously emotionless, she was suddenly tiny, frightened and alone. She couldn't remember anything that would prove she had seen him intimately. He had hairy toes - she remembered his feet clearly - wrapped in tan leather sandals with no socks, the long hairs winding upwards, man hair. Man foot hair. Hope could physically taste his penis, but couldn't describe its appearance - it had been purple, but aren't they all?

Jackie muttered insincere thanks and goodbyes, and rushed off to get a sandwich. Stunned by the speed of the officer's exit, Hope slowly dressed against the cold weather: coat, hat, scarf, finally dragging thermal gloves over her fingers.

The freezing mist reddened her cheeks as she walked the short distance to the car park, watching Jackie Lancer scurrying further along the busy road. Her eyes burned, years of anger and frustration boring into the woman's back. Jackie had disbelieved the truth, and rather than breaking her heart and hammering the pain deeper, it infuriated her.

Social Services Get Involved

Hands clasped in a vain attempt to ward off the cold, Karen waited on the doorstep with her trainee colleague, Avis. The sprawling rectory was a beautiful example of rustic architecture, the uneven stone dating back to the early eighteen hundreds, the garage a recent afterthought.

Still unable to face the accusing eyes and hushed whispers of his flock, Griffin asked Dorothy to answer the doorbell. "Mrs Hall?" She nodded. "My name's Karen Turner, I'm a social worker for the Bedford Child and Family Unit. I'm here about some allegations that have been made against Griffin Hall."

Resigned, her jaw set with irritation, Dorothy moved aside and the two women stepped into the warmth, the icy dampness steaming from their coats. "Griff, some more people are here regarding the ridiculous statement that hussy made." Bobbing her head indignantly, she returned to the kitchen to continue baking for the New Year's Eve party they hosted annually at the church hall.

Griffin sloped into the hallway, stooping in his sorrow, weary and drawn. His broad shoulders were hunched listlessly and his body gaunt from not eating after his appetite vanished in the early hours of Christmas Day. Karen studied the tortured figure she had read memos about and found him oddly attractive. He was many years older than her own twenty-nine, but his height was impressive and his body lean and defined. She felt an incredible sexual tension for him which stirred a longing she had not felt for years. When his eyes met hers, tearful in innocence, blood surged to her inner thighs in a rush of desire. This man was no paedophile.

Griffin led the women to his study and sagged onto the scaly leather chair, wheeling it forward, tucking his knees under the desk. He indicated for the two women to sit. Imploring, he said, "It's just the dirty lies of a psychotic woman, I tell you. I have no idea why she's doing this, but I know that I'm innocent and that God's truth will shine out." He clasped his chest to emphasise his torment and his eyelids drooped, shrew eyes peeping from underneath, a wounded man hounded unfairly.

150

Karen's heart reached out to him and she nodded gently, accepting his pain and frustration without question. "Rector, I understand how dreadful this must be for you, but unfortunately we're duty bound to be involved once a complaint such as this is registered with the police. To be honest, it's for your own protection as much as anything else."

Griffin sensed the trust billowing from the woman, an ally in his fight against the hideous accusations, and his esteem grew. He squared his shoulders, enhancing his height and the breadth of his chest. His commanding appearance - strong nose, firm chin, greying temples - teamed with the purity of the white collar inspired trust, and manipulating his current audience wouldn't be too hard: some mild flirtation, a few affable and cheeky smiles, mirroring their movements. They would be firmly on his side in no time.

His plan worked on smitten Karen; she adored him and wanted to bear his babies.

But not Avis. Griffin Hall made her skin crawl.

Claudia Views the Evidence

Claudia Horseferry spent the afternoon ploughing through statements taken from Hope's family, although Wanda Ferris, the woman's mother, had absolutely refused to get involved, professing the whole situation to be ridiculous. Charity and Faith agreed that Griffin Hall had visited their childhood home on several occasions, but had had little personal interaction with him as he had spent most of his time with Hope. They also stated he had been extremely close with their mother.

Faith had been genuinely concerned for her sister during the interview, but Charity had been arrogant, admitting her knowledge of the visits as an aside, concentrating the conversation mainly on herself. However, the evidence was there.

Now the peripheral evidence had been collected, Claudia checked that the video of Hope's interview had finished downloading on her computer. She relaxed on her seat with her feet resting on an open drawer and clicked 'play', immediately transfixed by the petite and delicate woman on the screen. Shyly attractive with a haunting presence, her inner power was intense and Claudia had no doubt she spoke the truth. The vicious and filthy account of an innocent child's torture ripped through the detective's heart.

When the video ended, Claudia debated the evidence and, regardless of apathetic Lancer's conviction that Hope Brown was a bored attention seeker, she was certain of the rector's guilt. Griffin Hall was a monster who must be locked away.

Jackie Lancer

Her shift had finished and she nipped to the corner shop for milk and bread before heading for her first-floor apartment. The air was pungent with tones of alcohol and stale cigarettes, which reminded her of the lonely night before, supping Christmas booze, bemoaning her dull existence. Of course, everything had seemed less dire once day had broken. Dry January, here I come, she thought.

She flicked on the kettle and took a mug from the cupboard, spooning in some coffee. But the bottle of wine on the side was singing to her and she relented, filling a tumbler to the brim, sipping the top. Taking it to the bathroom, she turned on the taps and tipped bubble bath into the flowing water, wobbling the water with her hand. Stripping naked, she threw the sweaty uniform she had not changed from the day before into the laundry basket.

The strike came from nowhere and Jackie reeled, baffled and dazed. A sudden, grinding thud to her back and she fell forward into the steaming water, blood spurting, colouring the bubbles. No pain, only confusion. An aching, yawning fatigue, consuming, overwhelming. Sliding under the scalding water, barely noticing her nerves screaming, a wave of peace spread through her and she closed her eyes.

Then realisation, self-preservation. She had been attacked, must defend herself. Jackie scrabbled up, flailing, fighting, searching for her assailant. Soap stung her eyes and they throbbed, blind. But the pathetic attempt was too late. A forceful punch to her chest knocked her back into the tub, a knife slicing her flesh. Breathless and terrified, her blood spattered the tiles.

Adrenaline flooded. She must resist her attacker, disarm him, save herself. Reaching out with clawed hands, nails ready to gouge.

Another blow knocked her down, head underwater, mouth full, lungs saturated. Struggling to breathe, a strong taste of iron.

Barely conscious, gasping, she struggled to sit, but another crack came and her fight was gone. Devastated in the crimson water, her mutilated abdomen spilling viscera, her life seeped away in pulsing rhythms. Jackie closed her eyes and saw blackness.

153

The lights remained on, the taps running, and eventually the spilled water seeped into the carpet and through the floorboards, staining the ceiling of the apartment below. The annoyed owners hammered on the door, shouting, but their neighbour didn't answer.

And later, when the water dripping into the bucket they had placed underneath the leak coloured pink, they called the police, concerned.

Too late for Jackie. She was long gone.

Session Fourteen

The snow had frozen overnight and was crisp and treacherous, grey with exhaust fumes and dirt. Dawn watched through the frosty window of the overheated room for Hope to arrive. A familiar bundle of outerwear came into view, treading carefully in flat boots, firming each step before trusting the leg with her weight. Her red nose and bright blue eyes peeped from the piles of black wool that drowned her as she made her way up the steps and pushed the door. Dawn moved the seats close to the radiator, eagerly awaiting the next hour.

The bustle entered without introduction, reminding Dawn that the receptionist was on sick leave with a nasty cold. She grinned widely and Hope returned the cheerfulness. "How was your New Year?"

Hope removed her coat to expose heavyweight jeans and a light jumper covered with a contrasting cardigan, a thick metallic chain weighted with a Celtic cross lying on top. She dropped her outerwear on the carpet without tidying the pile as she normally would and Dawn cocked her head. "Not feeling orderly today then?"

Hope laughed, kicking the clothes playfully. "No, life's too short. New Year was good thanks. Yeah, it was good. What about yours?"

Dawn rested her head on her hand, leaning on the arm of the chair. "Quiet this year. We played in Bensons early evening, then I went home. I didn't feel like following the lads to the party they..." Dawn faltered, transfixed by a metal hipflask Hope had dragged from her bag, unscrewing the lid and swigging. Again. And again. She screwed the lid firmly and dropped the flask back in her bag, finally noticing Dawn's incredulous interest. "Brandy, helps keep me warm on shitty days like this. Want some?" She gestured her bag.

It was naughty, but tempting. Dawn had driven to work as always and wasn't one to drink and drive, especially in such hazardous weather. Plus, she was at work. "Yes, actually. Go on then, I'll have some." Whatever. She wasn't due to drive for a few hours, and Hope was right: life's too short.

Dawn savoured the taste - warm, biting, soothing - the quality smoothness. She rarely drank spirits, let alone neat, and her reddening nose throbbed within seconds. Such unprofessional behaviour was wrong, but Hope seemed rebellious today, challenging and careless, and she wanted to be part of that wantonness, be a maverick too.

The misbehaviour continued until the final dregs had been drained by the giggling women and Hope replaced the flask in her bag. They sat for a while, faces flushed, basking in the wooziness. Finally, relaxed and laid back, Dawn began the session. "You seem carefree today, more than I've ever seen you. Like a huge weight has dropped from your shoulders."

Hope smiled, eyes twinkling and mischievous. "I reported him."

Dawn grinned warmly. "I'm so proud of you. Were the police helpful? Are they taking it seriously?"

"Well, I was interviewed by a copper from Norwich at first, Jackie Lancer, and I don't think she believed me, but I found out yesterday she's been taken off the case anyway so her opinion's irrelevant. The woman in Bedfordshire has been great though, really supportive."

"Good, it's obviously made a big difference to how you feel about yourself, you're much less tense."

"It's amazing, so cathartic, like twenty-five years of oppression has lifted. It's his word against mine, and obviously he's not going to admit anything, but my sisters have given statements that back my case. Mum refuses though, says she doesn't want to be involved."

"That's rough, you'd think she'd want to support you through a hard time like this."

"Hey, you know yourself what it's like, I mean, you fell out with your parents irretrievably over yours, didn't you?"

Dawn's smile waned, sad and reminiscent. "Yes, but I think that was what propelled me to ensure he was convicted. I wanted to show them he'd get his comeuppance with or without their help."

"I can understand that; I feel the same. But as I say, Faith and Charity are helping and I believe they've found Tracy so she can give a statement too."

156

"Fantastic, the more support you can get, the more they can push on him. Have you had any thoughts about what you want to talk about today?"

Hope smoothed her jeans, showing nervousness for the first time since arriving. "I'll tell you what I would like to get off my chest: my daughter, Penny." Dawn crossed her arms and smiled encouragingly. "She's gone really weird all of a sudden. Has Rick told you we're dating?"

Stunned, horrified. Her brother obviously - rightly - had concerns about telling her. Dawn stuttered, "No... no, he didn't. How... how long?"

In lust, maybe love, and enjoying it greatly, Hope was oblivious to Dawn's discomfort and continued brightly, "Well, this is the problem, we went out for the first time on Boxing Day, went to a restaurant in the town centre, Pinocchio's, do you know it?" Dawn nodded, the idea of Hope with her brother appalling. "Then we dated twice the following week. After that I was relaxed enough with how things were going to introduce him to my kids, so I invited him round for dinner."

Dawn shifted uncomfortably; she wanted Rick away from Hope, away from her dangerousness. She had no valid reason to object to them dating, but was torn between sisterly concern for Rick and jealousy that he was stealing Hope from her. The realisation stunned her.

"Well, the kids were all looking forward to meeting him, they know I'm happier in a relationship than single, and they all scrubbed up ready for his arrival. We prepared a really nice meal, we were excited. Anyway, Rick turned up at six, the table was set, everything ready to go, but as soon as Penny clapped eyes on him she threw a tantrum, crying, shouting. I couldn't believe it. She was calling him a bastard, telling him to fuck off out of her house. I was gobsmacked.

"After a while I calmed her down enough to tell me what was going on and she said she knew him because she'd been to see Reveal on one of the nights she'd slipped out of the house behind my back. I couldn't get angry because she would have stopped talking, but I was furious inside, I mean, what was a thirty-two-year-old bloke doing knowing my attractive thirteen-year-old? What would you do, Dawn?"

Dawn didn't answer, knowing exactly what her brother was capable of when it came to getting laid, and once again the thought

157

of him with Hope disgusted her. But not as much as the thought of him with a young child. She swallowed, captivated by the sickening revelations but wishing she could run away. Far, far away.

"I was angry. She'd sneaked out, lied to me, put herself at risk while I thought she was asleep in bed. And I was angry with him, he should have told me he knew her, although he swore blind he didn't. He had to, she was devastated and that had to come from somewhere. You know, I'm so worried about her at the moment, she's becoming unhinged. She's put on so much weight in the past few months, she looks terrible. She never stops eating, all day, she's eating everything and tons of it - cereal, toast, chocolate, biscuits, seconds at dinner. She's getting so fat. She used to be such a skinny little thing, scrawny and petite. I'm worried about her, it's like the opposite to anorexia."

Dawn's emotions were churning. "So what happened?"

"He went home. We're still seeing each other, but I won't bring him home again. Actually, he refuses to come back to mine any more." She quietened, wistful. "She's always been such a tiny thing, little and skinny. Always eaten like a sparrow, pecking at it until she's had enough and leaving the rest. Now it's like she can't fill her mouth enough."

Dawn nodded, pleased the conversation had steered from Rick, yet determined to have words with him later. As for the issue at hand, she had two choices: either believe the account verbatim and accept Penny was eating obsessively, or dismiss it discreetly, considering Hope's self-confessed problem with weight and fat. She decided to sit on the fence for a while.

"I know all children get puppy fat. The way I've seen it with the three of them growing up is that they get all podgy, then have a growth spurt. But Penny's fully grown, she's taller than me, and until she started putting the weight on she had a lovely figure, just right." Hope's hands subconsciously contoured Penny's body and Dawn hoped her client was exaggerating her daughter's size, else she would be grotesquely overweight. "I don't know what to do, she gets bigger by the day."

"Have you talked to her about it, asked if she's aware she's overeating?"

Hope nodded, frown lines deepening. "She says she doesn't know why, she just feels madly hungry all the time. I've told her to chew each mouthful properly, eat slower, all the ways to ensure you don't continue eating once you're full up. I can see her trying, but then she ruins it by bingeing."

"Are you concerned about bulimia?"

"No, she wouldn't be gaining so much weight if she was honking it down the loo after eating."

Dawn grimaced with the mental image and clasped her hands together, keen to advise responsibly. Her head swam with a mixture of alcohol and the revelations about Rick. "How long has the overeating been going on?"

Hope chewed her lip as she counted on her fingers, concentrating. "I'd say six months or so, five, six months. It wasn't so noticeable at first, just the odd extra bag of crisps here and there, but in the past month the weight gain has been so noticeable." Their eyes met; the answer was obvious. "Doctors, right?"

Dawn nodded. "Get her blood and urine tested, just as a precaution."

Hope scanned the carpet, worried. "Yes, I'll do that. Of course." The subject had concluded naturally and both women fidgeted, silent. Hope stroked her cashmere woollens, the silkiness comforting, while Dawn focused on the grain of the coffee table. Hope sighed deeply, a warning Dawn had learned from experience to mean the next sentence would be difficult. "It's Mum and Belinda's anniversary in six weeks, they'll have been married four years. We've just received an invitation to go to Cornwall for the weekend, they're having a party to celebrate."

Dawn surveyed Hope's forlorn expression and smiled ironically. "I can see you're overwhelmed with excitement with the idea."

Hope chuckled, standing, smoothing her tight clothes, strolling to the window to watch the cold greyness. She crossed her arms. "You know, when I first mentioned Mum and Belinda's wedding to you, I surprised myself that I sounded so prejudiced, because the truth is I have no problem with gay, or lesbian, or bi. I have no problem with race, gender, age, I don't do 'ism's'. Getting this invitation - and that was a shock in itself, Mum and I aren't on the best of terms since all this Griffin business raised its ugly head - it reminded me of their wedding."

Hope stared at the water cooler, swallowing; she was thirsty, but the idea of iced water in the depths of winter wasn't tempting. Glancing at her watch, she sat again. "This'll take a while, but I want

159

you to know how it happened, then maybe you can explain why it hurt so much, because, being honest, I'm struggling to understand my bitterness."

Dawn crossed her legs, head cocked, listening intently. "Tell me how it went, then we can analyse it."

Hope swallowed again, digging in her pocket for a mint, her mouth too dry to wait any longer for refreshment. "All of us - me, Faith, Charity, Happiness - had left home long before. Mum had no idea what the event was, at least that's what she said. We got an invitation just after Christmas, said Mum was hosting an important event on the eighteenth of February and we were all invited. It was quite exciting, cloak and dagger, and we were phoning each other constantly, trying to get an idea of what was going on. The invite stated formal dress so we all went shopping, spruced ourselves up.

"We went down to Cornwall the night before, the Friday. No one was allowed in the ballroom, there were people in there setting up, but we were all kept well away in Mum's private quarters. The refuge was in its early days then, she only set it up, well, only had the money to set it up after Honesty." She hesitated and Dawn despaired, sure they had got past the stage where Hope retreated now they had a firm mutual trust.

The pause lasted a minute - two, three - and Hope swallowed dryly, deliberating, controlling herself. Eventually, "The next morning we were instructed to stay in our rooms until ten forty-five exactly, when we were to make our way to the ballroom. It was all very mysterious and I was as excited as the kids. The caterers left trays loaded with toasts, jams, croissants, meats - you know, a sort of continental-stroke-English without the grease - outside our rooms and the kids piled in, as kids do, and finished the lot, greedy little buggers." A gentle laugh lit her eyes briefly and Dawn understood the memory was treasured.

"Well, eager to find out what was going on we all went to the ballroom at the right time. In all honesty, I thought it would be a formal opening for the refuge, so you can imagine how surprised I was when Brahms's Wedding March began playing." Hope popped another mint in her dry mouth.

"It was beautiful, no doubt about that. Mum's not very tasteful, but we've since discovered that Belinda is, she's a real homebody, mothering, caring. She did all the arrangements. Everything was white, the only contrast the cushions on the seats

160

and the flower arrangements that were scattered everywhere. It was regal but not ostentatious, you know, just enough without rubbing your nose in it Beckham style."

Hope paused, seeking reassurance and Dawn nodded. "Brahms was being played by a string quartet, not my kind of thing," Hope indicated her clothing, a direct imitation of Dawn's style, "as you can tell, but it was fitting. My instant assumption was she'd met another man and just hadn't mentioned him. She appeared - I was looking over my shoulder - and there she was, more beautiful than I'd ever seen her. Slim, elegant, demure even. She had a full length ivory dress made of Indian silk, and it was befitting to a mature woman, not a fairy tale meringue, just subtle, and she strode up to what we now realised was the altar."

Hope clutched her chest, fingers splayed across the sternum, protecting her heart from the shocking memory. "I felt so happy for her. In retrospect, I should have questioned that no groom was at the altar, how was I to know that Mum was the 'groom'? Now I know she's the dominant of the two it makes sense, but back then the shock was..." her fist tapped her chest by way of explanation. "Then I saw another bride. We'd never even met Belinda before, well, not properly. We'd seen her at the Christmas do and assumed she was one of the refuge women. She also looked beautiful, but I couldn't take it all in. Charity couldn't handle it, she walked out. Faith and me, we kept looking at each other, stunned. I couldn't take it in, any of it. All my head kept screaming was 'my mum's a lesbian, she's marrying the lesbian lover we've never been introduced to. Right now.' I just couldn't get to grips with it."

Hope coughed lightly, cracking, bone dry. "The meal was fantastic, the band, everybody was having a wonderful time. Charity had gone home in disgust, but that was no change as she's always off in a huff about something or other, living on her bloody high horse. But Faith, me, just looking at each other in disbelief."

"Happiness seemed to take it in her stride, from what you say."

Hope nodded vigorously. "Yes, she had a fantastic time. She was up dancing, did a stint on the karaoke. Hell, she's got a lovely voice."

Dawn's smile didn't reach her eyes. "I've heard; Vivity are on the radio non-stop."

Hope's eyes widened, guilty. "Oh my god, I'm sorry. I was going to get her to check out your band, I'm so sorry, I've been so busy, there's so much going on…"

Dawn raised her hand to stop the torrent. "Hope, don't worry."

Calming, she sighed. "Look, I'll be seeing Happiness at the anniversary, I'll have a word with her then if I haven't had a chance before. Have you got a demo I could take her or something?"

"I'll collect a few bits together for your session next week." Dawn glanced at the clock. "Anyway, we've got ten minutes left, fill me in on how the wedding felt to you."

Hope shrugged. "Well, that was it. A beautiful, stylish occasion, a massive shock. I think if I'd known she was a lesbian before it wouldn't have been a problem. It was the shock."

Dawn drummed her fingers against her lips, contemplative. "The shock. Hope, has it ever occurred to you that the shock was deliberate?"

"In what way?"

"I remember you mentioning ages ago that you and Al got married to shock people, maybe that's what your mum was doing to you. She seems fairly competitive towards you." Hope quietly considered the statement. "I've never heard you include Faith in any of the deeper conversations we've had about your family, but it seems to me that everybody else is attention grabbing in their own way. Charity with her snobbishness, you with the writing, Honesty with her recording, Happiness with hers. Mum wants to make you all notice her. What better way of doing it than a surprise wedding, the surprise not being the wedding."

Hope mused, able to appreciate what Dawn was saying, but unsure if it fitted. Did it fit? Were they all pathetic attention grabbers? Was she? She didn't feel like she was, but maybe. "I need to think about that one. I can see your reasoning, but I need to mull it over for a while. I've never considered that possibility."

Dawn raised her hand, halting the session. "Do that, think about things and we can talk about it next week." They stood, Dawn towering over Hope, who shrugged on her winter garments ready to face the harshness outside.

As Hope hurried along the corridor, a whisper, haunting, "I want to hurt him. I want him to suffer."

Dawn turned to the tiny voice that may or may not have been there. Nobody, it must have been her imagination. Was it? And who did she want to hurt? Was it Rick? Her heart speeded, adrenaline flowing, and she was terrified for her brother. Maybe she was being silly, maybe she meant Griffin. Maybe she had said nothing at all.

What was going on?

Hope's strength was impressive, but she was terrifying too. Dawn shuddered.

Another Night Out

Penny was sprawled along the length of the cream sofa, packet of biscuits in hand, eating without chewing, swallowing chunks in her desperation to cram the next mouthful in. The television chattered to itself in the corner, blending into the white noise. Olive was curled neatly on the recliner chair, a book way beyond her years gripping her in its horror. Bern, in pyjamas and dressing gown, played with his cars on the carpet, the beige weave transformed into a small town in his imagination.

In the kitchen, Hope removed the final metal sheet from the oven and turned the heat off. She wiped her hands on the cloth, fussing, irritated that the babysitter was late.

Fifteen minutes past the arranged time, Kirsty knocked on the door and Hope trotted to the hall, beaten by her small son who shot from the living room at full speed. On tiptoes to reach the catch, he dragged the door wide and huffed when he saw the fifteen-year-old blonde, eyes heavily blackened, hair poker straight, clothes fashionably tight. "Not you again." Bern's shoulders slumped and he let go of the door, mooching back to his carpet kingdom.

"Come in, Kirsty, make yourself at home." In an apparently single movement, Hope had closed the door, shrugged on her jacket, slipped her scarf, hat and gloves on, and grasped her handbag and car keys. Miserable Penny traipsed into the hall, her baggy T-shirt straining from the recent excessive weight gain, and Hope was concerned.

Penny sagged lazily against the wall, acknowledging the senior girl from her school with a light nod. "Why are you going out again, Mum?"

Hope had almost disappeared under the layers. "I have to, I'll be back about midnight, maybe."

Penny's eyes rolled dramatically, the pained adolescent act in full flow. "But you're always going out now, it's not fair. We never see you any more."

Hope tugged at Penny's top, dislodging a shelf of biscuit crumbs. "I have important things to do that can't be avoided,

164

sweetheart. Look, Penny," her daughter's bottom lip jutted defiantly, "try not to eat any more today."

Penny crossed her arms, indignant, head cocked in challenge. "Not that again."

Hope sighed with motherly resignation, wishing she could instil common sense into the child. "I know it's hard, you're growing and I know you're hungry. But in the past few months you must have put on over a stone, maybe even two. I'm worried." A rebellious glare at her mother, and Penny sidled to the kitchen, taking a hot sausage roll from the tray. She exaggeratedly savoured the first bite, the second, and Hope shook her head, breaking the obstinate exchange.

Sighing, she nodded farewell to Kirsty and headed for the car, starting the engine and turning the blowers on full blast to clear the windows of the thick ice on the outside and condensation on the inside. She took the scraper, bitterness biting the ends of her fingers, and scrubbed at the sheets of melting ice. Eventually the windows were clear and Hope climbed in, grateful of the warmth and eager to begin her journey.

Dorothy is Suspicious

Sluggish, her battered sheepskin slippers scraping the carpet, Dorothy came downstairs and watched a pile of post drop through the letterbox. Her housecoat barely kept her warm; winter was in full swing and it was freezing in the old cottage. She bent stiffly to collect the letters, focusing on the one at the bottom, which she was certain had been there before the postman delivered the others. There was no stamp or frank; it had been hand delivered and was addressed to her husband. The writing was undoubtedly female and Dorothy's jaw stiffened jealously. She marched to the kitchen and rested the letter against the salt pot, ready to question Griffin. Pouring oil into the unwashed frying pan, the salty smell of bacon wafted as the layer of lard at the bottom spat.

Twenty minutes later Griffin entered, snug in his threadbare woollen dressing gown, and sat without acknowledging his wife. She had become used to his manner over the years and it didn't bother her, but his ignoring the envelope did; she was desperate to see what it held. She dished out the bacon and eggs.

Griffin grunted as his wife placed the steaming food before him, grease glistening in the cold sunlight from the window, but when she grasped the teapot to pour, she noticed the letter was gone and her heart lurched. The behaviour was suspicious; was he having a clandestine affair? She choked, part cough, part retch, and excused herself, shuffling from the room. Unaware of her torment, Griffin fingered the envelope in his pocket, desperate to finish breakfast and retreat to his study to read Eva's words.

Stirrings

He read the letter for the third time, savouring each tempting word, fingertips stroking the paper that her hands had rested on the day before, and his groin stirred. It had been many years since he had felt such affection for a woman, in fact he wasn't sure he ever had. Dorothy was his wife and he loved her for that, but they had never been sexually close, not even once to consummate the marriage. They had excused their childlessness to concerned parishioners with bad luck rather than the truth.

Griffin's hand wandered inside his gown, reaching for himself, and once more he read the letter, planning his reply mentally as he played his forbidden game. His pleasure was quickly over and he took his pen, the words tumbling onto his personalised paper:

'Dearest Eva, thank you again for your letter, I'm really enjoying our friendship and I'm so pleased we've been getting closer and more trusting over the past couple of weeks. I have imagined you time over, wandering what you look like, sound like, feel like. Eva, I want to meet you, after all, you know me, yet I have no idea who you are.

I don't know if this is out of line, but I suspect I'm falling just a little bit for you. You stir me in ways no other woman has. I feel like a naughty schoolboy sometimes, but I cannot deny that my heart yearns for you. Please can we meet, and soon. Yours, with fond affection, Griff.'

He took an envelope, shifting his reading glasses to focus on the address of the hotel Eva was currently staying at and copying it neatly. He imagined Eva would receive the letter and profess undying love to him, they would meet up and have a torrid, passionate affair, providing him with enough sexual memories to see him through the rest of his mundane life, before she toddled back to America, back to her life, leaving him to grow old with Dorothy in their comfortable way.

His penis grew again and it brought a proud smile to his face. After all, he was nearing fifty, but age hadn't dented his drive in the

167

slightest. He dropped the pen and reached inside once more, preferring to play, eyes closed, imagination wild, than to work.

The Unexpected

Claudia clicked the video off with the remote control and stretched her long, thickset legs, leaning firmly on the chair to recline it as far as it would go. Until yesterday it looked likely that the nasty accusations against Rector Griffin Hall would be swept under the carpet, but now another woman had come forward claiming he sexually abused her at an early age.

Eager for the details, Claudia had rushed a video interview first thing in the morning, scared to wait in case the mystery woman disappeared in a puff of smoke, a figment of her imagination. But Eva Brunel was very real and a pretty little thing too.

Regardless that she had only conducted the interview that morning, Claudia started the footage for the fifth time. A light fuzzing, a quick sound-check, and the camera focused on the unexpected witness. Claudia heard herself questioning the woman, studying her body language and voice patterns, and again had no doubt that the details Eva was remembering were truthful.

Griffin obviously had a penchant for petite women, a trait shared by Eva, Hope Brown and Mrs Hall, all of whom were five feet or under. Eva's severe black bob framed her delicate features, and she wore small, barely-there glasses which accentuated the austere haircut. Her quality business suit impacted the image, but there was a fragility about her and Claudia doubted Eva had a wild side; she was too in control. Every recollection she told was considered carefully before it escaped, but the answers weren't premeditated, simply honest.

Eva's account of her traumatic abuse was astoundingly similar to Hope's, the only difference being the year and location it took place. Griffin had befriended her at an after-school club in her childhood town of Newmarket where he worked for the parish of St Andrews as a vicar. She had mentioned to him that her home life was difficult and he had suggested visiting her mother.

The abuse started after he had been visiting for a few weeks. Her mother had left her in Griffin's care for an hour or so in order to get some groceries and he had taken her upstairs and forced her to have vaginal sex, before finishing him off orally. Claudia winced

169

at the revelation, as she had done each time she had watched the interview. She had worked for the Rape and Sexual Abuse team for years, climbing the career ladder, training intensively, but had never become hardened to the horrific details the victims related.

Eva's account was concise and detailed and she also bizarrely recollected Griffin's hairy toes, leading Claudia to question the significance, for which Eva had no answer.

Eva was an only child and her mother had died twenty years before, leaving her an orphan. An aunt, also now deceased, had subsequently brought her up, and there were no witnesses to Griffin's visits. However, that she was prepared to testify against him, and with such a shockingly similar accusation, strengthened the case against the rector.

Claudia watched the video to the end, then reread Eva's statement. Although Claudia was certain they had enough evidence to warrant a conviction, she wished there were a witness on Eva's side and debated digging deeper into the woman's childhood to maybe find a friend or parishioner who could corroborate the accusations.

Claudia sipped her cold coffee with a grimace, resolving to get enough evidence to arrest the man; what they had currently was circumstantial.

Session Fifteen

They had politely greeted, shaking off the cold layers of winter wear, and were cradling steaming mugs of coffee in their reddened hands, Hope's from the bitter wind, Dawn's from the excessive heating in the building. Hope sipped before speaking. "Friday the thirteenth."

"Unlucky for some?"

"Definitely unlucky for some. I had a call from the detective in Bedford who's dealing with the investigation, Claudia Horseferry." Dawn sat to attention, eager. "They have new information and are hoping to arrest him within the week."

Dawn was shocked, but supportive. "So what's the new information, have they given you any details?"

Hope nodded sincerely, smiling enigmatically. "It's amazing, another woman, Eva Brunel, has come forward, says he abused her when she was a child. She read about my case and decided it was time she shared her story too."

"Oh my God, that's fantastic news, not for the woman who was abused, obviously, but for your case. He might actually go down for it. Do you know anything about her?" And it occurred to Dawn that the police shouldn't have given the name of the other witness, surely it was confidential. And where would she have read about the case?

Hope shook her head, rich mahogany waves tumbling from side to side. "No, nothing at all, except her abuse happened after mine."

Dawn grinned, delighted for her client. "You never know, when word gets out more women may stand up and admit he's abused them. I doubt he stopped at two."

Suddenly Hope's eyes were fiery, burning the grin from Dawn's face. "How many fucking witnesses do you want? Don't you think two victims is enough?" Astounded, Dawn felt like a victim herself. "I'll tell you what, I had so much hope when I came in ten minutes ago and you've just dashed everything."

A moment of unease passed before Dawn remembered her place in the room, that she was in charge and her client was

171

misbehaving. She forced a confident appearance and calm voice. "What brought that on?" Firm. Back in control.

Hope's expression wavered between anger and timidity, before becoming blank, emotionless. "I'm sorry, it means so much that Griffin pays for what he did, for destroying me. I'm terrified the judge will throw it out of court."

"I understand. Do you want to discuss it in here?"

Shaking her head again, the well-conditioned hair a contrast to the greasy rat's tails she'd had before her confidence increased. Dawn regarded Hope, her outfit, the new woman - or the old woman without the consuming depression? Maybe she was subconsciously mimicking a woman she admired.

Hope buried the moment. "No. I'll keep you informed of how the case is going, but I don't want to discuss it. He did what he did, he's going to pay, and Eva and I will do our part in getting revenge."

Dawn shuddered and it occurred to her that Hope never mentioned conviction, or jail, or justice, only revenge, as if custody wasn't enough for his crime. Should she pursue this, or just make a mental note for the next time it came up in conversation? She let it go, but not without relief that she wasn't in Griffin's shoes.

"I'll tell you what I do want to get off my chest." There was a wicked glint in her eyes; was Hope teasing her? "Working as a prostitute after Olive was born."

Dawn's mouth opened and closed lamely, tongue-tied. Hope's challenging derision tempted her to doubt the statement was truthful; Hope loved to shock and wasn't averse to dropping a bomb for a reaction. She laughed. Irritated, Dawn waved dismissively, crossing legs and arms against the provocation. "You've got to stop doing things like that. It doesn't help you and it's counterproductive for me."

Hope giggled more, wiping her eyes, hand over mouth. "You should see your face." Dawn hated to be played like a fool, a game Hope excelled at, and was tempted to throw her toys from the pram and stomp out; she wasn't in the mood. But her job was to stay and take the flak. "Thing is, I'm not lying. Maybe the term prostitute was an exaggeration but it's the same thing whatever you call it."

Dawn glared at her. "Enough is enough, let's just stop it with the games, okay. Last week you were going to think about how competitive your family is with each other, why don't we take it from there and stop the silliness, it's wasting your time and mine."

Defiant, ruffled. Hope sat straight, commanding and angry, her personality swelling, dominating. "Fuck it, Dawn, I was giving it away for nothing, which I now accept was a result of low self-esteem following the sexual abuse I didn't know I'd suffered. I was sleeping with them all, practically a different one each night, and I was drinking and smoking, and I'd been made redundant, and I was trying to bring two kids up on my own, and I was strapped for cash. One day I was in bed being humped by god knows who and thought I might as well get paid for it rather than give it away for free."

Hope stared, confrontational, but Dawn was calm, pale underneath the bright, sparkling make up. "No. No."

"You're taking a moral high ground on me now, huh? Make me out to be some fucking dirty tart? Is that it, have I dropped in your estimation now? Go on, Dawn, say it like it is, say what you think." Acrimony oozing, a coiled spring.

Suddenly exhausted by the stand-off, Dawn shrank, hands between her knees, shoulders sloping. Deflated, wounded. Hope noticed her torment and ceased fire, calming. "I'm ashamed of it now, that's why I got annoyed before. I know it was a symptom and I know the reasons I went into it, so I don't want to beat myself up about it, but the truth is I do. I lie in bed remembering how dirty I felt, how dirty the money felt. I couldn't spend it. I fucked them to earn money to make us more comfortable but the money was filth, I couldn't spend it." She quietened, pained.

Ignoring her training, Dawn took Hope's hand, stroking gently, holding eye contact. Soothing the hurt. "How old were you?"

Hope calculated for a moment. "Twenty-three. I only did three; I was finding it too hard to live with myself. I got paid a hundred and twenty pounds each time, working through an escort agency, Pussycats in Reading. I made an appointment and went along in a tight, black, Lycra mini. High boots, black stockings. My hair looked great and my make-up was subtle but dusky. The woman looked me up and down and told me I'd get plenty of work. I felt really good right then. Appreciated. Sexy."

Hope's eyes watered and she sighed, setting the empty mug down. "The first guy was sixty. I had to go to his house, which was

173

about twenty miles away in High Wycombe." A deep breath, the memory hurting. "I didn't think about what I was about to do the whole journey, I just wondered how an old guy could manage to perform. I guessed he'd be wrinkly, a little floppy dick, dribbling like a dirty old man. I mean, he was near on forty years older than me."

The eye contact lost, she disappeared inside herself. "He wasn't like that. Right from the first moment he was kind, treated me with respect, nice. He was a masseur and he asked me to - asked me, Dawn, he didn't order me - asked me to strip to my undies, said he'd give me a full body massage to relax me. Well, this didn't fit the knowledge I had of the trade, I guessed he was a lucky 'employee' of Pussycats, got a shag for a reduced rate, something like that."

Dawn held a hand up, the light catching her metallic green nails. "You mean he sort of tested the new girls to see if they were up to the job?"

"Exactly that." Nodding, her eyes returned to the denim stretched over her knees. "I always want to be the best regardless of what I'm doing, so I decided I wanted a glowing report. I closed my eyes - I was lying face down on his couch - and let his fingers work their magic on me while I imagined a more handsome face, a fitter body, a different man. He really turned me on, well, his hands and my fantasy, and after a blissful half an hour we walked to the bed and got to work. I gave him a show; I bet it was the best sex he'd ever had. I was so horny I came too and that made him happier than anything, he was truly moved, asking again and again if it was him who'd made me come. Of course I said yes for his pride, but my imagination did most of the work."

Hope swallowed, dry, and cleared her throat. "He paid me, I left. I went home, kissed the kids, stuffed the money at the back of my drawer, knocked back a whisky and went to bed. It was as if I had no emotion, I'd detached myself completely and, you know, I was proud to be able to do that."

"Proud is an odd word to use. Why would you be proud of disassociating your feelings?"

Hope chose her words carefully. "I suppose it was about control, maybe self-preservation. If I thought about what I was doing I felt dirtier than ever before, but if I was indifferent I could keep doing the job, keep earning the money so the girls and I could eat, at least until I found another job."

174

"I wonder though how much of this was really about money and how much about not valuing your body, yourself."

Hope's sorrowful blue eyes invited sympathy and understanding. "I can see that now, but not at the time. Over the next few days the voice in my head niggled me, told me I was nothing more than a filthy prostitute. I'd found my calling, this was all I was, I deserved. Trash. Filth."

Hope paused and Dawn knew better than to prompt. "Three days after the old guy I got a call for another one, this time in Newbury, a guest house near a roundabout. Reception told me to go straight up and when I opened the door there was this revolting, flabby, slimy fat guy on the bed. He was naked and his floppy two-inch penis was in his hand, fat fingers rolling it around like a piece of Playdoh. I couldn't keep the disgust off my face and he noticed, grinning those fat slug lips underneath the greasy black moustache. I wanted to be sick."

"So what happened?"

"He told me to strip off, so I did, and knelt on the bed beside him. He started groping my tits, it was vile, but then he pushed me away a bit and said, 'I like big tits, these don't do anything for me. Wank me off.' Hope clasped her chest protectively. "So I did. I took the floppy dick, looked the other way, and did the business. I took my money and ran. Drove home at ninety, straight to the shower with a large whisky, and I scrubbed and scrubbed, even inside because he'd had his fat fingers in there. I had to get every trace of that revolting shit away from me. I scrubbed until it hurt, then got pissed. Really badly pissed."

Hope took a while to prepare the next watershed, Dawn trying to comprehend the complexity of the issue. "The third was the end for me. I got a call about a week later, a professor at Oxford University…"

"*The* Oxford University?"

"The very same. He wanted me to go to his offices. Pussycats warned me he was a difficult customer, always trying to slip the condom off, and that terrified me. No bloody way was I screwing a man who had a call girl habit without protection. Anyway, he let me in. It was a huge office with a kitchen and bathroom, a suite, really. Everything was dingy brown, dark wood everywhere, yellowing upholstery and curtains, and the air was thick with stale smoke. I mean, I was a smoker myself back then, but I found it heavy.

175

"There was no talking. He looked me up and down, smiling, lecherous, and I did my part, posing sexily, showing him the goods. He didn't waste time, took me straight to a sofa and tugged my dress up, feeling the suspenders, groping my crotch. He unzipped himself, pulling my knickers to one side, trying to force himself in, but I pulled away, made sure I got a condom on him. He tried again, but his hands were fiddling down there and luckily, just before he tried to get in again, I felt there too and he'd slipped the condom off. It happened a couple of times more and I got annoyed. I told him he either kept it on or I was going.

"So he did it with one on. It seemed to last forever, humping away, grunting like a filthy beast. I just lay there, took my mind away completely, thinking about how I was going to send my CV to as many companies as I could find the next day. And that's what I did. I got a job almost straight away and I never slept with a guy for money again. I'd earned three hundred and sixty pounds and it stayed stuffed at the back of my drawer. It stayed there until I was moving to Norfolk, then I divided it between the three kids - Bern was born by then - put it in their savings accounts. I could never spend it."

Dawn sighed, grateful the uncomfortable story had been told, but hoping they would move away from it soon. "And now? You're much stronger now, you've gained so much esteem in the past couple of months, and you know there was an underlying cause to your, to your…"

"Promiscuity. It's okay, I accept what I was."

Dawn cringed at the word she had been avoiding. "Do you forgive yourself now you have a better idea of how tormented your mind was?"

Hope smiled, shy, innocent. "I've never told anyone else, I was too ashamed, embarrassed. It was a disgusting thing to resort to and you're right, I think low self-worth was more of a factor than needing the money. I mean, we were poor, but I didn't put much effort into finding a job before I resorted to that."

Dawn relaxed, her back stiff. "You mentioned you'd been made redundant, that must have knocked you a bit, had some part in you taking the route you did."

Rueful, resigned to never changing the past, never cleansing the truth. "I have no doubt it did. I wasn't so much made redundant as sacked for not sleeping with the boss."

"No way."

Hope cupped her hand over her mouth and giggled, fingers forcing the grin away. "Sorry Dawn, it's just you make me laugh when you're shocked."

The consternation was replaced by irritation. "Oh no, don't do this again. Come on."

Serious. "I'm not kidding. Ray had me fired, it's true, it was only your response that made me laugh. Look, I'll tell you about it, but I'm okay with it." She shook her head, digesting the next line before firing. "No, that's not true, I'm bitter about it, because what happened was wrong. But at the end of the day, the pay-off was good and I got a car out of it too. I managed to disguise it on my CV, so it's just something I put down to experience."

"That sounds fair. Tell me if you want, it's up to you."

Hope nodded, deftly taming her bouncy waves, the superb condition reflecting the light. "I will, it may make you understand my determination a little better. Then again, it might not." She rolled her eyes. "In a nutshell then. I was on a one day a week training scheme, it was summer and I was about to take the exam; I would have been a Certified Financial Planner if I passed. Anyway, that's irrelevant. His name was Ray and he was new, my last boss had left. He was ugly, gross, slimy, but he took a fancy to me, made it obvious when we were alone, and that was quite often. He wanted us to get together and I wasn't interested, so he had me fired."

"Come on, you can't brush over it that easily. He must have had some grounds, surely?"

Hope glanced at the clock and stood, collecting her woollens together, languidly dressing for the cold as she finished the story. "No grounds. He suggested we have sex, I said no, and three days later I was asked to leave. Simple as that. I was given a decent cheque and they said I could keep my company car."

Hope's abject dismissal of the episode worried Dawn and the fact she had turned to prostitution afterwards, albeit only a couple of times, showed the episode was far more traumatic than Hope admitted to. She sighed, desperate to bring out the hidden layer before her client slipped away, leaving the moment lost and unchallenged. Subconsciously, Dawn moved beside the door, a physical barrier to stop Hope escaping. "I'm sorry, but getting paid off doesn't make you so low that you start selling your body."

177

Glowering, Hope joined her counsellor by the door and her words tumbled forcefully, harsh, unflinchingly final. "I'd love to know how the fuck you think you know how I or anyone else feels. Maybe I wanted to try selling sex, maybe it was a new experience and I was bored, maybe I wanted men drooling over me, making me feel sexy and desirable. Maybe you just don't have a fucking clue about how I feel now, then or anytime." Quiet, in Dawn's face, intimidating. "By the way, do your best tonight, you have star guests to play to." Hope swept through the door and Dawn took a moment to comprehend the statement that hung in the air.

She gathered her composure, determined not to allow Hope's anger to affect the rest of her day, but a tinge of nervousness crept up, questions tumbling from nowhere. Who were the star guests? Had Hope arranged for Vivity to watch Reveal's gig at the Horse and Crown? Or was it somebody more important still, a record producer, talent scout? Maybe it was FMI. Dawn scooped the demo tape that Reveal had recorded in November from the table into her handbag; she wouldn't need to give it to Hope now.

As Hope's parting words sank further, work didn't seem important any more. Today could be the big day. Gathering her wits, excitement, apprehensions, Dawn decided to cancel the afternoon appointments and get the lads together for rehearsal; she was going to make sure their set tonight would be the best yet. She rushed from the room to ask Gayle to reschedule the two clients.

Dawn's Hope

The atmosphere was buzzing in the small room, the members of Reveal nervously hoping they would impress whoever was coming to see them play. Chaz was drinking heavily, the only way to control the apprehension in his addicted mind, which irked his bandmates, who knew his performance was badly affected when he started on the whisky. Ed, the quiet one, raised their concerns as Chaz sank the golden fluid from the bottle. "Cut it out, mate, tonight's important, you need to be on top form."

His slurred reply brought worried glances between the sober four, realisation dawning that he wasn't in any state to play that night. Eyes locking, Dawn and Rick simultaneously thought of the same name and a hurried call to Steve Pickard ensued as Dawn gently settled Chaz on a seat, covering him with her heavy anorak for warmth; her maternal instinct towards her former boyfriend was possibly why their relationship hadn't worked. His muffled thanks were lost in the quilted khaki and she glanced at her brother, questioning success or failure with his eleventh-hour call. His bright eyes and thumbs up reassured her immediately.

The band playing before them started in the background, a catchy rhythm of upbeat blues, and the four hopefuls were filled with excited anticipation. They spent the next thirty minutes fixing stage make-up, teasing hair and posing in the mirror, enthusiastically grateful to Steve when he arrived brandishing his superior Fender American P-Bass. He was a star player, regularly strumming session guitar in recording studios across the country for chart-topping bands, and they were relieved he was free to help them out.

Steve sneered at Chaz's slumbering form in the corner and Dawn, instantly protective, remembered why she detested him: arrogant, superior and insincere. But tonight he was doing them a huge favour and she would have to grin and bear him for the sake of the band's future.

The raucous applause determined that the talented youngsters, Free Angels, had finished their set and they anxiously left the room, praying they wouldn't screw up. Cocky and swaggering, Steve led them to the stage, his silver guitar reflecting the lights as he paraded to the tumultuous cheering. He bowed, ignorant to the other band members; as far as he was concerned he was the star of the show.

Dawn felt Hope's presence as she stepped onto the stage, nurturing, mothering, feeding her the strength to perform to perfection, and she lapped up the frenzy of Reveal's loyal fans. LeMan settled on his stool and brandished his drumsticks with a flourish, hammering a catchy roll, leading the other instruments in. Despite his personality, Steve's talent was impressive, with a depth and directness Chaz had never mastered. A real showman, he whooped across the tiny stage, tantalising the audience.

The introduction to their cover of ZZ Top's *Sleeping Bag* over, Dawn put her heart and soul into singing, to fronting the band, and they were the tightest they had ever been, performing immaculately. The raucous crowd soaked them up with glee.

Breaking Dawn's Heart

Air thick with sweat and body odour, everybody babbled excitedly, congratulating each other on their superior show, and Dawn and the boys were confident that if a record company scout had been in the audience, he or she would have been impressed.

A knock on the door silenced them, nervous eyes darting, suspecting this could be the make or break visitor. Rick mustered some courage and swept to the door with the lumbering gait he and Dawn shared, pulling it wide to expose a group of people, fronted by a stunning and sexy Hope. "Hi everyone, great show tonight." She gestured to her sister, beaming with pride. "This is Happiness, lead singer with Vivity, and her bandmate Tony." The acne suffering teen smiled shyly, heavy make-up useless against the mounds on his face. "And this is Barry Powell of Powell and Associates, who find bands for many of the larger labels."

Dawn gasped, while Hope dragged a plump girl from behind, hugging her chubby shoulders protectively. "This is my eldest daughter, Penny." Recoiling, Rick shook lightly while he lit a cigarette, ignoring the 'No Smoking' signs that adorned the walls, and Dawn noticed the vicious glare Penny shot him. The proud mother continued, "And this is Dawn, my good friend, Rick, my boyfriend, Ed, LeMan, and..." Hope eyed Steve, her brow furrowed, and he swaggered forward, hand out.

"Steve Pickard. I'm not one of the band, but I can be." His slug lips splayed over his bristly cheeks in a self-confident smile.

Barry shrugged his overcoat from his shoulders, marching into the room purposefully. He pointed a manicured hand at Steve, yellow fingers betraying his twenty-a-day habit. "I want you." Stale tobacco wafted as he moved his hand to Rick. "I want you." LeMan was next. "You. You make me laugh, you're a right character, a nutter, so you're in."

LeMan punched the air. "Good choice, my son, good choice. You won't regret it."

Barry chuckled, his long, black ponytail swaying. "I'm sure I won't." He pointed to Ed. "I want to try you, but you're going to have to crazy up your act a bit. I'll do a one-month contract with you, and if you don't perk up, you're out."

Dawn's heart beat heavily against her ribs, trembling, hopeful but nervous. The hand moved in her direction and she was lightheaded, holding her breath. "Look, you're a fine-looking girl, I mean, I'd have you, and your voice is great, there's a lot of power in there." He patted her sternum, uninvited, and Dawn felt ants crawling over her skin. "But you're old. You're just old. We need hot totty fronting a band, not a has been."

Shocked, Dawn's mouth hung, bile in her throat. "But I'm the youngest in the band."

"Sorry, love, you're past it. But if you've got a foxy mate who can take your place, let me know. She doesn't have to be able to sing, we can speed the voice up if necessary. She just needs to look pretty, dance sexy, be a natural flirt." Barry handed a business card to the four selected band members, each uncomfortable with Dawn's rejection yet celebrating their own success, and he spun on his Berluti brogues, strutting confidently away.

Distraught, Hope reached for Dawn's arm, but she snatched it away, bubbling with anger. Grabbing her jacket and bag, she squeezed through the embarrassed visitors at the door, trotting along the corridor, desperate for air. She leant against the bricks outside, doubled over, bitter tears flooding raw agony as she forced herself to accept that her dream career would never happen, that she would be a counsellor for the rest of her boring life. Grief for her ambition, for herself.

Eventually the tears subsided and she became aware of a presence. "I'm sorry." Dawn glared, fierce yet hopeless, her eyes red and skin blotchy. "Really, I had no idea that was going to happen. I'm so sorry." The displaced rage became wretched sorrow again and Hope took her hand. "Look, Barry is an acquaintance of mine, I've known him a few years. He can be tough in business, but he has a heart of gold. Let me talk to him. Don't give up hope yet, okay?"

Dawn shrugged, unable to speak in case the tears returned, and then Hope was gone, back to her sister, her daughter, her boyfriend. To the celebration she was no part of.

The Celebration

Word of their impending record contract spread instantly and the landlord of the Horse and Crown was quick to send his congratulations in the form of his best house Champagne. LeMan, reckless as ever, gave the bottle a shake before letting the pressure inside fire the cork, the eager liquid spraying the delighted revellers, froth oozing down the green bottle.

Cheering and self-congratulating, the group sipped their sparkling drinks and Hope cheerfully glanced at her daughter, her smile disappearing when she saw Penny staring unwaveringly at her boyfriend. Rick was gorgeous, a real catch. He was kind and considerate, a gentleman, an amazing lover, and she was tempted to hope there may be a future with him. But the unexplained - and as far as she could tell unwarranted - tension between him and her daughter would have to be dealt with.

Not tonight though; she had revenge on her mind.

Griffin Gets Excited

Unable to sleep, Griffin sat in the darkness, his eyes adjusting gradually until he could just about make out Dorothy's huge body rising and falling rhythmically in her slumber. He tugged the covers back and slipped his legs over the side of the bed, the carpet soft underfoot as he located his slippers. He needed a drink.

Shoulders hunched as they always were nowadays, he moved silently across the room, feeling for the door handle. He tiptoed down the creaking stairs, old floorboards objecting to his meagre weight, and switched the kitchen light on. Although he filled the kettle, he was tempted by the brandy in the cupboard. Glancing at the door to ensure his wife hadn't followed him, he filled a juice glass to the brim with the warming liquid. Gulping, the fire burned his throat, settling in his belly, heating from within.

A noise came from the garden and he strolled nervously to the window by the front door, peering into the blackness with trepidation. The moon shone brightly through the frosted glass panels, highlighting a familiar envelope on the mat, and Griffin, forgetting the cold and his state of undress, turned the key and tugged the door wide. Now unconcerned about disturbing his wife, he shouted, "Eva? Come back, I need to see you. Eva?"

The clump of Dorothy's footsteps on the stairs restored his sanity immediately and he slammed the door, swooping down for the envelope, folding it, tucking it into his pocket. Blushing and guilty, he turned to face his wife, the woman who adored him, cosseted him, mothered him.

"What's going on?" She yawned, bleary-eyed.

"Um, nothing." Griffin remembered the forbidden brandy and slowly edged towards the kitchen. "I came down for a drink, um, I've just boiled the kettle for a cocoa."

Hands on cumbersome hips, head cocked, she suspected his nervousness had something to do with the bimbo he was seeing behind her back - she had heard his plaintive cries - and she marched after him. Griffin reached the kitchen and squinted against the light. "I was making the cocoa and I heard a noise by the front

184

door. I thought intruders were trying to break in so I shouted after them."

She spotted the alcohol on the side and tutted her disapproval, determined to eke out the truth, and he winced, suddenly five years old again, about to be belted by his drunken father. "And you just happened to know the intruder was called Eva?"

"I, I, I…" His brain whirled, desperately searching for a believable lie. "I wasn't shouting Eva, you silly woman, I said 'come here'. I was angry, how dare they try and break into a man of the cloth's house. It's not the first time this has happened."

"Griff, I know very well you're lying, and there's no point tipping that away behind your back, I've already seen it and it's shameful. Save it, you're going to need it by the time I've finished with you." Griff righted the glass to rescue the remaining brandy, wishing he had the courage to down it in front of her. "Let me feel your pockets."

He couldn't let Dorothy see the letter, she would go crazy, and years of torment - of being ordered about, of reprimands and scolding, of unmet sexual desire - caught up with him. He was sick of her controlling his every move and something inside snapped; the punch was instantaneous, unplanned, he was out of control. Her face reddened, blood trickling from her nose as she bounced against the wall. He wanted to stop, but was relishing her pain, her punishment. Suddenly he was back. He stopped lashing out and the stunned woman doubled over, gasping with fear and disbelief. For the first time in their marriage she was lost for words, trapped in a nightmare. Terrified, she scurried away, back to her bed, back to the world she knew.

Slumping onto a chair by the table, Griffin rested his weary head in his hands, astonished by his violence. What was happening to him? It was all that bloody Hope Ferris's fault. She was destroying him, taking his life blood, making him misbehave. Then he remembered the letter and sagged as the tension melted. He grasped at his pocket, the comforting crackle reminding him he had an ally in the furious war for the truth.

The letter had been sprayed with a gentle perfume and the aroma reminded him of times to be had when he finally met the evasive Eva. His hand moved between his legs as he eagerly devoured what his future lover had written with her dainty hand.

And when he read her promise to meet him, his imagination exploded, spilling his juice over the cotton underpants.

His ardour quelled, Griffin continued with the letter and his jaw dropped at the conditions she had imposed on their liaison. He read the terms again - reading, rereading - worried about fulfilling the task, but recalling his anger minutes before, and why he had been so angry. A new strength and determination came from deep inside.

Dorothy Rethinks Her Life

The haunting moonlight bathed her through the window and she tugged the eiderdown over her battered face, the rollers in her thinning hair resting on the pillow, ends digging into her scalp.

She wanted to cry but the tears wouldn't come, still disbelieving. Had her husband of twenty-three years really just beaten her? Her husband, the Rector of Polton. Or had it been a bad dream?

The answer presented itself too quickly for a reaction. She smelled the freshness of the new pillow as it stifled her breath, the pulsing in her head reaching a crescendo as she struggled for air, for life.

Griffin held the pillow tightly over his wife's face long after she stopped resisting, a cumbersome beached whale on the virgin bed. Eventually he relaxed, studying the bruised woman who had made his life hell for so long, the early years of tempting her to have sex with him, the latter years resentful of the passionless marriage.

Curious, he dragged the quilt to her feet and his genitals stirred. The elusive vagina that had taunted him for nearly quarter of a century was in reach and he wanted to fuck it. He tugged the nightdress up, breathing heavily, eager, wrenching the oversized knickers down her legs, desire flooding as he moved her legs to expose her lips. One finger, two, feeling her virginity breaking, and he thrust his pulsing penis into the forbidden garden. His orgasm was instant and he lay on the warm body, waiting for his erection to return. Once more, and then he would call the police, tell them he had found his wife murdered; he could muster tears from somewhere.

Hope's Interrogation

She was cold, despite several shots of whisky that had flushed her cheeks and nose. She had spent the evening scheming, planning her onslaught, and was too exhausted to sleep. Rick snored gently beside her, a comforting lullaby, and she snuggled close, soaking in his warmth. He stirred, turning towards her, returning the cuddle. "Where have you been, babe, I hate sleeping without you by my side."

Hope stroked his overnight bristles lovingly in the darkness. "I love you."

He had always dismissed love as a redundant emotion, but now it surged. Hope was different, he had never met anyone like her. He'd had thousands of women - young, old, white, black, fat, skinny - but Hope was the one who made life worthwhile. Unplanned, it came from nowhere: "Marry me?"

Gasping, she cupped her open mouth, head spinning with questions and worries. Eventually she found her voice. "What's the problem between you and Penny?"

Groaning, he turned over. "She's just a kid. She's watched us play a few times. I think she's got a teenage crush on me and that's why she hates me and you dating."

Hope contemplated for a while. "Why didn't you tell me before?"

He rolled to face her again, smiling, relieved she had accepted his explanation. "I didn't want to upset you." He shifted up onto an elbow, his free hand caressing her. "Answer me though, babe, will you marry me?"

She chuckled. "Maybe I will if you'll help me out with something." He only heard 'yes' and relaxed, his breaths becoming regular, slipping to a dream world with a happy future of togetherness.

Hope rested contentedly in the crook of his arm and waited patiently until she was certain he was asleep. Raising herself on one arm carefully to avoid waking him, Hope studied his handsome face in the sliver of moonlight that shone through a crack in the curtains. She had one condition to matrimony which would prove the depth of his love for her. Trailing a finger tenderly along his jaw, she took a deep breath and whispered, "I want you to kill someone for me."

Disposing A Body

The brandy bottle now empty, Griffin paced the kitchen, trying to come to terms with what he had done, pondering what to do with Dorothy's body now he had decided that to inform the police would be a mistake. Having already dragged her from the bed, the walls shaking when she hit the floorboards, he was aware of how heavy and awkwardly cumbersome her stiffening form was.

Did he roll her in a carpet, dump her in a bin or a skip? Dissolve her in acid? Dig a giant hole and bury her?

He took the handwritten letter from the side, the distinguished writing black against the pale-pink paper, and read for a final time before screwing the page up, tossing it into the fire. 'Get rid of your wife and I'll be yours'. The words haunted him; he wanted Eva, but he already missed Dorothy. Would Eva cook him breakfast every morning like she had? Would she bring him cocoa in bed? Listen to the ideas for his sermons? Was this just about sex or was there more?

Clasping his forehead, he retraced his steps to the bedroom, wishing the body would have disappeared to solve his problem, but it was still slumped on the crinkled bedroom rug as large in death as it had been in life. Griffin sat on his bed, legs up and crossed, relaxing against the pillow, and stared at the body until it became blurry. Eyelids heavy - closing, opening, closing - he eventually reached for the switch to extinguish the bedside light, hoping the answer would come in his sleep.

Penny's Truth

Bern's chuntering was the only sound in the room, his hands whizzing trains along an imaginary rail track on the carpet. Hope was at the table, eyes puffy from lack of sleep, hair unkempt from tossing and turning throughout the early hours, and she played her toast from one hand to the other, hungry, but too choked to eat. She dropped it on the plate.

Penny, lemon pyjamas stretching at the seams and her gown tied loosely over her belly, trudged into the kitchen and flopped onto a chair, reaching for the steaming teapot. "Did *he* stay again last night?" Challenging, she had been preparing for an argument since awaking ten minutes before.

Hope sighed, resenting the intrusion on her privacy. She had wondered if Penny had guessed she was sneaking him in at night and there seemed little point continuing the charade. "I wish you'd try and get on with him, especially now he's asked me to marry him."

Penny stood instantly, stunned, then tempestuous. "That's disgusting."

Hope smiled; she had been after a reaction and here it was. Penny opened the fridge, greedy fingers picking at leftovers, swallowing the food before the taste registered. With her mouth stuffed, she said, "Mum, he's a womaniser, he's well known for it. He shags everybody. Everybody."

Hope raised an eyebrow, the comment unexpected and hurtful. "I see." She contemplated for a while, torn between two loves, and finally dragged the chair beside her from under the table, patting it. "Okay, tell me what you know about him. I can see there's bad blood between you, so I need you to tell me why you hate him so much."

Penny perched on the edge of the seat, a thousand worries on her young shoulders, and picked at the peeling skin beside her nails. "I can't, Mum. He's just a womaniser, he charms the pants off all the girls. He must have slept with hundreds of girls."

191

Hope remained matter-of-fact. "Maybe so, but he hadn't met me before and I'm different. When he says he loves me I know it's true."

Penny shook her head slowly and rose from the seat, waggling her bleeding fingertip, resigned. "Have it your way, Mother, just don't say I didn't warn you when he dumps you, or fucks someone else, or gives you some disease or whatever."

Appalled and bewildered by her daughter's obscenity, Hope was concerned. "Penny, there's more to it than that and you know it. Why can't you just tell me the truth?"

The child's defences came down instantly, tears prickling her melancholy eyes, and she struggled to speak. Hope's maternal instinct surged and she pulled her daughter close for a comforting hug. "I promise whatever it is, I won't be angry. Has he tried it on with you or something? Is it something like that?"

Tears flooding copiously, her plump body racked with sobs, Penny melted into her mother's protective arms, while Hope stroked her mousy hair tenderly, lovingly. For five long minutes she comforted her daughter, and eventually Penny was cried out. Sniffing, wiping her eyes, she said in a tiny voice, "I had sex with him last year."

Hope pulled away, eyes wide, horrified. Her daughter, her child - her baby - had lost her virginity to a bastard twenty years older. Her partner a paedophile. She grasped Penny's shoulders and their eyes locked, but no words came. Thoughts whizzed tauntingly through Hope's mind, echoing back and forth with no substance, stabbing her heart repeatedly.

Ashamed and devastated to have broken her mother, Penny shrugged from the standoff and slumped back on the chair, Hope's astounded glare burning her lowered head. The impact of her disclosure had been greater than she had expected and her mother deserved an explanation.

Penny's eyes, a paler blue than her mother's yet just as stunning, implored Hope for understanding, searching for a way to begin the sordid story. Mumbling, she said, "It was in the summer half term. Saz and Nessa said they were going to see Reveal at the youth club, them and some other girls I didn't know. I wanted to go, but you said no."

She faltered, sour with guilt, and Hope stroked her hair. "I remember. It was just after Lee had invited me to Rio. My head was all over the place."

Encouraged, Penny continued, "Well, Saz, Nessa, the rest of the gang, they all teased me, calling me a baby 'cos I couldn't go, so I told them you'd changed your mind and that I'd meet them there." The pleading eyes were back, shaming her mother. "I had to go, Mum, they were taking the piss so much, I couldn't stand it any more."

Hope nodded, finding every word painful, every sentence hammering her failure as a mother home. Penny began to cry again. "Sweetheart, I promised you I wouldn't be angry and I'm not. In fact, I'm ashamed of myself, not you."

Wiping her nose on her sleeve, her voice cracking. "I told you I was going to bed early, said I had a headache or something, and I tied an extension lead to my bed, lobbed it out the window and slid down. They gave me so much cred when I got there, it was worth it."

Hope studied the grain of the oak table, agonising at the thought of the danger her daughter had put herself in. Why had she said no? If she had agreed, at least Penny would have had a safe lift there and back and this would never have happened.

Penny swallowed, her throat dry. "Reveal were brilliant, the first band I ever saw…"

"You've seen more since?"

She nodded, her secret life now public and reprehensible. "I was totally into it, the noise, the atmosphere, and I thought the guys were hot. After a while Saz managed to get someone to buy us some drinks, I had a couple of vodka Red Bulls and it gave me some confidence. I got up to the front and Rick was even hotter close up, so when he started making eye contact with me, I flirted." Uncomfortable sharing her sex life with her mother, she shifted, grasping the edges of the chair with chubby nail-bitten fingers.

"When they stopped playing I hung around and I couldn't believe it when he came over, thought he'd just think I was a geeky little kid. He bought me drinks, quite a few, and I was getting lightheaded, and I was flattered that he, like, this hot guitarist in a big band, that he was interested in me."

Hope sneered. "Rubbish, they're just a two-bit no-hope group. He's no star." Penny was momentarily forgotten as she mulled the sickening behaviour of the man she had considered marrying minutes before.

"He was a star to me, like, at least I thought he was." Hope forced herself quiet to let her abused child continue. "When he suggested we go on to a party, me, Saz and Nessa, we jumped at the chance."

Incredulous. Disgusted. "Surely he could see you were just schoolgirls?"

"You hate me now, don't you?"

Hope held her tormented child close, reassuring, exonerating the guilt. "I love you more than ever, actually."

Penny continued, timid. "It wasn't just his fault, because we told him we were sixteen, told him we were leaving school this year."

Bern's chattering, engrossed in his imagination, was the only sound, neither mother nor daughter knowing what to say next. Penny withdrew from the cuddle. "It wasn't really a party though. We went back to Rick's place and LeMan and Chaz came too. They gave us beer and whisky, and soon LeMan and Saz were snogging. Then LeMan got some more drinks, we were all giggly now, the booze had gone to our heads. He got a little plastic bag out of his pocket, it had some white tablets in it. He said they'd make us feel good. Sexy. So we all took one. He told us to take it with lots of beer because they didn't taste so nice."

Hope choked back her repulsion; her day - her life - was ruined now. "Do you know what the tablets were?"

"I didn't at the time, but Saz told me a few months later they were Ecstasy." The child-woman peeped at her mother from under her fringe, dismayed, self-conscious, and they each became aware of a new closeness, a solid bond. "It did make me feel good, Mum. I felt happy. I felt sexy, and after a while I wanted him, I wanted more than a kiss, I wanted to go further and he wasn't about to say no. When Chaz and Saz disappeared into the spare bedroom, Rick looked at me and I just wanted him. He took me to his bedroom, asked me if it was my first time. I said no, said I'd done it twice before, because I wanted him to think I was cool."

"Was that a lie?" A silent prayer to the God she didn't believe in.

"Yes."

"Thank God for that."

194

Swallowing, the memory painful. "We did it on the bed. It was horrid, it hurt, made me bleed, and halfway through I wanted him to stop."

Responsible, sensible mother again. "Did he force you? Did he use a condom?"

Penny shook her head and Hope's face fell. "He didn't force me. I asked him to use a condom, but he begged me not to, said he didn't feel as much with one on, so we didn't." Their eyes met again. "Mum, I regret it, I really do. But at the time I thought he loved me, I thought we'd start dating." She quietened. "I thought he loved me." Her face twisted, bitter. "I didn't think he'd just ignore me afterwards and it really upset me. He didn't call, nothing. I'm more grown up now, I can see him for the pig he is. That's why I don't want you to marry him. He's a bastard."

The profanity no longer irritated Hope now she understood the source of the acrimony. The vile man she no longer loved had fucked her daughter. And then fucked her. Crossing the thin line, hatred surfaced and she wanted revenge, for herself, for her child. Whispering, laden with furious pain, "You must have only been twelve at the time." Penny nodded, rueful tears spilling. "We need to report him to the police. I'll help you. I'll support you."

Penny shook her head, horrified. "No. Mum, I lied about my age, I led him on, and I wanted him as much as he wanted me. It wasn't all his fault."

Hope left the table and switched the kettle on, eager for normality, if there were such a thing any more, and contempt for the handsome man who slept peacefully in her bed burned fiercely. She busied herself with mindless chores, her delicate features stony and vengeful, and after five minutes of seething, she quietly mounted the stairs carrying two mugs of tea.

Rick was deeply asleep, his chiselled face resting on her pillow, gorgeous yet despicable. She set the drinks on her bedside table and sat on the edge of the bed, watching his manly chest, naked and shimmering with sweat. Her fingers crept to the duvet, softly dragging it down to expose his manhood, the same one that had penetrated both her and her daughter, and she shuddered with revulsion. She took the flaccid penis and placed it carefully in her mouth, her tongue working, flicking, arousing, and soon he was in a half-sleep, groaning with desire, unsure if the sensation was his imagination tricking him. His question was answered when he felt

195

the hot mouth leave his body, soon replaced by another hot wetness, and Hope writhed on top, bringing him to the point of ecstasy.

The sensations amazing, Rick breathed heavily, in, out, pushing his groin as far forward as possible, deepening the impact, and he knew he was there, he was there, he was about to explode. She pulled away and his eyes sprung open, confused.

"Babe, why did you stop? I was about to…"

She leant forward, seductive eyes flashing sex at him, and cupped his face tenderly. "Rick, I'll marry you, and I'll finish the job, but you need to agree to do something for me before either happens."

She dipped her hips, inserting him again and his relieved groan was loud, but she lifted away once more leaving him gasping. Unable to stand the teasing any longer, he panted, "Babe, anything. Tell me what it is and I'll do it, I promise, just get back on my dick."

In complete control, resisting his grasping hands, fingers clawing at the soft skin of her buttocks, pulling her back. "I want you to kill someone."

She may as well have asked him if he wanted a coffee; he agreed easily, pulling her down, encasing his penis, the immediate orgasm mind blowing and explosive, pulsing, lasting forever.

Hope smiled. She had him where she wanted him.

The Awaited Phone Call

It was a struggle, but Griffin had managed to drag Dorothy's stiffening body down the stairs and her ample flesh covered the hall carpet, the nightdress having risen, exposing her recently raped genitals. He paced uneasily from front door to back, needing to hide the body before any villagers stopped by on their travels.

His shoulders ached from towing the weight, long unused muscles objecting, and he stretched, momentarily free of the pain. He hadn't decided what to do with her yet, but would have to manhandle her into the car boot somehow, which meant clearing a space in the garage for the car. The whole situation was a mess and he reminded himself of the words that had led to the present: "You get rid of her, and then we can meet up. I don't want an extramarital affair, I want commitment, truth and love."

A ringing snapped him back to reality and the aching was instantly forgotten, a spurt of energy propelling him to the telephone, grasping it to his ear. "Eva?"

"Have you done it?"

He had not heard her voice before - sweet and innocent - and a tingle ran along his spine. "I did. Eva, I want you. I want you so badly"

"You can have me. I've booked a room for tomorrow in the Cambridge Garden House Hotel, Mill Lane, Cambridge, obviously. It's room number three-sixty-nine and you're booked under the name of John Smith. I'll be there at eight."

The dial tone replaced the voice and his erection began to shrink. "Eva, don't go." He thrust the receiver down, irritated by her haste, by his predicament; not only did he have to dispose of a body, he now had to find a hotel in an unfamiliar city. Without his wife's controlling swipe to chastise him, he cursed, again, again, before kicking her weighty frame in frustration.

Claudia is Frustrated

"I'm sorry, but Miss Brunel checked out three days ago and we have no forwarding details." Claudia gritted her teeth and slammed the phone down. She had been poring over the statements of the two accusing women to find enough evidence to substantiate an arrest, but there wasn't enough; the judge would laugh her out of court. Hope's witnesses proved that Griffin Hall had visited the family home, but not the sexual abuse.

There were no witnesses at all for Eva, and when she had questioned the incredulous rector, referring to Eva by her childhood name, Maeve Rowbottom, which she had since changed by deed poll, he insisted he had never heard of the girl. If he was lying, it was a spectacular and believable performance, yet Eva had been so sincere in the interview.

Quite simply, if she couldn't find someone to corroborate Eva's story, the arrest wasn't going to happen. Not unless another victim came forward. And now Eva had disappeared. Checking her file for the number, Claudia grasped the phone again and dialled, holding her breath while it rang, willing the call to be answered. "Hello."

"Hope?"

"What?"

She had clearly called at a bad time. "It's Claudia Horseferry, have you got a minute?"

"Don't be long, I'm just heading out."

Her curtness niggled the detective, but she realised she had no idea why she had called and she stammered. "Thing is, if we want an arrest we need some solid evidence, which we don't have."

"What? What about this Eva woman? I thought she'd sealed the case, that's what you told me."

Her face reddened, ashamed to have promised the impossible. The best thing was to come clean. "I know and I shouldn't have, but I want to see him go down for what he did to you as much as you do. I need you or Eva..." Claudia halted. She had referred to the other accuser by name, which was unprofessional, but then it occurred to her that Hope had said Eva's

198

name first. Was her imagination playing tricks? It must be; she was sure she hadn't revealed the other woman's details before.

Impatient, Hope was angry. "You need me or Eva what?"

Claudia drew a sharp breath. "I need one of you to come up with more witnesses because we just don't have enough. We need something more solid, but the other lady has moved from the hotel she was staying at with no following address. Unless I can find her, it's down to you."

Hope was quiet, her breathing audible on the line. Eventually, "I've got to go, I've got an appointment." The dial tone purred and Claudia replaced the receiver, slamming her fist against the desk. Grabbing her mug, she marched to the kitchen to fix a drink. Her phone chimed and she deliberated whether to answer or not, but after ten rings she traipsed back. "Detective Inspector…"

"It's Eva Brunel, the hotel told me you were looking for me."

Claudia gasped at the coincidence, momentarily blessing the hotel's efficiency, before it dawned on her that she hadn't left her name during the conversation with the hotel, and this time she knew she wasn't going crazy. How did Eva Brunel know she had been trying to find her?

A Temporary Resting Place

The doorbell flooded Griffin with terror; the visitor would see Dorothy's grotesque and lifeless body if they were to look through the letterbox. He forced his voice to stay level. "One minute, please." Grasping the oversized ankles, strength fuelled by panic, he dragged the body away from the stairs, finding it easier once she was on the kitchen tiles. Glancing around furiously, aware that the visitor may peer through the huge kitchen window any moment, he pulled the door of the pantry open and with a final heroic effort hauled the body inside, folding the resistant arms and legs. He gave the door giving a hefty shove and the latch clicked.

Wiping the death odour from his hands, puffing, he waited until his breathing had regulated and headed for the front door, fixing a serene smile. "Ah, Mrs Higgins, how lovely to see you. Do come in."

Hope Needs Charity

Helen, who usually helped with the childminding, was trapped in Putney, sorting through cupboards and boxing her belongings, having exchanged contracts the week before. Hope didn't ask her selfish sister for a favour often, but in Helen's absence she needed help. She dialled the number and waited. "Charity?"

"Oh, Hope, you won't believe what's happened: I'm pregnant again."

"Great news, wow, I'm so pleased for you. You'll have to look after yourself now, make sure this one stays put." The comments were heartfelt, but Hope had other concerns.

"You bet I will, I've stopped eating wheat, sugar, dairy…"

"Charity," Hope wasn't usually rude and her sister was taken aback by the interruption, "look, we'll talk about that on Sunday, but right now I need to ask you a favour: I'm in a bit of trouble and I need the kids to stay at yours on Saturday night."

Charity was quiet for a while, then, "I can't, sorry. The stress of three kids as well as Ava might bring on another miscarriage. I just can't take the risk."

"Fuck that, Charity." The fierceness of the fury stunned Charity, amazed by the side of her timid sister she had never seen before. She scrabbled for a seat. "How many times have I had Ava when you and Keith go swanning about the country, about the world. I have never asked you to mind the kids, not once. This is the first time in my thirteen years as a mother that I have asked you to reciprocate the favours I do for you. Now let's get this straight, my children are staying at your house tomorrow night whether you fucking like it or not. I'll drop them off at midday and we'll draw a line under this. If you really feel you can't cope, get one of your fucking nannies or babysitters in and I'll cover the cost." Hope slammed the phone down and chuckled; she rarely lost her temper but it made her laugh when she did.

Rick's approach made her jump; she hadn't realised he was in the room. "Whoa, babe, are you due on or something?" She held her breath, willing her irritation at his presence away. "What's going on tomorrow? Why are you taking the kids to your sister's?"

Biting back the bile, Hope tenderly stroked the short bristles that defined his strong chin. "I've booked us a romantic night away, just the two of us. A big bed, room service and minibar. Just us, to celebrate our engagement."

Grinning, he tugged her close to his naked chest, the black hairs tickling her nose, muscles firm and manly. But her daughter had also stroked this chest, touched this torso. She pulled away, revolted. "No time for this, sorry, I'm already late for my appointment with Dawn."

Rick had seen the fleeting tell of disgust on her face and was concerned, confused. "Babe?"

Gritting her teeth, Hope reached up and pecked him on the lips, thrusting a sheet of paper into his hand. "By the way, I forgot to ask you, I'm playing a joke on someone and they would recognise my voice, so I wondered if you could make this call while I'm out. What you need to say is all written down. You'll do it, won't you?"

His eyes flashed, licking his lips. "Only if you promise to give me another blow job later." He winked and she forced a smile, grabbing her keys and leaving.

Session Sixteen

Today, Dawn greeted Efficient Hope, who bustled in, her day planned to the last minute, the counselling another chore to tick off. "Sorry I'm late, the traffic was a nightmare and I was late leaving anyway. I had that policewoman who's dealing with the abuse on the phone, she reckons they haven't got a strong enough case to arrest him after all. I'm furious, I thought it was all cut and dried."

Dawn regarded her client, bitter with dislike, and made no comment. Hope scanned her face, puzzled. "You're still mad about the record contract, aren't you?"

Dawn pursed her lips, confirming Hope's question. She had been dreading the coming hour for a week, ever since the harsh rejection, the unfair sexism. The lads no longer contacted her - texts and emails - throughout the day, which hurt more than Barry Powell's disgraceful rebuke. She couldn't help but blame Hope, which was irrational, but feelings often were. Her irritation was clear. "I take it you didn't talk to Barry about including me in the contract."

Hope focused on the carpet, avoiding the confrontational stare. "I did, actually. He's a stubborn man, Dawn, he's not about to give in. I'm so sorry, I had no idea this would happen and I feel like I've let you down."

Dawn sat straight, tall. "I have to get this off my chest, Hope, and if it hurts you, I'm sorry. But, yes, I think what that man did was disgusting, and yes, I'm angry with you at putting me in that situation. I also hate the fact you're dating my brother, it feels wrong, and I know you only got with him to piss me off."

Hope took the cup of water from the table and sipped, sad but understanding. "That's not true, but all the same our relationship is over, we won't be dating any more after this weekend. He won't be seeing anyone." A chill hung in the overheated room and Dawn shuddered. The minutes ticked by in silence.

Finally, Dawn broke the spell. "What do you mean by that?"

Flippant and unemotional. "Nothing. I've heard some stuff about him and it's put me off."

A surge of protectiveness washed over Dawn. "What have you heard?" Hope ignored the question and Dawn's anger rose along with her voice. "This is my brother you're talking about, if there are rumours going around I want to know what they are." Hope glared at her, irascible herself. "Tell me, Hope, I want to know."

"Okay, I'll tell you, if you insist." The blueness bored into Dawn, mouth twisted and scornful. "He fucked my daughter last year when she was only twelve. Good enough for you?"

Dawn was on her feet, marching the room, and Hope held her breath with uncertainty. Seconds ticked by, beating a drum against the tension, and eventually Dawn's common sense returned. "What are you going to do?" Unusually, she could only hope that her client was playing games.

"Nothing, Penny doesn't want to prosecute, but obviously I can't see him any more."

Rick's behaviour was contemptible, but the relief that he wouldn't be facing prison, wouldn't be under Hope's wicked influence any more, was overwhelming. Dawn's jaw fell; wicked? Where had that come from? Hope was a victim, as a child herself and as a mother to her child. Why had she thought her wicked?

A sense of trepidation, a gut feeling, and Dawn couldn't rationalise her suspicions. But the fear she felt on her brother's behalf was real. She swallowed, debating the situation, aware she had to phrase her statement carefully to get a result. "Are you willing to tell me what happened? I mean, it must be a terrible revelation for you to hear."

Through gritted teeth and with fire in her eyes, Hope related the story her daughter had told. Every now and then she clasped the top of her left arm, leading Dawn to suspect her client hadn't consulted a doctor as she had suggested a few weeks before. "I'm worried that you keep grabbing your arm, are you in pain?"

Hope shrugged, wincing. "It's fine, it's just heartburn. I forgot to take my Gaviscon tablets this morning."

A ringing halted the conversation and Hope searched her pockets, stopping only when Dawn, apologetic, answered her mobile. "Rick, I've told you not to call me at work, I'm in the middle of a session." Listening carefully - face paling, frowning - she cut the call without speaking. Stony faced, she gazed through the window.

"What's going on?"

A silent minute passed, Dawn's jaw tense, eyes watering, and finally she said, "We were supposed to be rehearsing this afternoon. They promised me they wouldn't sign anything unless I was included on the contract." She swallowed, holding back tears. "The bastards have found a new singer to take my place."

"You're joking."

But Dawn wasn't laughing.

Rick's Ambitions

Chaz had worked hard to stay sober, but Barry absolutely refused to include him in the contract. Distraught but understanding, he wanted to remain a part of the excitement and offered his services as a sound technician, with a sombre promise to lay off the whisky. Forlorn, he watched Steve Pickard expertly tune his guitar by ear, following the indulgent show with an elaborate riff that ensured everybody was aware of his prowess.

Each player warmed up, practising, perfecting, gradually falling into a spontaneous jam while they awaited the new band member. She rushed in ten minutes late, pink and puffing. A long, black coat shrouded her small frame and she shrugged it off to reveal a black PVC mini and a breast spilling, long-sleeved lacy top that enhanced her perfect figure. She wore fishnet tights on her slim legs teamed with patent leather boots that enhanced the statement outfit. Their instruments forgotten, the boys stood, gaping. Throwing her head forward - aware of her audience - she mussed her hair, tossing it back with abandon.

Barry Powell leaned smugly against the brick wall, manicured fingernails raking through the untied locks that flowed down his back, eagerly watching the new band member perform. LeMan tapped his sticks together to count the song in and the music began. Barry was transfixed as she stepped up to the microphone, her sweet voice a bonus. Not as strong or gravelly as Dawn's, it had a unique softness, a haunting quality, echoing, taunting, commanding the performance. And her presence was amazing, bright eyes hooking and trapping. The lads were great, but she was the star.

Dawn hovered in the doorway, crushed and abandoned. The woman on the stage - her replacement - was impressive in a way she could never be, a clearer voice, prettier face, overwhelmingly seductive, not masculine like she was. Dawn was consumed by her failure, by Reveal's undoubtable future success.

Dawn stayed for the rehearsal, her heart aching but unable to tear herself away and go home to drown her sorrow. The boys played better than ever before and the final song was tremendous, a tumultuous crescendo before ceasing abruptly. The five musicians took an unnecessary bow and Barry clapped loudly, smoke billowing from the cigar trapped between his lips. He shook his fist in victory and shouted, proud, excited. Greedy. "Eva Brunel, you are so in this band."

Dawn's heart hammered. Eva Brunel? Hadn't she heard that name before? Something important. Where did she know it from? Racking her brain, she walked away, from the band, from the music she had cowritten, from her dream.

Eva smiled, winking, and left the stage, but when the lads followed her she had gone. Intrigued by the mysterious singer, the ensuing conversation covered only one topic. Ten minutes, eight cans of lager and four cigarettes later, the four rock stars in-the-making had discussed nothing but gorgeous Eva Brunel, battling light-heartedly about who would be the lucky man to snag her.

Gradually the conversation returned to music, to the recording contract. Next week they would be officially signing the deal and they cracked open another lager each to celebrate.

Hope Receives a Call

The conversation earlier had been uncomfortable and Claudia was nervous about speaking to Hope again, but this time she had good news. She dialled the number and introduced herself tentatively, testing the water.

"What." Indifferent.

She took a deep breath and cleared her throat. "We have another witness, a really good one. A school friend of the other lady is willing to testify in court to actually witnessing her assault on two occasions." Hope smiled at the welcome words. "He also said..."

"He?"

"Yes, he was a friend of hers at junior and senior school. He's also stated that Hall touched him inappropriately on both occasions, so now there are three of you. Mind you, the man was adamant he doesn't want to prosecute for himself, just be a witness to the investigations."

"So what happens now? Have you said anything to Griffin about it?"

"I've been to his house again and he denies it, of course. Said he's never even heard the man's name, but to be honest with you I've become hardened to his pleadings of innocence. Three victims are more than coincidence." Claudia had hoped the positive news would clear the air but the silence hung, awkward. Keeping her voice bright, she continued, "The man's coming in to do a video statement on Monday, and if it's as strong as the story he told me on the phone, I'll be able to arrest Griffin Monday afternoon."

"Yeah, whatever." The line went dead and Claudia held the phone away from her ear, staring at it, incredulous. However, she understood this was a difficult time for Hope and so far, the law hadn't been on her side.

Tired Hope

The day had been exhausting, but Hope's mind refused to switch off. She was biding her time with Rick, intent that the revenge she had planned for both herself and her daughter would be destructive and terrifying. But first she needed his help.

He sat in the bed beside her, periodically chuckling at the Bill Bryson novel. Her own book hadn't gripped her in the same way and she laid it on the bedside table, unable to concentrate, the single malt affecting her focus. She rubbed her face, bored and tired - fed up - and snuggled under the covers.

But her brain refused to sleep. Memories, conversations, plotting. Plus, the problematic self-diagnosed heartburn was griping her chest and shoulder. Hope rolled onto her side, annoyed at her sleeplessness and irritated by Rick's sniggering.

After five minutes of trying to relax, she sighed impatiently and half-sat, downing the glass of whisky, and her throat burned as she swallowed.

The alcohol soon soothed her into an intoxicated sleep, the off switch finally found, and Rick set his book on the side and watched her, swelling with love. He had never been so sure about anything before, he adored her. She was amazing, different. And tomorrow night he would have her to himself; no feeding and bathing the kids, putting them to bed, shouting for them to be quiet. Just Hope and him. Alone.

A Final Resting Place

Griffin hadn't been able to work, unable to concentrate on life's tedium while his dead wife lay in the larder. He had spent much of the day pacing, considering what to do with her body. It was a no-brainer to remove her from the house during the night, but simply how to get her twenty-stone bulk into the boot of his car, and quietly to avoid nosy neighbours, was a dilemma.

He had chosen to take her to the outskirts of the nearby village of Beeston, which had a perfectly remote area along the bank of the River Trent that wasn't overlooked. It was a beautiful setting too, a tribute to the fondness he had for the woman. He would push her into the water, reasoning that such a vast weight would sink without trace.

He had cleared enough space in the integral garage earlier in the day to fit his car inside, the connecting door to the kitchen close to the larder, and laid some plastic bags inside the boot to avoid leaving any trace of her on the carpet. He drank his cocoa, mustering courage to open the cupboard and begin the daunting task, but just the thought overwhelmed him and he stopped short of the door. He needed something to calm his nerves.

The empty brandy bottle and glass from the previous night sat on the worktop and he kicked himself for having finished it. Then he remembered the box of communion wine. Dragging a bottle from under the stairs, he tipped a large measure into the dirty tumbler, sipping it readily, and once the glass was empty, he steeled himself, breathing deeply before reaching for the door handle.

The acrid stench that hit him was vile. Decay? Surely it was too early for that. Heady, gassy, cloying and thick. The smell of death. He wanted to run, from the house, from the town, the country. From the world. Instead he grabbed the purple-white mottled wrists, gripping firmly and tugging with all his strength. The carcass was so heavy he half expected the chubby joints to snap and leave him carrying just the hands, but they remained firm and five minutes later he had dragged her to the garage. Now he had to somehow lift her into the car.

Goosebumps appeared on his bare chest and Griffin shivered, cold under the sweat of exertion. He returned to the kitchen and chucked a couple of logs into the Aga, bathing in the heat that sparked almost immediately. Pouring another drink, he sank it in one, unconcerned about driving under the influence; that was the least of his worries.

Soon his skin flushed, the alcohol, roaring fire and hard labour contributing to the colour, and he pondered, anxious, wishing the mess would go away. And from nowhere a solution appeared: he would tie rope around her body and feed it through the rafters to hoist her up.

It took an hour of backbreaking toil to winch the body high enough to swing into place and he pushed the colossal form across, using the last of his strength, gratefully releasing the thick rope. The body slumped down, the head bent unnaturally at a right angle to the ample chest, which created several new chins, and flabby legs spilling over the rear lights. Retching, he breathed himself calm, sickened by the sight of the hideous woman he had once loved. Not any more. Monstrous and discoloured, as ungraceful in death as she had been in life. He bent the limbs, joints grating with objection, to fit inside and with a final glare of contempt, he slammed the lid.

He poured another glass of wine to settle his nerves, head woozy and muscles aching, and scrubbed his hands at the sink, washing away the nauseating odour. A glance at the clock: three A.M., the witching hour. It was time.

Griffin opened the wooden garage doors, cursing under his breath as they squeaked, and stepped into the freezing mist, listening, searching, ensuring there was no witness to his sordid movements. Satisfied he was alone, he climbed into the car and clicked the door closed quietly, turning the key until the engine purred into life.

Griffin began the short drive, heart pounding against his chest, wary of cars, of pedestrians - sounds, lights, unexpected shadows - but he arrived safely and reversed as close to the riverbank as the reeds would allow, killing the engine. Now the problem was how to get the body from the car without any tools to assist him and he willed himself superhuman strength.

He searched the area furtively, the trickling water the only sound, and tiptoed to the boot, scared of attracting attention. Opening the lid, the same repulsive fetor filled his nostrils, settling

211

on his tongue and seeping into his pores. He backed away, turning his back on the arduous task for long enough to breathe some freshness into his lungs.

Holding his breath, bracing himself, Griffin unfolded the legs and draped them over the rear end, leaving them to flop gruesomely while he debated how to move the bulk of the body. He tried to lift her by the wrists, but he had barely been able to drag her on a flat and unhindered surface before, let alone lift the necessary twelve inches to clear the boot. Her shoulders raised a little, but not enough, and he dropped her hands, frustrated. Three times more he tried, aborting each attempt with growing anger, and eventually threw an infuriated punch at Dorothy's bloated and bruised face.

A dog barking brought Griffin to his senses and he strained to hear where it had come from. There were no nearby houses, and with growing despondency he supposed a dog walker must be close. Panicking. Urgent now. Could he muster the desperate strength to remove the body, or should he fold her back inside and get the hell out of there? Summoning a determination he had never known before, he firmly gripped the waxy skin and inched the gargantuan body higher, higher, groaning with the strain. The fat under her skin slid this way and that, loosening his hold, and he grasped her nightdress, the seams straining as he lifted her slowly to the edge. With a final, tremendous heave, her torso flopped over and fell inelegantly into the reeds, legs slumping on top, a mound of blubber slipping into the icy water that lapped at her curlers.

Relieved, exhausted, Griffin shoved Dorothy with his brogue, watching the pointed leaves entangle her body and claim her for their own. The dog barked again, nearer this time, and he glanced around, heart thundering. With a last glance at the disappearing corpse, he jumped into the car and fired the engine, accelerating out of the mud, squealing away in the opposite direction to the dog.

And now the abominable task was done, he laughed. Great, bellyaching guffaws that tightened his abdomen until it screamed with pain. Drowning the radio with maniacal howling until tears flooded down his cheeks.

Finally, the relief subsided, leaving him ready to take the next step in his new and unexpected life.

There was only one thing he wanted now: Eva.

Richard Shearsmith crouched beside his aging red-setter on the riverbank and watched the rear lights of the car disappear. He would wait a few minutes in case the car returned, and then investigate where it had been parked. The eager dog strained at the lead, sniffing the air. "Still, Bernie, quiet." He flicked through the photos he had taken on his mobile, sure his tired imagination was playing up, but there it was, clear on the screen: silhouetted images of what looked remarkably like a body.

Minutes later, as he neared the edge of the river, the overwhelming smell and Dorothy's gruesome face bobbing on the surface of the water confirmed his suspicions. He dialled 999.

By daybreak, Dorothy's body had been photographed in-situ from all possible angles and examined by a pathologist, while Mr Shearsmith watched with disbelief at the exceptional start to his day. The preliminary investigations done, a team of six beefy men hauled the body from the reeds and it was taken by ambulance to the mortuary.

Although he hadn't been able to see the number plate of the car, which he thought was a Vauxhall, Shearsmith relinquished his phone to the police in the hope his intriguing pictures would help them to identify the person who had disposed the body.

Rick's Delusions

Rick had never wanted children, lacking whatever it was that made people yearn for babies and family life. But then again he had never wanted marriage either. He studied Hope's face across the breakfast table - the prettiness, her stunning figure - and his heart leapt. He had never experienced such an intense feeling before and had no doubt she was The One. She finished her tea and got up, grabbing a few overnight bags from beside the door, and he dropped his toast on the plate and followed her to the car, where she put the holdalls into the boot. He reached her as she turned and wrapped his arms around her, kissing her forehead tenderly. She glanced up, smiling, and a warm loveliness flooded his body.

Not only did he desperately want marriage now, he also ached for this woman to bear his child.

She efficiently gathered the children together, squeezing an inordinate number of cases and bags into the boot, and ensured all the house doors and windows were locked and secure. Finally, they were ready to go and Rick sat on the passenger seat while Hope bundled the children in the back, helping Bern to buckle his seatbelt. She checked the kids were behaving in the rear-view mirror, and started the engine.

The journey to Beccles was uneventful and Hope nervously wondered what mood Charity would be in after the argument the day before. She noticed Rick gazing at her from the corner of her eye several times, but filled with a consuming hatred for him now, she looked straight ahead, concentrating on the road and traffic. As much as she detested him, she needed his help, and currently he was putty in her hands.

Charity remained in her bedroom for the duration of Hope's short visit, the nanny informing her guests that she was suffering from severe morning sickness. Hope knew it was a lie, but had more important things on her mind than petty sulks and sibling drama. She briefed the harassed childminder on her children's wants and needs and hastened back to the car, eager for the fun to begin.

Hope reversed from the drive, aware of Rick's adoring eyes again and her instinct was to slap him; he made her skin crawl.

Restraining herself, she counted the cat's eyes in the road as a distraction.

"Hope, I want to ask you something."

Screaming obscenities in her mind at the smooth and charming tones of the man she had once loved, she wanted to spit at him, smear it, wipe the smile from his smug face. "Go on." Forcing a light tone.

He grinned at her and she reminded herself repeatedly that after they had executed her plans tonight she would never have to see him again. "Let's have a baby, me and you, babe."

Without checking the mirrors, Hope swerved to the roadside, pulling the handbrake, staring straight ahead. She gripped the steering wheel, sickened by the man who had fucked her firstborn. Rick shuffled on his seat, worried, knuckles whitening as the silence progressed. "Babe, it was just a suggestion. I mean, we don't have to."

Hope jumped from the car and doubled over on the verge, retching violently. Heaving, heaving, expelling the last of her stomach contents, turning inside out. Tears tumbled down her face from exertion and pain. And now she had a dilemma. It would scupper her plans if she told Rick the reason for her extreme reaction, but how could she explain the vomiting. She pulled a tissue from her handbag and blotted her face, buying time, while Rick looked on with concern. He stroked her hand as she climbed back in the car. "Babe?"

And there it was. So what if it was a lie; she would be rid of him by tomorrow anyway, and it would guarantee his collaboration later. She faced him, bashful, a shy smile. "I was going to tell you tonight, but I may as well do it now seeing as you've just witnessed the morning sickness."

Hope let the sentence hang, and soon an overjoyed smile spread across his face. "You mean...?" She nodded and suddenly his arms crawled over her body, hugging her tight, wet lips kissing every inch of her face. Repulsed, she deadened her emotion and resisted the urge to scream. It was necessary; she needed his help.

His affection tired eventually and Hope wasted no time in restarting the car, speeding away to avoid his revolting touch any more.

Griffin's Relief

Despite having a full seven hours sleep, the enormity of the past few days had drained him and he was still exhausted when he awoke mid-afternoon to the sound of knocking on the front door. Yawning, he plodded down the stairs and was stunned to find two constables waiting. "Mr Griffin Hall?"

His heart raced so loudly he imagined his visitors would hear and he felt faint. How had they found Dorothy so quickly? Did they know he was her killer, or were they simply informing him of her death? He nodded lamely, scared, and it occurred to him that if they took him away he may never meet Eva Brunel.

"I'm afraid we have some bad news, can we come in please?"

Now fully awake, Griffin stepped back and the constables entered, following him to the kitchen and sitting as directed. "I'm sorry, Mr Hall, it's about your wife, Dorothy." The mention of her name shook him and it dawned on him that the room, usually full of bustling life and sumptuous aromas, felt empty without Dorothy's homely presence. He felt a brief longing until Eva and her passion, her mystery, returned to his thoughts. As his erection stirred underneath the table, he wondered if Eva was a competent cook. "Mr Hall?"

Remembering the present company, Griffin snapped to attention, thinking quickly. "I'm sorry, I was just thinking about my wife, she's not been home all night."

The constables glanced at each other, confused by the odd reaction. "We have found a body. We believe it may be your wife." Griffin's expression remained blank and once again the constables exchanged quizzical looks. "Are you okay, sir? Do you understand what I have just told you?"

Griffin nodded, awaiting handcuffs and a caution before his removal to a cell, destined to never meet the lovely Eva, never enter her, never bite the bosoms he suspected were ample and firm. His life was over.

"Do you want me to contact someone to be with you?"

His voice cracked, the world on his weary shoulders. "No."

216

"We'll need someone to identify the body within the next couple of days. Do you think you'll be prepared to do so?"

The officers stood and moved to the door, and Griffin realised they weren't planning to arrest him. Intense relief flooded and he beamed a grin, close to tears. "Yes, no problem, give me a day or so. Thank you both for coming, for letting me know about Dorothy, it's much appreciated. Good day." He gestured to the front door, bustling the stunned officers back into the coldness outside.

He watched them drive away through the window and immediately fetched a suitcase from above the wardrobe, throwing in his washbag and enough clothes for a day or two.

Dropping the case in the boot of his car, he climbed in and reversed from the drive; he couldn't wait to meet the woman of his dreams any longer.

Suspicious of the rector's reaction to the news of his wife's death, the two officers had parked around the corner to watch the house for a while and their perseverance paid off when he drove past, smiling smugly. MacIntyre nodded to Scott as he started the engine and said, "Not the behaviour of a bereaved man, eh?"

Griffin turned left at the end of the road and Scott radioed the control room to request an unmarked car take over the pursuit. "You're right. He's either not all there, or he killed that woman."

The Detectives

The pathologist had suspected murder immediately on seeing Dorothy Hall's body by the river and had fitted an urgent post mortem into his busy schedule. Meanwhile, Detective Chief Inspector Williams had ordered his team to prepare the incident room accordingly. The initial post mortem results in his hand, he addressed the detectives. "Although the cause of death is asphyxiation, Dorothy was subjected to a violent attack before her death; her facial injuries are severe and consistent with blunt force trauma. The area around her mouth was pale with cyanosis apparent on her face, which suggests suffocation with a soft object, such as a pillow, for example. Evidence shows she was raped after her death," Williams waited for the disgusted murmuring to die down, "possibly repeatedly, but the DNA recovered has no match on our database. Turner estimates Dorothy died less than twenty-four hours before the PM, probably the early hours of Friday morning.

"The preliminary analysis of the photographs taken by the man who witnessed the body being dumped show that the perp is probably male, judging by the build, but we cannot see a clear face. The car was a dark coloured Vauxhall Vectra saloon but the number plate isn't clear. Obviously, we will be expanding the photos further.

"However, some possible good news, for us anyway," Williams explained the bizarre actions of the deceased's husband earlier that morning which strongly suggested he'd had a hand in her untimely death, "and I'm sure it will come as no surprise that he drives a dark blue Vauxhall Vectra 1.8i."

"So we know who the killer is, then?"

"Suspect, Paduch, we still need proof. Scott and MacIntyre went to pick him up earlier and both he and the car have gone. We've put out feelers but so far there have been no sightings."

Hope Arrives

The journey had been long and tedious and the early sunset glowing bright orange through the windscreen had given Hope a headache. Irritable and grumpy, she parked at the hotel and collected the holdalls from the boot, and Rick knew better than to speak. He took the bags from her and went inside quickly to escape the cold, waiting by the wall while she booked them in.

Room one-twenty was delicious, a king-size bed heading one wall with crisp white sheets and a red and black striped runner. A television, built-in wardrobe and dressing table stretched along the opposite wall and the bathroom was beside the door. Through the polished glass patio doors was a balcony with ornate railings, which led to a stunning view of the immaculately kept grounds and hills beyond.

Rick had never stayed anywhere so luxurious and he darted around the room like a child, opening drawers, playing with gadgets, checking out the well-stocked minibar.

The surroundings were irrelevant to Hope until her immediate problem was sorted; she swallowed two painkillers with a glass with water, grimacing at the bitter aftertaste. Rick stopped playing with the radio and turned to the woman he loved. "Better?"

She shook her head, scraping her tongue across her teeth to try and remove the lingering sourness. "I will be in a minute, but I need something to take the revolting taste away; they were on my tongue too long."

Rick smiled and took two tiny bottles from the bar, pouring the whisky and Baileys into a glass. He swirled the glass to blend them, producing a creamy, fierce drink, and passed it to Hope. "Try this."

She took it gratefully, sipping, rinsing it around her mouth until the bitterness was gone. Regarding the glass with a curious smile, she took another sip. "That's delicious, I've never thought about mixing those two."

Rick winked and leapt onto the bed, lounging lazily on one elbow, and patted the covers with a glint in his eye, beckoning her seductively. Hope knew the expression well and the thought of going there again sickened her. She knocked back the drink to steel herself, build a solid wall around her emotions. "Hey, go easy, babe, you're carrying my baby, remember. I don't think you're supposed to drink, are you?"

"You poured it." Hope lay on her back next to him, focusing on the ceiling - just as she would when he began to grind into her - and waved a hand, dismissive. "I don't believe in all that shit, anyway. I drank through my other pregnancies and the kids turned out fine." The lie was justified; she needed Dutch courage to set her plans in place, and she wasn't pregnant anyway. It was crucial she kept Rick on her side for now, she would enjoy disposing of him later.

Bracing herself for the gruesome task ahead, Hope leaned over and unbuttoned his jeans, lowering the zip to release his penis, moving her hand rhythmically. He was ready in no time and yanked at her trousers, her knickers, finding her warmth and filling it. Hope counted the cracks in the ceiling.

He exploded within a minute; she was grateful it was over. Now he would fall into a deep sleep like always and she would have a chance to begin work, but - she glanced at the clock on the television - she needed him to sleep for at least two hours. "Rick, don't fall asleep just yet, let's have a couple of drinks and we can cuddle up together afterwards."

Rick yawned, sighing, awash with tiredness but aware this special weekend alone together was rare. He nodded. Hope trotted to the bar and replicated her previous drink, preparing a double for Rick - spirits always lulled him to sleep easily - and soon his breathing was regular and deep. Hope grinned, the revenge she had waited so long for was about to start.

Biding her time, Hope refilled her glass and tugged the patio door wide, instantly hit by a blast of icy cold. Shivering, she stepped out and soaked up the stark scenery. The balcony was framed by empty branches, soon to be budding with baby leaves, and the River Cam, its rippling soothing and peaceful, trickled behind the garden, the gentle waves reflecting the moonlight.

Eventually the cold became too much to bear and Hope returned to the suite, immediately heading for the shower to wash away the grime of the road and Rick's foul juice from inside her.

Griffin Gets Ready for Eva

Rubbing off the steaming wetness, Griffin discarded the towel and pulled on his greying Y-fronts, wishing he had bought a more glamourous pair. Regardless, it was what was inside them that mattered. Glancing at his watch - ten to eight - his heart speeded; the lovely Eva would be arriving soon.

He dressed in brown tweed trousers and a beige shirt, a tie, and tugged an olive jumper that Dorothy had knitted over the top, parading before the mirror to check his reflection. A knock on the door startled him and running this way and that, panicked, he grabbed his comb and raked it through the damp, greying curls. He sprang to the door on the second knock, straightening to his full height before opening the door.

Griffin gasped; she was a picture. Tiny, stunning, helpless yet strong. And demure, but with a mischievous glint in her eye.

Sexy.

Gibbering nonsensically, he moved aside to let Eva through, a flow of warmth flooding his groin. Usually the growing bulge would embarrass him, but today he was proud to show off his manhood. Hidden inside a knee-length leather trench coat, Eva sashayed to the mirror, preening herself, teasing her severe bob into place. She dropped her handbag onto the floor and the heavy thud intrigued Griffin.

Catching his eye to ensure he was paying attention, she slowly slipped the coat from her shoulders and he gasped, grasping the straining trousers which now made his restrained erection painful. Clad in a PVC mini skirt and a long-sleeved, lacy top that squeezed her bosom into an impressive cleavage, her shapely legs enhanced by fishnet stockings and sexy patent leather boots with stilettoed heels, Eva was every man's dream.

She sat on the bed and folded her legs to one side, flicking glossy hair from her face. Her eyes taunted him, sexed him, insinuating the pleasures to come. "Nice to meet you at last, Griffin."

He sat beside her, speechless at her beauty, salivating over the raunchy outfit he couldn't wait to remove. But first he felt a wave of

221

tenderness and reached forward, gently stroking the raven locks, her cheek, her dainty chin, the outline of her rosebud lips. His hand moved down slowly to reach the peachy softness of her neck and he felt her body tense. "It's okay, Eva, I won't hurt you."

She pulled back. "It's too quick, we've only just met for the first time. I need to know you a bit better."

His temper was sudden, lip curled into a snarl. "Oh, come on, we've been corresponding for ages. I thought that was the point of meeting up."

Serene and unperturbed, Eva grasped his hand, a calming influence, and his tension ebbed away. "It is, and we will, but later." She gestured to her leather bag, "In fact, I've brought some," she smiled, winking, "toys."

Now he was pacified, Eva strolled to the minibar and opened some red wine, emptying the small bottle between two glasses. She presented one to Griffin and sipped the other. Returning to his side, she curled her legs up tightly to appear even tinier than before and peered at him sweetly from under her fringe with a gentle, tinkling laugh. "Well?"

Transfixed by her daintiness, Griffin raised his glass. "Lovely. Perfect."

Chuckling again, she shoved him playfully. "Not the wine, silly, what's your view on sex toys, on games and roleplay?" She glimpsed down and saw the bulge in his trousers returning, clearly answering her question. Leaning back seductively on one elbow, she trailed her finger wispily along his thigh and caught his eye. "You may be a man of God, but I can tell you've got a naughty streak. I'm right, aren't I?"

Griffin shuddered, every nerve in his body heightened with the titillation, and composed himself enough to whisper, "It depends on what you call naughty." He reached across to cup her breast but she pushed his hand away softly. Maintaining eye contact, she slowly sat and faced him, pulling a knee to her chest to expose her naked genitals underneath the skirt.

He gasped, instinctively reaching for them, desperate to feel inside, but she deflected his hand and climbed off the bed, setting her glass on the bedside cabinet. She unzipped her bag and brought out some ankle and handcuffs, followed heavy duty chains and a leather whip. She glanced at Griffin "Well, would you call these naughty?"

His fascinated gaze moved from the bondage equipment to the intense blue eyes, staring into her soul, and his voice crackled huskily. "Yes, I would. And yes, I've got a wickedly naughty streak." He coughed to clear his throat. "What else have you got in there?"

Eva chuckled, a light breeze, and brought out a blindfold, a ball gag, a large vibrator, a feather and a can of spray cream, adding them neatly to the display on the carpet. "There's more, but we'll save that for later. So now tell me I didn't come here with sex on my mind."

"You bitch, you horny, sexy bitch." He nodded at her long and neatly manicured blood-red nails. "Do you use them?"

She clawed the air. "You bet." Standing, she dropped the chains and cuffs on the bed. "I'm in charge now, Griffin. I'm your dominatrix, you're my slave and you'll do whatever I tell you to do. If you feel uncomfortable the code-word for me to stop is 'hope', okay?" He nodded greedily. "Lie down on your back."

Grinning, Griffin threw himself back on the bed, head sinking comfortably into the pillow. Slow and tantalizing, Eva undressed him, nails stroking his skin, barely there and erotic. Now naked and fully erect, his pulsing tower standing upright impressively, he moved his arms and legs to the four corners of the bed and she expertly cuffed him, attaching the chains and feeding them under the wooden bed frame, locking the links together with a hefty padlock. She stood back with hands on hips and surveyed her handiwork. "Perfect. Give me a minute, I'll just freshen up a bit."

Eva disappeared into the en-suite and locked the door. Griffin could hear the taps running and it turned him on that she was cleaning herself for his pleasure. Without a doubt, she was about to give him the time of his life, the best sex, the roughest and most violent. Unlike other men, erections had never presented themselves easily, only forthcoming in the presence of a young girl or boy, and on the times he had acted on that they had always screamed, which brought on his orgasm. And his only experience of Dorothy, who had been disgusted by sex, was necrophilia. The idea of fucking a willing adult woman - Eva - was tantalising; he wanted to punch her, slap her, bite, make her squeal with pain while she writhed on his dick.

The chain flushed and he bounced back to reality, the fantasy waning. Within seconds he was flaccid again.

223

Eva came from the bathroom wearing a PVC bra and panties with black silk gloves stretched up her arms. Back straight and head held high, she strode confidently to the titillating toys and took the aerosol cream, the feather, the whip and blindfold, which she tied behind his head. Griffin memorised Eva's sexy body as the blackness consumed him. After a few moments of tentative anticipation, he sighed on feeling a sensation under his chin, which he guessed was the feather. He closed his eyes, relishing the spasms that racked his body when the tickling traced over an erogenous zone. Finally, flicking firmly, it reached his testicles and his whole body tingled, desperate for what was to come.

A gentle fizz, a coldness, and cream mingled with the thick grey and black hairs that littered his chest and abdomen, his burning heat melting it rapidly from foam to liquid. The chill now surrounded his testicles, his penis, and he pushed his groin high, ecstatic, an animal moan easing from his lips, begging. "Lick it off. Lick it off. Eva, lick it off."

A sudden, stinging crack on his hip startled him and he flinched as it stung, searing through his buttocks. Another, and he whelped in pain. "No. Stop."

Her voice was all around him, surrounding, cloying, sinking into his pores: "I didn't say you could talk. You only speak when I tell you to, is that clear?"

He nodded fervently. "Yes, yes."

"You spoke again. Now I punish you." Eva scrambled from the bed and roughly shoved the ball gag in his mouth, fixing it firmly behind his head. He tried to object but his muffled words were unintelligible. Her nails scraped down his chest leaving red welts and Eva noticed his erection subside. Much as she enjoyed his fear, she needed him to be hard and with a grimace slipped a latex glove over the silk on her hands, grasping his penis, holding it at arm's length, masturbating him. He grew and Eva raised the whip high, cracking it over his shoulder, making him recoil as far as his restraints would allow. A lascivious grin spread over his face and she knew she had won round one.

It took moments for him to explode, thrusting his hips up, manhood throbbing, shooting juice to mingle with the molten cream on his belly. More. More. He squirmed on the bed, the ecstasy not subsiding, writhing and grimacing, until finally his body relaxed. By the time Eva reached the bathroom to scrub at her skin, scour any trace of him away, his breathing had slowed, a soft rasping as sleep beckoned.

Having showered in the hottest water, any trace of Griffin washed down the plughole, Eva was ready for round two and she smiled. Leaving the latex glove beside him on the bed, she took her coat from the carpet and shrugged it on. Taking her bag and the room keys as she left, she locked the door quietly behind her.

Manhunt

Regardless of Griffin's absence, DCI Williams had been granted a warrant to search the rectory and a constable guarded the gate while officers carried out their search. Williams immediately noted the empty brandy and wine bottles on the kitchen side - Dutch courage? - and a faint slide mark on the tiles, which started underneath the larder door, turned a crescent and finished at the internal door to the garage. He stooped and wiped his finger on the mark, sniffing. It was sweet, maybe honey or golden syrup, and he was unsurprised to find a pool of the substance on the pantry floor with a few grey hairs stuck to the edges, which he bagged.

A thick rope hung from a rafter in the garage and Williams examined it closely. One side was frayed slightly and closer inspection showed a few fibres caught in the nylon strands. He called the photographer through.

In the main bedroom, one bed was neatly made, an empty coin tray on the bedside cabinet; Griffin's bed? The covers of the other lay on the floor, still tucked under the mattress on one side. A small, damp patch on the sheet reminded Williams that Dorothy had been raped post mortem, possibly several times.

The study was next and he opened the leather bound A4 diary that lay on the desk. 'Eva Brunel. 8pm. Cambridge Garden House Hotel, Mill Lane.' He tapped the book with his finger. "There's the motive then: he was having an affair with some woman called Eva Brunel."

Claudia looked up from where she sat on the floor, searching the bin for possible evidence. "Did you say Eva Brunel?"

He nodded, flicking through the diary. "Yep, he's meeting her tonight in Cambridge. Well, I assume the hotel's in Cambridge by its name."

Claudia abandoned the bin and joined her boss by the desk, reading the diary entry with wide eyes. "Jack, Eva Brunel is one of the two women who have accused Hall of sexual abuse when they were children." Williams stroked the day-old stubble that covered his chin as he digested her revelation, and she eventually continued, quiet. "I knew something was odd about her, she was too calm, too business-like."

"Where are you going with this?"

"That we should be worried about him, not condemning him. Eva's clearly out for revenge, not justice, and we need to stop her. Does it say where they're meeting?"

Trusting his colleague's instincts, Williams fished his keys from his pocket. "Yes. Come on, let's take a drive, you can request backup on the way there."

The Promise

Rick had slept for over two hours and lay dozing on the bed, still relaxed from the mind-blowing sex. Hearing a key in the door, he looked up and gasped when he saw Eva. "What the fuck are you doing here? Get out, if Hope sees you she'll go mental."

Hope was stern as she tugged the raven, bobbed wig from her head, her mahogany curls flattened until she shook them out, and Rick's jaw dropped. "What's this? You're Eva? Our new singer is you?" He shook his head, wondering if he was dreaming, but she was still there. "What the hell are you playing at, Hope Brown?"

Heading for the minibar, Hope shrugged the heavy coat from her shoulders to reveal the skimpy PVC outfit Rick recognised from Eva's audition and tugged the gloves off. She poured two large brandies and thrust one at Rick, who was now sitting, sheets covering his nakedness. "Fucking hell, babe, you had me taken in there, but I have to admit you look hot. Come here." He reached out but she dodged his hand, slugging the brandy.

"Remember when we got engaged, I agreed on condition you did me a favour?" Hope sat neatly on the end of the bed, swirling the dregs of her drink in the bottom of the glass.

"Yep, and I phoned that policewoman…"

"Claudia Horseferry."

"That's the one. I told her everything you wrote down and I'm certain she bought it."

Hope sneered. "That wasn't the favour, I clearly stated to you on two occasions that I wanted you to kill someone."

Now he sat bolt upright, pushing the covers off. "Like fuck you did. I wouldn't agree to that."

"Oh, you did. And I fucked you again straight after you said yes so you could orgasm. Remember now?"

Rick had jumped out of bed and was tugging his underpants on, furious. "For fuck's sake, Hope, I would have agreed to anything to get you to fuck me again, you know that."

Fire shot from her eyes, searing his soul. "Exactly, and that's why I fucked you, so you'd agree, and now I've agreed to marry you and I'm having your baby," she patted her tummy, "so you'll keep your side of the bargain."

Rick stomped to the window, dismissive. "Fuck off, babe, I'm not killing anybody, baby or not. You want someone dead, hire a

228

fucking hit man." He stomped to the minibar. "It's not like you're short of a bob or two. But I'm not getting involved." He grabbed a can of lager and cracked it open, swigging thirstily from the can, and gradually it dawned on him that the only noise he could hear was his own gulping. He lowered the can, the sinister silence disconcerting, and tentatively glanced at the bed.

An opened knife roll lay on the covers with one missing, leaving a glaring space, and he looked fearfully at Hope, who gripped a long and narrow boner knife so firmly her knuckles were white. He gulped, heart hammering. "What are you doing?"

Whispered, growling, "Call me babe, Rick, it's more your style."

"What's that supposed to mean?"

"You work it out. Do you want me to have your baby? Do you want this baby in here?" She hammered her belly with her fist and Rick winced.

"Hope, I mean, babe, don't do that, I don't want you hurting the baby."

She hitched the mini skirt high to reveal her nakedness and spread her legs, the knife close to her genitals. Rick gasped, springing forward.

"Back off." Louder, guttural.

He stopped, hands in the air, bewildered. "Babe, come on, you're hormonal. Put the knife down. Put it on the bed. Come on, babe, we'll get through this."

"Help me to kill the guy who raped me and forced me to give him oral sex when I was Bern's age. I've managed to get him here by pretending to be Eva, now I want to torture him for what he did to me. If you refuse, Rick, I'm going to cut your child from my body in front of you. Don't try calling my bluff." She indicated the scars on her arms with her eyes. "Cutting myself is a relief, I'll enjoy doing it, it'll give me piece of mind. It's you who won't be able to deal with it." Hope whipped the knife across her arm, beads of blood surfacing immediately, and Rick clenched his fists, pained. "Say bye-bye to baby, sweetheart."

"You're a fucking nut job." She slashed again - deeper, more blood - and he leapt forward, wrestling the knife from her hand. She probed for another knife but he whisked them off the bed, out of her reach, throwing the boner to join them.

Hope snarled, tears brimming. "You will fucking help me, Rick Faraday, Griffin Hall has to pay for what he did."

She pounded his chest, flailing, striking - again, again - wild, overwhelmed by years of frustration and pent up anger, of sadness for a stolen life.

He stood for a while, taking the blows, accepting her need to unleash emotion, but eventually he pushed her onto the bed, trapping her with the weight of his body. Still she struggled. "Babe, calm down, come on, it's okay." Freeing her arms, she pummelled him, his back, chest, face, head, a trapped animal fighting for liberty, and he grappled again, catching the flailing wrists and gripping firmly. This time he shouted, "Okay, enough already. I'll help you, I'll do whatever you need if it makes you happy." The struggling ceased instantly.

They lay together for a while, panting, sweaty, emotionally charged minutes passing as the adrenaline ebbed from their bodies. Eventually Rick broke the silence. "So, are you going to tell me the plan?"

Hope wriggled from under him and sat, hanging her head with a mixture of weariness, shame and alcohol. She reached for the dregs of her drink, savouring the warmth before grabbing Rick's untouched glass. Quiet and emotionless now her anger was spent, she said, "He's bound, blindfolded and gagged in a room two floors up."

"Hope, what have you got yourself into."

She eyed him, disbelieving, and a surge of rage overwhelmed her. "I want to slice at his body the way his abuse made me slice mine for so many years. I want him to see how it feels to be riddled with cuts like I have been so often, how the scabs catch on your clothes and pinch and hurt."

Rick didn't know whether to hold her, comfort her, or to remain still and listen. He chose the latter. "Then what?"

Hope downed the last of his drink and waited for the burning in her throat to ease enough for her to speak without choking. "Paracetamol. Aspirin." She leant forward and dragged her bag over, removing a handful of tablet boxes, which she chucked on the bed. "Ibuprofen, Diazepam, Temazepam, Prozac, Seroxat. There's more, but I'm sure you get the idea. They're all tablets I've overdosed on in the past and I cannot describe how revolting they

230

taste when you vomit them back. Maybe Griffin will be able to explain, maybe he's better with words than me."

Returning to the bag, she retrieved some thin, fraying rope tied into a slip knot - a rudimentary noose - and Rick resisted the urge to laugh at its inadequacy. Hope was deadly serious. "I've deliberately made one that will break with his weight. I just want him to feel that fear briefly, make him wonder if he'll ever breathe again, just like I have in the past."

Rick inhaled deeply and held the breath with trepidation, anxious of the answer to his next question. "So you're not going to kill him, just torture him until he realises what you've been through because of him?"

Hope chuckled without mirth. "No, I'm not going to kill him."

He sighed, relieved.

"You are."

Hope poured some vodka now they had finished the brandy and whisky, adding orange juice, and she went to the bathroom to change into some comfortable clothes.

Once he had heard the door lock, Rick dragged the bedcovers over his head to muffle his voice and dialled a number on his mobile. It rang. "Come on." And rang. "Come on. Oh, at last. Dawn, it's me." He desperately hoped his whispering was inaudible in the en-suite.

Furious still at being dropped from the band she had started, Dawn was terse. "What do you want?"

"I'm in Cambridge with Hope and she's gone completely mental, says she's got that guy who abused her in another room, that she's tied him up and she's going to torture him then make me kill him."

"Fuck," Dawn was already slipping her trainers on, car keys in hand, "I knew she was up to something."

"Get the police here, we're in room one-twenty, Cambridge something hotel."

"What hotel, Rick? Think."

"I don't know, I didn't take any notice. Garden, maybe. Cambridge Garden Hotel, something like that, on a road called Mill Lane in central Cambridge."

"Calling the police now, bro, and I'm on my way. Try and stall her somehow, the best way is to get her talking about herself. Help will be with you soon."

Rick lay on the bed, frantically contemplating a way to keep Hope in the room long enough for the police to arrive. The bathroom door opened and she stepped out, and Rick's jaw dropped, aghast; the thirty-two-year-old had transformed herself into a virginal teenager, mahogany pigtails that reflected the light hanging over each shoulder, complementing the black hair-ties that held them in place. Her legs were clad in black stockings under a grey schoolgirl miniskirt, the lacy tops just meeting the hem, and she wore high-heeled lace ups. Her white blouse was unbuttoned to expose cleavage and a burgundy school blazer finished the outfit.

"What the hell are you playing at?"

She glared at him, challenging, hateful. "You'll see. Come on, let's go."

He needed to stall her, but how? He racked his brains and an idea presented easily; he would play on Hope's weakness. He patted the bedcover. "Come and sit down first, we'll both need something to calm our nerves before we get to work. Let's have a drink first, then we can go. He won't be going anywhere if you've tied him up..."

"Handcuffed."

"Okay, handcuffed him. Come on, let me fix you a drink."

Hope's suspicions were raised immediately and her heart thudded. "You've spoken to someone, haven't you?" Now the pressure was on to finish her revenge before fleeing back to East Anglia, to the kids, to a cleansed life. "You bastard. Who did you call?"

Rick forced a smile. "Call? I don't know what you mean."

Hope crouched to fold the knife roll, fixing it securely, and threw it into her bag with the tablets and noose. She pointed to the door and nodded. "We're going now." His mind whirled, desperate to stay in the room until help arrived. She growled, fuming. "I said we're going now. Move, you bastard."

Thinking quickly, Rick crossed his arms in defiance. "No. You can't exactly make me, can you. I mean, you're a short-arse and I'm six foot four."

The blue of her eyes became black pools of vitriol, teeth clenched, a threatening sneer. She rummaged in her bag, searching, and the hairs on the back of Rick's neck rose, goose-bumps prickling his skin.

She had a gun. Cocking the hammer, pointing in his direction. He shuddered, arms dropping to his side as he moved carefully from the bed, making no sudden movements. He walked slowly to the door, eye contact constant, and opened it wide. Hope tugged on her coat to conceal the school uniform and hid the gun in her bag as they left the room.

The corridor was empty and they waited for what felt like hours until the lift cranked to the first floor, the opening doors revealing an empty cell. The journey up passed in silence and Hope guided Rick to room three-six-nine by nudging his back with the barrel of the gun.

A muffled, pained whine came through the door and Rick hoped somebody had heard the noise and reported it to the receptionist. Hope unlocked the door and pushed him into the room and the groaning increased, Griffin thrashing about on the bed as much as his restraints would allow. Regardless that he was male, Rick's eyes were drawn to the penis flopped across Griffin's thigh; it was colossal, the biggest he had seen despite being flaccid. Rick uncomfortably imagined how massive it would be erect and winced at the thought of the monstrous tool penetrating a seven-year-old. Suddenly he had intense sympathy for his girlfriend and remorse for not supporting her more. "That's the guy who fucked you when you were a baby?"

Hope marched to the bed, the gun hanging loosely by her side. She pulled her arm back, striking Griffin with the barrel and he roared in pain through the ball gag. "Shut up, bastard. I'm your dominatrix and I told you not to make any noise unless I tell you to." He stilled immediately and silence hung in the air, a thin stream of blood trickling through his greying hair. Hope glanced at Rick, nodding to an easy chair in the corner opposite the door. "Go and sit down." He obeyed, leaning forward, forearms on knees, trying not to show his fear.

Hope crawled onto the bed and lowered her head over Griffin's impressive beast, the ends of her bunches tickling him temptingly. She stared at Rick and he was hypnotised by the intensity of the glare, unable to break the spell, mesmerised. Flicking her tongue above Griffin's penis, seductive and tantalising, Rick was both revolted and intrigued. She hovered close but not touching, never taking it into her mouth, and memories of her sucking flooded and stirred him. He didn't want to be aroused - the display was sick - but the act was stimulating nonetheless, and soon his own manhood had grown. He wanted her.

Any fear, concern, had dissipated and Rick desperately hoped the police wouldn't find them after all. If he had realised Hope was planning a sexy act he wouldn't have called Dawn. His erection stood firm, and longing for the warm tongue pulsed through him.

Checking the ball gag was firmly lodged in Griffin's mouth, she climbed off the bed and removed the blindfold. Posing coyly, a finger on her lip, other hand behind her back, swaying childishly. "Sorry Griffin, Eva had to go. She asked me to take over. Remember me?"

Terrified, Griffin's brow furrowed, his muffled cries for help thwarted by the gag, and Rick was captivated by her scheming. He had no desire to help the religious man before him; the man was a monster. He fucked children.

Dark lashes framing the stunning blue, lowered and coy, Hope said, "You like schoolgirls, don't you? Do you remember when you first had sex with me? When you forced your cock into my face for the first time?" She slapped him, the skin reddening instantly. Now louder, angry. "Well, do you?" Griffin nodded exaggeratedly, pleading eyes begging forgiveness.

Hope rolled a sleeve up to show the silver and purple scars that covered her forearm. "See those?" Griffin nodded, apprehensive. "That's the life I had to look forward to after you pleasured yourself using my tiny body." She tapped her head. "What was just a perverse orgasm to you fucked me up in here. For life. And I can bet you that all the other little children you've fucked are dealing with their rapes in a similar way. Makes you feel good, does it?"

Griffin frantically shook his head.

Hope collected the knives from the bag and unrolled them out of Griffin's sight, and he strained to see. She slipped the discarded latex glove on and climbed onto the covers, her grip working his penis. It remained flaccid. Hope pressed harder, sped up, but Griffin's excitement had gone.

Lazing back in the chair with his foot over his knee, an audience to a seedy show, Rick was enjoying himself. "Suck him. No man can resist that."

Hope shot a contemptuous look, sick that she had considered marrying the arsehole, and worked her hand harder, faster, gripping firmly, willing life into the droopy member. But it lay, weak and weary, and she dropped it with frustration.

"Go on, Griffin," Rick's voice was soft, lulling and melodic, "you've got a little schoolgirl over you and she's gagging to suck your dick, you know how much the young ones turn you on. Don't you just want to force it inside her until she tears?"

His plan worked within seconds - the big man was back - and he watched the expert hand pleasuring the rector, oblivious that Hope had taken a knife.

Until an animal roar that the gag couldn't quell.

She pulled away from his penis and fresh blood trickled onto the covers.

The depths of her revenge on another level, a Hope never seen before, she spat on him, slashing his chest again and again, comforted by his blood spilling on the sheets.

Rick's hopes crashed, fear returning. She was going to make him kill a man.

Room One-Twenty

The aging concierge limped slowly towards room one-twenty, followed by two officers, who were amused by the bizarre report of a disturbance. Receiving no response to his knock, the concierge unlocked the door and they entered, finding the room empty, although the television chatted quietly. The crumpled bed and used glasses on the desk showed someone had recently been there, and PC Collins rapped half-heartedly on the bathroom door before entering, while his colleague checked the balcony, leaning over the rail to check the terrace below.

Satisfied all was well, that the crazy woman who had called from a different county was a timewasting nutter, the officers were about to leave when Collins winked at his colleague, tipping his head towards the minibar.

Reception

Williams and Horseferry pushed through the main doors and trotted to the reception desk. Julie, a glamorous brunette with a St. Tropez orange hue and brightly made-up face, smiled winningly. "Can I help you?"

Both had automatically reached for their badges and Julie's smile waned to an inquisitive pout. "Could you please tell us which room Griffin Hall is staying in?"

Efficient, Julie's French-manicured nail traced the guestbook and she shrugged a fake smile. "We have no Mr Hall staying here tonight, I'm afraid. Sorry I couldn't be any more help." She closed the book, dismissing the detectives.

Claudia bristled. "We haven't finished yet. Can you see if an Eva Brunel is registered?"

With a long, harassed sigh, Julie retrieved the book exaggeratedly, huffing as she opened it once more. "What name was that?"

"Eva Brunel."

"No, I'm sorry," the false smile returned, "we have no Eva Brunel booked in tonight either." And now sarcastic, "Is there anything else I can help you with?"

Claudia's patience was wearing thin and she held her hand out. "Just give me the book, we'll look ourselves."

Tipped head. Smile. Fluttered lashes. "I'm sorry, but it's not hotel policy…"

"Give me the fucking book, Barbie."

Seething, Julie passed the book across and Claudia took it to a nearby coffee table, sitting on the oversized sofa. Williams followed. "Nice PR, Claud."

She chuckled. "Piss off, Jack." Together they scrutinized the names, unlike flippant Julie who had appeared to speed read. Claudia gasped. "Shit, I haven't found Hall or Brunel, but Hope Brown is registered."

"Who?"

"I told you this in the car, colander brain; two women have accused Griffin of sexual assault when they were children. Eva's one

237

of them and Hope Brown is the other. I don't know what's going on here, but it's getting pretty fishy."

"What room?"

She focused again. "One-twenty."

Williams stood, straightening his jacket. "Then let's go and investigate."

But when they reached the room they only found two guilty officers holding cans of beer. Embarrassed, Collins explained about a woman's frantic call to the emergency services, how her brother had told her Griffin Hall was handcuffed in a room, that Hope Brown had flipped and Rick Faraday was scared for his life.

Williams crossed his arms. "So you find the room empty and hit the minibar?"

"Forget that for now," Claudia headed for the door, "I don't care if we have to disturb every guest at this hotel, but we've got to find whatever room Griffin's booked into. Come on."

Room Three-Six-Nine

Rick sat in the corner, tormented from witnessing the rector's torture, and every bone in his body wanted to escape, get the hell out of the nightmare, but volatile Hope had the gun in her hand, and even though her back was turned as she emptied tablets into a pile on the cabinet, he was scared to take the risk.

He surveyed the sadistic scene. She had superficially slashed Griffin all over, trails of blood oozing onto the covers, and tears of pain and fear soaked his hairline. Hope removed the gag with a warning not to scream and forced a handful of tablets into his mouth, tipping in water to make him swallow. He fought the urge, tongue pushing against the pills, but the instinct was too strong and at least half were swallowed. She poured in more water and he gulped the remaining drugs, screwing his face up with the bitter aftertaste.

Desperate to escape, Rick slowly edged the chair towards the door, inch by inch, praying Hope wouldn't notice. She gathered more tablets and dropped them in the hostage's mouth, following with water, and Rick silently closed the gap. Without looking up, Hope said, "Don't bother, it's locked."

Rick jumped to the handle, tugging, rattling, but the door wouldn't budge. "For God's sake, Hope, let me out. You don't need me here, I'm not part of this."

Leaning over Griffin, Hope fed another handful into his mouth, following with water. "But you are. You fucked my daughter. Did you think she wouldn't tell me? That she'd keep your filthy secret. Well, now you know, me and Penny, we're closer than that." More water, and the tablets went down.

Rick grabbed the handle again, pulling the door with all his strength, and Hope's tinkling laughter seemed sinister now, taunting, terrifying. He glanced over his shoulder and stilled instantly; she held the gun with both hands, aimed at him, and she had cocked the hammer. "Come here." Heart sinking, Rick obeyed, not struggling when she calmly untied the makeshift noose and bound his wrists behind his back, tying securely.

239

She scooped the last of the tablets up and dosed her now compliant prisoner. Rick debated whether to try and reason with her, and the only way he could see forward was to tell the truth. "Penny told me she was sixteen."

"I know."

"She looked it. In fact, she looked older. She said it wasn't her first time and she wasn't making it hard for me. I had no idea, Hope, if I had I'd never have gone there."

"Liar." Hope strolled to the minibar, reaching inside without looking.

"No, God's honour, she was twelve for fucks sake. It makes me sick to think of it."

It was gin, and she mixed in some tonic. "I know, but I also know that you begged her not to use a condom. How fucking irresponsible is that? She wasn't using contraception; you want to be grateful she didn't get pregnant."

Despite everything, he loved Hope and wanted to spend the rest of his life with her, but now he realised how much he had hurt her. He whispered, contrite. "When I saw you in the crowd at the gig, you were the only one there, you shone out, and I knew straight away you were the woman I wanted to marry. I still do. I can't take back the past, but I can promise you a good future."

Griffin breathed heavily and his head lolled to the side. "He's passed out. I thought he'd be sick, I always was."

Rick snorted with irony. "You can't hang him anyway unless you untie me and I doubt you're about to do that." She looked daggers at him and his head sagged with remorse. "Hope, I swear, if I'd known Penny was your daughter I'd never have come on to you, not until I'd explained things to you."

She was meting her revenge but it didn't feel as sweet as she had imagined, and Hope slid down the wall, sitting on the floor and hugging her knees to her chest. She rested her head on her legs. "Do you think he's going to die?"

"Do you care?"

"I'll get done for murder."

"It'd be manslaughter, you have good grounds, and you can claim diminished responsibility because of your depression."

"I don't care what you call it, I'll still be locked away."

"Then make it look like suicide. He's a child molester, he's about to get sprung, so he took his own life. Simple."

With great effort, Hope dragged herself up and slipped the disposable glove onto her hand, gripping Griffin's wrist for a pulse. Sighing, she dropped it. "Slow and weak." Sitting heavily on the bed, despondent. "I thought it would feel good, you know, cathartic, I thought I'd find the bit of me that was missing finally. But no. It doesn't make me feel better. I don't feel anything at all, like a void, a nothing."

Rick nodded to his fellow prisoner. "You've done him, he's finished. Come on, untie me, we can put this behind us and move on together. Please. You've done what you came to do, what you needed to do to free yourself from the memories, now let it go. We'll get married and have the baby, whatever you want."

"There is no baby. When you said you wanted a child with me earlier I was sick because the thought of having a baby with the guy who stole my child's virginity at twelve revolted me, but I couldn't tell you that at the time."

"Then we still get married, have a baby or not, whatever. We live however you want. You can keep writing if you want, or I can support you with Reveal's advance and royalties, it's up to you."

Ever hopeful, ever naïve, Hope reached behind him and untied the rope.

Williams and Claudia thanked the guest and moved across the corridor to room one-forty, knocking. Presently a woman, clothed only in a towel, her damp hair hanging limp over her shoulders, opened the door, curious. The detectives showed their badges and Claudia introduced them. "We're looking for three people: Griffin Hall, Eva Brunel and Hope Brown. Have you seen any of them?"

The woman shook her head. "No, sorry."

She sighed and walked a few steps to the next room. "Only another eighty-one to go."

Rick and Hope

Packing the last of their belongings into the suitcases, Rick turned, cuddling Hope tight to his chest. She couldn't help loving him, it wasn't an emotion with an on-off switch, and it must have been a terrible secret for him to keep. Plus, Penny had admitted how provocative she had been. "Why didn't you run off when I untied you back there?"

"I can't help it, Hope, I love you so much. Anyway, now you've tied me up once," he pushed her back, a playful glint in his eye, "you'll have to do it more often."

She chuckled, zipping her bag. "Let's go home."

The phone began ringing as they left the room and they glanced at each other, questioning whether to answer. With a shrug, Hope continued towards the lift and Rick closed the door, following. Travelling downstairs, checking their hair in the mirrored lift, neither noticed Hope's mobile vibrating and buzzing in her bag.

Charity Panics

Charity slammed the phone down, venting her frustration on anything in her way. A blood-curdling scream rang out behind her - again - and she couldn't stand it any longer. "Will you just shut that bloody noise up, Penny, you're having a baby, not a hippo-bloody-potamus."

Penny was slumped on the sofa, a tarpaulin - muddy side up - separating her from the quality upholstery, with amniotic fluid pooled around her hips. Terrified and tearful, she couldn't contain the scream as the contraction gripped her tight, stabbing, squeezing her, racking her body with pain. "I want my mum."

"Jesus, Penny, I told you, I can't bloody get hold of her. She's not answering the hotel phone or her mobile. Look, we have got to get you to hospital. From the ridiculous racket you're making I'd say you're about to give birth any minute."

And Charity realised how right she was as clear signs of the transitional stage of labour raged from Penny's lips: "I don't fucking care, okay, I don't fucking care, and I'll fucking scream if I fucking want to. I'm not going anywhere without my fucking mother."

Panicking, stressed, Charity snatched the phone and dialled nine-nine-nine. "Ambulance, and hurry."

Screaming. "I don't want a fucking ambulance. I want my fucking mother."

"Yes, it's my niece, she's having a baby on my sofa, and it's a Cantoni, cost over five thousand, and we only got it just before Christmas. If there's any stains I'll... Oh, yes, I'm Charity Rowbotham, the address is Brahms House, Waylaid Road, that's in Beccles... yes, N-R-thirty-four, nine-J-U."

Behind her, Penny panted, another contraction building. Charity glanced over, flustered and thoroughly pissed off, sticking a finger in her spare ear as the screaming restarted. "Good God, woman, fifteen minutes is too long. Surely you can hear her, she's almost there. She's only thirteen, I'd kill my Ava if she got pregnant at... sorry, yes, I said she was thirteen. Thank God for that, and make sure they do hurry, because there's no way I'm delivering a baby."

Slamming the receiver down, Charity turned to Penny. "Ten minutes, you'll have to hold it in."

"I don't want a fucking ambulance; I want my fucking mother. Oh, my god, not another one already, not another one, please. I can't stand this any more." Penny scrambled up, standing, leaning against the arm of the sofa, searing agony in her lower back. Instinct kicked in and she kneeled, leaning forward on outstretched arms, gravity pulling the pressure from her aching spine.

A guttural roar, a high-pitched scream that pierced Charity's ears. Penny's bitten nails ripped at the tarpaulin, knuckles white, writhing, squirming. And it eased. She breathed, sweat beading her brow. "I need my mum. I can't do this without my mum. Please get her, Auntie. Please."

Charity grabbed the handset again, fumbling fingers pushing the number of the hotel, unaware that Bern and Olive had sneaked into the room, scared by the noise their sister was making. They nervously watched her panting on all fours, her dignity long gone. Although he had been told where babies came from, Bern didn't care, preferring to play with his trains. "What are you doing, Penny?"

Olive nudged her brother. "She's having a baby, silly, it's going to come out of her bottom."

"Yuck, that's disgusting." Bern grimaced and, disinterested, ran from the room. Olive, however, decided to stay and watch so she could tell her friends about it afterwards and she trotted to the kitchen, returning with the biscuit tin and wafting it under Penny's nose.

The sickly sweet aroma made her retch. "Fuck off. Oh no, not another, please not another." Screaming, tears tumbling, stomach churning. She swiped the tin from Olive's hand, biscuits and crumbs scattering over the plush, cream carpet.

Horrified, Charity clasped her chest, gasping at the mess. "For God's sake, not on the Axminster, that cost nearly eight thousand pounds."

Meanwhile…

Claudia's feet ached and she was frustrated that, despite knocking on seemingly endless doors, they had not found anything untoward. They had decided to each take one side of the corridor to speed things up, but it wasn't any less tedious. She reached room three-six-nine and rapped on the door. Nothing, but a retching noise came from inside. Concerned, she shouted, "Are you okay in there? It's the police."

The reply was weak and inaudible, followed by more vomiting. Something felt wrong. "Jack, this one. We need to get in here, and quick."

"I'll go to reception to get…"

"No," she surprised herself with her urgency, "we need to break in."

Trusting her intuition, Williams braced himself for the painful bruise he was about to get and slammed his shoulder against the door, which fell open. Claudia rushed past him.

It stank inside, and Griffin lay on the bed, naked and curled into the foetal position, his pallid face swimming in frothy, foul, vomit. Apart from a pile of empty tablet blisters scattered on the bed, the room was tidy. Claudia whipped her phone out, requesting back up and an ambulance urgently, while Williams dragged the seriously ill man away from his stomach contents, manhandling him into the recovery position. "Pulse is slow and breathing's shallow. He's not got long if they don't get here quick."

Claudia spoke gravely to her phone. "That ambulance, we need it now, blues and twos, the guy's in a bad way." She cut the call and surveyed the scabbing cuts on his body, the red welts on his wrists and ankles. "It looks like he's been tied up, and I can't see a knife or anything else that could have made these scratches."

Unable to do anything more for the rector, the detectives independently scoured the room, searching for clues to explain the bizarre situation. Griffin's clothes were folded on the chair near the balcony, shoes neatly tucked underneath. No signs of a struggle, of anything untoward, except a drugged man with multiple superficial blade wounds. A man recently accused of paedophilia.

"I reckon he's tried to do himself in, Claud."

She shook her head. "No."

"Why?"

Claudia glanced around. "It's too tidy. If you're about to kill yourself, you don't fold your clothes up neatly ready for the next day."

"I suppose."

"And there's no alcohol. There's always alcohol at a suicide." She lifted Griffin's limp arm. "He's been tied up, too." Claudia glared at the man she had seen several times recently and felt nothing but scorn, revulsion. "Couldn't have happened to a nicer man. Still, it's our job to keep him alive if possible."

"The abuse was bad?"

Claudia rolled her eyes. "He's a sick fuck, alright. I tell you, Jack, if it was one of those girls who did this, or even both, I can't say I blame them."

Outside, running footsteps neared and Williams opened the door for the paramedics. They began their lifesaving, strapping monitors and probes to the patient, moving him minimally.

Suddenly, Claudia dashed to the door, grabbing Williams by the arm, dragging him alongside. "We're bloody idiots, Jack, we need to check room one-twenty again. Come on."

Too Late

The room was empty; if the register was correct and Hope Brown had been staying in the room, then she was long gone. Claudia was pleased, although she would never admit as much; Hope had been through enough. The detectives wandered around, scanning the scene, noting anomalies, memorising and photographing.

The phone rang and, curious, Claudia answered.

"Thank God for that, it's about bloody time, I've been ringing for ever. It's Penny, she's giving birth on my Cantoni sofa, you never even told me she was pregnant, and now..."

"Excuse me, you're through to Detective Inspector Horseferry, who are you trying to reach?"

"Oh, for God's sake, that bloody receptionist is such a bloody bimbo, I asked for room one-twenty."

"You've got one-twenty. Are you looking for Hope?"

"Oh, don't start bloody preaching to me, that's the last bloody thing I need right now, this is a disaster." Charity's panic was palpable.

Claudia stifled a laugh and tried again. "I mean, are you after Hope Brown?"

"Oh, right, I get you, um, yes, she's my sister, my niece's mother, Penny's, that is. She needs to get home, Penny's refusing to go to hospital without her and the baby's on its way, it's close. We've got two paramedics here, but even they can't persuade her so they've had to try and get some midwives to come for a home birth. If Hope doesn't get here soon that child is going to be born in my lounge, and quite apart from anything the smell in this room is disgusting already, I'll have to leave the windows open for the next year to get rid of the stench and it's freezing outside."

"You say Hope's daughter? I thought her children were young."

"They are, Penny's only thirteen, bloody little slut. She shouldn't even know what sex is at that age." A guttural roar in the background became a shrill scream and Claudia held the phone from her ear.

247

When it ended, she said, "So when Hope comes back from Cambridge she'll be going straight to your house?"

"Yes, and she'd better hurry up too, pass that on to her, will you."

Claudia scratched her head, an idea forming. "We don't know where she is, she's left the hotel. I can only assume she's on her way back to you already. Look, if you give me her car details we can put out an emergency trace, try and get a helicopter to bring her over on a mercy dash."

A huge sigh of relief and her voice became muffled; Claudia guessed she had turned away from the phone. "Penny, what's the registration number of your mum's car?"

Alive

Dawn rushed through doors and sprinted to the reception desk, demanding to know which room Hope Brown was in. The receptionist rolled her eyes, knowing the answer off by heart now. "One hundred and twenty. I think she's having a party, judging by the number of people going up there."

Williams and Claudia stepped from the lift and eyed Dawn. "Were you asking after room one-twenty?" Dawn nodded and Claudia approached her. "Why do you want that room? Who are you?" She showed her badge.

The counsellor reddened, nervous. "Dawn Faraday, I'm looking for my brother and his girlfriend."

Williams chuckled. "You're the woman who called the cops, worried Hope might be about to harm him? I don't think you need worry, I'm pretty sure he's fine. We're on our way to see them both now."

Dawn nodded, blonde curls bobbing, and relief washed over her; the words she had been desperate to hear were a symphony of joy: he's fine.

Rick, her baby brother, was alive.

Drama on the Roadside

The general location of Hope's car had been traced and a couple of officers waited in their car by the side of a country road south of the historical town of Diss. Finally, the car they had been watching for passed, brake lights illuminating the road as Hope desperately attempted to slow to the speed limit.

The driver fired the engine and turned the siren and lights on, filtering into the traffic, and his colleague radioed the control room with their location.

Hope swore under her breath when she noticed the flashing car behind, resigning herself to another three points on her licence. She bumped up the verge and waited while the patrol car parked in front, the lofty driver trotting urgently towards her, bending through the window. "Madam, are you Mrs Hope Brown?"

Her jaw dropped, nervous. "How on earth do you know my name?"

The policeman opened her door and beckoned her out, the whop-whop-whop of a helicopter deafening overhead. She squinted at the bright spotlights above, worried now; they must have found Griffin. *Prison it is, then.* Too quiet to be heard, she mumbled, "I had good reason."

"We need to get you to your sister's house immediately."

"What?" Shouting now, curiously watching the helicopter hovering over a nearby field. Her heart sped up, adrenaline surging, the pressure in her chest increasing, hurting. She hugged her body to quell the ache.

Bewildered, Rick climbed from the car. "What's going on? What are you doing?"

"And who are you, sir?" The officer, gigantic beside Hope, steered her towards a harness which swayed precariously from the helicopter, and she debated whether to struggle free or give up without a fuss. "He's my fiancé, I want him with me."

Swiftly, he wrapped the harness over her shoulders, feeding straps through her legs and buckling her securely, and Hope's anxiety increased. "No time, love."

"Isn't this overkill? It's not like I…" Killed him? Was Griffin dead? Was she a murderer? Breathing deeply to quell the burgeoning fear, wishing she had never found her abuser. Dreading the coming twenty years behind bars. Why had she gone so far?

The officer gave the pilot a thumbs up and Hope was whipped from her feet as the helicopter accelerated away, panicking, terrified tears blurring her view. Deafened by the whirring rotors, she didn't hear the policeman call after her: "It's okay, love, we'll bring him in the car."

Soon, she was winched up and helped aboard by the crew and she morbidly contemplated her fate.

New Life

Penny screamed, piercing and scared, wishing she were in her mother's protective arms. Her body urged her to push and instinct told her to comply, but when she did it felt like her body was tearing in two.

Charity paced the room with her head down, hand shielding her eyes from the revolting scene. "This is disgusting, Penny, why couldn't you wait until you got home to do this. God, the smell, it's making me feel sick, and all that bloody gore everywhere; foul. None of it better get on my furniture. Or my carpet for that matter."

"You fucking selfish bitch." Pant, pant, pant. "I'm squeezing a fucking rugby ball out and," pant, pant, pant, "all you can think about is your fucking furniture." The fire burned through her again, ripping her in half, and she roared like an animal.

Unable to do anything but soothe and encourage the child-woman until the baby's head crowned, the two midwives glanced at each other knowingly. Linda rubbed Penny's shoulder gently. "It's okay sweetheart, you're nearly there. Not long now and this will all be forgotten."

Penny shot a venomous glare at Linda. "Fucking forgotten, my arse. I'll never forget this pain, ever. Where's my mum?" The next contraction boomed without notice and she squeezed the midwife's hand until it turned purple, growling at first then shrieking.

The doorbell rang and Charity darted from the room, eagerly letting the officers in and indicating the lounge. "Follow the noise, boys."

They glanced uncomfortably at the naked child on the sofa as she screeched with agony and turned away. Post-contraction, Penny was irate. "Get those fucking men fucking out of here, I've got no fucking clothes on." Relieved, they returned to the hallway and Charity.

Another contraction mushroomed and Penny yelped, howling, crying, and Linda laid a hand on the little patch of silken black hair that appeared, wet from the womb. "Baby's crowning now, sweetheart, you're doing an excellent job. Give me one more push with the next contraction, but when I tell you to stop, just pant like a dog, okay."

"Oh no, oh no, oh no. Not more. Argh…" Penny's face contorted, scraping her sodden fringe from her eyes, exhausted.

Charity popped her head around the door. "They've found your mother, thank God. She'll be here any minute."

"Fuck off." Shrieking.

"Easy, sweetheart, pant, pant, don't push, baby's head's just coming, just keep panting for now. Good girl, you're doing an excellent job."

A wave of nausea flowed through Charity and she wished she had stayed in the hall. She clutched her head, staggering. "I think I'm going to faint." Her skin paled and Linda nodded to Becky, who guided Charity to her designer armchair, helping her sit.

"That's it, baby's head's through. Next time you feel the urge to push, go with it, sweetheart."

Seconds later, Linda felt the muscles tighten in Penny's abdomen and she cradled the baby's head. "Can you get the towel from the radiator please, Becky, just hold it out for baby." With a rasping growl Penny pushed for the final time and the tiny body slithered from hers into Linda's waiting hands. A shocked mewing echoed and Linda scanned the child for abnormalities. "Congratulations, Penny, you have a beautiful daughter." She clamped and cut the cord, swaddling the baby in the towel.

Drained, the teenager shuffled up, tentatively lowering herself onto the wet cushion, scared to sit in case it hurt, and took a shy peek at her homegrown miracle. A rush of love hit her, marvelling at the beauty of nature. Thick, dark hair covered the baby's head and her intense blue eyes focused on her mother, curious, intrigued. Penny smiled with pride. She was a mother and this was her child, and she would protect her for the rest of her life. She carefully took her baby from Linda and instinctively held her to her chest. "Hello, little one, I'm your mummy."

A minute ticked by, peaceful and serene.

Whop-whop-whop overhead, louder, louder.

Then a commotion from the kitchen. "Where is everybody?" Hope was urgent, scared. "What's going on?"

One of the policemen motioned to the lounge and Hope darted through, immediately shocked by the mess; tasteful and

253

expensively decorated, Charity's house was normally impeccably tidy... She noticed Charity curled on the chair, pale, a nurse holding her hand, and her heart leapt with fear.

"Mummy." Olive stood in the corner, eyes wide and traumatised.

Another nurse kneeling over something on a blue tarpaulin. "Oh my god, which one?" Hope rushed to see around the nurse and found a smiling Penny. And a baby. Penny with a baby? She looked back at Charity. "Is it yours?"

Back to Penny. Penny and a baby. "Where are your clothes?" Why was her daughter naked with a baby in her arms? "Will somebody tell me what the hell is going on?" Her eyes darted from one person to the next, questioning. Had Penny just had a baby? Had her thirteen-year-old just had a baby? A sickening in the pit of her stomach, bile rising, horror, and she stared at her daughter, incredulous. "Have you just had a baby?"

Penny grinned her childish smile. "Hi, Mum, meet your granddaughter."

Grasping, searching for support, Hope sat, stunned, and it dawned on her: "Rick?"

The new mother nodded, smiling, and Hope's chest tightened, breathless. Her husband to be, the father of her grandchild. Hideous. So wrong. Hope hugged herself, a vice gripping her torso, squeezing daggers through her core. Hatred borne of love burned for the man she could now never have, for the man who had impregnated her child. She should have killed him when she had the chance, and Griffin too, the men who had ruined her life. This hurt too much.

She had a thousand questions. "Why didn't you tell me you were pregnant?"

"I didn't know. I was so hungry all the time, I thought I was just putting on weight."

"Me too. I should have known, should have seen it." Hope dropped to the floor beside her daughter and examined her grandchild's pretty face, arm over Penny's shoulders. "I'll support you every step of the way and I promise I will love her, but I need some time for it to sink in."

Penny shrugged, gazing at the baby. "I've got to get used to it too."

"Good lord, we've got our work cut out. I could do with a drink if anybody's offering."

Speeding

The car hurtled along the roads, overtaking the traffic when the opportunity arose. Williams was breaking the speed limit, but Claudia shared his urgency to find Hope before she disappeared again. The officers at her sister's house had been instructed to keep her there, or accompany her if she needed to go to hospital with her daughter.

As they neared Beccles, Williams put his foot down, eager to get the job done. Claudia felt like a traitor; she was duty bound to prosecute Hope if she had forced the tablets on Hall against his will, but the mitigating circumstances were significant. However, the magnitude of her punishment rested on whether the rector lived or died.

Spurred by her musing, Claudia radioed for an update on his condition. "Not good, I'm afraid. They've pumped his stomach, but he's still comatose.
Covered in wires and machines. They're running toxicology tests and the only treatment they can give him is a charcoal solution. At first they thought he would come round, but he hasn't."

"So what's going to happen then?"

"I don't know to be honest, there's a lot of people toing and froing. All I know is he's in a bad way."

"Thanks." Claudia ended the conversation and updated Williams on the patient's condition. "If he dies she'll be sent down, Jack."

He waved a hand, dismissive. "You're jumping the gun, Claud. We don't know for sure that she had anything to do with Griffin, she may not even know he was staying at the hotel. Maybe it's just a huge coincidence."

She snorted, sarcastic. "Come on, Jack, you don't believe that for a second. Both Hope and Eva were at that hotel today, it's no coincidence that their mutual childhood abuser suddenly ends up struggling for his life."

Stopping at a roundabout, Williams focused on Claudia. "Just remember we're the only ones who know everything at the moment."

She gasped. "Really? You'd do that?"

"If you wanted me to." He pulled into a gap in the traffic. "The girl deserves a break after what you've told me."

She sighed, her guilt ebbing away. Williams was genuine, a truly caring person, and she hoped she was reading between the lines correctly, that he would deny all knowledge of Hope's suspected presence at the hotel. After all, it wasn't as if they had seen her. It seemed like the right thing to do, more palatable. Justice would be served.

Shocked by her conspiratorial thoughts, Claudia clicked the radio on as a distraction, but Williams turned it off. "No," he paused, thinking, "I want you to tell me what he did to her, every sordid, sick detail. That way I'll understand where you're coming from on this."

"Your daughter's seven, isn't she?" He nodded. "I'll tell you, Jack, but I want you to imagine it's happening to Caitlyn, not Hope. Then you'll really understand her pain."

The New Father Arrives

On their way to Beccles, an officer explained to Rick why Hope had been rushed away and he mentally calculated the dates, realising with horror that he was probably the infant's father. Not only would Hope be furious, but he would be a father to an unwanted baby and a co-parent with a child he didn't like. Worse, would they prosecute him for having sex with a minor? He prayed earnestly to whoever that the baby was premature - not his.

They arrived at Charity's house and he leapt from the car, desperate and terrified. Pushing past the officers in the hallway, throwing himself to the lions, he opened the door and awaited his retribution. The silence was disconcerting and he searched for Hope, whose back was to him, shielding Penny from his view. He stood, lame, unsure what to do.

Charity noticed him and grimaced. "I hope you're going to tidy this bloody mess up."

Hope turned and her steel eyes drilled pure hatred into him. He winced, but mustered bravado, slowly approaching his girlfriend, the grandmother of his lovechild. And Penny, the chubby girl he had met as an attractive groupie and shagged for a laugh. It wasn't funny now, though. Her Mona Lisa smile, the maternal love for his child beaming from her eyes. The baby's head was obscured by the midwife, who was helping to latch her onto her mother's barely formed breast. He felt no longing for the brat; he only wanted a child with Hope, not her daughter.

Bewildered, sadness pouring from despondent and dulled eyes, he wanted to hug his girlfriend, reassure her, but her glare was unforgiving. "Congratulations, Rick, meet your daughter."

The bitterness slapped him on both cheeks. "Hope, we need to talk. In private."

"Damned right, we do." She briefly hugged Penny and headed for the door, but an officer blocked her. "Excuse me, I need to get past."

"I'm sorry, ma'am, we've been asked to keep you on these premises. A detective wants to speak to you."

"A detective? I've just about had enough of today. I've just been stopped by policemen, tied to a helicopter and dropped off in my sister's garden only to be met with a granddaughter I didn't even realise was on the way," she shot daggers at Rick, "whose father happens to be the man I'm supposed to be marrying."

Charity gasped, edging closer to hear more, while Hope took deep and calming breaths. They didn't work; she saw red. "Unless you have an arrest warrant, you cannot hold me against my will. Now, if you'll get your arse out of my fucking way, I'd like to go in the kitchen with the father of my grandchild who didn't bother to give me these details when he fucked me earlier today." She shoved the policeman aside and grasped Rick's hand, leading him to the kitchen. Shooting daggers at the three constables who propped up the granite breakfast bar was enough for them to move diplomatically to the hall. Hope slammed the door.

She played with her fingernails, uneasy, not sure where to start. "Obviously we can't see each other now you're the father of my grandchild."

"Only biologically." She glowered at him and he winced. "Look, I'll see Penny okay, her baby. But the only babies I want to have are with you." He grasped her arms, earnest. "I know it's hard for you to hear, but I have a reputation and it's deserved, I've slept with shitloads of women. But every time I moved from one to the next it was because she wasn't right. That's stopped with you. Completely. Because you *are* right."

"Don't think…" A loud rapping silenced her and the door burst open. "Who are you?"

"I'm Claudia Horseferry, nice to meet you at last. Can we have five minutes?"

"Your timing could be better, that's for sure. Can't it wait?"

"We need to talk about Griffin."

Her heart hammered in her chest. The past couple of hours had been so demanding, so emotional - a rollercoaster - she had all but forgotten the sordid events of the evening. She caught Rick's eye, her terror evident, the world as she knew it falling apart, and he whispered, "Stick with our story," and louder, "you'll be fine, babe, it'll be good news. They've probably arrested him."

Williams hovered by the back door, still horrified by the details he had heard from his colleague during the journey, while Claudia closed the internal door to block out prying ears. She

259

indicated the breakfast bar and they sat. "Hope, we understand you booked into The Cambridge Garden House Hotel earlier today."

Hope nodded. "So what, I had a night out planned with my partner."

"What was the real reason for going?" Hope stared at Rick for support, scared. "Were you aware that Griffin Hall was also a guest at the hotel?"

She paled, jaw dropping, and stuttered, "No." Rick was in awe of her acting skills.

Claudia shifted awkwardly. Whom did she want justice for? The paedophile's victim, or the victim's victim. "Do you know of an Eva Brunel?"

Hope shrugged, playing games. "Yes, I know her well."

Claudia hadn't expected the answer and she momentarily lost her train of thought. "How do you know her?"

"I am her. Black wig, glasses, different make up and clothes. I even fooled Rick and we spend every night together."

Flummoxed, the idea had never occurred to Claudia and she reddened at having been fooled so easily. She didn't understand, and all she could manage was, "Why?"

Hope gritted her teeth and her eyes watered, frustrated. "You said it was his word against mine, and after twenty-five years you know as well as I do he'd never get done for it."

Williams and Claudia shared an embarrassed glance. "No, you're probably right, but he could have been placed on the sex-offenders register."

Annoyed, Hope waved dismissively. "Bollocks. Clean living rector with docile little wifey versus me, controversial writer with hard-hitting, finger-pointing studies that name and shame. Plus, the memory of the abuse raised, equally controversially, by regression. No case, Claudia, and you know it."

It was the truth and Claudia was ashamed of the law she lived to uphold. "So you invented Eva as another witness and transformed yourself into her for my benefit." She felt like a gullible idiot.

"It was easy. When you told me my evidence wasn't enough, it dawned on me that I could get some revenge on him, pay him back for the years he stole of my life. It was just some fun at first. I wrote to him - well, Eva did - said she'd read about the investigation and wanted him to know she was totally on his side." Jack and

Claudia remained quiet, enthralled. "I just need to get a drink; I'm dry as a bone."

Hope collected a glass from a cupboard and filled it to the brim with chilled fifty-pounds-a-bottle Chardonnay as if it had come from the bargain bin. She gulped some and returned to the table. "I didn't expect a response, so I was stunned when the hotel whose stationary I'd used while I was staying there forwarded his reply. I realised I could have some real fun, get my revenge by leading him on."

With their backs to the door, no one but Rick noticed Dawn creep in, socked feet on tiptoes. He was relieved to see her, aware of her closeness to his girlfriend, and she mouthed to him: 'Are you okay?' A nod relaxed her and she crouched silently by the wall.

"We exchanged a few letters and he was clearly becoming emotionally attached to Eva. Well, backtracking a bit, I needed to see Griffin as he is now, not how I remembered him. I don't know why it was important to me, it just was. I went to his church on Christmas Eve, intending to stay in the background and not say a word, but when I saw him I was rooted to the spot. Seeing him there, the self-righteous liar, I felt sick. I could feel the bile rising, the thought that the smarmy man who was standing in front of me, pretending to be virtuous and moralistic, had shoved his cock in my mouth, inside me, when I was just a tiny child. I vomited over him. It was disgusting, but it was my body's response to seeing the bastard I abhorred.

"Anyway, getting back to Eva, seeing him in the church meant he'd seen my face, and then I'd stupidly gone to the rectory and created a scene, humiliating Griffin by telling his parishioners the truth, humiliating his wife, simply because she irritated me."

Claudia swallowed. "You do know Dorothy Hall is dead, don't you?"

Hope's head fell, the glossy mahogany curls tumbling to frame her cheeks. "I didn't think he'd do it. I said if he killed her he could have me - Eva. I was bored of the game, I thought he'd say 'oh, sorry love, can't do that one, see ya'. But suddenly he'd done it, he'd actually gone and done it. That's when things got above my head. Eva was due to meet up with him, and he was going to try and seduce her."

"You could have just left it there, not met and not written any more." Williams felt compelled to speak having seen Dorothy's mottled body, knowing of her undignified rape.

Hope sighed, refilling the empty tumbler. "It was like an obsession, I didn't want to go, but I did too. Maybe it was about finding closure or something, I don't know."

Annoyed by the time-wasting, the deceit, being taken for a fool, Claudia bristled. "Hope, with that third witness making a statement…"

Rick raised his hand. "That was me. I didn't know what was going on at the time, but now it all makes sense." He smiled at Hope. "Nice one, babe."

Disheartened, Claudia's shoulders sagged, the reality becoming clearer. "Three witnesses, all one person. You wouldn't have been able to cope with the identity changes when the case came to court, you knew we wouldn't be able to convict him, so you plotted your revenge in another way."

"It isn't as cut and dried as that, there were other circumstances that concerned me. I was worried about Penny; she was putting on weight fast. Obviously, we know why now, but we didn't then. I was terrified about the pains I'd been getting in my arm, that crushing vice thing in my chest."

Rick took Hope's hand. "You never told me you were getting pains."

"I told you to see a doctor." Hope and the officers spun to see Dawn and she wished she had kept quiet.

"What the hell are you doing here? First Claudia, then you, this is getting bizarre." Hope was incredulous.

Rick jumped in. "I phoned her on the way back after you'd gone on the helicopter. I was scared about the baby situation and wanted her with me for moral support." Dawn eyed him, aware he only lied if there were danger in the truth. The hairs on her arm stood high, goose-bumps surfacing as a deep and sinister fear spread over her. His expression silenced her and she discreetly nodded her assent.

Williams and Claudia dismissed the lie, knowing from their conversation with Dawn exactly why she had made the long journey so suddenly, and they tried to imagine why he was shielding Hope after his earlier panic. Was she still unstable? Dangerous?

Naïve, content with the explanation, Hope smiled. "Getting back to what happened, well, the last straw was discovering my fiancé had slept with my daughter last year when she was twelve." Dawn cringed and Rick held his head in his hands, ashamed. "I went mad inside, I was furious, disgusted. They'd both known all the time I'd been with him, yet neither was willing to tell me until the other day. I didn't tell him I knew. I just said we were going away on our own at the weekend to celebrate our engagement and he bought it. I was going to use him to help me get revenge on Griffin."

Williams listened keenly, eager to hear what had happened to the paedophilic Rector Hall, the circumstances that had led to his hospitalisation.

"When we got to the hotel, I needed Rick to be asleep so I could change into Eva Brunel, and the best way I could think of was raunchy sex and a glass of brandy; he can't hold his alcohol very well." Rick shot her a wounded look. "The plan worked so I got changed and went to the room I'd booked for Griffin under a false name. I'd picked room three-sixty-nine for the irony.

"Once I got there he kept trying to paw me about, feel me up, and his trousers never stopped bulging. Obviously, I had no intention of letting him anywhere near me so I talked my way out, promising him the hottest sex he would ever have, but later. I'd brought chains, handcuffs - standard bondage crap - and he made no effort to stop me putting them on him after he'd stripped naked. I had him trapped, just where I wanted him, and now I could go and collect Rick to help me."

Williams held up a hand to halt the flow. "Help you do what?" A singeing, stark blue glare; he felt like an admonished child.

"I changed into a sexy schoolgirl outfit, another touch of irony; I've got a pretty sarcastic sense of humour. I think that must have been when Rick called Dawn for help." Rick recoiled, stunned she had known he was lying all along.

"Why do you think he called Dawn for help then? He's just told you he called from the police car later?" Claudia was intrigued.

"Because I told him I knew about him screwing my daughter, and that I was getting my revenge on him. I guess he was scared, especially when he tried to run off and found the door locked." She grinned at the memory, which annoyed Rick.

Hope described the indecent uniform she had worn to titillate both men, while Dawn reflected on the meetings she'd had with Hope - angry days, sad days, efficient days - and one thread was constant: sex. She realised that Hope used flirtation and a promise of sexual favours to get whatever she wanted. She was sassy, and anyone, male or female, who wanted to have sex with her was in her power.

Casting her mind back, she could see that Hope had discreetly flirted with her from the very first session. Her brother was besotted, a lovesick fool, as a result of Hope's clever manipulation. On Christmas Eve, she had worn provocative clothes to meet a paedophilic rapist. And the two detectives were drawn to her, the coy expression, flickering eye contact while describing the suggestive outfit that mocked her abuse.

Everybody ended up trapped in Hope's web.

Shuddering, Dawn felt a sense of foreboding. Something - she had no idea what - was going to happen. Hope was hunting her prey, lulling it into security before she went for the jugular. She tried to catch her brother's attention, but he was as enthralled with Hope as the detectives were. Dawn wanted to run, but she couldn't - wouldn't - leave her brother.

"He had no idea I wasn't Eva, and no idea I was in the uniform because I'd blindfolded him before I left. We came in, me and Rick, and we started to tease him, took his mask off so he could see that it was me. He had a ball gag in his mouth so he couldn't shout for help."

Williams's phone chirruped and he jumped, engrossed in the tale. He took it to a corner while Claudia looked on, and Rick whispered to Hope: "Stick to the story."

Williams ended the call and sat again. "Griffin Hall has died. Hope, if you had anything to do with this you know you'll be looking at a prison term."

Straightening, indignant. "Rubbish. That guy screwed me and probably many other girls against our will when we were children. He murdered his wife. He was the lowest of the low."

"I realise there are mitigating circumstances, but all the same..."

Hope growled, low and threatening, and the animal rawness shocked everybody. "I'm not going to any prison. Talavera is the one and only prison I will ever set foot in."

Puzzled, Williams and Claudia's eyes met and an invisible mist settled over the room, thick and cloying. Dawn hugged her knees, a chill running through her. Rick had seen Hope's dangerous anger before, but Dawn knew the background, the ingrained hurt that made it so easy for her to erase her emotions at will, and this time she was under pressure, not in the comfort of the counselling room. If she were to lose control, Rick was in the most danger, having just become a father to Hope's child's baby. Dawn had no doubt the woman teemed with bitterness, regardless of how close the couple currently seemed.

She studied her brother under the threatening veil that danced around the room, floating in swirls, pervading every pore and charging the air with peril. Rick was a stunner and had been since the moment he was born. Dark chocolate eyes framed by long black lashes, foppish dark hair, tousled and cute, that took years off his age. Physically, he was a monster, tall and well-proportioned. She understood why women fell for him in droves. He was young and unattached and his reasoning during their frequent arguments - if it's there on a plate I'm going to eat it - made sense, despite her higher morals. A wave of sisterly protection swamped her; she didn't trust Hope for a second.

Hope. There was something beautiful in her anger, the crystal clear blue firing through black lashes. Her mahogany hair enhanced her pale skin, topping the frail body that packed so much power, the distressed mind containing lifelong wounds which fuelled her vehemence. She could understand why her brother had fallen for her, her uniqueness trapped everybody she met, including herself. And now the special bond she and Hope had shared for three months was the only thing that could save Rick... of that, Dawn was certain.

She stood, towering beneath the suspended ceiling, the scattering of halogen spotlights reflecting from her mass of unkempt golden curls, and met Hope's stare as she approached the breakfast bar. She sat opposite her client and immediately Claudia was forgotten. They were the only people in the room and both knew the counselling session they were about to begin would be the final one.

Dawn chose her words carefully, the opening line was vital, and the wallflower witnesses instinctively knew to keep out of the discussion while the counsellor guided her client. Only Dawn knew how much danger Rick was in, that the fury raging inside the wounded woman was indifferent to love and devoid of compassion and common sense. She sensed that Hope had finally dropped over the edge.

Charity Fusses

Both midwives had gone and Penny slept peacefully on the sofa, crisp white upholstery almost saved from ruin by the muddy tarpaulin Charity had removed under Linda's orders. Charity had argued her case strongly, unable to understand why nobody else cared that the sofa was new and hugely expensive, but the no-nonsense midwife had dismissed her pleading: 'Conversation over. A baby cannot be born on a filthy tarpaulin, it's unhygienic. Get rid of it, you can claim on insurance for the sofa.'

The baby lay sleeping in Penny's comforting arms, protected from harm, nestled between her mother and the back of the sofa, healthy and bonny. Charity fussed around the room, astounded by the clutter, the stained carpet and cushions, and again wished Keith wasn't in Houston on business.

"What are they bloody doing in that kitchen?" Huffing, Charity opened the bureau and rooted through the alphabetically ordered pockets, and at last, "There it is: house insurance."

The Final Session

"How are you feeling, Hope? You've had some shocks tonight. I imagine you're scared and confused."

Her jaw tense and lips taut, the white knuckles of the clenched fists described her inner emotions without words. "They are not putting me in prison again. I'll die first." Rick clasped her hand supportively, but she shoved him away.

"Why do you think you might go to prison?"

"That bastard has ruined me in his lifetime and now he's going to ruin me in death too. He wasn't meant to die. I wanted him dead at first, I admit, but I realised it wouldn't make me feel any better." She clasped her hand to her breast, "I have to let go in here," long, red-stained fingernails tapping her head, "and in here." Fire glared at Claudia, who shuffled uncomfortably under the intensity. "That bitch screwed me up, telling me they were going to arrest him, then letting me down. He deserved to be punished for what he did. Dawn, I was just seven, I was a baby. My childhood ended there." The flames moved to Rick, burning deeply, making him flinch. "Just like your vile brother did to my own baby."

Keep her talking, but change the subject; while the venom was aimed at Rick he was in danger. "So you went to Cambridge to punish him?"

"Chained down on that bed, naked, skinny. Weak arms covered in wiry black hair, yellow toenails, that disgusting phallus flopped over his thigh. I saw him for what he was: pathetic, a mere bully who got his power kicks from abusing little girls. I wanted to make him see that every time he steals a baby virgin the scars last for life, not just for the moment of his depraved orgasm. You know, he forced it into my tiny seven-year-old mouth so hard my lips split in three places, I had the ugly scabs to remind me for weeks."

Williams squirmed, thinking of his own daughter and her blissful, unharmed childhood. "Even when he was flaccid it was monstrous, so you can imagine how massive it was when it was erect. Fucking abnormal, that's what, he was a mutant."

268

Rick had quietly taken Gayle's role and prepared drinks in the background, the kettle bubbling gently to make coffee for Williams and Claudia, pouring brandy for the other three. Hope downed hers without wincing and shoved the glass towards Rick, who poured a second and left the bottle with her. "I had a gun."

Claudia and Williams were immediately on edge, desperate to know where the gun was now, whether they were all in danger, but common sense told them to bury their questions; they would be answered in time. Hope glared at Claudia, as if she had heard her thoughts: "If you must know, I bought the gun from some sleazy guy for cash after my ex-husband raped me. I swore nobody would ever humiliate me like that again. And you don't need to know where it is now."

Incredulous, Claudia's face paled, and having had her own mind read by Hope in the past, Dawn knew how intimidating it was. The blue returned to her, calming in their rapport. "It was totally unplanned, but I hit him with it, cut his forehead. I saw him on the bed and he revolted me. I detested him, wanted to hurt him."

Hope's head dropped and she peered coyly at Dawn, shame tinged with naughtiness. "Like you said, for as long as I can remember I've manipulated men to get what I want by using sex as a tool. Men will do anything if they think they're going to get laid."

Flabbergasted, Dawn knew she hadn't stated that conclusion aloud, and she became fearful of even thinking. She glanced at Rick, innocent to his girlfriend's uncanny powers, his arms crossed tightly and face sullen.

If Hope knew of the concern she had created, she didn't let on. "Griffin was a pervert, so I thought the suggestion of filthy sex was the best way to get him going."

"Premeditated?"

"Of course, I even brought a disposable glove so I didn't have to touch his revolting skin."

"What skin, why were you touching him?"

"I was masturbating him. Get him going, then hurt him."

Dawn cupped her chin in her hand, contemplative. "Let me get this straight: he's chained up by a woman he's sexually abused, she's just whipped him with a gun, and he still gets a stiffy? No, Hope, I'm not buying that one."

"That was your brother, not me."

Dawn's eyes widened, horrified at the thought of her brother's involvement in the disgusting game, and Rick chuckled, throwing a cigarette at Hope and taking one himself. He held it in his lips, talking from the corner of his mouth. "She was working him but it wouldn't rise to the occasion, so I described a little girl in school uniform playing with his knob, and it worked straight away. That's the power of the imagination for you." He lit the cigarette.

Sickened, Dawn returned her attention to Hope. "I still don't get it. Why masturbate him, I mean, that's giving him pleasure, why did you want to do that?"

Her fairylike tinkle echoed against the stark cupboards that lined the white walls. "No, I was making him think he was enjoying it to make my next strike hurt even more. It did, it was ace; I slashed his chest with a knife. Not deep enough to do damage, but enough to bleed."

"Like you do when you're frustrated?"

"To show him how it feels to self-harm, that the physical pain of cutting yourself is severe, which shows how deeply the pain is up here," she tapped her head again, "if you're willing to experience that pain just to get rid of the anger inside."

Claudia had so much to ask, but when she leaned forward, mouth poised in question, Dawn's eyes warned her off.

"I slashed him in all the places I've cut myself." She moved her clothing aside to reveal scars, some white, some reddish purple. "Arms, legs, chest, belly, bum, shoulders. He was bleeding everywhere."

"What was he doing? Griffin?"

"Crying. Trying to scream but the gag stopped him. His feebleness made me hate him more. Anyway, the bit you're both here for." Hope addressed the detectives. "I forced him to take the tablets that killed him." She thought Claudia would jump up and arrest her, but was surprised when her shoulders sagged, sad and resigned. "I've taken five overdoses in my time, I'm always sick within half an hour, that's why it's never worked."

"You wanted him to be sick?"

She took a swig of the brandy, swilling it, pondering. "I guess. I didn't want it, maybe, but I expected it. I also had a noose prepared that would only hold his weight for seconds, but I had to use the rope on Rick to stop him from running away. All the same, I doubt it would have gone that far, anyway."

270

Dawn reflected for a minute. "Why a noose? You've never tried to hang yourself, have you?"

"No, but I've thought about it, just never had the courage to do it." Hope took her drink and distanced herself from the group, sitting on the worktop across the room. "As he lay there, his eyes drooping, pathetic, everything suddenly felt okay, like the darkness had lifted. I'd done what I needed to do, I didn't need to take it any further. I was avenged.

"On the way home, Rick begged me to stay with him, swearing he didn't know Penny was underage when he screwed her, and she agrees with that too, says she told him she was sixteen. Just briefly I felt true happiness, something I've never experienced before. I was totally in love, and the consuming anger at the abuse had disappeared, I hoped for ever. Even the pains in my chest went away." As if reminded she was acting a role, Hope clasped her left arm, wincing, breathing deeply.

She lowered her head, eyes blackening and emotion dying. "We drove home holding hands, we were blissful. I loved him more than anything then, we were going to get married, have a baby, commit ourselves to us."

The rage returned, lips twisting and eyes deadly, glaring at Claudia. "Then I'm stopped by you bastards and flown off, then faced with a grandchild I wasn't expecting. That's bad enough, but it's his filthy spawn. The same filthy spawn I wanted to make me another child. It made me sick. It makes me sick. Every ounce of happiness flooded out of me, my exciting future a pointless dream. I loved him and now I could never have him. And all because he couldn't keep his dick to himself. He'd thrown our relationship away before it had even started, because my child was already carrying his."

The hand clenching her arm moved to her chest and grasped, face contorted, and Claudia was concerned. "Are you okay, Hope?"

"It's just heartburn, it'll pass in a minute." Claudia wasn't convinced and moved her legs from under the table to face Hope. "It's like life was playing a game with me: it gave me a moment of true happiness, of pure contentment, and then whisked it away, mocking me, contemptuous. My granddaughter, I've no affection but hatred, because she's stolen my man away from me. I'll always do my best for her, but how can I ever love her, she'll always remind me of what I've lost."

271

Forlorn, Hope jumped from the worktop, uncharacteristic tears now rolling down her cheeks. She stood beside Claudia, holding her hands outstretched, submissive. "So there you are. I've admitted I murdered Griffin and I know you have no choice but to arrest me."

Claudia glanced at Williams and saw that he too was uncomfortable with the grey area between right and wrong, justice and revenge. Silence hung and nobody moved, all deep in thought.

Suddenly, too quick to comprehend, Hope doubled over and Claudia reached forward to grab her, holding her up. Gasping, sweating, face screwed tightly with pain, lips turning blue. And then Claudia understood. She lay the groaning woman on the floor, checking her pulse. "Get an ambulance, she's in cardiac arrest. Now."

Williams rushed away from the commotion and called for help, while Dawn and Rick stood by helplessly, distressed, wide eyed and desperate. "She's going to be okay, right?"

Claudia ignored him, feeling the rapid and irregular pulse in Hope's clammy neck. Then Hope calmed, the writhing subsiding, and she was asleep, peaceful and serene. Checking her airways, Claudia dragged her into the recovery position, manipulating her deadweight limbs to make her comfortable, and monitored her carotid pulse, slow and weak.

Williams stood over them, useless. "The paramedics are on their way."

The Big Decision

Hope felt as if she were floating, warm sun bathing her, lost in a bright light and feeling no pain. She was tired, unsure if she was asleep in the nothingness surrounding her. The silence was blissful, unaware of the commotion and panic around her, the heavy hands that pumped her chest, forcing her blood to circulate, the tube in her throat to give her oxygen. The only sensation was harmony. Now she had a choice: should she stay, or should she go?

The brightness was welcoming, so balmy and friendly, tempting her to let it consume her, and she wanted to go. But what was that distant noise on the edge of her new reality? Something familiar… The cries of a newborn baby. Instantly she remembered why she had to say goodbye.

"She's crashing."

"Preparing for defib. Two hundred. Clear."

Hope's body jerked forward and Penny wailed, beside herself, clutching the baby to her shoulder like a teddy bear.

"Two fifty. Clear."

Hope's eyes flickered, confused, and the paramedic stopped working her chest, groping for her pulse instead. The pain that the coma had dulled returned and she grimaced. "Hurts."

"I know, love, the doctors will give you some pain relief when we get you to hospital."

Hope focused on her child-mother daughter, comforting the baby, tears cascading down her face, and tried to smile. Behind her was Rick, fearful eyes also spilling. She knew he loved her in a way he had never loved before, but her emotions were in turmoil. She loved him but hated him still. And a future was impossible. If the newspapers discovered the truth, both being in the public eye now, they would have field day.

Strong hands - teamwork - lifted her onto a stretcher, which was hoisted onto a waiting trolley, wheeling urgently to an ambulance outside. Hope turned away from the concerned faces, heartbroken. She wanted to die and they had saved her. Now she would have to bear responsibility for the revenge that had freed her from her demons, and accept that her daughter was the teenage mother of a child that she would undoubtedly become prime carer of if Penny were to have a semblance of a life in the next few years.

Hope glanced bitterly at the paramedic beside her as the ambulance sped away, sirens blaring and flashing blue lights. Satisfied the woman was busy, her back turned, Hope reached for the gun in her pocket, drawing it out with limp fingers. Slowly - it was so heavy in her weakness - she put it to her head, and relaxed, relieved. She closed her eyes and pulled the trigger.

The Kitchen

Seven people were in the room but the stillness was uncanny. The baby, adorable in contented sleep, lay in her mother's arms, the stunned child terrified of losing her own mother, overwhelmed by guilt that the coronary may have been brought on by her pregnancy.

Dawn sat in the corner, dazed, yet still charged with the recent excitement. Beside her, Rick waded in his sorrow, stung by Hope's words, the knowledge that she would never be with him too much to bear.

Fuming at having her house used for both mediation and maternity, Charity nursed a steaming hot chocolate, the only beverage that didn't make her queasy in the early months of pregnancy. She wanted them gone, the whole lot of them. Out of her kitchen, out of her house. Then she would sterilize everything.

Williams rose slowly, repeating the volcanic events that had happened within just a few hours in his mind - the comatose paedophile, the extensive and unexpected journey, the hideous revelations, both of Griffin's actions and of Hope's attempt at retribution - and he waved to the equally pensive Claudia, nodding towards the door. She smiled, feeling for the car keys in her pocket, gratefully joining him, and they said nothing on their way out. Nobody would have heard if they had.

The chill of the January dawn smacked them as they closed the front door and they tugged their clothes tight, trotting to the car to escape the bitter frost. Williams fired the engine to warm the cab up, blowers melting the icy windscreen. He searched Claudia's face, unsure whether to speak, but his curiosity had been his downfall on many occasions. "What are we going to do?"

She shrugged. "Nothing."

"You know our jobs will be on the line if the truth ever gets out."

She regarded him, catching his eye. "We attended the hotel when we were alerted that a woman may be committing a crime, and came across a man who'd taken an overdose. Turns out it was a prank call, but lucky because it meant we could get the man to hospital. The man in question was facing a probable life sentence for the murder of his wife, and this, coupled with the accusation of a serious sexual offence looming over him, was too much for him. He had self-harmed before taking a fatal overdose." She reversed the car and began the long drive back to Cambridge.

Neither detective spoke during the journey, and when they arrived at the police station, Claudia laid a hand on his. "Thank you."

"You were abused too, weren't you?" The suggestion had come from nowhere, but she nodded. Neither would ever tell the truth; Hope had already served her life sentence.

A Startled Paramedic

The bang made her jump and she instinctively searched in the direction of the sound, jaw dropping when she saw the gun. "Jerry, come here." Her colleague leapt up the steps and followed her pointing finger. On the floor lay a Colt Python.

"Where the hell did that come from?" He inched forward.

"It just fell off that shelf when I was tidying up for the next callout."

Shaking his head, Jerry jumped from the ambulance, glancing at an empty police car nearby, striding towards the hospital to find the officers. "Don't touch it, I'm just going to find a copper."

Client to Counsellor

Hope's recovery had been arduous and painfully slow. Thirty-two was an unusually young age to suffer a coronary, and the cause had been diagnosed as a severe arrhythmia. But after months of toing and froing to one hospital appointment after another, amiodarone was prescribed, which stabilised the condition with barely any side effects. Hope was finally able to settle into new motherhood properly.

With an inner peace that had never surfaced before, she cradled her third daughter, who was growing bigger and bouncier by the day, and glanced lovingly at the baby's father. No more stress, her aggression gone, she smiled more and deliberated less. Removing the empty bottle from the sleeping child's mouth, Hope strolled to Rick and he took Penny's daughter - whom they had registered in their own names - into his waiting, comforting arms.

Nobody had known about Penny's pregnancy, so a cover-up was simple. In fact, more discussion and criticism had been directed at Hope's figure, blasted by journalists for being so skinny during the pregnancy they assumed she'd had, accused of starving her baby for the sake of fashion. The disparaging reports didn't affect Hope in the slightest as she smiled through life, calm and free of angst.

Getting Charity to keep their newsworthy secret had been a struggle - at first she wanted to scream the sick tale from the rooftops - but as her own pregnancy progressed, she developed an uncommon softness to her materialistic character. Hope had reasoned that keeping the skeleton locked away was the best thing for baby Rhia and her birth mother.

Hope and Rick snuggled together, sharing their baby, content, gazing through open patio doors that led to the landscaped garden, bright summer flowers and contrasting greens dancing in the warm breeze. A family in love. At peace.

The front door slamming broke the spell and three pairs of shoes clumped through the hall. Hope caught Rick's eyes and they laughed; the kids were home.

They separated as the children piled into the room, all shouting at once - at each other, at their parents, at nobody - and the familiar evening mayhem began. Laden with shopping bags and haggard, Dawn sloped in, dropping them on the carpet and slumping onto a seat.

"Everything okay?" Hope regarded her ex-counsellor, her sister-in-law. Dawn sighed exaggeratedly and Hope nodded to the door. "Want to talk about it? We can get a bit of quiet in the kitchen while I'm cooking dinner."

Dawn prepared giant mugs of coffee while Hope peeled a mountain of potatoes, gossiping, debating. Laughing. The counsellor and her client, roles reversed as Dawn related her clumsy love life. After the emotional events of January, the two women had reached a place they had tentatively considered during the first intense three months of meeting. The constraints of counselling, of one-sided conversation and selfishness, was gone.

Hope's vengeance had nearly destroyed them, but the situation was over now, resolved.

Dawn and Hope shared a look of love, each welcoming the future joys still to come. Not only as family, but friends.

Biography

Best-selling author of Unlikely Killer, Deadly Angels, Bonfire Night, Black Park, Rings of Death and Bloody Mary, Ricki continuously studies the mind, the psychology, of people with great interest, and writes to educate and involve.